ALSO BY ELLIOT ACKERMAN

Red Dress in Black & White

Places and Names

Waiting for Eden

Dark at the Crossing

Istanbul Letters

Green on Blue

ALSO BY ADMIRAL JAMES STAVRIDIS

Sailing True North

Sea Power

The Accidental Admiral

Partnership for the Americas

Destroyer Captain

Coauthored by Admiral James Stavridis

Command at Sea

The Leader's Bookshelf

Watch Officer's Guide

Division Officer's Guide

2034

A NOVEL OF THE NEXT WORLD WAR

Elliot Ackerman

Admiral James Stavridis

PENGUIN PRESS   NEW YORK   2021

PENGUIN PRESS
An imprint of Penguin Random House LLC
penguinrandomhouse.com

LIBRARY OF CONGRESS CATALOGING-IN-PUBLICATION DATA
Names: Ackerman, Elliot, author. | Stavridis, James, author.
Title: 2034 : a novel of the next world war / Elliot Ackerman,
Admiral James Stavridis, USN (Ret.).
Other titles: Twenty thirty-four
Description: New York: Penguin Press, 2021.
Identifiers: LCCN 2020020779 (print) | LCCN 2020020780 (ebook) |
ISBN 9781984881250 (hardcover) | ISBN 9781984881267 (ebook)
Subjects: LCSH: Naval battles.—Fiction. | Cyberspace operations
(Military science)—Fiction. | GSAFD: War stories.
Classification: LCC PS3601.C5456 A615 2021 (print) |
LCC PS3601.C5456 (ebook) | DDC 813/.6—dc23
LC record available at https://lccn.loc.gov/2020020779
LC ebook record available at https://lccn.loc.gov/2020020780

ISBN 9780593298688 (export)

Printed in the United States of America

ScoutAutomatedPrintCode

Book design by Daniel Lagin

"For there is no folly of the beast of the earth
which is not infinitely outdone by the madness of men."

—Herman Melville

Contents

2034

2034

1

The *Wén Rui* Incident

14:47 March 12, 2034 (GMT+8)
South China Sea

It surprised her still, even after twenty-four years, the way from horizon to horizon the vast expanse of ocean could in an instant turn completely calm, taut as a linen pulled across a table. She imagined that if a single needle were dropped from a height, it would slip through all the fathoms of water to the seabed, where, undisturbed by any current, it would rest on its point. How many times over her career had she stood as she did now, on the bridge of a ship, observing this miracle of stillness? A thousand times? Two thousand? On a recent sleepless night, she had studied her logbooks and totaled up all the days she had spent traversing the deep ocean, out of sight of land. It added up to nearly nine years. Her memory darted back and forth across those long years, to her watch-standing days as an ensign on the wood-slatted decks of a minesweeper with its bronchial diesel engines, to her mid-career hiatus in special warfare spent in the brown waters of the world, to this day, with these three sleek Arleigh Burke–class destroyers under her command cutting a south-by-southwest wake at eighteen knots under a relentless and uncaring sun.

Her small flotilla was twelve nautical miles off Mischief Reef in the long-disputed Spratly Islands on a euphemistically titled *freedom of navigation patrol*. She hated that term. Like so much in military life it was designed to belie the truth of their mission, which was a provocation, plain and simple. These were indisputably international waters, at least according to established conventions of maritime law, but the People's Republic of China claimed them as territorial seas. Passing through the much-disputed Spratlys with her flotilla was the legal equivalent of driving donuts into your neighbor's prized front lawn after he moves his fence a little too far onto your property. And the Chinese had been doing that for decades now, moving the fence a little further, a little further, and a little further still, until they would claim the entire South Pacific.

So . . . time to donut drive their yard.

Maybe we should simply call it that, she thought, the hint of a smirk falling across her carefully curated demeanor. Let's call it a *donut drive* instead of a *freedom of navigation patrol*. At least then my sailors would understand what the hell we're doing out here.

She glanced behind her, toward the fantail of her flagship, the *John Paul Jones*. Extending in its wake, arrayed in a line of battle over the flat horizon, were her other two destroyers, the *Carl Levin* and *Chung-Hoon*. She was the commodore, in charge of these three warships, as well as another four still back in their home port of San Diego. She stood at the pinnacle of her career, and when she stared off in the direction of her other ships, searching for them in the wake of her flagship, she couldn't help but see herself out there, as clearly as if she were standing on that tabletop of perfectly calm ocean, appearing and disappearing into the shimmer. Herself as she once was: the youthful Ensign Sarah Hunt. And then herself as she was now: the older, wiser Captain Sarah Hunt, commodore of Destroyer Squadron 21—*Solomons Onward*, their motto since the Second World War; "Rampant Lions," the name they gave themselves. On the deck plates of her seven ships she was affectionately known as the "Lion Queen."

She stood for a while, staring pensively into the ship's wake, finding and losing an image of herself in the water. She'd been given the news from the medical board yesterday, right before she'd pulled in all lines and sailed out of Yokosuka Naval Station. The envelope was tucked in her pocket. The thought of the paper made her left leg ache, right where the bone had set poorly, the ache followed by a predictable lightning bolt of pins and needles that began at the base of her spine. The old injury had finally caught up with her. The medical board had had its say. This would be the Lion Queen's last voyage. Hunt couldn't quite believe it.

The light changed suddenly, almost imperceptibly. Hunt observed an oblong shadow passing across the smooth mantle of the sea, whose surface was now interrupted by a flicker of wind, forming into a ripple. She glanced above her, to where a thin cloud, the only one in the sky, made its transit. Then the cloud vanished, dissolving into mist, as it failed to make passage beyond the relentless late-winter sun. The water grew perfectly still once again.

Her thoughts were interrupted by the hollow clatter of steps quickly and lightly making their way up the ladder behind her. Hunt checked her watch. The ship's captain, Commander Jane Morris, was, as usual, running behind schedule.

10:51 March 12, 2034 (GMT+4:30)
Strait of Hormuz

Major Chris "Wedge" Mitchell hardly ever felt *it*. . . .

His father had felt *it* a bit more than him, like that one time the FLIR on his F/A-18 Hornet had failed and he'd pickle-barreled two GBU-38s "danger close" for a platoon of grunts in Ramadi, using nothing but a handheld GPS and a map. . . .

"Pop," his grandfather, had felt *it* more than them both when, for five exhausting days, he'd dropped snake and nape with nothing more than an optical sight on treetop passes during Tet, where he dusted-in so low the flames had blistered the fuselage of his A-4 Skyhawk. . . .

"Pop-Pop," his great-grandfather, had felt *it* most of all, patrolling the South Pacific for Japanese Zeros with VMF-214, the famed *Black Sheep* squadron led by the hard-drinking, harder-fighting five-time Marine Corps ace Major Gregory "Pappy" Boyington. . . .

This elusive *it*, which had held four generations of Mitchells in its thrall, was the sensation of flying by the seat of your pants, on pure instinct alone. (*Back when I flew with Pappy, and we'd be on patrol, it wasn't all whizbang like you have it now. No targeting computers. No autopilot. It was just your skill, your controls, and your luck. We'd mark our gunsights on the canopy with a grease pencil and off we'd fly. And when you flew with Pappy you learned pretty quick to watch your horizon. You'd watch it close, but you'd also watch Pappy. When he'd toss his cigarette out of the cockpit and slam his canopy shut, you knew he meant business and you were about to tangle with a flight of Zeros.*)

The last time Wedge had heard that little speech from his great-grandfather, he'd been six years old. The sharp-eyed pilot had only the slightest tremor in his voice despite his ninety-plus years. And now, as the clear sun caught light on his canopy, Wedge could hear the words as distinctly as if his great-grandfather were riding along as his back-seater. Except the F-35E Lightning he flew only had a single seat.

This was but one of the many gripes Wedge had with the fighter he was piloting so close to Iranian airspace that he was literally dancing his starboard wing along the border. Not that the maneuver was hard. In fact, flying with such precision took no skill at all. The flight plan had been inputted into the F-35's onboard navigation computer. Wedge didn't have to do a thing. The plane flew itself. He merely watched the controls, admired the view out his canopy, and listened to the ghost of his great-grandfather taunting him from a nonexistent back seat.

Jammed behind his headrest was an auxiliary battery unit whose hum seemed impossibly loud, even over the F-35's turbofan engine. This battery, about the size of a shoebox, powered the latest upgrade to the fighter's suite of stealth technologies. Wedge hadn't been told much about the addition, only that it was some kind of an electromagnetic disrupter. Before he'd been briefed on his mission, he'd caught two civilian Lockheed contractors tampering with his plane belowdecks and had alerted the sergeant at arms, who himself had no record of any civilians on the manifest of the *George H. W. Bush*. This had resulted in a call to the ship's captain, who eventually resolved the confusion. Due to the sensitivity of the technology being installed, the presence of these contractors was itself highly classified. Ultimately, it proved a messy way for Wedge to learn about his mission, but aside from that initial hiccup every other part of the flight plan had proceeded smoothly.

Maybe too smoothly. Which was the problem. Wedge was hopelessly bored. He glanced below, to the Strait of Hormuz, that militarized sliver of turquoise that separated the Arabian Peninsula from Persia. He checked his watch, a Breitling chronometer with built-in compass and altimeter his father had worn during strafing runs over Marjah twenty-five years before. He trusted the watch more than his onboard computer. Both said that he was forty-three seconds out from a six-degree eastward course adjustment that would take him into Iranian airspace. At which point—so long as the little humming box behind his head did its job—he would vanish completely.

It would be a neat trick.

It almost seemed like a prank that he'd been entrusted with such a high-tech mission. His buddies in the squadron had always joked that he should've been born in an earlier time. That's how he'd gotten his call sign, "Wedge": the world's first and simplest tool.

Time for his six-degree turn.

He switched off the autopilot. He knew there'd be hell to pay for flying throttle and stick, but he'd deal with that when he got back to the *Bush*.

He wanted to feel *it*.

If only for a second. And if only for once in his life.

It would be worth the ass-chewing. And so, with a bunch of noise behind his head, he banked into Iranian airspace.

⌐

14:58 March 12, 2034 (GMT+8)
South China Sea

"You wanted to see me, Commodore?"

Commander Jane Morris, captain of the *John Paul Jones*, seemed tired, too tired to apologize for being almost fifteen minutes late to her meeting with Hunt, who understood the strain Morris was under. Hunt understood that strain because she herself had felt it on occasions too countless to number. It was the strain of getting a ship underway. The absolute accountability for nearly four hundred sailors. And the lack of sleep as the captain was summoned again and again to the bridge as the ship maneuvered through the seemingly endless fishing fleets in the South China Sea. The argument could be made that Hunt was under that strain three times over, based on the scope of her command, but both Hunt and Morris knew that the command of a flotilla was command by delegation while the command of a ship was pure command. *In the end, you and you alone are responsible for everything your ship does or fails to do.* A simple lesson they'd both been taught as midshipmen at Annapolis.

Hunt fished out two cigars from her cargo pocket.

"And what're those?" asked Morris.

"An apology," said Hunt. "They're Cubans. My dad used to buy them from the Marines at Gitmo. It's not as much fun now that they're legal, but still . . . they're pretty good." Morris was a devout Christian, quietly evangelical, and Hunt hadn't been sure whether or not she'd partake, so she was pleased when Morris took the cigar and came up alongside her on the bridge wing for a light.

"An apology?" asked Morris. "What for?" She dipped the tip of the cigar into the flame made by Hunt's Zippo, which was engraved with one of those cigar-chomping, submachine gun–toting bullfrogs commonly tattooed onto the chests and shoulders of Navy SEALs or, in the case of Hunt's father, etched onto the lighter he'd passed down to his only child.

"I imagine you weren't thrilled to learn that I'd picked the *John Paul Jones* for my flagship." Hunt had lit her cigar as well, and as their ship held its course the smoke was carried off behind them. "I wouldn't want you to think this choice was a rebuke," she continued, "particularly as the only other female in command. I wouldn't want you to think that I was trying to babysit you by situating my flag here." Hunt instinctively glanced up at the mast, at her commodore's command pennant.

"Permission to speak freely?"

"C'mon, Jane. Cut the shit. You're not a plebe. This isn't Bancroft Hall."

"Okay, ma'am," began Morris, "I never thought any of that. Wouldn't have even occurred to me. You've got three good ships with three good crews. You need to put yourself somewhere. Actually, my crew was pretty jazzed to hear that we'd have the Lion Queen herself on board."

"Could be worse," said Hunt. "If I were a man, you'd be stuck with the Lion King."

Morris laughed.

"And if I were the Lion King," deadpanned Hunt, "that'd make you Zazu." Then Hunt smiled, that wide-open smile that had always endeared her to her subordinates.

Which led Morris to say a little more, maybe more than she would've in the normal course: "If we were two men, and the *Levin* and *Hoon* were skippered by two women, do you think we'd be having this conversation?" Morris allowed the beat of silence between them to serve as the answer.

"You're right," said Hunt, taking another pull on her Cuban as she leaned on the deck railing and stared out toward the horizon, across the still impossibly calm ocean.

"How's your leg holding up?" asked Morris.

Hunt reached down to her thigh. "It's as good as it'll ever be," she said. She didn't touch the break in her femur, the one she'd suffered a decade before during a training jump gone bad. A faulty parachute had ended her tenure as one of the first women in the SEALs and nearly ended her life. Instead, she fingered the letter from the medical board resting in her pocket.

They'd smoked their short cigars nearly down to the nubs when Morris spotted something on the starboard horizon. "You see that smoke?" she said. The two naval officers pitched their cigars over the side for a clearer view. It was a small ship, steaming slowly or perhaps even drifting. Morris ducked into the bridge and returned to the observation deck with two pairs of binoculars, one for each of them.

They could see it clearly now, a trawler about seventy feet long, built low amidships to recover its fishing nets, with a high-built prow designed to crest storm surge. Smoke billowed from the aft part of the ship, where the navigation bridge was set behind the nets and cranes— great dense, dark clouds of it, interspersed with orange flames. There was a commotion on deck as the crew of maybe a dozen struggled to contain the blaze.

The flotilla had rehearsed what to do in the event they came across a ship in duress. First, they would check to see if other vessels were coming to render assistance. If not, they would amplify any distress signals and facilitate finding help. What they wouldn't do—or would do only as an absolute last resort—was divert from their own freedom of navigation patrol to provide that assistance themselves.

"Did you catch the ship's nationality?" asked Hunt. Inwardly, she began running through a decision tree of her options.

Morris said no, there wasn't a flag flying either fore or aft. Then she stepped back into the bridge and asked the officer of the deck, a beef-fed lieutenant junior grade with a sweep of sandy blond hair, whether or not a distress signal had come in over the last hour.

The officer of the deck reviewed the bridge log, checked with the combat information center—the central nervous system of the ship's sensors and communications complex a couple of decks below—and concluded that no distress signal had been issued. Before Morris could dispatch such a signal on the trawler's behalf, Hunt stepped onto the bridge and stopped her.

"We're diverting to render assistance," ordered Hunt.

"Diverting?" Morris's question escaped her reflexively, almost accidentally, as every head on the bridge swiveled toward the commodore, who knew as well as the crew that lingering in these waters dramatically increased the odds of a confrontation with a naval vessel from the People's Liberation Army. The crew was already at a modified general quarters, well trained and ready, the atmosphere one of grim anticipation.

"We've got a ship in duress that's sailing without a flag and that hasn't sent out a distress signal," said Hunt. "Let's take a closer look, Jane. And let's go to full general quarters. Something doesn't add up."

Crisply, Morris issued those orders to the crew, as if they were the chorus to a song she'd rehearsed to herself for years but up to this moment had never had the opportunity to perform. Sailors sprang into motion on every deck of the vessel, quickly donning flash gear, strapping on gas masks and inflatable life jackets, locking down the warship's many hatches, spinning up the full combat suite, to include energizing the stealth apparatus that would cloak the ship's radar and infrared signatures. While the *John Paul Jones* changed course and closed in on the incapacitated trawler, its sister ships, the *Levin* and *Hoon*, remained on course and speed for the freedom of navigation mission. The distance between them and the flagship began to open. Hunt then disappeared back to her stateroom, to where she would send out the encrypted dispatch to Seventh Fleet Headquarters in Yokosuka. Their plans had changed.

04:47 March 12, 2034 (GMT-4)
Washington, D.C.

Dr. Sandeep "Sandy" Chowdhury, the deputy national security advisor, hated the second and fourth Mondays of every month. These were the days, according to his custody agreement, that his six-year-old daughter, Ashni, returned to her mother. What often complicated matters was that the handoff didn't technically occur until the end of school. Which left him responsible for any unforeseen childcare issues that might arise, such as a snow day. And on this particular Monday morning, a snow day in which he was scheduled to be in the White House Situation Room monitoring progress on a particularly sensitive test flight over the Strait of Hormuz, he had resorted to calling his own mother, the formidable Lakshmi Chowdhury, to come to his Logan Circle apartment. She had arrived before the sun had even risen in order to watch Ashni.

"Don't forget my one condition," she'd reminded her son as he tightened his tie around the collar that was too loose for his thin neck. Heading out into the slushy predawn, he paused at the door. "I won't forget," he told her. "And I'll be back by the time Ashni's picked up." He had to be: his mother's one condition was that she not be inflicted with the sight of Sandy's ex-wife, Samantha, a transplant from Texas's Gulf Coast whom Lakshmi haughtily called "provincial." She'd disliked her the moment she had set eyes on her skinny frame and pageboy blonde haircut. A poor man's Ellen DeGeneres, Lakshmi had once said in a pique, having to remind her son about the old-time television show host whose appeal she'd never understood.

If being single and reliant upon his mother at forty-four was somewhat humiliating, the ego blow was diminished when he removed his White House all-access badge from his briefcase. He flashed it to the uniformed Secret Service agent at the northwest gate while a couple of early morning joggers on Pennsylvania Avenue glanced in his direction, wondering if they should know who he was. It was only in the last eighteen months, since he'd taken up his posting in the West Wing, that his mother had finally begun to correct people when they assumed that her son, Dr. Chowdhury, was a medical doctor.

His mother had asked to visit his office several times, but he'd kept her at bay. The idea of an office in the West Wing was far more glamorous than the reality, a desk and a chair jammed against a basement wall in a general crush of staff.

He sat at his desk, enjoying the rare quiet of the empty room. No one else had made it through the two inches of snow that had paralyzed the capital city. Chowdhury rooted around one of his drawers, scrounged up a badly crushed but still edible energy bar, and took it, a cup of coffee, and a briefing binder through the heavy soundproof doors into the Situation Room.

A seat with a built-in work terminal had been left for him at the head of the conference table. He logged in. At the far end of the room was an LED screen with a map displaying the disposition of US military forces abroad, to include an encrypted video-teleconference link with each of the major combatant commands, Southern, Central, Northern, and the rest. He focused on the Indo-Pacific Command—the largest and most important, responsible for nearly 40 percent of the earth's surface, though much of it was ocean.

The briefer was Rear Admiral John T. Hendrickson, a nuclear submariner with whom Chowdhury had a passing familiarity, though they'd yet to work together directly. The admiral was flanked by two junior officers, a man and a woman, each significantly taller than him. The admiral and Chowdhury had been contemporaries in the doctoral program at the Fletcher School of Law and Diplomacy fifteen years before. That didn't mean they'd been friends; in fact, they'd only over-lapped by a single year, but Chowdhury knew Hendrickson by reputation. At a hair over five feet, five inches tall, Hendrickson was conspicuous in his shortness. His compact size made it seem as though he were born to fit into submarines, and his quirky, deeply analytic mind seemed equally customized for that strange brand of naval service. Hendrick-son had finished his doctorate in a record-breaking three years (as op-posed to Chowdhury's seven), and during that time he'd led the Fletcher softball team to a hat trick of intramural championships in the Boston area, earning the nickname "Bunt."

Chowdhury nearly called Hendrickson by that old nickname, but he thought better of it. It was a moment for deference to official roles. The screen in front of them was littered with forward-deployed military units—an amphibious ready group in the Aegean, a carrier battle group in the Western Pacific, two nuclear submarines under what remained of the Arctic ice, the concentric rings of armored formations fanned out from west to east in Central Europe, as they had been for nearly a hun-dred years to ward off Russian aggression. Hendrickson quickly homed in on two critical events underway, one long planned; the other "devel-oping," as Hendrickson put it.

The planned event was the testing of a new electromagnetic dis-rupter within the F-35's suite of stealth technology. This test was now in progress and would play out over the next several hours. The fighter had been launched from a Marine squadron off the *George H. W. Bush* in the Arabian Gulf. Hendrickson glanced down at his watch. "The pilot's been dark in Iranian airspace for the last four minutes." He went into a long, top secret, and dizzyingly expository paragraph on the nature of the electromagnetic disruption, which was occurring at that very moment, soothing the Iranian air defenses to sleep.

Within the first few sentences, Chowdhury was lost. He had never been detail oriented, particularly when those details were technical in nature. This was why he'd found his way into politics after graduate school. This was also why Hendrickson—brilliant though he was—did, technically, work for Chowdhury. As a political appointee on the National Security Council staff Chowdhury outranked him, though this was a point few military officers in the White House would publicly concede to their civilian masters. Chowdhury's genius, while not technical, was an intuitive understanding of how to make the best out of any bad situation. He'd gotten his political start working in the one-term Pence presidency. Who could say he wasn't a survivor?

"The second situation is developing," continued Hendrickson. "The *John Paul Jones* command group—a three-ship surface action group—has diverted the flagship from its freedom of navigation patrol nearby the Spratly Islands to investigate a vessel in duress."

"What kind of vessel?" asked Chowdhury. He was leaning back in the leather executive chair at the head of the conference table, the same chair that the president sat in when she used the room. Chowdhury was munching the end of his energy bar in a particularly non-presidential fashion.

"We don't know," answered Hendrickson. "We're waiting on an update from Seventh Fleet."

Even though Chowdhury couldn't follow the particulars of the F-35's stealth disruption, he did know that having a two-billion-dollar Arleigh Burke guided missile destroyer playing rescue tugboat to a mystery ship in waters claimed by the Chinese had the potential to undermine his morning. And splitting up the surface action group didn't seem like the best idea. "This doesn't sound good, Bunt. Who is the on-scene commander?"

Hendrickson shot a glance back at Chowdhury, who recognized the slight provocation he was making by using the old nickname. The two junior staffers exchanged an apprehensive look. Hendrickson chose to ignore it. "I know the commodore," he said. "Captain Sarah Hunt. She is extremely capable. Top of her class at everything."

"So?" asked Chowdhury.

"So, we'd be prudent to cut her a little slack."

⌐

15:28 March 12, 2034 (GMT+8)
South China Sea

Once the order to render aid was given, the crew of the *John Paul Jones* worked quickly. Two RHIBs launched off the fantail and pulled alongside the burning trawler. The stocky blond lieutenant junior grade had been placed in charge of this tiny flotilla of inflatable boats, while Hunt and Morris observed from the bridge, listening to the updates he sent over his handheld radio with all the baritone hysteria of plays being called at the line of scrimmage. Both senior officers forgave his novice lack of calm. He was putting out a fire with two pumps and two hoses in hostile waters.

Hostile but completely calm, rigid as a pane of glass as the drama of the fire and the trawler played out a couple of hundred yards off the bridge. Hunt found herself staring wistfully at the water, wondering again if perhaps this might be her last time seeing such a sea, or at least seeing it from the command of a naval vessel. After a moment's thought, she told the officer of the deck to send a signal to her other two destroyers to break off the freedom of navigation patrol and divert on-scene. Better to have a bit more firepower in close.

The *Levin* and *Hoon* reversed course and increased speed, and in a few minutes they had taken up positions around the *John Paul Jones*, sailing in a protective orbit as the flagship continued a dead slow approach toward the trawler. Soon, the last of the flames had been extinguished and the young lieutenant junior grade gave a triumphant announcement over the radio, to which both Hunt and Morris volunteered some quick congratulations followed by instructions for him to board and assess the extent of the damages. An order that he followed. Or at least tried to follow.

The crew of the trawler met the first boarding party at the gunnels with angry, desperate shouts. One went so far as to swing a grapple at a boatswain's head. Watching this struggle from the bridge of the *John Paul Jones*, Hunt wondered why the crew of a burning ship would so stridently resist help. Between radio transmissions, in which she encouraged a general de-escalation, she could overhear the trawler's crew, who spoke in what sounded like Mandarin.

"Ma'am, I suggest we cut them loose," Morris eventually offered. "They don't seem to want any more help."

"I can see that, Jane," responded Hunt. "But the question is, why not?"

She could observe the boarding party and the crew of the trawler gesticulating wildly at one another. Why this resistance? Hunt saw Morris's point—with each passing minute her command became increasingly vulnerable to intercept by a People's Liberation Army naval patrol, which would undermine their mission. But wasn't this their mission as well? To keep these waters safe and navigable? Ten, maybe even five years before, the threat level had been lower. Back then, most of the Cold War treaties had remained intact. Those old systems had eroded, however. And Sarah Hunt, gazing out at this trawler with its defiant crew, had an instinct that this small fishing vessel represented a threat.

"Commander Morris," said Hunt gravely, "pull your ship alongside that trawler. If we can't board her from the RHIBs we'll board her from here."

Morris immediately objected to the order, offering a predictable list of concerns: first, the time it would take would further expose them to a potential confrontation with a hostile naval patrol; second, placing the *John Paul Jones* alongside the trawler would put their own ship at undue risk. "We don't know what's on board," cautioned Morris.

Hunt listened patiently. She could feel Morris's crew going about their tasks on the bridge, trying to ignore these two senior-most officers as they had their disagreement. Then Hunt repeated the order. Morris complied.

As the *John Paul Jones* came astride the trawler, Hunt could now see its name, *Wén Rui*, and its home port, Quanzhou, a provincial-level anchorage astride the Taiwan Strait. Her crew shot grapples over the trawler's gunnels, which allowed them to affix steel tow cables to its side. Lashed together, the two ships cut through the water in tandem like a motorcycle with an unruly sidecar. The danger of this maneuver was obvious to everyone on the bridge. They went about their tasks with a glum air of silent-sailor-disapproval, all thinking their commodore was risking the ship unnecessarily for a bunch of agitated Chinese fishermen. No one voiced their collective wish that their commodore let her hunch go by the boards and return them to safer waters.

Sensing the discontent, Hunt announced that she was heading belowdecks.

Heads snapped around.

"Where to, ma'am?" Morris said by way of protest, seemingly indignant that her commander would abandon her in such a precarious position.

"To the *Wén Rui*," answered Hunt. "I want to see her for myself."

And this is what she did, surprising the master-at-arms, who handed her a holstered pistol, which she strapped on as she clamored over the side, ignoring the throbbing in her bad leg. When Hunt dropped onto the deck of the trawler, she found that the boarding party had already placed under arrest the half dozen crew members of the *Wén Rui*. They sat cross-legged amidships with an armed guard hovering behind them, their wrists bound at their backs in plastic flex-cuffs, their peaked fishing caps pulled low, and their clothes oily and stained. When Hunt stepped on deck, one of the arrested men, who was oddly clean-shaven and whose cap wasn't pulled low but was worn proudly back on his head, stood. The gesture wasn't defiant, actually quite the opposite; he was clear-eyed. Hunt immediately took him for the captain of the *Wén Rui*.

The chief petty officer who was leading the party explained that they'd searched most of the trawler but that a steel, watertight hatch secured one of the stern compartments and the crew had refused to unlock it. The chief had ordered a welding torch brought from the ship's locker. In about fifteen minutes they'd have everything opened up.

The clean-shaven man, the trawler's captain, began to speak in uncertain and heavily accented English: "Are you command here?"

"You speak English?" Hunt replied.

"Are you command here?" he repeated to her, as if perhaps he weren't certain what these words meant and had simply memorized them long ago as a contingency.

"I am Captain Sarah Hunt, United States Navy," she answered, placing her palm on her chest. "Yes, this is my command."

He nodded, and as he did his shoulders collapsed, as if shrugging off a heavy pack. "I surrender my command to you." Then he turned his back to Hunt, a gesture that, at first, seemed to be a sign of disrespect, but that she soon recognized as being something altogether different. In his open palm, which was cuffed behind him at the wrist, was a key. He'd been holding it all this time and was now, with whatever ceremony he could muster, surrendering it to Hunt.

Hunt plucked the key from his palm, which was noticeably soft, not the calloused palm of a fisherman. She approached the compartment at the stern on the *Wén Rui*, popped off the lock, and opened the hatch.

"What we got, ma'am?" asked the master-at-arms, who stood close behind her.

"Christ," said Hunt, staring at racks of blinking miniature hard drives and plasma screens. "I have no idea."

Γ

13:47 March 12, 2034 (GMT+4:30)
Strait of Hormuz

When Wedge switched to manual control, the Lockheed contractors on the *George H. W. Bush* immediately began to radio, wanting to know if everything was okay. He hadn't answered, at least not at first. They could still track him and see that he was adhering to their flight plan, which at this moment placed him approximately fifty nautical miles west of Bandar Abbas, the main regional Iranian naval base. The accuracy of his flight proved—at least to him—that his navigation was as precise as any computer.

Then his F-35 hit a pocket of atmospheric turbulence—a bad one. Wedge could feel it shudder up the controls, through his feet, which were planted on the rudder pedals, into the stick, and across his shoulders. The turbulence threatened to throw him off course, which could have diverted him into the more technologically advanced layers of Iranian air defenses, the ones that expanded outward from Tehran, in which the F-35's stealth countermeasures might prove inadequate.

This is *it*, he thought.

Or at least as close to *it* as he had ever come. His manipulation of throttle, stick, and rudder was fast, instinctual, the result of his entire career in the cockpit, and of four generations' worth of Mitchell family breeding.

He skittered his aircraft on the edge of the turbulence, flying for a total of 3.6 nautical miles at a speed of 736 knots with his aircraft oriented with 28 degrees of yaw respective to its direction of flight. The entire episode lasted under four seconds, but it was a moment of hidden grace, one that only he and perhaps his great-grandfather watching from the afterlife appreciated in the instant of its occurrence.

Then, as quickly as the turbulence sprung up, it dissipated, and Wedge was flying steadily. Once again, the Lockheed contractors on the *George H. W. Bush* radioed, asking why he'd disabled his navigation computer. They insisted that he turn it back on. "Roger," said Wedge, as he finally came up over the encrypted communications link, "activating navigation override." He leaned forward, pressed a single innocuous button, and felt a slight lurch, like a train being switched back onto a set of tracks, as his F-35 returned to autopilot.

Wedge was overcome by an urge to smoke a cigarette in the cockpit, just as Pappy Boyington used to do, but he'd pushed his luck far enough for today. Returning to the *Bush* in a cockpit that reeked of a celebratory

Marlboro would likely be more than the Lockheed contractors, or his superiors, could countenance. The pack was in the left breast pocket of his flight suit, but he'd wait and have one on the fantail after his debrief. Checking his watch, he calculated that he'd be back in time for dinner in the pilots' dirty shirt wardroom in the forward part of the carrier. He hoped they'd have the "heart attack" sliders he loved—triple cheeseburger patties with a fried egg on top.

It was while he was thinking of that dinner—and the cigarette—that his F-35 diverted off course, heading north, inland toward Iran. This shift in direction was so smooth that Wedge didn't even notice it until another series of calls came from the *Bush*, all of them alarmed as to this change in heading.

"Turn on your navigation computer."

Wedge tapped at its screen. "My navigation computer *is* on. . . . Wait, I'm going to reboot." Before Wedge could begin the long reboot sequence, he realized that his computer was nonresponsive. "Avionics are out. I'm switching to manual override."

He pulled at his stick.

He stamped on his rudder pedals.

The throttle no longer controlled the engine.

His F-35 was beginning to lose altitude, descending gradually. In sheer frustration, a frustration that bordered on rage, he tugged at the controls, strangling them, as if he were trying to murder the plane in which he flew. He could hear the chatter in his helmet, the impotent commands from the *George H. W. Bush*, which weren't even really commands but rather pleadings, desperate requests for Wedge to figure out this problem.

But he couldn't.

Wedge didn't know who or what was flying his plane.

07:23 March 12, 2034 (GMT-4)
Washington, D.C.

Sandy Chowdhury had finished his energy bar, was well into his second cup of coffee, and the updates would not stop coming. The first was this news that the *John Paul Jones* had found some type of advanced technological suite on the fishing trawler they'd boarded and lashed to their side. The commodore, this Sarah Hunt, whose judgment Hendrickson so trusted, was insistent that within an hour she could offload the computers onto one of the three ships in her flotilla for further forensic exploitation. While Chowdhury was weighing that option with Hendrickson, the second update came in, from Seventh Fleet Headquarters, "INFO" Indo-Pacific Command. A contingent of People's Liberation Army warships, at least six, to include the nuclear-powered carrier *Zheng He*, had altered course, and were heading directly toward the *John Paul Jones*.

The third update was most puzzling of all. The controls of the F-35, the one whose flight had brought Chowdhury into the Situation Room early that snowy Monday morning, had locked up. The pilot was working through every contingency, but at this moment, he was no longer in control of his aircraft.

"If the pilot isn't flying it, and we're not doing it remotely from the carrier, then who the hell is?" Chowdhury snapped at Hendrickson.

A junior White House staffer interrupted them. "Dr. Chowdhury," she said, "the Chinese defense attaché would like to speak with you."

Chowdhury shot Hendrickson an incredulous glance, as if he were willing the one-star admiral to explain that this entire situation was part of a single, elaborate, and twisted practical joke. But no such assurance came. "All right, transfer him through," said Chowdhury as he reached for the phone.

"No, Dr. Chowdhury," said the young staffer. "He's here. Admiral Lin Bao is here."

"Here?" said Hendrickson. "At the White House? You're kidding."

The staffer shook her head. "I'm not, sir. He's at the Northwest gate." Chowdhury and Hendrickson pushed open the Situation Room door, hurried down the corridor to the nearest window, and peered through the blinds. There was Admiral Lin Bao, resplendent in his blue service uniform with gold epaulets, standing patiently with three Chinese military escorts and one civilian at the west gate among the growing crowd of tourists. It was a mini-delegation. Chowdhury couldn't fathom what they were doing. The Chinese are never impulsive like this, he thought.

"Jesus," he muttered.

"We can't just let him in," said Hendrickson. A gaggle of Secret Service supervisors gathered around them to explain that the proper vetting for a Chinese official to enter the White House couldn't possibly be accomplished in anything less than four hours; that is, unless they had POTUS, chief of staff, or national security advisor–level approval. But all three were overseas. The television was tuned to the latest updates on the G7 summit in Munich, which had left the White House without a president and much of its national security team. Chowdhury was the senior NSC staffer in the White House at that moment.

"Shit," said Chowdhury. "I'm going out there."

"You can't go out there," said Hendrickson.

"He can't come in here."

Hendrickson couldn't argue the logic. Chowdhury headed for the door. He didn't grab his coat, though it was below freezing. He hoped that whatever message the defense attaché had to deliver wouldn't take long. Now that he was outside, his personal phone caught signal and vibrated with a half dozen text messages, all from his mother. Whenever she watched his daughter she would pepper him with mundane domestic questions as a reminder of the favor she was performing. Christ, he thought, I bet she can't find the baby wipes again. But Chowdhury didn't have time to check the particulars of those texts as he walked along the South Lawn.

Cold as it was, Lin Bao wasn't wearing a coat either, only his uniform, with its wall of medals, furiously embroidered epaulettes in gold, and peaked naval officer's cap tucked snugly under his arm. Lin Bao was casually eating from a packet of M&M's, picking the candies out one at a time with pinched fingers. Chowdhury passed through the black steel gate to where Lin Bao stood. "I have a weakness for your M&M's," said the admiral absently. "They were a military invention. Did you know that? It's true—the candies were first mass-produced for American GIs in World War Two, specifically in the South Pacific, where they required chocolate that wouldn't melt. That's your saying, right? *Melts in your mouth, not in your hand.*" Lin Bao licked the tips of his fingers, where the candy coloring had bled, staining his skin a mottled pastel.

"To what do we owe the pleasure, Admiral?" Chowdhury asked.

Lin Bao peered into his bag of M&M's, as if he had a specific idea of which color he'd like to sample next but couldn't quite find it. Speaking into the bag, he said, "You have something of ours, a small ship, very small—the *Wén Rui*. We'd like it back." Then he picked out a blue M&M, made a face, as if this wasn't the color he'd been searching for, and somewhat disappointedly placed it into his mouth.

"We shouldn't be talking about that out here," said Chowdhury.

"Would you care to invite me inside?" asked the admiral, nodding toward the West Wing, knowing the impossibility of that request. He then added, "Otherwise, I think out in the open is the only way we can talk."

Chowdhury was freezing. He tucked his hands underneath his arms.

"Believe me," added Lin Bao, "it is in your best interest to give us back the *Wén Rui*."

Although Chowdhury worked for the first American president who was unaffiliated with a political party in modern history, the administration's position with regards to freedom of navigation and the South China Sea had remained consistent with the several Republican and Democratic administrations that had preceded it. Chowdhury repeated those well-established policy positions to an increasingly impatient Lin Bao.

"You don't have time for this," he said to Chowdhury, still picking through his diminishing bag of M&M's.

"Is that a threat?"

"Not at all," said Lin Bao, shaking his head sadly, feigning disappointment that Chowdhury would make such a suggestion. "I meant that your mother has been texting you, hasn't she? Don't you need to reply? Check your phone. You'll see she wants to take your daughter Ashni outside to enjoy the snow but can't find the girl's coat."

Chowdhury removed his phone from his pants pocket.

He glanced at the text messages.

They were as Lin Bao had represented them.

"We have ships of our own coming to intercept the *John Paul Jones*, the *Carl Levin*, and the *Chung-Hoon*," continued Lin Bao, speaking the name of each destroyer to prove that he knew it, just as he knew the details of every text message that was sent to Chowdhury's phone. "Escalation on your part would be a mistake."

"What will you give us for the *Wén Rui*?"

"We'll return your F-35."

"F-35?" said Chowdhury. "You don't have an F-35."

"Maybe you should go back to your Situation Room and check," said Lin Bao mildly. He poured the last M&M from his packet into his palm. It was yellow. "We have M&M's in China too. But they taste better here. It's something about the candy shell. In China, we just can't get the formula quite right. . . ." Then he put the chocolate in his mouth, briefly shutting his eyes to savor it. When he opened them, he was again staring at Chowdhury. "You need to give us back the *Wén Rui*."

"I don't *need* to do anything," said Chowdhury.

Lin Bao nodded disappointedly. "Very well," he said. "I understand." He crumpled up the candy wrapper and then pitched it on the sidewalk.

"Pick that up, please, Admiral," said Chowdhury.

Lin Bao glanced down at the piece of litter. "Or else what?"

As Chowdhury struggled to formulate a response, the admiral turned on his heels and stepped across the street, weaving his way through the late-morning traffic.

⌐

16:12 March 12, 2034 (GMT+8)
South China Sea

The pair of high-speed fighter-interceptors came out of nowhere, their sonic booms rattling the deck of the *John Paul Jones*, taking the crew completely unawares. Commodore Hunt ducked instinctively at the sound. She was still aboard the *Wén Rui*, picking over the technical suite they'd uncovered the hour before. The trawler's captain returned a toothy grin, as if he'd been expecting the low-flying jets all along. "Let's get the crew of the *Wén Rui* secured down in the brig," Hunt told the master-at-arms supervising the search. She ran up to the bridge and found Morris struggling to manage the situation.

"What've you got?" asked Hunt.

Morris, who was peering into an Aegis terminal, now tracked not only the two interceptors, but also the signatures of at least six separate ships of unknown origin that had appeared at the exact same moment as the interceptors. It was as if an entire fleet, in a single coordinated maneuver, had chosen to unmask itself. The nearest of these vessels, which moved nimbly in the Aegis display, suggested the profile of a frigate or destroyer. They were eight nautical miles distant, right at the edge of visible range. Hunt raised a set of binoculars, searching the horizon. Then the first frigate's gray hull ominously appeared.

"There," she said, pointing off their bow.

Calls soon came in from the *Levin* and the *Hoon* confirming visuals on two, then three, and finally a fourth and fifth ship. All People's Liberation Army naval vessels, and they ranged in size from a frigate up to a carrier, the hulking *Zheng He*, which was as formidable as anything in the US Navy's Seventh Fleet. The Chinese ships formed in a circle around Hunt's command, which itself had encircled the *Wén Rui*, so that the two flotillas were arrayed in two concentric rings, rotating in opposite directions.

A radioman positioned in a corner of the bridge wearing a headset began to emphatically gesture for Hunt. "What is it?" she asked the sailor, who handed her the headset. Over the analog hum of static, she could hear a faint voice: "US Naval Commander, this is Rear Admiral

Ma Qiang, commander of the *Zheng He* Carrier Battle Group. We demand you release the civilian vessel you have captured. Depart our territorial waters immediately. . . ." There was a pause, then the message repeated. Hunt wondered how many times this request had been spoken into the ether, and how many times it would be allowed to go unanswered before the attendant battle group—which seemed to be drawing ever closer—took action.

"Can you get a secure VoIP connection with Seventh Fleet Headquarters?" Hunt asked the radioman, who nodded and then began reconfiguring red and blue wires into the back of an old-fashioned laptop normally used on the quiet midwatches for video games; it was primitive and so perhaps a more secure way to connect.

"What do they want?" asked Morris, who was staring vacantly at the ring of six ships that surrounded them.

"They want that fishing trawler back," said Hunt. "Or, rather, whatever technology is on it, and they want us out of these waters."

"What's our move?"

"I don't know yet," answered Hunt, who glanced over at the radioman, who was toggling the VoIP switch, checking it for a dial tone. While she waited, her leg began to ache from the activity of climbing around the ship. She reached in her pocket, rubbed the ache, and felt the letter from the medical board. "You got me Seventh Fleet yet?" she asked.

"Not yet, ma'am."

Hunt glanced impatiently at her watch. "Christ, then call the *Levin* or the *Hoon*. See if they can raise them."

The radioman glanced back at her, wide-eyed, as if searching within himself for the courage to say something he couldn't quite bear to say.

"What is it?" asked Hunt.

"I've got nothing."

"What do you mean, you've got nothing?" Hunt glanced at Morris, who appeared equally unnerved.

"All of our communications are down," said the radioman. "I can't raise the *Levin*, or the *Hoon*. . . . I've got nobody."

Hunt unclipped the handheld radio she had fastened to her belt, the one she'd been using to communicate with the bridge when she'd been belowdecks on the *Wén Rui*. She keyed and unkeyed the handset. "Can you get up on any channel?" Hunt asked, betraying for the first time the slightest tinge of desperation in her voice.

"Only this one," said the radioman, who raised the earphones he'd been listening to, which relayed a message on a loop:

"US Naval Commander, this is Rear Admiral Ma Qiang, commander of the *Zheng He* Carrier Battle Group. We demand you release the civilian vessel you have captured. Depart our territorial waters immediately. . . ."

⌐

14:22 March 12, 2034 (GMT+4:30)
Strait of Hormuz

All the screens in the cockpit were out. The avionics. The weapons. The navigation. All of it—dark. Wedge's communications had gone silent a few minutes before, which had left him feeling a remarkable sense of calm. No one from the *Bush* was calling. It was just him, up here, with an impossible problem. The plane was still flying itself. Or, rather, it was being flown by unseen forces who were smoothly and carefully maneuvering the jet. His descent had stalled. By his estimation, he was cruising at around five thousand feet. His speed was steady, five hundred, maybe five hundred and fifty knots. And he was circling.

He pulled from his flight bag the tablet on which he'd downloaded all the regional charts. He also checked the compass on his watch, the Breitling chronometer that had belonged to his father. Referencing the compass and the tablet together, it didn't take him long to calculate exactly where he was, which was directly above Bandar Abbas, the site of the massive Iranian military installation that guarded the entrance to the Arabian Gulf. Or the Persian Gulf, as they call it, thought Wedge. He watched the parched land below slowly rotate as he flew racetracks in the airspace.

There was, of course, the off chance that this override of his aircraft was due to some freak malfunction in the F-35. But those odds were long and running longer with each minute that passed. What was far more probable, as Wedge saw it, was that his mission had been compromised, the controls of his plane hacked, and he himself turned into a passenger on this flight that he increasingly believed would end with him on the ground in Iranian territory.

Time was short; he would be out of fuel within the hour. He had one choice.

It likely meant he wouldn't be smoking a celebratory Marlboro on the fantail of the *Bush* anytime soon. So, he reached between his legs, to the black-and-yellow striped handle, which was primed to the rocket in his ejection seat. This is *it*, he nearly said aloud, as he thought of his father, grandfather, and great-grandfather, all in the single instant it took him to pull the handle.

But nothing happened.

His ejector seat had been disabled too.

The engine on the F-35 let out a slight, decelerating groan. His plane began to cast off altitude, corkscrewing its descent into Bandar Abbas. One last time, Wedge stamped on the rudder pedals, pushed and then pulled the throttle, and tugged on the stick. He then reached under his flight vest, to where he carried his pistol. He grabbed it by its barrel, so that in his grip he wielded it like a hammer. And as his aircraft entered its glide path toward the runway, Wedge began to tear apart the inside of his cockpit, doing his best to destroy the sensitive items it contained, beginning with the small black box situated behind his head. This entire time, it hadn't stopped its humming.

Γ

08:32 March 12, 2034 (GMT-4)
Washington, D.C.

Air Force One, with the president on board, was slicing across the Atlantic on its way back from the G7 summit, its last round of meetings having been curtailed due to the burgeoning crisis. Touchdown at Andrews was scheduled for 16:37 local time, more than an hour after Chowdhury had sworn to his mother that he'd be home to facilitate his daughter's pickup with his ex-wife. Taking a reprieve from one crisis, he stepped outside the Situation Room and turned on his cell phone to deal with another.

"Sandeep, I refuse to stand in the same room as that woman," answered his mother as soon as Chowdhury had explained. He pleaded for her help. When she asked for the details of what was holding him up he couldn't say, recalling Lin Bao's familiarity with his texts. His mother continued to protest. In the end, however, Chowdhury insisted on remaining at work, adding, lamely, that it was "a matter of national security."

He hung up the phone and returned to the Situation Room. Hendrickson and his two aides sat on one side of the conference table, staring blankly at the opposite wall. Lin Bao had called, delivering news that had yet to filter from the *George H. W. Bush*, through Fifth Fleet Headquarters in Bahrain, up to Central Command, and then to the White House: the Iranian Revolutionary Guards had taken control of an F-35 transiting their airspace, hacking into its onboard computer to bring it down.

"Where's the plane now?" Chowdhury barked at Hendrickson.

"In Bandar Abbas," he said vacantly.

"And the pilot?"

"Sitting on the tarmac brandishing a pistol."

"Is he safe?"

"He's brandishing a pistol," said Hendrickson. But then he gave Chowdhury's question greater thought. The pilot was safe, insomuch as to kill him would be a further and significant provocation, one it seemed the Iranians and their Chinese collaborators weren't ready to make, at least not yet. What Lin Bao wanted was simple: a swap. The *John Paul Jones* had stumbled upon something of value to the Chinese—the *Wén Rui*, or more specifically the technology installed on it—and they wanted that technology back. They would be willing to arrange a swap through their Iranian allies, the F-35 for the *Wén Rui*.

Before Chowdhury could reach any conclusions, Lin Bao was again on the line. "Have you considered our offer?" Chowdhury thought of his own larger questions. Ever since the mid-2020s, when Iran had signed onto the Chinese "Belt and Road" global development initiative to prevent financial collapse after the coronavirus pandemic, they had helped project Chinese economic and military interests; but what was the scope of this seemingly new Sino-Iranian alliance? And who else was a party to it? Chowdhury didn't have the authority to trade an F-35 for what would seem to be a Chinese spy ship. The president herself would decide whether such a swap was in the offing. Chowdhury explained the limitations of his own authority to Lin Bao, and added that his superiors would soon return. Lin Bao seemed unimpressed.

"While you're holding the *Wén Rui* we are forced to interpret any stalling as an act of aggression, for we can only assume you are stalling so as to exploit the technology you've seized illegally. If the *Wén Rui* isn't turned over to us within the hour, we and our allies will have no other choice but to take action."

Then the line went silent.

What that action was, and who those allies were, Lin Bao didn't say.

Nothing could be done within an hour. The president had already indicated that she wouldn't be moved by ultimatums. She had summoned the Chinese ambassador to meet that evening and not before, which according to Lin Bao would be too late. While they assessed their options, Hendrickson explained gravely to Chowdhury that the only naval force they had within an hour's range of any other Chinese ships was the *Michelle Obama*, an attack submarine that had been trailing a Chinese merchant marine convoy up and around the Arctic deltas that had once been the polar ice caps. The *Obama* was tracking two Russian submarines, which had closed to within ten miles off the stern of the merchant convoy. While Chowdhury considered this development, puzzling over the appearance of the Russians, he was reminded of a story about Lincoln.

"It was during the darkest days of the Civil War," Chowdhury began, ostensibly speaking to Hendrickson, but really speaking to himself. "The Union had sustained a series of defeats against the Confederates. A visitor from Kentucky was leaving the White House and asked Lincoln what cheering news he could take home. By way of reply, Lincoln told him a story about a chess expert who had never met his match until he tried his luck against a machine called the 'automaton chess player' and was beaten three times running. Astonished, the defeated expert stood from his chair and walked slowly around and around this amazing new piece of technology, examining it minutely as he went, trying to understand how it worked. At last he stopped and leveled an accusing finger in its direction. 'There's a man in there!' he cried. Then Lincoln told his visitor to take heart. No matter how bad things looked there was always a man in the machine."

The phone rang again.

It was Lin Bao.

15:17 March 12, 2034 (GMT+4:30)
Strait of Hormuz

Wedge was furious. He couldn't help but feel betrayed as he sat on the taxiway at Bandar Abbas. Of course, he hadn't chosen this taxiway, or where to land, or even to open his canopy and shut off his engine. His plane had betrayed him so completely that the overriding emotion he felt was shame. On his descent he had managed to destroy the black box behind his head by using his pistol as a hammer. He had also destroyed the encrypted communications on board, as well as the most sensitive avionics, which controlled his suite of weapons. Like a crazed, captive animal, he'd been banging away at the inside of his cockpit ever since losing control.

He continued his work once he landed.

As soon as his cockpit was open, he'd stood up in it and fired his pistol into the controls. The gesture filled him with a surprising upsurge of emotion, as though he were a cavalryman putting a bullet through the brain of a once-faithful mount. The few dozen Revolutionary Guards dispersed around the airfield struggled to understand the commotion. For the first several minutes, they chose to keep their distance, not out of fear of him, but out of fear that he might force a misstep into what, up to this point, had been their well-orchestrated plan. However, the more Wedge destroyed—tearing at loose wiring, stamping with the heel of his boot, and brandishing his pistol in the direction of the guardsmen when he felt them approaching too closely—the more he forced their hand. If he completely destroyed the sensitive items in his F-35, the aircraft would be of no use as a bargaining chip.

The on-scene commander, a brigadier general, understood what Wedge was doing, having spent his entire adult life facing off, either directly or indirectly, with the Americans. The brigadier slowly tightened the cordon around Wedge's aircraft. Wedge, who could feel the Iranians closing in, continued to flash his pistol at them. But he could tell that each time he pulled it out, the guardsmen on the cordon became increasingly unconvinced that he'd actually use it. And he wouldn't have used it, even if it'd had any ammunition left, which it didn't. Wedge had already plugged the last round into the avionics.

The brigadier, who was missing the pinky and ring finger of his right hand, was now waving at Wedge, standing in the seat of his jeep, as the other jeeps and armored vehicles on the cordon grew closer. The brigadier's English was as mangled as his three-fingered hand, but Wedge could make out what he was saying, which was something to the effect of, "Surrender and no harm will come to you."

Wedge didn't plan on surrendering, not without a fight. Though he couldn't say what that fight would be. All Wedge had was the empty pistol.

The brigadier was now close enough to issue his demands for surrender without needing to shout them at Wedge, who replied by standing in the cockpit and chucking his pistol at the brigadier.

It was an admirable toss, the pistol tumbling end-over-end like a hatchet.

The brigadier, who to his credit didn't flinch when the pistol sailed right above his head, gave the order. His men stormed the F-35, dismounting their vehicles in a swarm to clamber up its wings, and then over its fuselage, where they found Wedge, crammed in his cockpit, his feet on the rudder pedals, one hand on the throttle, the other on the stick. Absently, he was scanning the far horizon, as if for enemy fighters. A Marlboro dangled from his lips. When the half dozen members of the Revolutionary Guard leveled the muzzles of their rifles around his head, he pitched his cigarette out of the cockpit.

16:36 March 12, 2034 (GMT+8)
South China Sea

The flotilla's communications had been down for the past twenty minutes, an eternity.

Between the *John Paul Jones*, the *Carl Levin*, and the *Chung-Hoon*, Hunt had only been able to communicate through signal flags, her sailors flapping away in the upper reaches of the ship as frantically as if they were trying to take flight for land. Surprisingly, this primitive means of signaling proved effective, allowing the three ships to coordinate their movements in plain sight of the *Zheng He* Carrier Battle Group that encircled them. The only message that came over any of the ship's radios was the demand to surrender the *Wén Rui*. It continued to play on a maddening loop while Hunt and one of her chief petty officers troubleshot the communications suite on the *John Paul Jones*, hoping to receive any sliver of a message from Seventh Fleet, something that might bring clarity to their situation, which had so quickly deteriorated.

That message wouldn't come, and Hunt knew it.

What she also knew was that whatever was happening to her was happening within a broader context, a context that she didn't understand. She'd been placed into a game in which her opponent could see the entire board and she could see but a fraction of it. The crew on all three of her ships were at general quarters. The master-at-arms had yet to offload the suite of computers from the *Wén Rui*, though that task would be completed within the hour. Hunt had to assume that her opponent, who was watching her, understood that, and so whatever was going to happen would happen before that hour was up.

Another twenty minutes passed.

Morris, who had been belowdecks checking on the *Wén Rui*, scrambled back to the bridge. "They're almost done with the transfer," she told Hunt, catching her breath. "Maybe five more minutes," she announced optimistically. "Then we can cut the *Wén Rui* loose and maneuver out of here."

Hunt nodded, but she felt certain that events would take a different course.

She didn't know what would happen, but whatever it was, she had only her eyes to rely on in order to see the move that would be played against her. The ocean remained calm, flat as a pane of glass, just as it had been all that morning. Hunt and Morris stood alongside one another on the bridge, scanning the horizon.

Because of the stillness of the water, they saw their adversary's next move when it came only seconds later. A single darting wake below the surface, jetting up a froth as it made its steady approach, closing the distance in seconds: a torpedo.

Six hundred yards.

Five hundred.

Three hundred and fifty.

It sliced through the torpid water.

Morris shouted the instinctual commands across the bridge, sounding the alarm for impact, the sirens echoing throughout the ship. Hunt, on the other hand, stood very still in these ultimate seconds. She felt strangely relieved. Her adversary had made his move. Her move would come next. But was the torpedo aimed at the *Wén Rui*, or at her ship? Who was the aggressor? No one would ever be able to agree. Wars were justified over such disagreements. And although few could predict what this first shot would bring, Hunt could. She could see the years ahead as clearly as the torpedo, which was now less than one hundred yards from the starboard side of the *John Paul Jones*.

Who was to blame for what had transpired on this day wouldn't be decided anytime soon. The war needed to come first. Then the victor would apportion the blame. This is how it was and would always be. This is what she was thinking when the torpedo hit.

Γ

17:13 March 12, 2034 (GMT-4)
Washington, D.C.

Chowdhury leaned forward out of his seat, his elbows planted on the conference table, his neck angled toward the speakerphone in its center. Hendrickson sat opposite him at a computer, his hands hovering over the keyboard, ready to transcribe notes. The two had received orders from the National Command Authority, which was now handling the situation from Air Force One. Before the Chinese ambassador's visit to the White House that evening, the national security advisor had laid out an aggressive negotiating framework for Chowdhury to telegraph to Lin Bao, which he now did.

"Before we agree to transfer the *Wén Rui* to your naval forces," Chowdhury began, glancing up at Hendrickson, "our F-35 at Bandar Abbas must be returned. Because we are not the ones who instigated this crisis, it is imperative that you act first. Immediately after we receive our F-35, you will have the *Wén Rui*. There is no reason for further escalation."

The line remained silent.

Chowdhury shot Hendrickson another glance.

Hendrickson reached over, muted the speaker, and whispered to Chowdhury, "Do you think he knows?" Chowdhury shook his head with a less-than-confident no. What Hendrickson was referring to was the call they'd received moments ago. For the past forty minutes, Seventh Fleet Headquarters in Yokosuka had lost all communications with the *John Paul Jones* and its sister ships.

"Hello?" said Chowdhury into the speaker.

"Yes, I am here," came the otherworldly echo of Lin Bao's voice on the line. He sounded impatient, as though he were being forced to continue a conversation he'd tired of long ago. "Let me repeat your position, to assure that I understand it: for decades, your navy has sailed through our territorial waters, it has flown through our allies' airspace, and today it has seized one of our vessels; but you maintain that you are the aggrieved party, and we are the ones who must appease you?"

The room became so quiet that for the first time Chowdhury noticed the slight buzzing of the halogen light bulbs overhead. Hendrickson had finished transcribing Lin Bao's comments. His fingers hovered above the keyboard, ready to strike the next letter.

"That is the position of this administration," answered Chowdhury, needing to swallow once to get the words out. "However, if you have a counterproposal we would, of course, take it into consideration."

More silence.

Then Lin Bao's exasperated voice: "We do have a counterproposal. . . ."

"Good," interjected Chowdhury, but Lin Bao ignored him, continuing on.

"If you check, you'll see that it's been sent to your computer—"

Then the power went out.

It was only a moment, a flash of darkness. The lights immediately came back on. And when they did, Lin Bao wasn't on the line anymore. There was only an empty dial tone. Chowdhury began messing with the phone, struggling to get the White House operator on the line, while Hendrickson attempted to log back on to his computer. "What's the matter?" asked Chowdhury.

"My log-in and password don't work."

Chowdhury pushed Hendrickson aside. His didn't work either.

2

Blackout

Anyone who lived through the war could tell you where they were the moment the power went out. Captain Sarah Hunt had been on the bridge of the *John Paul Jones*, fighting to keep her flagship afloat while trying to ignore the panicked cries coming from belowdecks. Wedge had his wrists flex-cuffed in the small of his back as he was driven blindfolded under armed escort across the tarmac of Bandar Abbas airfield. Lin Bao had recently departed Dulles International Airport on a Gulfstream 900, one of a suite of private jets made available to members of the Central Military Commission.

Lin Bao had, over the course of his thirty-year career, flown on these jets from time to time, either as part of a delegation to an international conference or when escorting a minister or other senior-level

41

official. However, he'd never before had one of these jets sent for him alone, a fact that signified the importance of the mission he'd now completed. Lin Bao had placed his call to Chowdhury right after takeoff, while the flight attendants were still belted into their jump seats. The Gulfstream had been ascending, cresting one thousand feet, when he hung up with Chowdhury and sent an encrypted message to the Central Military Commission, confirming that this final call had been placed. When he pressed send on that message the response was immediate, as though he had thrown a switch. Below him, the scattered lights of Washington went dark and then came right back on. Like a blink.

Lin Bao was thinking of that blink while he watched the eastern seaboard slip beneath the Gulfstream, as they struck out into international airspace and across the dark expanse of the Atlantic. He thought about time and how in English they say, *it passes in the blink of an eye.* While he sat alone on the plane, in this liminal space between nations, he felt as though his entire career had built to this one moment. Everything before this day—from his time at the academy, to his years shuffling from assignment to assignment in the fleet, to his study and later grooming in diplomatic postings—had been one stage after another in a larger plan, like a mountain's ascent. And here he stood at the summit.

He glanced once more out of his window, as if expecting to find a view that he might admire from such a height. There was only the darkness. The night sky without stars. The ocean below him. Onto that void, his imagination projected events he knew to be in progress half a world away. He could see the bridge of the carrier *Zheng He*, and Rear Admiral Ma Qiang, who commanded that battle group. The trajectory of Lin Bao's life, which had made him the American defense attaché at this moment, had been set by his government years ago, and it was every bit as deliberate as the trajectory set for Ma Qiang, whose carrier battle group was the perfect instrument to assert their nation's sovereignty over its territorial waters. If their parallel trajectories weren't known to them in the earliest days of their careers, when they'd been contemporaries as naval cadets, they could have been intuited. Ma Qiang had been an upperclassman, heir to an illustrious military family, his father and grandfather both admirals, part of the naval aristocracy. Ma Qiang had a reputation for cold competence and cruelty, particularly when it came to hazing underclassmen, one of whom was Lin Bao. In those days Lin Bao, an academic prodigy, had proven an easy target. Despite eventually graduating first in his class, with the highest scholastic record the faculty could remember, he'd arrived as a sniveling, homesick boy of half-American, half-Chinese descent. This split heritage made him particularly vulnerable, not only to derision but also to the suspicions of his classmates—particularly Ma Qiang.

But that was all a long time ago. Ultimately, it was Lin Bao's mixed heritage from which his government derived his value, eventually leading him to his current position, and it was Ma Qiang's competence and cruelty that made him the optimal commander of a fleet that at this moment was striking a long-anticipated blow against the Americans. Everyone played their role. Everyone did their part.

Part of Lin Bao wished he were the one standing on the bridge of the *Zheng He*, with the power of an entire carrier battle group arrayed in attack formation behind him. After all, he was a naval officer who had also held command at sea. But what offset this desire, or any jealousy he felt about his old classmate Ma Qiang's posting, was a specific knowledge he possessed. He was one of only a half dozen people who understood the scope of current events.

Ma Qiang and the thousands of sailors under his command had no idea that on the other side of the globe an American F-35 stealth fighter

43

had been grounded by a previously unknown cyber capability their government had deployed on behalf of the Iranians, nor how this action was related to his own mission. Those qualities Lin Bao had always admired in the Americans—their moral certitude, their single-minded determination, their blithe optimism—undermined them at this moment as they struggled to find a solution to a problem they didn't understand.

Our strengths become our weaknesses, thought Lin Bao. Always.

The American narrative was that they had captured the *Wén Rui*, a ship laden with sensitive technologies that Lin Bao's government would do anything to retrieve. For the *Wén Rui*'s capture to precipitate the desired crisis, Lin Bao's government would need a bargaining chip to force the Americans' hand; that's where the grounded F-35 came in. Lin Bao knew that the Americans would then follow a familiar series of moves and countermoves, a choreography the two nations had stepped through many times before: a crisis would lead to posturing, then to a bit of brinksmanship, and eventually to de-escalation and a trade. In this case, the F-35 would be traded for the *Wén Rui*. Lin Bao knew, and his superiors knew, that it would never occur to the Americans that pilfering the sensitive technology on the F-35 was a secondary objective for their adversary and that whatever was on the *Wén Rui* was of little value. The Americans wouldn't understand, or at least not until it was too late, that what Lin Bao's government wanted was simply the crisis itself, one that would allow them to strike in the South China Sea. What the Americans lacked—or lost somewhere along the way—was imagination. As it was said of the 9/11 attacks, it would also be said of the *Wén Rui* incident: it was not a failure of American intelligence, but rather a failure of American imagination. And the more the Americans struggled, the more trapped they would become.

Lin Bao remembered a puzzle he'd seen in a novelty shop in Cambridge, when he'd been studying at Harvard's Kennedy School. It was a tube made of a woven mesh material. The man behind the counter of the store had seen him looking at the puzzle, trying to figure out what it was. "You stick your fingers in either end," he had said in one of those thick Boston accents Lin Bao always struggled to understand. Lin Bao did as he was told. When he went to remove his fingers, the woven mesh cinched down. The more he tugged, the more tightly his fingers became stuck. The man behind the counter laughed and laughed. "You've never seen that before?" Lin Bao shook his head, no. The man laughed even harder, and then said, "It's called a Chinese finger trap."

⌐

05:17 March 13, 2034 (GMT+4:30)
Bandar Abbas

Brigadier General Qassem Farshad sat on a plastic foldout chair in an empty office next to one of the holding cells. It was early in the morning and he was in a sour mood. But no one seemed to notice because his appearance was always fearsome. His reputation equally so. This made it difficult to gauge his moods, as his expression at rest seemed to convey mild annoyance or even low-level rage, depending on who was looking at him. Farshad had scars, plenty of them. Most prominent was his right hand, where he'd lost his pinky and ring finger when assembling an IED in Sadr City on his first assignment as a young lieutenant. This misstep had almost cost him his job within the elite Quds Force. But Farshad's namesake, Major General Qassem Soleimani, the commander of the Quds Force, had intervened, blaming the incident on the incompetence of the Jaish al-Mahdi militiamen whom Farshad was advising.

This was the only time in his more than thirty years working within the Quds Force that Farshad had ever used his special connection with Soleimani to his advantage. His father, who had achieved the rank of lieutenant colonel, had died subverting an assassination attempt on Soleimani's life weeks before Farshad was born. The particulars of that incident had always remained shrouded in mystery, but the idea that Soleimani—one of the great protectors of the Islamic Republic—owed a debt to the elder Farshad lent the younger's career an aura of mystique as he ascended the ranks of the Revolutionary Guards. This mystique endured even after Soleimani's death, magnified by Farshad's inherent competence and daring.

The history of his exploits was etched across his body in scar tissue. When advising Syrian government forces in the Battle of Aleppo, a piece of shrapnel from a mortar had sliced a tidy diagonal gash from above his eyebrow to below his cheek. When advancing on Herat after the 2026 collapse of Afghanistan's last Kabul-based national government, a sniper's bullet had passed through his neck, missing his jugular and arteries, leaving a coin-sized entrance hole at one side of his neck and the same-sized exit wound at the other. That scar made his neck appear like Frankenstein's with the bolts removed, which inevitably led to a nickname among the younger troopers. And lastly, in the battle that was the pinnacle of his career, he'd led a regiment of Revolutionary Guards in the final assault to retake the Golan Heights in 2030. In this, his crowning achievement, the one that would earn him his nation's highest award for valor, the Order of the Fath, the retreating Israelis had fired a cowardly but lucky rocket that had struck beside him, killing his radio operator and severing his right leg below the knee. He still limped slightly from this wound, although Farshad hiked three miles each morning on a well-fitted prosthetic.

The missing fingers. The scar on his face. The leg lost below the knee. All those wounds were on his right side. His left side—apart from the scar on his neck—had never been touched. If his troopers called him "Padishah Frankenstein" (which translated to English as "Great King Frankenstein"), the intelligence analysts at Langley had given him a different nickname, one that corresponded with his psychological profile. That name was "Dr. Jekyll and Mr. Hyde." Farshad was a man with two sides, the one with the scars and the one without. He was capable of great kindness but also great rage. And that rageful side, the one that easily moved him into his reckless tempers, was very much present now as he waited in the empty office next to the holding cell at Bandar Abbas.

Five weeks before, the General Staff of the Armed Forces had issued Farshad his orders directly. His government planned to down an American F-35 and Farshad was to interrogate the pilot. He would have two days to extract a confession. The plan was to create one of those videos his government could use to shame the Americans. After that, the pilot would be released, and the aircraft's technology exploited and then destroyed. When Farshad protested that this was the work of an interrogator far junior to him in rank, he was told that he was the most junior person who could be entrusted with so sensitive a task. This could, the General Staff had explained, bring their two nations to the brink of war. The incident his government would precipitate was delicate. And so Farshad had been ordered to remain at this remote airfield for more than a month, waiting for the Americans to fly their plane overhead.

I've been reduced to this, Farshad thought bitterly. *The most junior man who can be trusted.*

Gone were his days of active service. Farshad had accumulated all of the scars he ever would. He remembered General Soleimani's end. When the Americans killed him, cancer had already developed in his throat and was slowly eating the great commander alive. Several times over those months, the disease had confined his father's old friend to his bed. During a particularly dire episode, he had summoned Farshad to his modest country house in Qanat-e Malek, a hamlet three hours' drive outside of Tehran where Soleimani had been born. The audience hadn't lasted long. Farshad was brought to the general's bedside, and he could see slow death in the smile that greeted him, the way Soleimani's gums had receded, the purple-white shade of his chapped lips. He told Farshad in a raspy voice that his father had been the lucky one, to be martyred, to never grow old, this was what all soldiers secretly desired, and he wished a warrior's death for the son of his old friend. Before Farshad could answer, Soleimani abruptly dismissed him. As he traveled out of the house, he could hear the old man retching pathetically from behind his closed door. Two months later, Soleimani's great adversary, the Americans, would grant him the most generous of gifts: a warrior's death.

Waiting in the empty office in Bandar Abbas, Farshad thought again of that last meeting with Soleimani. He felt certain his fate wouldn't be like his father's. His fate would be to die in his bed, like the old general nearly had. And if he was in a sour mood that day at Bandar Abbas, it was because of this. Another war was brewing—he could feel it—and it would be the first war in his life from which he wouldn't walk away with a scar.

A young trooper with a freshly washed and perfectly creased uniform stood at the door. "Brigadier Farshad, sir . . ."

He looked up, his gaze eager to the point of cruelty. "What is it?"

"The prisoner is ready for you now."

Farshad stood slowly. He pushed his way past the young trooper, toward the cell with the American. Whether he liked it or not, Farshad still had a job to do.

21:02 March 12, 2034 (GMT-4)
Washington, D.C.

Sandy Chowdhury knew the situation was bad. Their government email accounts, their government cell phones, even the vending machine that took credit cards and operated off a government IP address—all of it was down. No one could log in. Not a single password worked. They'd been locked out of everything. *This is bad, this is bad, this is bad*; it was all Chowdhury could think.

He couldn't contact Central Command or the Indo-Pacific Command, and his imagination raced as he projected a host of possible outcomes for the F-35 they'd lost, as well as the fate of the *John Paul Jones* and its sister ships in the South China Sea. In this gathering panic, Chowdhury's thoughts wandered unexpectedly.

A memory kept reoccurring.

When he was in high school in Northern Virginia, he'd run hurdles. He was quite good too, until an accident curtailed his track career. He'd broken an ankle on the anchor leg of the 4x400-meter relay. It was junior year, at the regional championships. When he fell on the track, he could feel his skinned knee and palms, the burn of sweat in those cuts, but he couldn't feel his badly broken ankle. He simply sat there in the middle of the race, his competitors passing him by, staring dumbfounded at his foot as it dangled numbly from the bottom of the joint. He knew how much it would soon hurt, but it hadn't started hurting yet.

That was what this moment was like; he knew something had broken, but he felt nothing.

Chowdhury, Hendrickson, and their modest staff scrambled about, tapping at keyboards, unplugging and re-plugging phones that refused to give a dial tone, troubleshooting systems that refused to be troubleshot. Air Force One had been scheduled to land at Andrews more than an hour ago, but there was still no word as to its status. There was no way to get a call into Andrews. Their personal cell phones worked, but no one wanted to dial through an unsecure line, particularly after Lin Bao had proven to Chowdhury that his own phone had been compromised.

Time passed strangely in the hours after the blackout. Everyone knew the minutes were critical, everyone could intuit that events of the type that shape history were unfolding at this very moment. But no one understood their form; no one understood what those events were or what that history would be. So much was happening—the *Wén Rui*, the F-35, Air Force One, which had seemed to vanish—and yet they had no news. Frantic as they were to understand the scope of this attack, they couldn't even make a secure phone call. Everything had been compromised.

They carried on in a general, ineffectual frenzy, with Chowdhury and Hendrickson bunkered up in the Situation Room, leaning over its conference table, scribbling on legal pads, hatching plans and then discarding them. Until after a few hours Chowdhury's boss, Trent Wisecarver, the national security advisor, stood in the open doorway.

At first they didn't notice him.

"Sandy," he said.

Chowdhury glanced up, stupefied. "Sir?"

Decades before, Wisecarver had played tailback at West Point, and he still looked the part. His shirtsleeves were rolled up over his thick forearms, his tie was loosened around his trunk of a neck, and his flop of salt-and-pepper hair was uncombed. He wore a pair of frameless eyeglasses (he was severely myopic) and looked as though he'd slept in his rumpled Brooks Brothers suit. "How much cash do you have?"

"Sir?"

"Cash. I need eighty bucks. My government credit card isn't working."

Chowdhury fished through his pockets, as did Hendrickson. Between them they came up with seventy-six dollars, three of which were in quarters. Chowdhury was passing the handful of coins and the crumple of bills to Wisecarver as they marched from the West Wing out toward the White House vestibule and North Lawn, where, pulled up on the curved driveway by the fountain, there was a metro taxi. A uniformed Secret Service guard handed Chowdhury the taxi driver's license and registration and then returned to his post. Chowdhury's boss curtly explained that his plane had been forced to divert to Dulles and land under the guise of a civilian aircraft. That meant no escort to meet them, no Secret Service motorcade, no elaborate security detail. POTUS herself was due back at Andrews within the hour. From Air Force One her communications proved limited, she could reach the four-star commanding general at Strategic Command and had spoken to the VP, but these carve-outs in their communications hierarchy were clearly designed by whoever instigated the attack as a way to avoid an inadvertent nuclear escalation. Beijing (or whoever did this) surely knew that if she had no communications with her nuclear capability, protocols were in place for an automatic preemptive strike. She did, however, have no direct communications with the secretary of defense, or any of her combatant commanders in the field other than Strategic Command. Establishing contact with them was Wisecarver's job. Refusing to wait for official travel arrangements when his plane landed, he had rushed into the main terminal at Dulles and gotten in a cab so he'd have communications working at the White House by the time POTUS arrived. And here Wisecarver was, without a dime to pay the fare.

Chowdhury examined the taxi's registration. The driver was an immigrant, South Asian, with a last name from the same part of India as Chowdhury's own family. When Chowdhury stepped to the taxi's window to hand back the documents, he thought to mention something about it but decided not to. This wasn't the time or the place. Wisecarver then paid the driver, meticulously counting out the fare from the wad of cash and coins, while the twitchy Secret Service agent he'd traveled with scanned in every direction for threats, whether real or imagined.

10:22 March 13, 2034 (GMT+8)
Beijing

Lin Bao hadn't slept much on the flight. When the Gulfstream touched down, he was shepherded by a heavily armed official escort—dark suits, dark sunglasses, concealed weapons—to the Ministry of National Defense headquarters, an ominous building in the heart of the smog-choked capital. Lin Bao guessed his escorts were officers of the Ministry of State Security but couldn't be sure. Without a *hello* or *goodbye* or any pleasantry whatsoever, they brought him up to a windowless conference room on the building's sixth floor and shut the door behind them.

Lin Bao waited. The conference table in the room's center was massive, designed to receive international delegations and to host negotiations of the highest sensitivity. In a vase at the center of the table were some flowers, peace lilies, one of the few species that required no sun-light to grow. Lin Bao ran his fingers beneath their white, silky petals and couldn't help but appreciate the irony of the choice in this place.

Also on the table were two silver platters, piled with packets of M&M's. He noticed the writing on the packets: it was in English.

Two double doors at the opposite end of the conference room swung open. Startled, Lin Bao sat up straight.

Mid-level military officers flowed into the room, dropping down a projection screen, establishing a secure video-teleconference connection, and arraying fresh pitchers of water on the table. Then, like a tidal surge, they moved back through the door as quickly as they had appeared. In their wake a diminutive man entered the room, his chest glinting with a field of medals. He wore a tobacco-colored dress uniform made of fine but poorly cut fabric, the sleeves extending almost to his knuckles. His demeanor was gregarious and his earlobes pendulous, framing his very round face whose full cheeks creased in a fixed smile. His arm was extended in a handshake like an electric plug in search of a socket. "Admiral Lin Bao, Admiral Lin Bao," he repeated, turning the name into a song, a triumphal anthem. "Congratulations. You have done *very* well."

Lin Bao had never met the Defense Minister General Chiang, but that face was as familiar as his own. How often had he seen it hung in one of those hierarchical portrait collages that adorned the anodyne military buildings in which he'd spent his career? It was the minister's smile that set him apart from the rest of the party officials who so assiduously cultivated their dour expressions for the photographer. His habitual courtesy, which could have been interpreted as weakness, was the smooth sheath that contained the force of his office. Minister Chiang gestured toward the silver platters spread across the conference table. "You haven't touched your M&M's," he said, barely suppressing a laugh.

Lin Bao felt a sense of foreboding. If he assumed that Minister Chiang and the Central Military Commission had recalled him for a debriefing, he was quickly disabused of this belief. They knew everything already, including the smallest of details. Every exchange. Every gesture. Every word. Down to a single comment made about M&M's. This was the point of the platters: to let Lin Bao know that nothing escaped their attention, lest he come to believe that any individual might assume an outsize role in this enterprise, lest he ever think that any one person could become greater than a single cog in the vast machinery of the People's Republic—their republic.

Minister Chiang reclined in his plush office chair at the head of the conference table. He gestured for Lin Bao to sit beside him. Although Lin Bao had served nearly thirty years in his country's navy, this was the first time he'd ever met directly with a member of the Central Military Commission. When he'd studied at Harvard's Kennedy School as a junior officer and later at the US Naval War College in Newport as a mid-level officer, and when he'd attended exercises with his Western counterparts, he was always fascinated by the familiarity so common among senior- and junior-level officers in their militaries. The admirals often knew the first names of the lieutenants. And used them. The deputy assistant secretaries and secretaries of defense had once been Annapolis or officer candidate school classmates with the commanders and captains. The egalitarian undercurrents ran much deeper in Western militaries than in his own, despite his country's ideological foundation in socialist and communist thought. He was anything but a "comrade" to senior officers or officials, and he knew it well. While at the war college in Newport, Lin Bao had studied the Battle of Kursk, the largest tank engagement of the Second World War, in which one of the great flaws of the Soviet army was that only command-variant tanks possessed two-way radios. The Soviets couldn't see any reason for subordinates to speak up to their commanders. The subordinate's job was solely to follow orders, to remain a cog in the machine. How little had changed in the intervening years.

The screen at the far end of the conference table flickered to life. "We've won a great battle," explained Minister Chiang. "You deserve to see this." The secure connection was perfect, its sound clear, and the image as unfiltered as if they were staring through a window into another room. That room was the bridge wing of the carrier *Zheng He*. Standing center frame was Ma Qiang.

"Congratulations, Admiral," said Minister Chiang, showing his small, carnivorous teeth. "I have an old friend of yours here with me." He gestured to Lin Bao, who awkwardly leaned into the frame so that he might nod once respectfully.

Ma Qiang returned the gesture, but otherwise ignored Lin Bao. He launched into a situation update: his carrier battle group had sunk two American destroyers, which they'd identified as the *Carl Levin* and the *Chung-Hoon*. The former had suffered a massive explosion in its magazine, leaving few survivors among the crew of nearly three hundred, while the latter had taken all night to sink. In these first hours of the morning, Ma Qiang's ships had picked up a few American survivors. The final ship in the flotilla, the crippled *John Paul Jones*, was taking on water. Ma Qiang had already called for the captain to surrender, but she had flatly refused, replying with an expletive-laced transmission that, at first, Ma Qiang's translator hesitated to put into Mandarin. The *Zheng He* Carrier Battle Group had been on station for the last thirty-six hours and Ma Qiang was growing increasingly concerned that the Americans, having heard nothing from their flotilla, might send a contingent of ships to investigate. He sought permission to strike the fatal blow against the *John Paul Jones*. "Comrade Minister," Ma Qiang said, "I have no doubt as to our success against any American naval reinforcements, but their arrival would lead to the escalation I've been instructed to avoid. I have a flight of J-31 interceptors ready for launch against the *John Paul Jones*. Total mission time with recovery is fifty-two minutes. We're awaiting your order."

Minister Chiang rubbed his round and very smooth chin. Lin Bao watched the screen. In the background, beyond the hurried comings and goings of the sailors on the bridge, he could see the horizon. A haze hung about the ocean. It took Lin Bao a moment to understand what had caused it—this haze was all that was left of the *Carl Levin* and *Chung-Hoon*. And it would, he suspected, soon be all that was left of the *John Paul Jones*. Ma Qiang's concern was merited, Lin Bao thought. This operation from its inception had always been limited in scope. Its objective—the final, uncontested control of the South China Sea— could only be undermined in one of two ways: first, if their forces failed to destroy this US flotilla; and second, if through a miscalculation this crisis escalated beyond a single, violent demonstration.

"Admiral," Minister Chiang began, addressing Ma Qiang, "is it your belief that the *John Paul Jones* can be saved?"

Ma Qiang paused for a moment, spoke to someone off screen in a hushed voice, and then returned his attention to the teleconference. "Comrade Minister, our best estimates are that the *John Paul Jones* will sink within three hours if unaided." Lin Bao could see that the *Zheng He* was turning into the wind to be in the most advantageous position to launch its aircraft. Suddenly on the distant horizon a stitch of dark smoke appeared. At first it was so faint that Lin Bao mistook it for an imperfection in the teleconference's connection. Then he understood: it was the *John Paul Jones* burning a dozen miles off.

Minister Chiang began stroking his chin as he weighed whether to order this final blow. A decisive engagement was essential, but he needed to proceed with caution lest a miscalculation cause the incident to spiral into a broader conflict, one that could threaten his nation's interests further afield than the South China Sea. He leaned forward in his seat. "Admiral, you are cleared for launch. But listen closely; there is a specific message we must deliver."

06:42 March 13, 2034 (GMT+4:30)
Bandar Abbas

"This fucking place stinks."

The dank air. The putrid scent. If Wedge hadn't known any better, he would've thought he'd been detained in the public restroom of a Greyhound bus terminal. Blindfolded, he sat cuffed to a steel chair bolted to the floor. He couldn't see anything except for the irregular permutations of shadow and ashy light that played around the room from what he suspected was a window near the ceiling.

A door creaked open, heavy on its hinges. From the sound, Wedge could tell it was metal. A set of uneven steps approached, like someone with a slight limp. Then a scrape on the floor as a chair was dragged over. Whoever sat across from him sat clumsily, as if the movement were awkward for them. Wedge waited for the person to say something, but there was only the smell of their cigarette. Wedge wouldn't be the one to speak first. He knew the Code of Conduct for POWs, an exclusive club into which he'd been inducted only hours before.

"Major Chris 'Wedge' Mitchell . . ." came the voice across from him.

Then his blindfold was yanked off. Overwhelmed by the light, even though the room was poorly lit, Wedge struggled to see. He couldn't quite focus on the dark figure across from him, who continued, "Why are you here, Major Wedge?"

Slowly, his eyes adjusted. The man asking questions was dressed in a green uniform with gold embroidered epaulettes of some significance. He had an athletic build like a runner and a hostile face with a long, hook-shaped scar that traced from above his eyebrow to below his cheek. His nose was compressed into a triangle, as if it had been broken and reset many times. In his hands he held the name patch that had been Velcroed onto Wedge's flight suit.

"It's not Major Wedge. It's just Wedge. And only my friends call me that."

The man in the green uniform frowned slightly, as if this hurt his feelings. "When we finish here, you will be wanting me as a friend." He offered Wedge a cigarette, which he refused with a wave. The man in the uniform repeated his question. "Why are you here?"

Wedge blinked his eyes. He inventoried the bare room. A single window with bars in one corner, which cast a square of light on the damp concrete floor. His chair. A metal table. And another chair where this man now sat. Based on his epaulettes, Wedge guessed he was a brigadier. In the far corner of the room was a pail, which Wedge assumed was his toilet. In the near corner was a mat, which he assumed was his bed. Above the mat a shackle with a chain was bolted into the wall. He realized they planned to restrain him while he slept—if they let him sleep. The room was medieval, except for a single camera. It was hung high in the center of the ceiling, a red light blinking at its base. It was recording everything.

Wedge felt a sinking sensation in the pit of his stomach. He found himself thinking of his great-grandfather, the stories of gunsights marked in grease pencil on his canopy, and Pappy Boyington, the greatest of Marine aces. Pappy had wound up as a prisoner too, finishing the war in a Japanese POW camp. He also thought of his grandfather slinging snake and nape up north in I Corps while kids back home smoked dope and burned their draft cards. Lastly, and in some ways most bitterly, he thought of his own dad. Wedge feared the old man might hold himself responsible if his son wound up rotting in this prison. Wedge had always wanted to be like his dad, even if it killed him. For the first time he entertained the idea that it might.

The brigadier asked him once again why he was there.

Wedge did what he'd been trained to do, what the Code of Conduct demanded: he answered the brigadier's question by giving only his name, rank, and service number.

"That's not what I asked you," said the brigadier. "I asked why you are here."

Wedge repeated himself.

The brigadier nodded, as if he understood. He circled the room until he stood behind Wedge. The brigadier rested both his hands on Wedge's shoulders, allowing the three fingers of his mangled right hand to crawl crab-like toward the base of Wedge's neck. "The only way we can resolve this situation is to work together, Major Mitchell. Whether you like it or not, you've trespassed. We have the right to know why you are here so we can resolve this. Nobody wants things to escalate further."

Wedge glanced toward the camera in the center of the ceiling. He repeated himself for a third time.

"Would it help if I turned that off?" the brigadier asked, looking up at the camera. "You could tell just me. Everything doesn't have to be recorded."

Wedge knew from his survival training that the brigadier was trying to ingratiate himself and build trust, and then through that trust to elicit a confession. The goal of an interrogation wasn't information but rather control—emotional control. Once that control was taken—preferably by building rapport, but just as often through intimidation, or even violence—the information would flow. But something didn't add up with this brigadier: his rank (he was too senior to be a first-line interrogator), his scars (he had too many of them to have spent a career in intelligence), and his uniform (Wedge knew enough to recognize that he wasn't standard Iranian military). What Wedge felt was nothing more than his intuition, but he was a pilot, reared from a long line of pilots, all of whom had been taught to trust their well-cultivated intuition, both in and out of the cockpit. And it was his trust in this intuition that led him to go on the offense, to make a desperate attempt to gain control of the situation.

The brigadier asked Wedge one more time why he'd come.

This time Wedge didn't answer with his name, rank, and service number. Instead, he said, "I'll tell you, if you tell me."

The brigadier appeared surprised, as if his reason for being there was obvious. "I'm not sure that I understand."

"Why are you here?" asked Wedge. "If you tell me, then I'll tell you."

The brigadier was no longer standing behind Wedge but had returned to his seat across from him. He leaned curiously toward his prisoner. "I'm here to question you," the brigadier said tentatively, as if this fact embarrassed him in some way he didn't recognize until the very words had escaped his mouth.

"Bullshit," said Wedge.

The brigadier came out of his seat.

"You're no interrogator," continued Wedge. "With a face like that you want me to believe you're some intel weenie?"

And that entire face, aside from the scar tissue, began to turn shamefully red.

"You should be out in the field, with your troops," said Wedge, and he was smiling now, with a reckless grin. He'd taken a gamble and from the brigadier's reaction he knew he'd been right. He knew he had control. "So why are you in here? Who'd you piss off to get stuck with this shit duty?"

The brigadier was towering over him. He swung back and struck Wedge so hard that he knocked his chair out of the floor where it had been bolted. Wedge toppled over. He hit the ground lifeless as a mannequin. As he lay on his side with his wrists still bound to the chair, the blows fell on him in quick succession. The video camera with its solid red light, high up in the center of the ceiling, was the last thing Wedge saw before he blacked out.

11:01 March 13, 2034 (GMT+8)
South China Sea

They charged out of the east, two silvery flashes on the horizon, and made an orbit around the badly wounded *John Paul Jones*. Nearly half the crew, more than one hundred sailors, had perished since that morning, either incinerated in the blast from the pair of successive torpedo impacts or entombed in the flooded compartments belowdecks that their shipmates had been forced to secure with them still trapped inside. There were very few wounded, mostly dead, as was usually the case in naval engagements, where there was no battlefield for the injured to rest upon, only the consuming sea.

When the two planes didn't come in straight for the attack, a collective silence fell over the crew, like a breath sucked in. Within that breath was a fleeting hope that these planes had been sent from Yokosuka, or perhaps launched from a friendly carrier dispatched to their aid. But as soon as the crew of the *John Paul Jones* glimpsed their wings, which were laden with munitions, and observed that the two aircraft kept a cautious distance, they knew they weren't friendly.

But why didn't they strike? Why didn't they drop their ordnance and finish the job?

Captain Sarah Hunt couldn't waste her time on speculation. Her full attention remained where it had since the first torpedo hit the day before. She needed to keep her flagship afloat. And it was, sadly, her ship now. Commander Morris hadn't been seen since the second impact. Hunt hadn't heard from the *Levin* or *Chung-Hoon* either. She'd only watched, helplessly, as each was crippled and then sunk. This was the fate that would soon befall her and the surviving members of her crew. Although they'd contained most of the fires on the *John Paul Jones*, they were taking on more water than they could pump out. As the weight of the water contorted the steel hull, it creaked mournfully, like a wounded beast, as minute by minute it came closer to buckling.

Hunt stood on the bridge. She tried to occupy herself—checking and rechecking their inoperable radios, dispatching runners for updates from damage control, replotting their position on an analog chart since anything that required a GPS had failed. She did this so her crew wouldn't despair at their captain's inactivity, and so that she herself wouldn't have to imagine the water slipping over the mast. She glanced up, at the twin attack planes from the *Zheng He*. How she wished they would stop taunting her, that they would stop their impudent circling, drop their ordnance, and allow her to go down with her ship.

"Ma'am . . ." interjected one of the radiomen standing beside her, as he pointed toward the horizon.

She glanced up.

The flight of two had changed their angle of attack. They were darting toward the *John Paul Jones*, flying low and fast, staggered in echelon. When the sun glinted off their wings, Hunt imagined it was their cannons firing. She grimaced but no impacts came. The flight of two was closing the distance between them. The weapon systems on the *John Paul Jones* had been taken out of action. On the bridge there was silence. Her command—the hierarchy that was her ship and its crew—it all melted away in these, their final moments. The radioman, who couldn't have been more than nineteen, glanced up at her, and she, surprising herself, placed her arm around him. The flight of two was so close now, so low, that she could observe the slight undulation of their wings as they passed through the uneven air. In a blink their ordnance would drop.

Hunt shut her eyes.

A noise like thunder—a boom.

But nothing happened.

Hunt glanced upward. The two planes turned aerobatic corkscrews around each other, climbing higher and higher still, losing and finding themselves in striations of cloud. Then they descended again, passing a hundred feet or less above the surface of the ocean, flying slowly, right above stall speed. As they passed in front of the bridge, the lead plane was so close that Hunt could see the silhouette of the pilot. Then he dipped his wing—a salute, which Hunt believed was the message he'd been sent there to deliver.

The planes ascended and flew back the way they came.

The ship's bridge remained silent.

Then there was a crackle of static. For the first time in more than a day, one of their radios turned on.

⌐

12:06 March 13, 2034 (GMT+8)
Beijing

The video teleconference shut off. The screen withdrew into the ceiling. Lin Bao and Minister Chiang sat alone at the vast conference table.

"Do you think your friend Admiral Ma Qiang is upset with me?"

The question took Lin Bao off guard. He never imagined that someone in Minister Chiang's position would concern himself with the emotional state of a subordinate. Not knowing how to answer, Lin Bao pretended that he hadn't heard, which caused Minister Chiang to ruminate a bit about why he'd asked.

"Ma Qiang is an excellent commander, decisive, efficient, even cruel. But his effectiveness can also be his weakness. He is an attack dog only. Like so many military officers, he doesn't understand nuance. By sparing the *John Paul Jones*, he believes that I've denied him a prize. However, he doesn't understand the true purpose of his mission." Minister Chiang arched an eyebrow. What the *true purpose* of that mission was hung in the air as an unanswered question, one that Lin Bao wouldn't dare ask aloud but instead asked through his silence, so that Minister Chiang continued, "Tell me, Lin Bao, you studied in the West. You must've learned the story of Aristodemus."

Lin Bao nodded. He knew the story of Aristodemus, that famous Spartan who was the sole survivor of the Battle of Thermopylae. He'd learned it at the Kennedy School, in a seminar pompously titled "The History of War" taught by a Hellenophile professor. The story went that in the days before the final stand of the famous Three Hundred, Aristodemus was stricken with an eye infection. The Spartan king, Leonidas, having no use for a blind soldier, sent Aristodemus home before the Persians slaughtered what was left of his army.

"Aristodemus," said Lin Bao, "was the only Spartan who survived to tell the story."

Minister Chiang leaned back in his armchair. "This is what Ma Qiang doesn't understand," he said, showing his teeth in an amused half smile. "He wasn't sent to sink three American warships; that was not his mission. His mission was to send a message. If the entire flotilla was destroyed, if it disappeared, the message would be lost. Who would deliver it? Who would tell the story of what happened? But by sparing a few survivors, by showing some restraint, we will be able to send our message more clearly. The point here is not to start a needless war but to get the Americans to finally listen to us, to respect the sovereignty of our waters."

Minister Chiang then complimented Lin Bao on his effectiveness as the American attaché, noting how well he'd managed the baiting of the *John Paul Jones* with the *Wén Rui*, and how American culpability in the seizure of that intelligence vessel disguised as a fishing trawler would undermine the international outcry that was certain to begin at the United Nations and then trickle from that ineffectual international organization to others that were equally ineffectual. Then, being in a pensive mood, Minister Chiang held forth on his vision of events as they might unfold in the coming days. He imagined the surviving crew members of the *John Paul Jones* recounting how they had been spared by the *Zheng He*. He imagined the Politburo Standing Committee brokering a deal with their Iranian allies to release the downed F-35 and its pilot as a means of placating the Americans. And lastly, he imagined their own country and its navy possessing unfettered control of the South China Sea, a goal generations in the making.

By the time he'd finished his explication, Minister Chiang seemed in an expansive mood. He placed his hand on Lin Bao's wrist. "As for you," he began, "our nation owes you a great debt. I imagine you'd like to spend some time with your family, but we also need to see to your next posting. Where would you like to be assigned?"

Lin Bao sat up in his chair. He looked the minister in the eye, knowing that such an opportunity might never again present itself. "Command at sea, Comrade Minister. That's my request."

"Very well," answered Minister Chiang. He gave a slight backhanded wave as he stood, as if with this gesture alone he had already granted such a wish.

Then as Minister Chiang headed for the door, Lin Bao plucked up his courage and added one caveat, "Specifically, Comrade Minister, I request command of the *Zheng He* Carrier Battle Group."

Minister Chiang stopped. He turned over his shoulder. "You would take Ma Qiang's command from him?" Then he began to laugh. "Maybe I was wrong about you. Perhaps you are the cruel one.... We'll see what can be arranged. And please, take those damn M&M's with you."

⌐

16:07 March 22, 2034 (GMT-4)
Washington, D.C.

For ten days Sandeep Chowdhury had slept on the floor of his office. His mother watched his daughter. His ex-wife didn't harass him with a single email or text message even after internet and cellular service resumed. His personal life remained mercifully quiet. He could attribute this détente to the crisis consuming the country's attention and his family's knowledge that he was playing a central part in its management. On the political left and political right, old adversaries seemed willing to dispense with decades of antipathy in the face of this new aggression. It had taken the television networks and newspapers about a day, maybe two, to understand the magnitude of what had occurred in the South China Sea and over the skies of Iran:

A flotilla wiped out.

A downed pilot.

The result was public unity. But also, a public outcry.

This outcry had grown louder and louder, to the point where it had become deafening. On the morning talk shows, on the evening news, the message was clear: *We have to do something.* Inside the administration a vociferous group of officials led by National Security Advisor Trent Wisecarver subscribed to the wisdom of the masses, believing that the US military must demonstrate to the world its unquestioned supremacy. "When tested, we must act" was the refrain echoed by this camp in various corners of the White House, except for one specific corner, the most important one, which was the Oval Office. The president had her doubts. Her camp, of which Chowdhury counted himself a member, had no refrain that they articulated within the administration, or on television, or in print. Their doubts manifested in a general reluctance to escalate a situation that seemed to have already spun out of control. The president and her allies were, put simply, dragging their feet.

Ten days into this crisis, the strategy of de-escalation seemed to be failing. Like the sinking of the *Lusitania* in the First World War, or the cries of "Remember the *Maine!*" at the outbreak of the Spanish-American War, a new set of names had replaced these historical ones. Within days, every American knew about the sinking of the *Carl Levin* and the *Chung-Hoon*, as well as the survival of the *John Paul Jones*, which hadn't really survived but had been scuttled by the submarine that had rescued its few dozen remaining crew members, to include the commodore of the flotilla, whom the Navy had kept out of the limelight as she faced a board of inquiry.

If Sarah Hunt had, at least up to this point, managed to remain relatively anonymous, the opposite held true for Marine Major Chris "Wedge" Mitchell. After the Battle of Mischief Reef, as the media dubbed the one-sided engagement, senior Chinese officials reached out to the administration. Minister of Defense Chiang was particularly engaged, insisting that this crisis was one large misunderstanding. As a gesture of goodwill, he offered himself to the Americans as an intermediary between them and the Iranians. He would personally negotiate the return of the F-35 and the release of its pilot. When a delegation of Chinese emissaries arrived with this message at the US embassy in New Delhi—their own embassy in Washington having been shut down in the wake of the crisis—the administration replied that it was the height of dishonesty to pretend that the F-35 would be turned over before the pilfering of its many sensitive technological secrets by the Chinese and

Iranians. As for the pilot, the administration was under an intense amount of pressure to recover him.

Three days after Major Mitchell went missing, his name was leaked by someone in the administration to a cable news network. An anchor at that network then paid a visit to the Mitchell family home outside of Kansas City, Missouri, where she found quite a story: four generations of Marine fighter pilots. The anchor conducted her interview in a living room with nearly one hundred years of memorabilia hanging on the walls, from captured Japanese battle flags to a blood-splattered flight suit. On camera, Major Mitchell's father described his son, while from time to time staring vacantly into the backyard, out toward a tree with the two rusted steel anchor points of a swing set drilled into its thickest branch. The elder Mitchell spoke about the family, the decades of tradition, all the way back to his own grandfather, who had flown with the vaunted *Black Sheep* squadron in the Second World War. The segment integrated photos of the young, handsome Major Chris "Wedge" Mitchell alongside photos of his father, and of his "Pop," and of his "Pop-Pop," the passage of generations linking the America of this time to the America of another time, when the country had been at the height of its greatness.

The video went up online, and within hours, it had been watched millions of times.

At a National Security Council meeting in the Situation Room on the fifth day of the crisis, the president asked if everyone had seen the segment. They all had. Already, *#FreeWedge* had begun to trend heavily on social media. One only had to look out of any West Wing window to see the proliferation of black POW/MIA flags that overnight picketed the Washington skyline. The president wondered aloud why the plight of this one pilot seemed to resonate more profoundly than the deaths of hundreds of sailors in the South China Sea. The room grew very quiet. Every staffer knew that on her desk for signature were the letters of condolence to the families of the *Levin*, *Chung-Hoon*, and *John Paul Jones*. Why, she asked rhetorically, does he matter more than them?

"He's a throwback, ma'am," Chowdhury blurted out.

He didn't even have a seat but was standing against the wall among the other backbench staffers. Half the cabinet turned to face him. He immediately regretted that he'd opened his mouth. He glanced down at his hands, as if by looking away he might convince the room that someone else had spoken, that his comment had been some strange act of ventriloquism.

In a firm but measured tone the president asked him to explain.

"Wedge is a link in a chain," Chowdhury began hesitantly, gaining confidence as he went. "His family ties us back to the last time we defeated a peer-level military. The country can intuit what might be coming. Seeing him reminds people of what we as a nation are capable of accomplishing. That's why they're so invested in him."

No one either agreed or disagreed with Chowdhury.

After a few beats of silence, the president told the room that she had one goal, and one goal alone, which was to avoid an escalation that would lead to the type of peer-to-peer conflict Chowdhury had mentioned. "Is that clear?" she said, leveling her gaze at those around the conference table.

Everyone nodded, but a lingering tension made it evident that not everyone agreed.

The president then stood from her seat at the head of the table and left, a trail of her aides following behind her. The hum of conversation resumed. The various secretaries and agency heads engaged in sidebar discussions, leaning in to one another as close as conspirators as they filtered out into the corridor. A pair of junior aides swept into the room and checked that no sensitive notes or errant document had been left behind.

As Chowdhury migrated back to his desk, his boss, Trent Wise-carver, found him. "Sandy . . ." Like a child who can tell whether he is in trouble from the inflection of a parent's voice, Chowdhury could tell immediately that Wisecarver was upset with him for speaking out of turn in the meeting. Chowdhury began to equivocate, apologizing for his outburst and making assurances that it wouldn't happen again. More than a decade before, Wisecarver's young son had perished in the coronavirus pandemic, an event many attributed to Wisecarver's hawkish political awakening and that made him adept at projecting fatherly guilt onto those subordinates he treated as surrogate children.

"Sandy," repeated Wisecarver, though his voice was different now, a bit softer and more conciliatory. "Take a break. Go home."

⌐

03:34 March 20, 2034 (GMT+4:30)
Tehran

At first Wedge thought he was home. He'd woken up in a dark room, in a bed, with clean sheets. He couldn't see a thing. Then he noticed a single bar of light beneath what must have been a shut door. He lifted his head to take a closer look. That's when the pain hit him. And with the pain came the realization that he was very far indeed from home. He returned his head to the pillow and kept his eyes open to the dark.

He couldn't quite remember what had happened at first, but slowly, details began to emerge: his starboard wing dancing along the border . . . losing flight control . . . his attempt to eject . . . his descent toward Bandar Abbas . . . his smoking a Marlboro on the tarmac . . . the man with the scars . . . the pressure of that three-fingered grip against his shoulder. It took an entire night for these details to resurface.

He ran his tongue through his mouth and could feel the gaps among his teeth. His lips felt fat and blistered. Light began to suggest itself at the rim of the curtains. Wedge was soon able to take in his surroundings, but his vision was blurred. One of his eyes was swollen shut, and he could hardly see through the other.

Without his vision, he'd never fly again.

Everything else would heal. Everything else could be undone. Not this.

He tried to reach his hand to his face, but his arm couldn't move. His wrists were cuffed to the frame of the bed. He pulled and then pulled again, his restraints rattling as he struggled to touch his face. A hurried procession of footsteps advanced toward his room. His door opened; balanced in the brightly lit threshold was a young nurse wearing a hijab. She held her finger to her mouth, shushing him. She wouldn't come too close. She formed both hands into a pleading gesture and spoke softly in a language Wedge didn't understand. Then she left. He could hear her running down the corridor.

There was light in his room now.

Hanging from a metal arm in the far corner was a television.

Something was written on its bottom.

Wedge relaxed his throbbing head against the pillow. With his unswollen eye, he focused on the television and the piece of text embossed at its base. It took all of his concentration but, slowly, the letters became sharper, shoring up around the edges. The image gathered itself, coming into focus. Then he could see it, in near twenty-twenty clarity, that fantastic and redeeming name: PANASONIC.

He shut his eyes and swallowed away a slight lump of emotion in his throat.

"Good morning, Major Wedge," came a voice as it entered. Its accent was haltingly British, and Wedge turned his attention in its direction. The man was Persian, with a bony face cut at flat angles like the blades of several knives, and a precisely cropped beard. He wore a white orderly coat. His long, tapered fingers began to manipulate the various intravenous lines that ran out of Wedge's arms, which remained cuffed to the bed frame.

Wedge gave the doctor his best defiant stare.

The doctor, in an effort to ingratiate himself, offered a bit of friendly explication. "You suffered an accident, Major Wedge," he began, "so we brought you here, to Arad Hospital, which I assure you is one of the finest in Tehran. Your accident was quite severe, but for the past week my colleagues and I have been looking after you." The doctor then nodded to the nurse, who followed him around Wedge's bedside, as though she were the assistant to a magician in the midst of his act. "We very much want to return you home," continued the doctor, "but unfortunately your government isn't making that easy for us. However, I'm confident this will all get resolved soon and that you'll be on your way. How does that sound, Major Wedge?"

Wedge still didn't say anything. He simply continued on with his stare.

"Right," said the doctor uncomfortably. "Well, can you at least tell me how you're feeling today?"

Wedge looked again at the television; PANASONIC came into focus a bit more quickly this time. He smiled, painfully, and then he turned to the doctor and told him what he resolved would be the only thing he told any of these fucking people: His name. His rank. His service number.

09:42 March 23, 2034 (GMT-4)
Washington, D.C.

He'd done as he'd been told. Chowdhury had gone home. He'd spent the evening with Ashni, just the two of them. He'd made them chicken fingers and french fries, their favorite, and they'd watched an old movie, *The Blues Brothers*, also their favorite. He read her three Dr. Seuss books, and halfway through the third—*The Butter Battle Book*—he fell asleep beside her, waking after midnight to stumble down the hall of their duplex to his own bed. When he woke the next morning, he had an email from Wisecarver, subject: *Today*, text: *Take it off.*

So he dropped his daughter at school. He came home. He made himself a French press coffee, bacon, eggs, toast. Then he wondered what else he might do. There were still a couple of hours until lunch. He walked to Logan Circle with his tablet and sat on a bench reading his news feed; every bit of coverage—from the international section, to the national section, to the opinion pages and even the arts—it all dealt in one way or another with the crisis of the past ten days. The editorials were contradictory. One cautioned against a phony war, comparing the *Wén Rui* incident to the Gulf of Tonkin, and warned of opportunistic politicians who now, just as seventy years before, "*would use this crisis as a means to advance ill-advised policy objectives in Southeast Asia.*" The next editorial reached even further back in history to express a contradictory view, noting at length the dangers of appeasement: *"If the Nazis had been stopped in the Sudetenland, a great bloodletting might have been avoided."* Chowdhury began to skim, coming to, *"In the South China Sea the tide of aggression has once again risen upon the free peoples of the world."* He could hardly finish this article, which sustained itself on ever loftier rhetoric in the name of pushing the country toward war.

Chowdhury remembered a classmate of his from graduate school, a Navy lieutenant commander, a prior enlisted sailor who'd gotten his start as a hospital corpsman with the Marines in Iraq. Walking past his cubicle in the study carrels one day, Chowdhury had noticed a vintage postcard of the USS *Maine* tacked to the partition. When Chowdhury joked that he ought to have a ship that *didn't* blow up and sink pinned to his cubicle, the officer replied, "I keep it there for two reasons, Sandy. One is as a reminder that complacency kills—a ship loaded out with fuel and munitions can explode at any time. But, more importantly, I keep it there to remind me that when the *Maine* blew up in 1898—before social media, before twenty-four-hour news—we had no problem engaging in national hysteria, blaming it on 'Spanish terrorists,' which of course led to the Spanish-American War. Fifty years later, after World War Two, when we finally performed a full investigation, you know what they found? The *Maine* blew up because of an internal explosion— a ruptured boiler or a compromised ammunition storage compartment. The lesson of the *Maine*—or even Iraq, where I fought—is that you better be goddamn sure you know what's going on before you start a war."

Chowdhury closed his newsfeed. It was nearly lunch time. He walked home lost in thought. His desire for de-escalation didn't stem from any pacifistic tendencies on his part. He believed in the use of force—after all, he worked on the National Security Council staff. His fear of escalation was more instinctual. Inherent in all wars, he knew, was a miscalculation; by their nature it had to exist. That's because when a war starts both sides believe that they will win.

As he walked, he struggled to put words around his reservations as if he were writing a white paper to himself. His opening sentence came to him. It would be, *The America that we believe ourselves to be is no longer the America that we are. . . .*

He thought this was a true statement. He pondered just how fraught a statement it was, how an overestimation of American strength could be disastrous. But it was lunch time, and there was nothing he could do about such existential questions, at least at this moment. This crisis, like every other, would likely pass. Cooler heads would prevail because it seemed that they always did.

He rooted around in the fridge. Not much there.

In the background CNN was playing. The anchor announced some breaking news. "We have obtained exclusive video of downed Marine pilot Major Chris Mitchell. . . ."

Chowdhury banged the back of his head as he startled up from the fridge. Before he could get to the television, he heard the warning that the video was graphic, that it might prove disturbing to some audiences. Chowdhury didn't wait around to see it. He already knew how bad it was. He climbed in his car and rushed to the office, forgetting to turn off the television.

He texted his mother to see if she could pick up Ashni from school, lest he appear negligent to his ex-wife. His mother wrote back immediately and, uncharacteristically, didn't complain about yet another change in plan. She must have already seen the video, thought Chowdhury. He was listening to the radio on his fifteen-minute drive into work; MSNBC, Fox, NPR, WAMU, even the local hip-hop station WPGC—everyone was talking about what they'd just seen. The image quality was grainy, pixilated, but what they all fixated on was how Wedge—lying on his side, with that brute of an Iranian officer standing over him, kicking him in the ribs and head—kept repeating only his name, rank, and service number.

The divergence of views Chowdhury had read in the paper that morning was quickly yielding to a consensus. Every voice he heard on the drive into work agreed: the defiance displayed by this downed flyer was an example to us all. We wouldn't be pushed around, not by anyone. Had we forgotten who we were? Had we forgotten the spirit which made us that single, indispensable nation? Chowdhury thought of yesterday's debate in the Situation Room and the president's policy of de-escalation. With the release of this video, such a policy would become untenable.

When he barged into his office, the first person he saw was Hendrickson, whom he hadn't seen since the crisis began. The offices of the national security staff were packed with Pentagon augments who were helping with—or at times getting in the way of—the administration's response to the Iranians. "When did the video come in?" Chowdhury asked Hendrickson.

He pulled Chowdhury into the corridor. "It came in last night," he said in a conspiratorial whisper, glancing side to side as though he were about to cross the road. "A signals intercept from Cyber Command— weird that it didn't come from NSA. It seems this Iranian brigadier in the video lost his cool. He's well connected and his superiors didn't quite believe what he'd done until a video circulated internally of the interrogation. We picked it up in their email traffic. Cyber defense has never been a strong suit for the Iranians. They have a tendency to focus on offensive cyber, but kind of forget to guard the barn door."

"How did it get to the press?" asked Chowdhury.

Hendrickson gave him a look, one Chowdhury had seen many times before when they'd attended the Fletcher School and either Chowdhury or one of his classmates had asked a question with an answer so obvious that its very asking annoyed Hendrickson. Nevertheless, Hendrickson obliged with an answer. "How do you think? A leak."

Before Chowdhury could ask Hendrickson who he thought had leaked the video, Trent Wisecarver stepped out from the office and into the corridor where the two stood. His frameless glasses were balanced on the tip of his nose, as if he'd been reading. Under his arm were several binders marked TOP SECRET//NOFORN. Based on their thickness and on the fact that they were paper, not electronic, Chowdhury assumed them to be military operational plans of the highest sensitivity. When he saw Chowdhury, Wisecarver made a face. "Didn't I tell you to take the day off?"

16:23 April 09, 2034 (GMT+9)
Yokosuka Naval Base

Captain Sarah Hunt ventured out to the commissary on foot. For three weeks she'd been trapped on base without a car, living in a room at the bachelor officers' quarters, its only amenities a television that played the antiseptically boring American Forces Network and a kitchenette with a mini-fridge that didn't make ice. Why the Navy chose to perform her board of inquiry here, at Yokosuka, instead of her home port of San Diego, was a mystery to her. Her best guess was that they wanted to avoid any undue attention paid to the proceedings, but she couldn't be certain. The Navy wasn't in the business of explaining its decisions, not to anyone, and most certainly not to itself, at least at her level of command. And so she'd spent the intervening weeks since the Battle of Mischief Reef stowed away in this crappy room, reporting to a nondescript office building once or twice a day to give tape-recorded answers to questions and hoping that the deliberations in progress might clear her name so that the administrative hold she'd been placed under would soon lift, allowing her to retire in peace.

She'd begun to think that the board of inquiry might never reach its conclusion when an optimistic note arrived in the form of a voice-mail left by her old friend Rear Admiral John Hendrickson, in which he announced that he "happened to be on base" and asked if he could stop by for a drink. When he was a lieutenant on faculty at Annapolis, Hendrickson had volunteered as one of the softball coaches. As a midshipman, Hunt had been one of his star players. She'd been the catcher. And Hendrickson and the other players had affectionately nicknamed her "Stonewall" for the way she guarded home plate. On occasions too numerous to count, a runner rounding third would find herself flat on her back along the baseline, staring up at an expanse of sky, while Midshipman Sarah "Stonewall" Hunt stood triumphantly over her, ball in hand, with the umpire bellowing, "Ouutt!"

Sarah Hunt now stood in the checkout line of the commissary. She'd bought two six-packs of IPA, a jar of Planters mixed nuts, some crackers, some cheese. While she waited in line, she couldn't help but feel as though the other sailors were eyeing her. They knew who she was, stealing glances while trying to pretend that they didn't notice her. She couldn't decide whether this reaction was awe or contempt. She had fought in her country's largest naval battle since the Second World War.

She was, at this moment, the only officer who had ever held command at sea during a peer-level naval engagement, her three subordinate commanders having gone down with their ships. As she worked her way through the checkout line, she wondered how the sailors at Pearl Harbor felt in the days after that iconic defeat. Although eventually they had been celebrated, were the veterans of that battle first vilified? Did they have to suffer through boards of inquiry?

The cashier handed Hunt her receipt.

Back in her room, she put the nuts into a plastic bowl. She laid the crackers and cheese on a plate. She popped open a beer. And then she waited.

It didn't take long.

Knock, knock, knock . . . knock . . . knock . . . knock . . . knock, knock, knock . . .

Unreal, thought Hunt.

She called out for him to come in. Hendrickson opened the unlocked door, crossed the room, and sat across from Hunt at the small table in the kitchenette. He exhaled heavily, as though he were tired; then he took one of the beers that sat sweating condensation on the table, as well as a fistful of the salty nuts. They knew each other so well that neither had to speak.

"Cute with the knocks," Hunt eventually said.

"SOS, remember?"

She nodded, and then added, "But this isn't Bancroft Hall. I'm not a twenty-one-year-old midshipman and you aren't a twenty-seven-year-old lieutenant sneaking into my room."

He nodded sadly.

"How's Suze?"

"Fine," he answered.

"The kids?"

"Also fine . . . grandkid soon," he added, allowing his voice to perk up. "Kristine's pregnant. The timing's good. She just finished a flight tour. She's slated for shore duty."

"She still with that guy, the artist?"

"Graphic designer," Hendrickson corrected.

"Smart girl," said Hunt, giving a defeated smile. If Hunt had ever married, she knew it would've needed to be an artist, a poet, someone whose ambition—or lack thereof—didn't conflict with her own. She had always known this. That was why, decades before, she'd broken off her affair with Hendrickson. Neither of them was married at the time, so what made it an affair—because affairs are illicit—was their discrepancy in rank. Hendrickson thought after Hunt's graduation from Annapolis they could be out in the open. Despite Hunt's feelings for Hendrickson, which were real, she knew she could never be with him, or at least never be with him and have the career she wanted. When she explained this logic weeks before her graduation, he had told her that she was the love of his life, a claim that in the intervening thirty years he'd never disavowed. She had offered him only the same stony silence they now shared, which in that moment again reminded him of her namesake from those years ago—Stonewall.

"How you holding up?" Hendrickson eventually asked her.

"Fine," she said, taking a long pull off her beer.

"The board of inquiry's almost finished with its report," he offered.

She looked away from him, out the window, toward the port where she'd noticed over the past week an unusually heavy concentration of ships.

"Sarah, I've read over what happened. . . . The Navy should've given you a medal, not an investigation." He reached out and put his hand on her arm.

Her gaze remained fixed on the acres of anchored gray steel. What she wouldn't give to be on the deck of any of those ships instead of here, trapped in this room, at the end of a career cut short. "They don't give medals," she said, "to commodores who lose all their ships."

"I know."

She glared at him. He was an inadequate receptacle for her grievances: from the destruction of her flotilla; to her medical retirement; all the way back to her decision never to have a family, to make the Navy her family. Hendrickson had gone on to have a career gilded with command at every level, prestigious fellowships, impressive graduate degrees, and even a White House posting, while also having a wife, children, and now a grandchild. Hunt had never had any of this, or at least not in the proportions that she had once hoped. "Is that why you came here?" she asked bitterly. "To tell me that I should've gotten a medal?"

"No," he said, taking his hand off her arm and coming up in his seat. He leaned toward her as if for a moment he might go so far as to remind her of their difference in rank, that even she could push him too far. "I came here to tell you that the board of inquiry is going to find that you did everything possible given the circumstances."

"What circumstances are those?"

Hendrickson grabbed a fistful of the nuts, dropping them one at a time in his mouth. "That's what I was hoping you might tell me."

The board of inquiry wasn't the only reason Hendrickson had flown from Washington to Yokosuka. This should've been obvious to Hunt, but it hadn't. She was so ensconced in her own grief, in her own frustration, that she hadn't given much thought to broader events. "You're here to coordinate our response?" she asked.

He nodded.

"What's our response going to be?"

"I'm not at liberty to say, Sarah. But you can imagine."

She glanced back out to the port filled with ships, to the twin carriers at anchor studded with parked fighters on their decks, to the low-set submarines brooding on the surface, and then to the new semi-submersible frigates and the more traditional destroyers with their bladelike hulls facing out to sea.

This was the response.

"Where are you and your bosses going to send these ships?"

He didn't answer, but instead held forth on a range of technical issues. "You told the board of inquiry that your communications shut down. We haven't figured out how they did this, but we have some theories. . . ." He asked her about the frequency of the static she heard from her failing radios, about whether the Aegis terminal turned off or simply froze. He asked a series of more runic questions above the classification level of the board of inquiry. She answered—at least as best she could—until she couldn't stand it anymore, until Hendrickson's questions began to prove that whatever response he and his masters at the White House had planned against their adversaries in Beijing was fated to be a disaster.

"Don't you see?" she finally said, exasperated. "The technical details of what they did hardly matter. The way to defeat technology isn't with more technology. It is with no technology. They'll blind the elephant and then overwhelm us."

He gave her a confused, sidelong glance. "What elephant?"

"Us," she added. "We're the elephant."

Hendrickson finished off the last of his beer. It'd been a long day and a tough few weeks, he told her. He'd return in the morning to check on her and then he had a flight out the following afternoon. He understood what she was saying, or at least wanted to understand. But the administration, he explained, was under enormous pressure to do something, to somehow demonstrate that they wouldn't be cowed. It wasn't only what had happened here but also this pilot, he said, this Marine who'd been brought down. Then he ruminated on the curse of domestic politics driving international policy as he stood from his seat and made for the door. "So, we'll pick up again tomorrow?" he asked.

She didn't answer.

"Okay?" he added.

She nodded. "Okay." She shut the door behind him as he left.

That night her sleep was thin and empty, except for one dream. He was in it. And the Navy wasn't. It was the two of them in an alternative life, where their choices had been different. She woke from that dream and didn't sleep well the rest of the night because she kept trying to return to it. The following morning, she woke to a knock at her door. But it wasn't him; it wasn't his familiar SOS knock, just a plain knocking.

When she opened her door, a pimply faced sailor handed over a message. She was to report to the board of inquiry that afternoon for a final interview. She thanked the sailor and returned to her dim room, where the darkness congealed in the empty corners. She threw open the drapes to let in the light. It blinded her for a moment.

She rubbed at her eyes and looked down onto the port.

It was empty.

3

Blinding the Elephant

Qassem Farshad had taken the deal he was offered. Discipline against him had been decisive and swift. In less than a month he was delivered a letter of reprimand for his excesses during the interrogation of the American pilot, followed by an early retirement. When he had asked if there was anyone else he might appeal his case to, the administrative officer who'd been sent to deliver the news showed him the bottom of the page, which held the signature of the old man himself, Major General Mohammad Bagheri, chief of the General Staff of the Armed Forces. When Farshad received the letter, he'd been on suspension at home, at his family's country residence an hour outside of Isfahan. It reminded him of Soleimani's home in Qanat-e Malek. It was peaceful there, quiet.

Farshad tried to settle into a routine. In the first few days he hiked his three miles each morning and began to sort through boxes of notebooks he'd kept throughout his career. He had an idea to write a memoir, maybe something that would be instructive to younger officers. However, it was difficult for him to concentrate. He was afflicted by a phantom itching in his missing leg, something he'd never experienced before. At midday he would break from his attempts at writing and take a picnic lunch to an elm tree that sat in a field on the far end of his property. He would rest with his back to the tree and have a simple lunch: a boiled egg, a piece of bread, some olives. He never finished his meal. His appetite had recently waned, and he would leave the remains for a pair of squirrels who lived in the tree and who, with each passing day, edged closer and closer to him in search of his scraps.

He remembered and then re-remembered his last exchange with the old general, how Soleimani had wished him a soldier's death. Farshad couldn't help it; he felt as though his outburst in Bandar Abbas had let his father's old friend down. On the other hand, striking a prisoner had never before been grounds for dismissal for a Revolutionary Guards officer. In Iraq, in Afghanistan, in Syria, and in Palestine, all through his career, intelligence work was often done with fists. He knew many who'd ascended into positions of high command by virtue of their brutality alone. But Farshad's superiors had expected more from him. They had told him—in no uncertain terms—that he was the most junior person they could trust. And he had betrayed that trust. Although they might have thought that Farshad had momentarily lost control of himself in the presence of an impertinent American flyer, it was more profound than that.

Farshad hadn't lost control.

Far from it.

He had known exactly what he was doing. He had known exactly how important this American was, even if he hadn't understood every detail. What he had known was that by beating this American to a pulp, he was pushing his country closer to war with the same alliance of Western powers that had killed both his own father and the old general. Perhaps neither would be disappointed in me after all, thought Farshad. Perhaps they would be proud of me for taking our people one step closer to the inevitable confrontation with the West that our feckless leaders have long avoided. He thought of himself as seizing an opportunity that fate had thrust before him. But it seemed to have backfired and cost him the twilight of his career.

For days and then weeks, Farshad kept to his routine and eventually the phantom itching in his missing leg began to subside. He lived alone in his family's empty home, hiking his three miles, taking his walk at lunch. Each day, the pair of squirrels who lived in the tree came ever closer, until one of them, whose fur was a very rich shade of brown and who he assumed to be the male (as opposed to the female, whose tail was snowy white), had plucked up enough courage to eat from the palm of Farshad's hand. After lunch he would return home and write through the afternoon. At night he prepared himself a simple dinner, and then he read in bed. His existence was reduced to this. After a career in command of hundreds and at times thousands of men, it surprised him how he enjoyed being responsible for himself alone.

No one stopped by.

The phone never rang.

It was only him.

So the weeks passed, until one morning he noticed that the single road that bordered his property was filled with military transports, even the occasional tracked vehicle. Their exhausts belched smoke. Beyond the line of trees that partially screened his house he could see them stuck in a traffic jam of their own creation as officers and noncommissioned officers barked orders at their drivers, trying to move things along. They seemed in a frenzy to reach their destination. Later that morning, as Farshad was leisurely filling a notebook with his memories, the phone rang, startling him so much that his pen skipped across the page.

"Hello," he answered.

"Is this Brigadier Qassem Farshad?" came a voice he didn't recognize.

"Who is this?"

The voice introduced itself quickly, as though its name were designed to be forgotten, and then informed the brigadier that the General Staff of the Armed Forces had ordered a mobilization of retired and reserve officers. Farshad was then given the address of a mustering office. The building was in a nondescript part of Isfahan, far from the military's power centers in Tehran where he'd spent much of his career. Farshad finished transcribing the particulars of where he was to report, leaving his notes on a scrap of paper. He felt tempted to ask the voice for details about whatever incident had precipitated this mobilization, but he decided against it. He thought that he knew, or at least had an instinct. When Farshad asked if there was anything else, the voice said no, and wished him well.

Farshad set down the phone. He had a radio upstairs. He could've turned it on to find out specifically what had happened, but he didn't want to, at least not yet. It was midday and he wanted to pack up his lunch, take his walk, and sit beneath his tree, as had become his custom. Farshad knew that if he didn't report for duty there'd be no recourse. No one would dare say he hadn't done enough for the Islamic Republic.

A few weeks ago, his choice would've been an easy one; he would've packed his things and happily marched off to another war. But, surprisingly enough to him, he had come to appreciate this quieter life. He had even begun to imagine that he might settle here, in the country, with some measure of contentment.

He left the house for his walk.

His stride was loose, his pace quick.

Down the dirt-packed roads, past the fields of wildflowers, across the footbridge that traversed a stream of glacial melt, he walked and walked, much farther than he usually would on such a morning. Each breath filled his lungs and he felt strong, even at peace. He had no obligation to follow the orders given by the voice on the phone, at least no moral obligation. He had done enough. And if he died old in his bed, far greater soldiers than him had met that same humble fate. War had taken everything from him—first his father, and eventually his mother, who never recovered from that loss—and all that remained was this land that had belonged to his family. Why should war take this last measure of peace from him?

By the time Farshad reached his familiar tree, he was famished. He'd hiked nearly twice his usual distance. It was the first time in a long time that he could remember having such an appetite. With his back against the trunk of the tree, he ate. He savored each bite, angling his head upward as the blotchy sunlight filtered through the canopy of branches and fell onto his smiling face.

He was finished with his meal and on the cusp of a nap when the familiar pair of squirrels approached. He could feel the one, darker squirrel brush against his leg. When he opened his eyes, it was right there while the other, smaller squirrel, the female with the snow-white tail, lingered not far behind, watching. Farshad felt badly that he had no scrap of food to offer them. He brushed a few breadcrumbs off his shirt and placed them in his palm; it was the best he could do. The darker squirrel came closer than he had ever come before, perching on Farshad's wrist while he dipped his head into Farshad's cupped palm. Farshad was amazed. He didn't think it possible that anything, particularly a squirrel, could be so unafraid of him, so trusting.

In his amazement, Farshad didn't notice that the dark squirrel was hardly satisfied by meager crumbs. When the squirrel finished his little mouthful of food, he twitched his head toward Farshad and then, realizing that nothing else would be offered, sunk his teeth into Farshad's palm.

Farshad didn't flinch. He didn't curse and drop the squirrel or clutch his palm to his chest. His reaction was different, but similarly reflexive. He snatched the dark squirrel around the body and squeezed. The squirrel's mate, who had been waiting at a more cautious distance, began to run in frantic circles. Farshad squeezed harder. He couldn't stop, even had he wanted to. And a part of him did want to stop, the same part of him that wanted to stay here, under this tree. Nevertheless, he squeezed so hard that his own blood, the blood from the bite, began to seep out from between his fingers. The dark squirrel's body struggled and twitched.

Until it didn't—until to Farshad it felt as though he were squeezing an empty sponge. He stood and dropped the dead squirrel by the roots of the tree.

Its mate ran to it and glanced up at Farshad, who looked over his shoulder in the direction from which he'd come. He walked slowly back to the house, back to the slip of paper with an address on it.

⌐

06:37 April 23, 2034 (GMT+8)
Beijing

Lin Bao's new job, as the deputy commander for naval operations to the Central Military Commission, was a bureaucratic morass. Although the ministry was on a war footing, it only increased the intensity and frequency of the interminable staff meetings he needed to attend. Lin Bao often saw Minister Chiang at these meetings, but the minister had never again brought up Lin Bao's request for command of the *Zheng He*, let alone any command. And Lin Bao had no license to raise the topic. On the surface his job was suitable and important, but privately he sensed that he was a long way from a return to sea duty. Ever since the *Zheng He* Carrier Battle Group's great victory over the Americans, a panic had begun to grow within Lin Bao.

He couldn't pinpoint it to one thing, but rather to a collection of annoyances, the mundane trivialities that can, at times, make life unbearable. As the military attaché to the United States, his position had been singular and of the greatest import. Now, while his nation faced its greatest military crisis in a generation, he was stuck commuting each morning to the Defense Ministry. He no longer had the driver he'd enjoyed in Washington. When his wife needed the car to drop their daughter at school, he was forced to carpool into work. Sandwiched in the back seat of a minivan between two short officers who spoke of nothing but basketball and whose careers had dead-ended long ago, he could not imagine ever standing on the bridge of his own carrier.

These weeks had brought only exaltation for Ma Qiang. It had been announced that for his actions he would receive the Order of August First, the greatest possible military honor. Once the award was conferred on Ma Qiang, Lin Bao knew it was highly unlikely that he would ever take command of the *Zheng He*. Whatever disappointment he felt was, however, tempered by his appreciation that their recent undertaking against the Americans had initiated events beyond any one person's control.

And so Lin Bao continued his staff work. He continued to carpool into the ministry with officers he deemed inferior to himself. He never again brought up his ambition for command to Minister Chiang, and he could feel the mundane ferocity of time passing. Until it was soon interrupted—as it always is—by an unanticipated event.

The unanticipated event was a phone call to Lin Bao that came in from the South Sea Fleet Headquarters in Zhanjiang. That morning, a reconnaissance drone had spotted "a significant American naval force" sailing southward at approximately twelve knots toward the Spratly Islands, along a route that was often used for their so-called "freedom of navigation patrols." Immediately after the drone observed the American ships, communications between it and the South Sea Fleet Headquarters cut off. It was the commander of the South Sea Fleet himself who had contacted the Central Military Commission. His question was simple: should he risk sending out another drone?

Before Lin Bao could offer a thought on the matter, there was a slight commotion in his workspace as Minister Chiang entered. The mid-level officers and junior sailors who served as clerks sprung to attention as the minister breezed past them, while Lin Bao himself stood, clutching his telephone's receiver. He began to explain the situation, but Minister Chiang raised his outstretched palm, as if to save him the trouble. He already knew about the drone and what it'd seen. And he already knew his response, snatching the telephone's receiver so that now Lin Bao was only privy to one side of the conversation.

"Yes . . . yes . . ." muttered Minister Chiang impatiently into the line. "I've already received those reports."

Then the inaudible response.

"No," answered Minister Chiang, "another flight is out of the question."

Again, the inaudible response.

"Because you'll lose that flight as well," Minister Chiang replied tersely. "We're preparing your orders now and will have them out within the hour. I'd recommend you recall all personnel on shore leave or otherwise. Plan to be busy." Minister Chiang hung up. He took a single, exasperated breath. His shoulders slumped forward as if he were profoundly tired. He was like a father whose child has, once again, bitterly disappointed him. Then he looked up and with a transformed expression, as if energized for whatever task lay ahead, ordered Lin Bao to follow him.

They walked briskly through the vast corridors of the Defense Ministry, a small retinue of Minister Chiang's staff trailing behind. Lin Bao wasn't certain what Minister Chiang's countermove would be if it wasn't the deployment of another reconnaissance drone. They reached the same windowless conference room where they'd first met.

Minister Chiang assumed his position at the head of the table, leaning backward in his cushioned swivel chair, his palms resting on his chest, his fingers laced together. "I suspected this was what the Americans would do," he began. "It is disappointingly predictable. . . ." One of the underlings on Minister Chiang's staff was setting up the secure video teleconference, and Lin Bao felt certain he knew with whom they'd soon be speaking. "By my estimation, the Americans have sent two carrier battle groups—the *Ford* and the *Miller* would be my guess— to sail right through our South China Sea. They are doing this for one reason and one reason alone: to prove that they still can. Yes, this provocation is certainly predictable. For decades, they have sent their 'freedom of navigation patrols' through our waters despite our protests. For just as long they have refused to recognize our claim over Chinese Taipei and insulted us in the UN with their insistence on calling it Taiwan. All the while we've endured these provocations. The country of Clint Eastwood, of Dwayne Johnson, of LeBron James, it can't imagine a nation like ours would submit to such humiliations for any other reason but weakness. . . .

"But our strength is what it has always been—our judicious patience. The Americans are incapable of behaving patiently. They change their government and their policies as often as the seasons. Their dysfunctional civil discourse is unable to deliver an international strategy that endures for more than a handful of years. They're governed by their emotions, by their blithe morality and belief in their precious indispensability. This is a fine disposition for a nation known for making movies, but not for a nation to survive as we have through the millennia. . . . And where will America be after today? I believe in a thousand years it won't even be remembered as a country. It will simply be remembered as a moment. A fleeting moment."

Minister Chiang sat with his palms on the table, waiting. Across from him was the video teleconference, which hadn't yet established its secure connection. He stared at the blank screen. His concentration was intense, as if willing an image of his own future to appear. And then the screen turned on. Ma Qiang stood on the bridge of the *Zheng He*, exactly as he'd done six weeks before. The only difference was the yellow, gold, and red ribbon with a star in its center fastened above the pocket of his fire-resistant coveralls: the Order of August First.

"Admiral Ma Qiang," the minister began formally, "a reconnaissance flight from our South Sea Fleet has gone missing approximately three hundred nautical miles east of your current position." Ma Qiang straightened up in the frame, his jaw set. It was obvious he understood the implications of such a disappearance. The minister continued, "Our entire constellation of satellites are now under your command. The Central Military Commission grants you all contingent authorizations."

Ma Qiang nodded his head slowly, as if in deference to the great scope of the mission he was now set upon, which Lin Bao implicitly understood was no less than the destruction of two US carrier battle groups.

"Good luck."

Ma Qiang nodded once again.

The connection switched off and the screen went blank. Although the conference room was far from empty, with various staff members entering and exiting, it was only Lin Bao and Minister Chiang sitting at the table. The minister stroked his smooth round chin, and for the first time that morning Lin Bao detected a hint of uncertainty in his expression.

"Don't look at me like that," said Minister Chiang.

Lin Bao averted his eyes. Perhaps his expression had betrayed his thoughts, which were that he was observing a man who had condemned thousands of other men to their deaths. Did any of them really think that their navy, despite its advanced cyber capability, was up to the task of destroying two US carrier battle groups? The *Gerald R. Ford* and *Doris Miller* sailed with a combined force of forty vessels. Destroyers armed with hypersonic missiles. Utterly silent attack submarines. Semisubmersible frigates. Guided missile cruisers with small, unmanned targeting drones and long-range land-attack hypersonic missiles. Each possessed the latest technology manned by the world's most highly trained crews, all of it watched over by a vast constellation of satellites with deep offensive and defensive cyber capabilities. Nobody knew this better than Lin Bao, whose entire career had centered on his understanding of the United States Navy. He also understood the United States itself, the nation's character. It was woefully misguided for the leaders of his country to believe diplomatic niceties could de-escalate a crisis in which one of their allies had taken an American pilot prisoner and in which their own navy had destroyed three American ships. Did leaders like Minister Chiang really believe that the Americans would simply cede freedom of navigation in the South China Sea? American morality, that slippery sensibility, which had so often led that country astray, would demand a response. Their reaction of returning with two carrier battle groups was completely predictable.

Minister Chiang insisted that Lin Bao sit beside him while all through that day a procession of subordinates entered and exited the conference room, receiving orders, issuing updates. The morning extended into the afternoon. The plan took shape. The *Zheng He* maneuvered into a blocking position south of the Spratly Island Chain, deploying in attack formation toward the last recorded position of the *Ford* and *Miller*. The American carrier battle groups would in all likelihood be able to get off a single salvo of weaponry before the *Zheng He* could disable their guidance systems. After that, the proverbial elephant would be blind. The American smart weapons would no longer be smart, not even dumb; they'd be brain-dead. Then the *Zheng He*, along with three surface action groups, would strike the *Ford* and *Miller*.

That had been the plan.

But by late afternoon, there was still no sign of the Americans.

Ma Qiang was on the video teleconference again, updating Minister Chiang as to the disposition of his forces, which at that moment were deployed in a racetrack formation extending over dozens of nautical miles. As Ma Qiang spoke of current conditions at sea, Lin Bao glanced surreptitiously at his watch.

"Why are you looking at your watch?" snapped Minster Chiang, interrupting the briefing.

Lin Bao felt his face turn red.

"Do you have somewhere else to be?"

"No, Comrade Minister. Nowhere else to be."

Minister Chiang nodded back toward Ma Qiang, who continued on with his briefing, while Lin Bao settled exhaustedly into his chair. His carpool had left fifteen minutes before. He had no idea how he would get home.

⌐

04:27 April 26, 2034 (GMT+5:30)
New Delhi

The phone rang. "Are you up?"

"I'm up now."

"It's bad, Sandy."

"What's bad?" he asked Hendrickson, swallowing the dryness from his throat as he rubbed his eyes, his vision slowly coming into focus so he could read the digital display of his alarm clock.

"The *Ford* and the *Miller*, they're gone."

"What do you mean *gone*?"

"They got the drop on us, or shut us down, or I don't even know how to describe it. Reports are nothing worked. We were blind. When we launched our planes, their avionics froze, their navigation systems glitched out and were then overridden. Pilots couldn't eject. Missiles wouldn't fire. Dozens of our aircraft plunged into the water. Then they came at us with everything. A carrier, frigates and destroyers, diesel and nuclear submarines, swarms of unmanned torpedo boats, hypersonic cruise missiles with total stealth, offensive cyber. We're still piecing it all together. The whole thing happened middle of last night. . . . Christ, Sandy, she was right."

"Who was right?"

"Sarah—Sarah Hunt. I saw her weeks ago when I was in Yokosuka."

Chowdhury knew that the board of inquiry had cleared Hunt of all culpability in the Battle of Mischief Reef and the loss of her flotilla, but he also knew the Navy had wanted to consign her defeat to a fluke. That would be far easier than taking a hard look at the circumstances that led to it. It would now be impossible for the Navy—or the nation—to ignore a disaster on this scale. Thirty-seven warships destroyed. Thousands of sailors perished.

"How did we do?" Chowdhury asked tentatively. "Did our long-range air score any hits? How many of theirs did we sink?"

"None," said Hendrickson.

"None?"

The line went silent for a moment. "I've heard that we might have scored a hit on their carrier, the *Zheng He*, but we didn't sink any of their ships."

"My God," said Chowdhury. "How's Wisecarver reacting?"

He was up now, his bedside lamp on, stepping into each leg of his trousers, which he'd draped over the back of a chair. He'd arrived at these bland quarters in the embassy's visitors' annex two days before. While Chowdhury dressed, Hendrickson explained that the news hadn't yet leaked to the public: one of the benefits of the blackout the Chinese had employed was that it allowed the administration to control the news, or at least to control it until the Chinese used that information against them. Which they had, strangely, not yet done.

Hendrickson explained that the White House had succumbed to

panic. "Jesus, what will the country say?" had been the president's response on hearing the news. Trent Wisecarver had contacted NORAD and elevated the threat level to DEFCON 2, with a request to the president to elevate it to DEFCON 1. In an emergency meeting of the National Security Council he had also requested preemptive authorization for a tactical nuclear launch against the *Zheng He* Carrier Battle Group, provided it could be found and targeted. Remarkably, his request had not been rejected outright. The president, who only days before had wanted to de-escalate tensions, was now entertaining such a strike.

De-escalation had been the entire reason the administration dispatched Chowdhury to New Delhi. Negotiations surrounding the release of Major Chris "Wedge" Mitchell had progressed to the point where the Iranians agreed to transport him to their embassy in India, and a prisoner swap seemed imminent. Chowdhury believed—and the analysts at CIA backed him up—that the sole reason the Iranians were dragging their feet on the major's release was because they wanted his wounds to heal a bit more, particularly his face. The last contact Chowdhury had with the Iranians—a contact brokered through officials at India's Foreign Ministry—they'd assured him that Major Mitchell would be released within a week, as he now explained to Hendrickson.

"A week's too long," Hendrickson replied. "Once the Iranians learn what's happened—if they don't know already—they'll take Major Mitchell back to Tehran. You've got to get him out now, or at least try. That's why I'm calling—" There was a pause on the line as Chowdhury wondered how Hendrickson could possibly expect him to accomplish such a task. Then Hendrickson added, "Sandy, we're at war." The words might once have sounded melodramatic, but now they didn't; they had become a statement of fact.

04:53 April 26, 2034 (GMT+9)
Yokosuka Naval Base

Dawn vanished the fog as the day broke bright and pure. Three ships on the horizon. A destroyer. A frigate. A cruiser.

They were sailing slowly, barely moving in fact. The frigate and cruiser were very close together, the destroyer a little further off. This view from Sarah Hunt's window early that morning was a curious sight. Her flight to San Diego was scheduled for later that day. As she watched the three ships limping closer, she wondered if they would pull into port by the time she left. What she saw didn't make much sense to her. Where were the *Ford* and *Miller*?

A red flare went up, followed by one and then two more. On the deck of the destroyer was a signal lamp; it began to flash.

Flash, flash, flash . . . flash . . . flash . . . flash . . . flash, flash, flash . . .
Three short . . . three long . . . three short . . .

Hunt recognized the message immediately. She ran out of her barracks room toward Seventh Fleet Headquarters.

05:23 April 26, 2034 (GMT+8)
Beijing

Victory had been total. Beyond what they could have hoped for.

It almost unsettled them.

It had been past midnight when Ma Qiang reported contact with the vanguard of destroyers from the *Ford* Battle Group. He was able to neutralize their weapons systems and communications with the same offensive cyber capability his fleet had employed weeks before to great effect near Mischief Reef. This allowed a dozen of his stealthy unmanned torpedo boats to close within a kilometer of the vanguard and launch their ordnance. Which they did, to devastating effect. Three direct hits on three American destroyers. They sunk in under ten minutes, vanished. That had been the opening blow, delivered in darkness. When the news was reported in the Defense Ministry, the cheers were raucous.

After that, all through the night their blows fell in quick succession.

A single flight of four Shenyang J-15s launched from the *Zheng He* scored a total of fifteen direct hits divided between three destroyers, two cruisers, and a frigate, sinking all six. A half dozen torpedo-armed Kamov helicopters launched from three separate Jiangkai II–class frigates scored four out of six hits, one of which struck the *Ford* itself, disabling its rudder. This would be the first of many strikes against both American carriers. Those carriers responded by launching their aircraft while the surface ships responded by launching their ordnance, but they all fired blindly, into not only the darkness of that night but the more profound darkness of what they could no longer see, reliant as they had become on technologies that failed to serve them. Chinese cyber dominance of the American forces was complete. A highly sophisticated artificial intelligence capability allowed the *Zheng He* to employ its cyber tools at precisely the right moment to infiltrate US systems by use of a high-frequency delivery mechanism. Stealth was a secondary tool, though not unimportant. In the end, it was the massive discrepancy in offensive cyber capabilities—an invisible advantage—that allowed the *Zheng He* to consign a far larger force to the depths of the South China Sea.

For four hours, a steady stream of reports filtered in from the bridge of the *Zheng He* back to the Defense Ministry. The blows struck by Ma

Qiang's command fell with remarkable rapidity. Equally remarkable was that they fell at such little cost. Two hours into the battle, they hadn't lost a single ship or aircraft. Then, the unimaginable happened, an event Lin Bao never thought he would see in his lifetime. At 04:37 a single Yuan-class diesel-electric submarine slipped toward the hull of the *Miller*, flooded its torpedo tubes, and fired a spread at point-blank range.

After impact, it took only eleven minutes for the carrier to sink.

When this news arrived, there wasn't any cheering in the Defense Ministry as there'd been before. Only silence. Minister Chiang, who had sat diligently at the head of the conference table all through the night, stood and headed for the door. Lin Bao, as the second most senior officer in the room, felt obliged to ask him where he was going and when he might return—the battle wasn't over yet, he reminded the minister. The *Ford* was out there, injured but still a threat. Minister Chiang turned back toward Lin Bao, and his expression, which was usually so exuberant, appeared tired, contorted by the fatigue he'd hidden these many weeks.

"I'm only stepping out for some fresh air," he said, glancing at his watch. "The sun will be up soon. It's a whole new day and I'd like to watch the dawn."

05:46 April 26, 2034 (GMT+5:30)
New Delhi

After Hendrickson hung up with him, Chowdhury knew who he needed to call, though it was a call he didn't wish to place. He quickly calculated the time difference. Though it was late, his mother would still be up.

"Sandeep, I thought I wasn't going to hear from you for a few days?" she began, sounding slightly annoyed.

"I know," he said exhaustedly. And his exhaustion wasn't as much from his lack of sleep, or even his gathering realization of how dire circumstances had become for the Seventh Fleet, as it was from having to apologize to his mother. He'd said he wasn't going to phone on this trip. Yet when he needed her, as he did now, she had always been there. "There's been a problem at work," said Chowdhury, pausing dramatically, as if to give his mother's imagination sufficient time to conjure what a "problem at work" currently meant for her son, given the circumstances. "Can you put me in touch with your brother?"

The line went silent, as he knew it would.

There was a reason Chowdhury hadn't referred to retired Vice Admiral Anand Patel as "my uncle," but instead as "your brother." Because Anand Patel had never been an uncle to Chowdhury, and he hadn't been much of a brother to his sister Lakshmi. The cause of their estrangement was an arranged marriage between a teenage Lakshmi and a young naval officer—a friend of her older brother's—that ended in an affair, a marriage-for-love to Chowdhury's father, who had been a medical student with plans to study at Columbia University, which led to Lakshmi's departure for the United States while the family honor—at least according to her elder brother—was left in tatters. But that was all a long time ago. Long enough that it'd been twenty years since the young naval officer who was meant to be Lakshmi's husband died in a helicopter crash, and ten years since Sandy's father, the oncologist, had died of his own cancer. In the meantime, Lakshmi's brother, Sandy's uncle, had climbed the ranks of India's naval service, ascending to the admiralty, a distinction that was never spoken of in the Chowdhury household but that now might prove useful as Sandy scrambled to play the inside hand that would assure Major Mitchell's release. That is, if his mother would oblige.

"I don't understand, Sandeep," she said. "Doesn't our government have contacts in the Indian government? Isn't this the sort of thing that gets worked out in official channels?"

Chowdhury explained to his mother that, yes, this was the sort of thing that was usually worked out in official channels, and that, yes, their government did have any number of contacts inside the Indian government and military—to include certain intelligence assets that Chowdhury didn't mention. However, despite these formidable resources, oftentimes the key to severing the Gordian knot of diplomacy was a personal connection, a familial connection.

"That man is no longer family of mine," she snapped back at him.

"Mom, why do you think they picked me, *Sandeep Chowdhury*, to come here? Plenty of others could have been given this assignment. They gave it to me because our family is from here."

"What would your father say to that? You're American. They should send you because you're the best man for the job, not because of who your parents—"

"Mom," he said, cutting her off. He allowed the line to go silent for a beat. "I need your help."

"Okay," she said. "Do you have a pen?"

He did.

She recited her brother's phone number by heart.

09:13 April 26, 2034 (GMT+5:30)
New Delhi

The swelling on his face had gone down considerably. His ribs were doing much better. When Wedge took a deep breath it no longer hurt. There were some scars, sure, but nothing too bad, nothing that would turn off the girls he imagined hanging on his every word in the bars around Miramar Air Station when he made it home with his stories. A few days before, they'd given him a clean change of clothes, added some sort of stringy meat to his diet, and placed him on a government airplane with stewardesses, fruit juice, and bagged peanuts—all he could eat. He hadn't been alone, of course. A plainclothes entourage of guards with pistols brandished in their waistbands and mirrored sunglasses masking their eyes kept a watch over him. When Wedge clownishly tossed a few of the peanuts into the air and caught them with his mouth, the guards even laughed, though Wedge couldn't be certain whether they were laughing at or with him.

The plane had landed in darkness, a choice he assumed was intentional. Then he was whisked from the airport in a panel van with blacked-out windows. No one told him anything until late that night, when he was getting ready for bed in the carpeted room where they'd placed him, more like a drab hotel room than a cell, and nicer than anything Wedge had seen for weeks. Still, no one told him where he'd been flown to. All they told him was that tomorrow a representative from the Red Cross would pay a visit. That night, excited by the prospect, he hardly slept. The image of an attractive nurse, of the type that entertained GIs at USO tours in another era, relentlessly came to mind. He could see her generically beautiful face, her white uniform, her stockings, the cap with the little red cross. He knew that wasn't how Red Cross women looked these days, but he couldn't help it. His room was empty, though he assumed a guard was posted outside his door, and in the emptiness of that room his imagination became ever more expansive as he fantasized about this meeting, his first contact with the outside world in nearly two months. He could see her lipsticked mouth forming the reassuring words: *I'll get you home.*

When his door opened the next morning and a slight Indian man appeared, his disappointment was acute.

⌐

09:02 April 27, 2034 (GMT+4:30)
Isfahan

At the Second Army's administrative center nobody knew for certain what had happened in the South China Sea. The General Staff of the Armed Forces had issued a nationwide mobilization order; the country was going to war, or was at least on the brink of war, yet no one could say exactly why. When leaving his family's home, Farshad thought of wearing his uniform but decided against it. He was no longer a brigadier in the Revolutionary Guards, let alone a brigadier in the elite Quds Force. He was a civilian now, and even though it had only been a few weeks the break felt permanent—less a break, more an amputation. Whether this amputation was reversible Farshad would soon discover. He was waiting in a line that extended down a corridor on the third floor of this vast administrative annex. He was, he guessed, the oldest person in the line by several decades. He could feel the others stealing glances at this man with all the scars and three fingers on his right hand.

After less than an hour, he was escorted out of the line and up a set of stairs to an office on the fourth floor. "Now wait here," said a corporal, who spoke to Farshad as though he outranked him. The corporal stepped into the office only to emerge moments later and wave Farshad in.

It was a spacious corner office. Behind the large oak desk were a pair of crossed flags; the first was the flag of the Islamic Republic and the second that of the army. A uniformed man, a colonel in the administrative service, approached Farshad with his hand outstretched. His palm was smooth and his uniform had been starched and ironed so many times that it shined with a metallic patina. The colonel asked for the old brigadier, the hero of the Golan Heights, the recipient of the Order of the Fath, to sit and join him for tea. The corporal set the glasses out, first in front of Farshad and then in front of the colonel.

"It is an honor to have you here," said the colonel between sips of tea.

Farshad shrugged. An obsequious exchange wasn't the point of his visit. Not wanting to appear impolite, he muttered, "You have a nice office."

"I'm sure you've enjoyed nicer."

"I was a field commander," Farshad answered, shaking his head. "I can't remember ever really having an office." Then he took another sip of tea, finishing his glass in a single gulp and placing it loudly on the tray, as if to indicate that the pleasantries were over and Farshad wanted to get down to business.

From a drawer, the colonel removed a manila envelope and slid it across the desk. "This arrived late last night from Tehran via courier. I was told if you appeared here to hand it to you personally. . . ." Farshad opened the envelope: it contained a single document printed on thick stock, riddled with calligraphy, seals, and signatures.

"It is a commission as a lieutenant commander in the Navy?"

"I was instructed to convey that Major General Bagheri, the chief of the General Staff of the Armed Forces, has, himself, asked that you consider accepting this commission."

"I was a brigadier before," said Farshad as he dropped the letter of commission on the colonel's desk.

To this, the colonel had no response.

"Why are we mobilizing?" asked Farshad.

"I don't know," replied the colonel. "Like you, I don't have a full explanation, only my orders at this point." Then he took another envelope from his desk and handed it to Farshad. It contained a travel itinerary for a flight to Damascus with a transfer to Russia's naval base in the Syrian port city of Tartus, where he was to report for "liaison duties." Farshad couldn't tell if the assignment was legitimate or designed as an insult. That confusion must have shown in his expression: the colonel began to explain how from "an administrative standpoint" it would be very difficult to reappoint a reprimanded officer to a commensurate rank within the same branch of the armed forces. "I happen to know," the colonel continued, "that the senior ranks of the Revolutionary Guards are oversubscribed. Your service to the Islamic Republic is needed; this is the only vacancy that can be afforded to you." The colonel reached into his drawer again and removed a pair of shoulder boards embroidered with the gold piping of a navy lieutenant commander. He placed them on the desk between himself and Farshad.

Farshad stared contemptuously at the rank, which was a demotion for him three times over. Had it come to this? If he wanted a role in the impending conflict, would he have to prostrate himself in this way, and not even for a frontline assignment, but for some auxiliary job as a liaison with the Russians? And to be a sailor? He didn't even like boats. Soleimani had never had to suffer such an indignity, nor had his father. Farshad stood and faced the colonel, his jaw set, his hands balled into fists. He didn't know what he should do, but he did know what his father and Soleimani would have told him to do.

Farshad gestured for the colonel to hand him a pen, so that he could sign the acceptance of his commission. Then he gathered up his orders and his itinerary to Tartus and turned to leave. "Lieutenant Commander," the colonel said as Farshad headed toward the door. "Forgetting something?" He held up the shoulder boards. Farshad took them and again made for the door.

"Aren't you forgetting something else, Lieutenant Commander?"

Farshad looked back blankly.

Then he realized. He struggled to control a familiar rage from deep in his stomach, one that on other occasions had spurred him to violence. This fool in his over-starched uniform, with his corner office that he never left. This fool who'd no doubt gone from cushy assignment to cushy assignment, all the while posing as though he were a real soldier, as though he knew what fighting and killing were. Farshad wanted to choke him, to squeeze him by the neck until his lips turned blue and his head hung limply by the stump of his neck.

But he didn't. He buried that desire in a place where he could later retrieve it. Instead he stood up straight, at attention. With his three-fingered right hand, Lieutenant Commander Qassem Farshad saluted the administrative colonel.

07:26 May 06, 2034 (GMT+8)
Southeast of the Spratly Islands

Lin Bao could see early light on the water. It had been so long since he had been at sea. So long since he had held command.

Not so long, however, since their great victory in these waters, or since his government had released to the world news of its victory over the Americans—thirty-seven ships sunk from the Seventh Fleet, to include the carriers *Ford* and *Miller*—and that same stunned world had woken to a new reality—the balance of power on the ocean had shifted.

And not so long since he had received his orders from Minister Chiang himself to take command of the *Zheng He* Carrier Battle Group. He had left his wife and daughter in Beijing three days before and arrived at the South Sea Fleet Headquarters at Zhanjiang with his orders in hand.

Lin Bao was thinking of Ma Qiang as he flew out to meet what was now his ship. The two young pilots of his twin-rotor transport had invited him to sit in the cockpit's third jump seat. They were cheerful and proud of their assignment to deliver their new commander from Zhanjiang to his carrier, assuring him of a smooth flight and a perfect landing, "... which is good luck for a new commander," one of them said with a toothy grin as they finished their preflight. Observing the sea from the cockpit, Lin Bao wondered if Ma Qiang's body was somewhere beneath him. His old classmate's dying wish having been a burial at sea. This, Lin Bao knew, was all part of a legend that Ma Qiang had orchestrated throughout his life, up to his death, which conveniently had arrived at the moment of his greatest victory. Like the naval hero Admiral Horatio Nelson at Trafalgar, Ma Qiang had maneuvered his flagship recklessly close to the action, inviting the peril that would assure his glory. When one American aircraft, an old model F/A-18 Hornet, slipped the *Zheng He*'s defenses, the pilot did something distinctly un-American. The pilot had kamikazed into the *Zheng He*'s flight deck, right beneath the bridge.

The *Zheng He* now appeared on the horizon, as small as a postage stamp.

As his plane lined up its approach, Lin Bao imagined it wasn't all that different than the final journey taken by the Hornet. He recalled Minister Chiang's reaction to the news that several sailors, two junior officers, and Admiral Ma Qiang had been killed in this American kamikaze attack. "That was a very brave pilot," the minister had said of the American, saying nothing of Ma Qiang, whose glory-hunting seemed to annoy Minister Chiang far more than his death seemed to disturb him. To Lin Bao, he had only added, "I suppose you'll be getting your command after all." And if Minister Chiang had been privately dismissive of Ma Qiang and what he perceived to be the undue risks he'd taken, publicly the defense minister and the entire membership of the Politburo Standing Committee had extolled the virtues of Admiral Ma Qiang, the hero of what they had already enshrined as the Victory of the South China Sea.

Nothing like replacing a hero, thought Lin Bao, as the plane made its descent toward the flight deck. He could hear the familiar chatter of air traffic control through his headset as they held their glide path. Only two of the four arresting wires on the deck of the *Zheng He* were operational. The one-wire and four-wire had been damaged during the battle and still, more than a week later, had gone unrepaired, a deficiency Lin Bao made a note of as he imagined the work ahead when preparing this crew for the battles that surely awaited them.

Some low-level turbulence then caused their aircraft to pitch violently. As they descended below one thousand feet, Lin Bao noticed that the flight deck was crowded, or at least more crowded than usual, as off-duty members of the crew assembled to catch a glimpse of their new commander's landing. When their aircraft hit the deck, it touched down a little long. The pilots throttled the engine to give their aircraft the extra power for a second pass.

The pilot who had flubbed the landing turned toward Lin Bao in the jump seat and sheepishly apologized. "Very sorry, Admiral. That turbulence knocked us off our glide path. We'll get you in on the next pass."

Lin Bao told the pilot not to worry about it, though privately he added this failure to the deficiencies he was cataloging at his new command.

As they gained altitude, perhaps the pilot could sense Lin Bao's disappointment, because he continued to prattle on as he lined up their aircraft for a second approach. "What I was saying before, sir," the pilot continued, "about landing on the first pass being good luck for your command—I wouldn't put too much stock in that either."

Another jolt of turbulence hit the aircraft.

"I remember when Admiral Ma Qiang took command," the pilot added cheerfully. "Variable winds that day. His plane didn't land until the third pass."

13:03 April 28, 2034 (GMT+5:30)
New Delhi

If not for the Chinese government's decision to wait twenty-four hours before releasing the news of its victory in the South China Sea, Chowdhury never would have sprung Wedge from the Iranian embassy. In the days after that operation, Chowdhury had begun to see Wedge's detention as a first misstep in what had otherwise been a series of perfectly executed moves by the Chinese, beginning with the phone call from their M&M-eating defense attaché about the *Wén Rui* those weeks before.

The release of Major Mitchell had been a risky proposition. When Chowdhury first appeared in his room at the Iranian embassy, Wedge had looked decidedly disappointed. He later told Chowdhury that he'd been expecting a Red Cross nurse, not a string bean of a diplomat. This disappointment immediately dissipated when Chowdhury explained that the Indian government had that very morning negotiated with the Iranians for his release into their custody. Chowdhury added only one word: "Hurry." Chowdhury and Wedge were rushed out a back service entrance by two officers from India's Intelligence Bureau.

Later, when Wedge asked Chowdhury how his uncle had convinced the Iranian ambassador to release him into Indian custody, a move that certainly wasn't in the best interests of the Iranian government, Chowdhury had answered with a single Russian word: *kompromat.*

"*Kompromat?*" asked Wedge.

"Little boys," Chowdhury answered, explaining that India's Intelligence Bureau made it a point to develop and cache bits of leverage over any foreigner, particularly one of ambassadorial rank. And it just so happened that this ambassador was a pederast. When Chowdhury's uncle had gone to the Iranian ambassador with the facts, the ambassador's calculation had been simple. He would face a lesser reprimand from his government for being duped by the Indians than he would if his sexual proclivities ever became known. "That's why they released you, Major Mitchell."

"My friends call me Wedge," he said, a wide grin stretching across his still-bruised face.

Chowdhury left Wedge at the hospital with the embassy staff, who would arrange his flight back to the US, or to wherever else the Marine Corps saw fit to send him. Chowdhury needed to return to Washington, to his duties, and to his daughter. From the hospital he was taken by car to the visitors' annex of the embassy, where he would collect his things and head to the airport. When he arrived at his quarters, he was in such a rush to pack that he walked straight to the bedroom, right past his uncle, who was sitting on the living room sofa, waiting patiently.

"Sandeep, may I have a word?"

Chowdhury jumped when he heard the baritone voice behind him. "Sorry to startle you."

"How'd you get in here?"

The old admiral rolled his eyes, as if he were disappointed that his nephew would ask such a naive question. Patel had in a single morning used his connections within his country's intelligence services, diplomatic corps, and military to arrange the release of a downed American flyer from Iranian custody; if he could handle that, he could certainly handle one locked door. Nevertheless, Patel gave his nephew a proper answer: "A local member of your embassy staff let me in. . . ." Then, as if sensing this explanation wasn't quite sufficient, he added, "Someone we've done some favors for in the past." Patel left it at that.

Chowdhury agreed to have a drink with his uncle. The two of them stepped outside and into a waiting black Mercedes sedan. Chowdhury didn't ask where they were going and his uncle didn't tell him. They barely spoke on the drive, which was fine with Chowdhury. In the few days he'd been in New Delhi, he'd hardly left the embassy complex; now, for the first time in his life, he had an opportunity to absorb the city. He was struck by how much it differed from his mother's descriptions, and from the photos he'd seen growing up. Gone were the dust-choked streets. Gone were the ramshackle shanties overflowing into those same streets. And gone, too, were what his uncle once called "the inconvenient and combustible masses prone to rebellion."

The streets were clean. The homes were new and beautiful.

The shift in India's urban demographics had begun two decades before, under President Modi, who along with the other nationalist leaders of that era had sloughed away the old India by investing in the country's infrastructure, finally bringing the Pakistani threat to heel through a decisive victory in the Ten-Day War of 2024, and using that victory to build out India's military.

Chowdhury could have gleaned the history simply by looking out the car window, at the streets without litter, at the proliferation of glass high-rises, at the packs of impeccably turned-out soldiers and sailors ambling down the freshly laid sidewalks, on leave from their tank divisions or on liberty from their ships. Modi and his acolytes had brushed away all resistance to their reforms, hiding the vast social wreckage. This makeover was hardly complete—much of the countryside still had a distance to go—but clearly the road ahead was smoothing as the century unfolded.

Finally, they arrived at their destination, which wasn't a step forward but rather a step backward in time: the Delhi Gymkhana, his uncle's club. A long, straight driveway led to its canopied entrance, while on the left and right teams of mowers kept the vast lawns perfectly cropped. Off in the distance Chowdhury could make out the grass tennis courts and shimmer of turquoise water in the swimming pool. After his uncle exchanged pleasantries with the staff, who all greeted him with obsequious bows, they were led to the veranda, which looked out on the elaborate gardens, another legacy from the club's founding at the height of the British Raj.

They ordered their drinks—gin and tonic for Patel, a club soda for Chowdhury, which evoked a disappointed sigh from the admiral. When the server left them, Patel asked, "How is my sister?" She was fine, Chowdhury answered. She enjoyed being a grandmother; his father's death had been very hard on her—but then he cut himself off, feeling suddenly as if he didn't quite possess the license to inform on his mother to her estranged brother. The conversation might have ended there were it not for a commotion inside the club, near the television above the bar. The well-turned-out patrons, most of whom wore tennis whites, along with the jacketed waiters and busboys, had gathered to listen to the news. The anchors were piecing together early reports of a massive naval engagement in the South China Sea, touching their earpieces and staring vacantly into the camera as some new fact trickled across the wire, all of which built to a single, astounding conclusion: the United States Navy had been soundly defeated.

Only Chowdhury and his uncle didn't feel the need to crowd around the television. They took the opportunity to sit, alone, on the now-empty veranda. "It will take people a while to understand what this all means," Patel said to his nephew as he nodded toward the bar.

"We're at war; that's what it means."

Patel nodded. He took a sip of his gin and tonic. "Yes," he said, "but your country's defeat is just beginning. That's also what this means."

"Our navy is as capable as theirs, even more so," Chowdhury replied defensively. "Sure, we underestimated them, but it's a mistake we won't make again. If anything, they're the ones who've made the mistake." Chowdhury paused and changed the inflection of his voice. *"I fear all we have done is to awaken a sleeping giant and fill him with a terrible resolve."*

His uncle knew the quote. "Admiral Isoroku Yamamoto," replied Patel. "But this isn't Pearl Harbor. This is a very different situation. Look around you. Look at this club. When empires overreach, that's when they crumble. This club, with its fusty Britishness, is a monument to overreach."

Chowdhury reminded his uncle that his country had far from overreached; that it had suffered a single defeat, perhaps two if you counted the "ambush of our flotilla," as Chowdhury referred to what had happened to the *John Paul Jones* and its sister ships. "Also," he added, allowing his voice to enter a graver register, "we haven't even discussed our country's tactical and strategic nuclear capability."

The old admiral crossed his arms over his chest. "Listen to yourself. *Tactical and strategic nukes.* Do you hear what you're saying? With those weapons, no one wins."

Chowdhury glanced away, and then, speaking under his breath like a petulant teenager, he muttered, "Hiroshima . . . Nagasaki . . . we won that."

"*We*? Who is this *we*?" His uncle was becoming increasingly annoyed. "Your family lived not three miles from here in those days. And why do you think America prospered after the Second World War?"

"Because we *won*," answered Chowdhury.

Patel shook his head. "The British won too; so did the Soviets, and even the French."

"I don't see what you're getting at."

"In war, it's not that you win. It's *how* you win. America didn't used to start wars. It used to finish them. But now"—Patel dropped his chin to his chest and began to shake his head mournfully—"now it is the reverse; now you start wars and don't finish them." Then he switched the subject and began to ask again about his sister. Chowdhury showed him a photograph of his daughter; he spoke a bit more about his divorce, his mother's antipathy toward his wife—the Ellen DeGeneres clone, as his mother called her, though Patel didn't get the reference. After listening to his nephew, his only response was a question: "Would you ever consider returning home?"

"America is my home," answered Chowdhury. "Nowhere else on earth could I, the son of an immigrant, rise up to work in the White House. America is special. That's what I've been trying to tell you."

Patel sat, respectfully listening to his nephew. "Do you know what I most enjoy about belonging to this club?" he asked.

Chowdhury returned a vacant gaze.

"Come," said Patel, pushing back his chair, its legs stuttering across the tiled floor of the veranda. They stepped into a room immediately inside, which appeared to be a trophy room, the walls lined with glass-fronted cabinets that contained resplendent two-handled cups engraved with years that reached back into other centuries. Patel took Chowdhury to a framed photograph in the far corner. Three ranks of British army officers stood flanked by their turbaned sepoys. The date was nearly one hundred years ago, a decade before Indian independence. Patel explained that the photograph was of the Rajputana Rifles, whose British officers were members of this club, and that it was taken on the eve of the Second World War, before the regiment shipped out for the Pacific theatre.

"Most of the officers were killed in either Burma or Malaya," said Patel. Their sepia-toned expressions stared hauntingly back at Chowdhury. Then his uncle took a silver pen from his pocket, which he indexed on one face, that of a mustachioed orderly with a squat build and single chevron, who scowled at the camera. "Him, right there. You see the name?" Patel tapped his pen on the bottom of the photograph, where there was a roster. "Lance Naik Imran Sandeep Patel . . . your great-great-grandfather."

Chowdhury stood silently in front of the photograph.

"It isn't only in America where people can change their fortunes," his uncle said. "America is not so special."

Chowdhury removed his phone from his pocket and snapped a photograph of his ancestor's face. "How do you think your government will respond?" he asked, gesturing toward the television and the breaking news about what seemed to be the certainty of an impending war.

"It's difficult to say," his uncle told him. "But I believe we'll make out very well."

"Why do you say that?"

"Because we have learned the lessons that you have forgotten."

⌐

11:42 May 13, 2034 (GMT+9)
Yokosuka Naval Base

First it was her flight home that was canceled.

Then her orders.

A medical evaluation was scheduled for her at the naval hospital.

This time she passed it.

A below-the-zone promotion came next, to rear admiral (lower half)—a one-star. A new set of orders followed. The assignment shocked her. The Navy was giving her command of the *Enterprise* Strike Group, which included the carrier itself as well as nearly twenty other ships. This all took a week. In another week she'd meet the flotilla at Yokosuka. The night before the *Enterprise* arrived, Hunt had the first of the nightmares that would come to plague her.

In them, she is watching what is left of the *Ford* and *Miller* carrier strike groups limp into port, just three ships. She stands on the dock, where one of the ships, a destroyer, drops its gangplank. But the destroyer isn't part of the group that went out with the *Ford* and *Miller*; no, it's her old flagship, the *John Paul Jones*. Her crew files down the gangplank. She recognizes many of the young sailors. Among them is Commander Jane Morris. She is smoking a cigar, the same cigar they shared on the bridge of the *John Paul Jones* those weeks before. Which feel like a lifetime before. When Hunt approaches Morris, her former subordinate walks right past her, as if she doesn't exist. There's no malice in Morris's reaction; rather it is as though Hunt is the ghost and these ghosts are the living. Then, while Hunt is trying to gain Morris's attention, she glimpses a young petty officer coming down the gangplank and onto the dock. Hunt is drawn to him because unlike the other sailors he is wearing his dress whites, the wide bell-bottoms flaring out over his mirror-shined leather shoes. Two chevrons are sewn to his sleeve. His Dixie cup hat balances on his head at a jaunty angle. He can't be more than twenty-five years old. And although he's a young petty officer, he wears a dizzying array of medals and ribbons, such as the Navy Cross, lesser awards for valor, and several Purple Hearts, to include the one that got him killed. He's a SEAL. He crosses the dock, comes right up to Hunt, and takes her by the hand. He squeezes it three times— I / LOVE / YOU—just as her father used to do. He looks at her, still holding her hand, still waiting. He is clean-shaven, strong; his torso angles toward his waist in a V. And his palm is soft. She can hardly recognize him. In her memory he is always older, worn down; she never remembered her father's medals and ribbons as shining. But they shine now, spectacularly so. His blue eyes are fixed on hers. She squeezes his hand four times—I / LOVE / YOU / TOO.

He looks at her and says, "You don't have to do this."

Then he drops her hand and walks away.

She calls after him, "Do what?" but he doesn't turn around.

This is where the dream always ends. Hunt had just woken from it on the morning the *Enterprise* pulled into port. She was still shaken by the question in the dream as she met her crew on the docks of Yokosuka. She caught herself looking around, as if she might see him, or even Morris, wandering among the other sailors as they descended the gangplank. Her crew was young. Most of the officers and enlisted filled positions that were one or two grades senior to their rank, a result of the Navy struggling to account for its most recent losses at sea as well as what in recent years had become perennial manpower shortages. Hunt consoled herself with the idea that if the crew was young, then it was also hungry, and she would take enthusiasm over experience.

The *Enterprise* was scheduled for a week in port after an arduous transit from Fifth Fleet and the Arabian Gulf. Its sister carrier, the *Bush*, had recently suffered the ignominy of losing a pilot over Iranian airspace, and the crew of the *Enterprise* seemed determined to avoid a similar humiliation in the performance of their mission. As to the specifics of that mission, they remained unclear. They knew the Chinese navy possessed an offensive cyber capability that they'd yet to effectively counter, and that this capability reduced their high-tech platforms—whether it be navigation, communications, or weapons guidance systems—to little more than a suite of glitching computers. Nevertheless, they understood that whatever their specific mission was, it would certainly include the more general objective of destroying, or at least neutralizing, the flotilla of Chinese vessels that threatened to destabilize the balance of power in the region.

First, however, they would need to find the Chinese fleet, specifically the *Zheng He* Carrier Battle Group. If the *Wén Rui* incident and the sinking of the *Ford* and *Miller* demonstrated anything, it was that China's cyber capability could effectively black out a vast swath of ocean. While Hunt was having her retirement canceled by Seventh Fleet Headquarters, that same headquarters had scrambled reconnaissance drones across the South China Sea and even the far reaches of the Pacific in an effort to map the disposition of Chinese naval forces and infer their next move. A variety of drones were tasked, from the latest stealth variants of MQ-4C Tritons, to RQ-4 Global Hawks, to even the CIA's RQ-170 Sentinels, each fully integrated into America's network of satellites. However, as was the case with the F-35 at Bandar Abbas, the Chinese were able to take control of these drones once they came into a certain range, disabling their sensors and controls. The result was that all Hunt had from Seventh Fleet was a circular black hole with a radius of nearly eight hundred nautical miles. This included the waters around Japan, Vietnam, Taiwan, and the Philippines. Somewhere in that black hole was the *Zheng He* and the rest of the Chinese fleet. And she would be expected to find and destroy it.

She made a request to disable all of the avionics in one of her fighter squadrons, VMFA-323, the Death Rattlers, the only Marine squadron aboard the *Enterprise* and the only one that still used the antiquated F/A-18 Hornet airframe. She would be given two days to modify the aircraft in port, and then whatever extra time she could steal once she got underway. She would, in effect, be refashioning one of her squadrons as a "dumb squadron."

The squadron's commanding officer had stridently objected. He had told Hunt that he wasn't sure all of his pilots were up for this type of flying—without instruments, by the seat of their pants alone. She had dismissed his concerns, not because she didn't think they had merit but because she had little alternative. She knew that when they next fought, they would fight blind.

That was, of course, if she could find the *Zheng He*.

⌐

09:00 May 21, 2034 (GMT-4)
Quantico

Wedge just wanted to go home. Back to San Diego. Back to the beach. Back to 06:00 at the gym, to a 08:00 preflight, to a 09:00 first hop, then lunch, then a second hop at 13:30, then postflight and debrief, followed by drinks at the officers' club and a night spent in a bed that wasn't his own. He wanted to wear his Ray-Bans. He wanted to surf the point at Punta Miramar. He wanted to talk shit to his buddies in the squadron, and then back that shit up when they did dogfight maneuvers at Fallon Naval Air Station.

What he didn't want?

He didn't want to be in Quantico. He didn't want the master sergeant who Headquarters Marine Corps had assigned as his "escort while in the WDCMA" to keep following him around. "What the fuck is the WDCMA?" Wedge had asked the humorless master sergeant, who had shit for ribbons except a bunch of drill field commendations and about a dozen Good Conduct Medals. "Washington, D.C., Metro Area, sir," the master sergeant had said.

"Are you shitting me?"

"Negative, sir."

In the weeks since Wedge had arrived back in the States, or CONUS as the master sergeant insistently referred to it, the two had had this exchange numerous times. About Wedge's denied request to have dinner with an old college buddy who lived near Dupont Circle ("Are you shitting me?" "Negative, sir."), or the master sergeant insisting on coming with him to the base theater when he wanted to see a movie ("Are you shitting me?" "Negative, sir."), and, lastly—and perhaps most bitterly—each time his enforced stay in Quantico was extended by at first a day, then two, then a week, and then another ("Are you *mother-fucking* shitting me?" "Negative, sir.").

The reason, nominally, for Wedge's lengthening stay was a series of debriefings. Within the first week of coming home, he had breezed through meetings with officers from CIA, DIA, NSA, State, and even the National Geospatial-Intelligence Agency. He had explained to them in detail the malfunctions he'd had with the F-35, the series of trouble-shooting procedures he'd employed (to include putting a bullet into the avionics—"When all systems became unresponsive, I disabled them manually"—which was met with skeptical looks by the career bureau-crats and defense contractors), and he had gone on to explain his captiv-ity. Or at least what he could remember of it.

"Tell us a bit more about this Iranian officer."

"Guy had three fingers on his right hand, a short temper, and kicked the shit out of me. What more do you want to know?"

The bureaucrats scribbled studiously in their notepads.

Wedge was bored. That was the real problem. He spent most of his day sitting around, watching the news. "Thirty-seven ships," he'd often say aloud, as if from nowhere. Each time he said it he hoped that someone—maybe the buttoned-down master sergeant—would refute him and tell him that none of it had happened; that the *Ford* and *Miller* with all their escorts were still afloat; that the whole thing was a dream, an illusion; that the only reality was American greatness. Wedge knew a number of the now-dead pilots from flight school in Pensacola a de-cade before. "We got our teeth kicked in," Wedge would say of the battle, running his tongue over his own missing teeth. On his second week in Quantico, he had a four-hour dental appointment, and it was the dentist who revealed the real reason he was being held on base. After finishing her handiwork, a total of five replaced teeth, she held up the mirror so Wedge could take a look. "What do you think?" she asked. "You'll be in good shape for when they take you over to the White House."

Another week passed.

So that's what he'd been waiting for, a debriefing at the White House.

The master sergeant explained to Wedge his brush with celebrity while behind bars, even showing him the #FreeWedge threads on social media. The president was, after all, a politician, so it seemed little wonder she wanted to have a photo op with Wedge. It was a box she needed to check. But their meeting kept getting delayed. All Wedge had to do was turn on the news to see why. The Chinese fleet had disappeared. Vanished. Vamoose. The SECDEF, the chairman of the joint chiefs, even the national security advisor—that chicken hawk Trent Wisecarver—all of them held press conferences in which they made thinly veiled threats in response to "Sino aggression."

The Chinese were watching.

They didn't respond.

After weeks of saber rattling, the administration seemed as if it had tired itself out. The first day without a press conference was when Wedge finally received his summons to the White House. On the car ride north from Quantico, he kept checking and rechecking his service alpha uniform the Marine Shop had rush-tailored for him. The president, he was told, was going to present him with the Prisoner of War Medal. She would ask him a few questions, they'd have their picture taken, and he'd be done. As Wedge fiddled with the ribbons on his chest, he kept running his tongue over his new teeth.

"You look good, sir," the master sergeant said.

Wedge said thanks, and then stared out the window.

When they arrived at the West Wing visitor entrance, it seemed as though no one was expecting them. The Secret Service didn't have Wedge in the system for a visit that day. Wedge suggested to the master sergeant that maybe they should get a bite nearby; they could grab sliders and a couple of beers at the Old Ebbitt Grill or the Hay-Adams bar and then come back later. The master sergeant wasn't having it. He kept arguing with the Secret Service uniform division officer, who eventually called his supervisor. This went on for half an hour as phone calls were placed to the Pentagon and Headquarters Marine Corps.

Then Chowdhury walked past. He knew about Wedge's visit and volunteered to escort him inside. The master sergeant would have to wait, as Chowdhury was only authorized to escort one person at a time. While he and Wedge navigated through the cramped West Wing offices, Chowdhury apologetically explained, "Since the blackout none of our systems have come back online properly." He then found Wedge a seat where he could wait. "I know you're on the schedule for today, but things are pretty fluid at the moment. Let me find out when we're going to get you in." And then Chowdhury disappeared into a hive of activity.

Wedge knew a crisis when he saw one. Staffers hurrying in one direction down the corridor, only to turn around suddenly and head in the opposite direction. Heated conversations taking place in whispers. Phones urgently answered. The men hadn't shaved. The women hadn't brushed their hair. People ate at their desks.

"So you're him?" said a man who had crept up next to Wedge, a red binder tucked beneath his arm, his frameless glasses balanced on the tip of his nose, evaluating Wedge as though he were a painting of dubious provenance.

Instinctively, Wedge stood, making a sir sandwich of this introduction. "Yes, sir, Major Chris Mitchell, sir," he said, as though he was once again an officer candidate on the parade field in Quantico. Trent Wise-carver introduced himself not by name, but by his position, as in "I'm the president's national security advisor," and then he weakly shook Wedge's hand as though he couldn't muster enough regard for a heartier grip. "Major Mitchell," he continued, referring to the binder tucked beneath his arm, "you are on the schedule; however, this evening the president has an address to the nation that she's preparing for. So today has gotten a little busy. I must apologize, but I've been instructed to present you with your award instead." Wisecarver then unceremoniously handed over the red binder, as well as a blue box that contained the medal itself. He paused for a moment, searching, it seemed, for the appropriate words, and mustered a paltry "Congratulations" before excusing himself as he rushed off to his next briefing.

Wedge wandered out of the West Wing to the visitor area, where the master sergeant dutifully waited for him. Neither spoke as they stepped out onto Pennsylvania Avenue and into the public garage where they'd left their government car. The master sergeant didn't ask for the details of Wedge's presidential visit. He seemed to intuit the unceremonious nature with which Wedge had been handled, and as if trying to cheer up the major, he reminded him that the next day they could cut his orders. He was now free to rejoin a squadron. Wedge smiled at this, and as they drove down to Quantico the two of them filled the silence with music from an oldies station. Until that station and every other was interrupted by a public service announcement followed by the president's remarks.

The master sergeant turned up the radio.

Wedge stared out the window, into the night.

"My fellow Americans, hours ago our navy and intelligence services reported the appearance of a large Chinese fleet off the coast of Taiwan,

an ally of the United States. In the context of recent hostilities with Beijing, this represents a clear and present danger not only to the independence of that island nation but also to our own. Recent military setbacks have limited our options for dealing with this threat. But, rest assured, those options remain ample. To quote the words of our thirty-fifth president, John F. Kennedy, 'Let every nation know, whether it wishes us well or ill, that we shall pay any price, bear any burden, meet any hardship, support any friend, oppose any foe, in order to assure the survival and the success of liberty.' This statement proved true during the darkest hours of President Kennedy's administration, to include the Cuban Missile Crisis. And it proves true today.

"To the citizens and government of the People's Republic of China, I wish to speak to you directly: Through your cyber weapons you have degraded our ability to offer a more conventional, measured response. The path of war is not one we wish to travel, but if forced, travel it we will. We will honor our commitments to our allies. Turn your ships around, return them to port, respect the freedom of navigation of the seas, and catastrophe may still be avoided. However, a violation of Taiwan's sovereignty is a red line for the United States. A violation of that red line will be met with overwhelming force at a time and place of our choosing. To stand with our allies and to stand up for ourselves, I have preauthorized the employment of select tactical nuclear weapons to our commanders in the region. . . ."

Wedge turned off the radio.

Traffic was flitting by them on I-95. Here and there, cars had pulled over on the shoulder with their hazard lights flashing into the darkness. Inside, Wedge could see the silhouettes of drivers and passengers leaning forward, listening attentively to the address on the radio. Wedge didn't need to hear anything more. He understood what was coming.

The master sergeant muttered, "Jesus, tactical nukes," and then, "I hope they've got their shit wired tight at the White House."

Wedge only nodded.

They drove a bit more in silence.

Wedge glanced down on his lap, to where he held the red binder with the citation for his Prisoner of War Medal, as well as the blue box that contained the decoration itself.

"Let's see that medal of yours, sir," said the master sergeant.

Wedge opened the box.

It was empty.

Neither he nor the master sergeant knew quite what to say. The master sergeant sat up a little bit straighter in his seat. He affixed his hands firmly at ten and two o'clock on the steering wheel. "No big deal," he muttered after a moment, glancing once more into the empty box that rested on Wedge's lap. "There must've been an oversight today at the White House. Tomorrow, we'll unfuck it."

4

Red Lines

01:46 May 22, 2034 (GMT+2)
Barents Sea

For the third night in a row, Farshad struggled to sleep. His cabin was right above the waterline and he could hear the ice floes glancing off the bow, hitting like the tolling of a bell—*dong, dong, dong.* All through the night, the noise was relentless. When he had arrived in Tartus weeks before, a set of orders had awaited him. He wouldn't be assigned to liaison duties there, with the Russian Federation's short-sleeved, sun-bronzed Mediterranean Fleet, but far to the north with its Baltic Fleet. When he had stepped off the plane at naval headquarters in Kaliningrad, he didn't even have a winter coat. He assumed headquarters would assign him to one of the larger command ships, the *Kuznetsov,* or perhaps the battle cruiser *Pyotr Velikiy.* Instead, he found himself aboard the corvette *Rezkiy*, which rolled incessantly. Farshad found himself mildly seasick aboard this fast little tin can of a ship with its thin sides.

Dong, dong, dong—

He gave up and switched on the light.

His bed was cantilevered to the bulkhead of his cabin, which was so small that he couldn't open his door until he stowed the bed, and he couldn't stow the bed until he stripped it of its wool blanket, sheets, and pillow. This multistep process of putting away his bed, to open his door, to leave his cabin, was one of the myriad humbling routines that composed his life as a relatively junior liaison officer. Another was taking his meals in the cramped wardroom among his fellow officers, few of whom spoke anything but Russian and all of whom were at least a decade younger. This had caused Farshad to eat mostly between meals, or to eat *midrats*, which were the day's leftovers placed out at around midnight by the messmen.

Over his pajamas he shrugged on his peacoat, a gift from a kindly supply orderly in Kaliningrad. The incessant noise of the ice floes banging off the hull kept him company as he padded down the red-lit passageway, staggering between the ship's steel bulkheads, toward the wardroom where he hoped to scrounge a bite to eat.

Like Farshad's room, the wardroom was an exercise in spacial economy. It was no more than a two-table banquette with a small galley attached. Sitting at the banquette was Lieutenant Commander Vasily Kolchak, the *Rezkiy*'s executive officer. He was nursing a cup of tea tapped from the wardroom's samovar. A cigarette receded toward his knuckles as he read from a laptop. Behind him was the room's only adornment, an aquarium populated by yellow-orange fish who poked their eyes from a novelty shipwreck at its bottom. The messmen had already laid out the *midrats* in two stainless-steel vats, one filled with a dark-colored meat in a brown sauce and the other filled with a light-colored meat in a white sauce. A placard sat next to each dish, but Farshad couldn't read Russian.

"The white one is fish, some type of herring, I think," said Kolchak in English, glancing up from his laptop. "The dark one is pork."

Farshad paused for a moment, hovering over the two options. Then he sat across from Kolchak with an empty plate.

"Good choice," said Kolchak. The only other sound was the aquarium filter running in the corner. He wore a gold signet ring on his right pinky. With his left hand he played nervously with the blond, almost snow-white hair that brushed the tops of his ears. His small, shrewd eyes were cold and blue, their color slightly faded like two precious stones that had been cut generations ago. His nose was long, sharply pointed, and red on its tip; it seemed as though Kolchak was battling a cold. "I don't imagine you've seen the news," he said to Farshad. Kolchak's English accent sounded faintly British and old-worldly, as if Farshad were eavesdropping on the conversational mores of a previous century.

Kolchak clicked on a video from his laptop. The two of them listened to an address made a couple of hours before by the American president. When the video cut out, neither of them spoke. Finally Kolchak asked Farshad about his missing fingers.

"Fighting the Americans," he explained. Farshad then pointed to Kolchak's signet ring, which at a closer inspection he could see was adorned with a two-headed eagle. "And your ring?"

"It was my great-great-grandfather's. He was also a naval officer, the Imperial Navy." Kolchak took a long drag on his cigarette. "He fought in our war with Japan. Then the Bolsheviks killed him when he was an old man. This ring remained hidden in my family for many years. I'm the first to wear it openly since him. Time changes everything."

"What do you think the Americans will do?" asked Farshad.

"I should ask you," answered Kolchak. "You've fought against them before."

This slight gesture of deference caught Farshad off guard. How long had it been since someone had sought out his opinion? Farshad couldn't help it; he felt a certain measure of affection for Kolchak, who, like him, was the loyal son of a nation that had not always treated him or his family fairly. Farshad answered Kolchak by saying that American presidents had a mixed history when it came to the enforcement of self-imposed "red lines." He wondered if the United States would be willing to resort to nuclear weapons—even tactical nuclear weapons, as the president had suggested in her remarks—to prevent the Chinese from annexing Taiwan. "The United States was once predictable; not so much anymore," concluded Farshad. "Their unpredictability makes them very dangerous. What will Russia do if the United States acts? Your leaders have a great deal to lose. Everywhere I look I see wealthy Russians."

"Wealthy Russians?" Kolchak laughed. "There is no such thing."

Farshad didn't understand. He mentioned their ubiquitous mega yachts in the Mediterranean and Black Seas, their ostentatious villas on the Amalfi and Dalmatian coasts. Whenever Farshad traveled abroad and he saw some resplendent thing—a villa, a boat, a private jet idling on the tarmac, or a woman bejeweled beyond measure—and he asked to whom it all belonged, the inevitable response was always some Russian.

Kolchak was shaking his head. "No, no, no," he said. "There are no wealthy Russians." He stubbed his cigarette out in the ashtray. "There are only poor Russians with money."

While lighting another cigarette, Kolchak began to pontificate about the *Rodina*, his "Mother Russia," how in its many iterations, whether they be tsarist, imperialist, or communist, it had never enjoyed the legitimacy of other world powers. "During the empire our tsars spoke French at court," said Kolchak. "During communism our economy was a hollow shell. Today, under the federation, our leaders are viewed as criminals by the rest of the world. In New York City, or in London, they don't respect any of us, not even President Putin. To them, President Putin isn't the grandfather of our Federation; no, to them he is simply another poor Russian, a gangster at best, even though he has retaken our ancestral territories in Crimea, Georgia, and Greater Ukraine; even though he has crippled America's political system, so that now their president doesn't even have a party but has to run as one of these enfeebled 'independents.' We are a cunning people. Our leader is one of us and is equally cunning. You asked what Russia will do if the United States acts? Isn't it obvious? What does the fox do in the henhouse?" Kolchak's lips peeled back from his teeth in a smile.

Farshad had always understood, or at least understood intellectually, that his country and Russia had many shared interests. But with Kolchak, he began to understand the depth of their kinship, the degree by which their two nations had developed in tandem, sharing a trajectory. Both had imperial and ancient pasts; the Russian tsars, the Persian shahs. Both had endured revolutions; the Bolsheviks, the Islamists. And both had suffered the antipathies of the West: economic sanctions, international censure. Farshad also understood, or at least intuited, the opportunity now presenting itself to his Russian allies.

They had left their home port of Kaliningrad three weeks before. On the first week of their journey, the *Rezkiy* had tracked numerous ships from the US Third and Sixth Fleets, which aggressively patrolled the western Atlantic and these northern Baltic waters. And then, quite suddenly, their American antagonists had vanished. After the dual catastrophes in the South China Sea, the destination of the American fleet became obvious. Equally obvious was the opportunity presented by its absence. No fewer than five hundred fiber-optic cables, which accounted for 90 percent of North America's 10G internet access, crisscrossed these icy depths.

"If the Americans detonate a nuclear weapon," said Kolchak, "I don't think the world will much care if we tamper with a few undersea cables." He held Farshad in his gaze. "I also don't think the world would say much if our troops seized a sliver of Poland, to unite Kaliningrad to the Russian mainland." Kolchak pointed to a map on the wall. He traced out a corridor with his finger, which would give Russia direct overland access to its one Baltic port. Putin himself had often spoken about reclaiming this strip of land. "If the Americans detonate a nuclear weapon, they will become the pariah state they have always claimed we are."

"Do you think they'd ever go through with it?" Farshad asked Kolchak.

"Ten or even fifteen years ago, I would have said no. Today, I am not so sure. The America they believe themselves to be is no longer the America that they are. Time changes everything, doesn't it. And now, it is changing the world's balance in our favor." Kolchak checked his watch. He shut his laptop and glanced up at Farshad. "But it is late. You must get some rest."

"I can't sleep," said Farshad.

"How come?"

Farshad allowed the quiet to settle between them, so that Kolchak could perceive the faint *dong, dong, dong* of the ice floes glancing against the hull of the ship. "I find that sound unnerving," Farshad admitted. "And the ship constantly rolls."

Kolchak reached across the table and grasped Farshad affectionately by the arm. "You mustn't let either bother you. Go back to your room, lie down. The rolling you will get used to. And the noise? It has always helped me to imagine that the noise is something else."

"Like what?" Farshad asked skeptically.

Dong, dong, a couple more ice floes glanced against the hull.

"Like a bell, tolling out a change in the time."

⌐

23:47 May 22, 2034 (GMT+8)
South China Sea

A knock on his door.

Middle of the night.

Lin Bao groaned as he sat up. What can it be now? he wondered. Such interruptions to his sleep had become routine. Last night, the commanders of two destroyers in his battle group had a dispute as to their order in formation, which Lin Bao had to resolve; the night before that there had been an unexpected weather advisory, a typhoon that thankfully never materialized; then a missed communications window with one of his submarines; before that an excess of hard-water moisture in one of his ship's reactors. The list blurred in his sleep-deprived mind. If Lin Bao stood on the cusp of a great moment in his nation's history, it didn't feel that way. Lin Bao felt consumed by the minutiae of his command, and convinced that he might never again enjoy a full night's rest.

He did, however, feel a small surge of satisfaction that the complex mix of cyber cloaking, stealth materials, and satellite spoofing had kept his fleet well hidden. While the Americans surely suspected them of heading for the vicinity of Chinese Taipei, their old adversary had been unable to develop the precise targeting data required for a counter-maneuver. Eventually, the Americans would find them. But by then it would be too late.

"Comrade Admiral, your presence is requested in the combat information center."

Lin Bao awoke to another knock. "Comrade Admiral—"

Lin Bao flung open his door. "I heard you the first time," he snapped at the young sailor, who couldn't have been more than nineteen, and who looked as sleep-deprived as the admiral. "Tell them"—he coughed—"tell them I'm coming." The sailor nodded once and hurried down the corridor. As he dressed, Lin Bao regretted his outburst. It was a manifestation of the strain he was under. To exhibit that strain to his crew was to exhibit his weakness to them, and they were under a similar strain. For the past three weeks, ever since they had gone dark, the *Zheng He* Carrier Battle Group—along with the Navy's three other strike groups, elements of special forces from the People's Army, strategic land-based bombers, and hypersonic missiles from the air force—had all converged in a noose around Chinese Taipei, or Taiwan, as the West insisted on calling it. Although Lin Bao's command remained cloaked, he could almost feel the massive American global surveillance network groping for his precise location.

The operation, as designed by Minister Chiang and approved by the Politburo Standing Committee, was playing out in two phases, each of which adhered to one of Sun Tzu's famous axioms, the first being, *Let your plans be dark and impenetrable as night, and when you move, fall like a thunderbolt.* As dramatically as the Chinese fleet had vanished, it would soon reappear around Taiwan, moving like that proverbial thunderbolt. Never before had a nation concentrated its military strength with such stealth. It would take weeks, or even as much as a month, for the Americans or any other power to position combat assets to counter it. The second phase of Minister Chiang's plan was likewise based on Sun Tzu: *The supreme art of war is to subdue your enemy without fighting.* Minister Chiang believed that the sudden revelation of his forces off the coast would present the Legislative Yuan, the governing body of so-called Taiwan, with only one choice: a vote of dissolution followed by annexation into the People's Republic. Not a single shot would need to be fired. When Minister Chiang had proposed his plan to the Politburo Standing Committee, he had argued that surrounding Taiwan so suddenly would result in a bloodless checkmate. Although skepticism existed among certain committee members, including Zhao Leji, the much-feared octogenarian secretary of the Central Commission for Discipline Inspection, ultimately the majority placed its confidence in Minister Chiang.

Lin Bao entered the combat information center and found Minister Chiang waiting for him via secure video teleconference. "Comrade Minister," Lin Bao began, "it is good to see you." When the *Zheng He* had gone dark, the two had continued to email, but because of security concerns they hadn't spoken. Upon seeing each other again there was an embarrassed silence, as if each were taking a measure of the other's strain.

"It is good to see you too," began Minister Chiang, who then proceeded to laud Lin Bao and his crew on their exceptional conduct, not only in maneuvering the *Zheng He* Carrier Battle Group into position—a complex task to be sure—but also for repairing their ship while underway, so that it stood poised to achieve a great victory. On and on the minister went. The more congratulations he heaped on the crew of the *Zheng He*, the more it unsettled Lin Bao.

Something was wrong.

"Late last night, the Legislative Yuan scheduled an emergency session," said Minister Chiang. "I expect a vote for dissolution in the coming days. . . ." His voice began to peter out, to choke even. "Our plan seems to be coming together. . . ." He pinched the bridge of his nose and squeezed his eyes shut. He took a long, heavy breath, and then, in a more defeated tone, he added, "However, there is a concern. The Americans have threatened a nuclear strike—no doubt you've heard."

Lin Bao hadn't heard. He shot a glance at one of his intelligence analysts, who sat an arm's length away. For the last twelve hours they'd been in a communications blackout. The young sailor immediately pulled up the *New York Times* home page on an unclassified laptop. The headline was in the largest, boldest font: WITH RED LINE DRAWN, NUCLEAR WEAPONS AN OPTION, SAYS PRESIDENT. The story had been filed several hours earlier.

Lin Bao wasn't certain how to respond to Minister Chiang. All he could think to do was provide the latest disposition of the *Zheng He* Carrier Battle Group, so he began talking mechanically. He reviewed the readiness of his flight crews, the placement of his surface escorts, the arrangements of his assigned submarines. On and on he went. But as he covered these technical details, Minister Chiang began to nervously bite his fingernails. He stared at his hands. He hardly seemed to listen.

Then Lin Bao blurted out, "Our plan remains a good one, Comrade Minister."

Minister Chiang glanced up at him and said nothing.

Lin Bao continued, "If the Legislative Yuan votes to dissolve, the Americans can't launch a strike against us. They aren't brazen enough to attack us for a vote taken by someone else."

Minister Chiang stroked his round chin. "Perhaps," he said.

"And if they did strike, they can't attack our fleet. They don't have precise positional data, even for a tactical nuclear strike. Also, we're only a few miles off the coast of Taipei—the collateral damage to the ports would prove catastrophic. That is the genius of your plan, Comrade Minister. We subdue the enemy without ever fighting. As Sun Tzu said, it's *'the supreme art of war.'*"

Minister Chiang nodded and repeated, "Perhaps." His voice was thin, as if he needed a drink of water. Then their video teleconference was over. The Legislative Yuan had a vote to take. The Americans had drawn a red line, one that they might or might not enforce. There was little for Lin Bao and his crew to do, except to wait. It was now early morning. On his way back to his cabin, Lin Bao checked the bridge watch. His crew, despite their youth and inexperience, executed their duties vigilantly. Each understood the enterprise they were embarked upon. In the near distance was the Taiwanese coast, shrouded in a predawn fog. Their fleet was also concealed in this fog. The sun would soon rise and that fog would burn away. The island would reveal itself and so, too, would they. But Lin Bao was tired. He needed to get some rest.

He returned to his quarters and attempted but failed to sleep. Eventually, he tried reading. He scanned his bookshelf and saw his copy of *The Art of War*, which, ironically, he'd first read at the US Naval War College in Newport. As he browsed the well-annotated pages, he thought of the fog in Newport, the way it clung to the coast, its consistency, how a ship sliced through it, and how it reminded him of the fog here. He then came to a passage, one he'd read many times before but seemed to have forgotten in the intervening years: *If you know the enemy and know yourself, you need not fear the result of a hundred battles. If you*

*know yourself but not the enemy, for every victory gained you will also
suffer a defeat. If you know neither the enemy nor yourself, you will suc-
cumb in every battle.*

Lin Bao shut his eyes.

Did he know his enemy? He tried to remember everything he could
of America. He thought of his years studying there, living there, and of
his mother, that other half of him who was born there. When he shut his
eyes, he could hear her voice, how she used to sing to him as a child. Her
songs . . . American songs. He hummed one unevenly to himself, "The
Dock of the Bay"; its rhythm, he knew it so well. At last he fell into a deep
and peaceful sleep.

⌐

21:37 May 21, 2034 (GMT-4)
Washington, D.C.

The morning before it was delivered, a copy of the president's Oval Office address had been circulated widely and thoroughly staffed. It had
traveled through the interagency coordination process—State, Defense,
Homeland Security, even Treasury had all weighed in with their comments. The press secretary, senior political advisors, and select members of the national security staff, including Chowdhury, had been privy
to the rehearsals, which had taken place with the president sitting behind the Resolute Desk. Chowdhury thought she looked good, very
composed, steady.

That evening, when it came time for her to deliver her remarks,
Chowdhury was sitting at his desk while his colleagues gathered around
one or another of the ubiquitous televisions that littered the cramped
West Wing. Chowdhury wasn't watching; after the many rehearsals he

hadn't felt the need to. It was only when he heard a collective murmur that he glanced up. Neither he nor any of his colleagues had known that the president planned to announce the authorization of a potential nuclear strike. Before they had a chance to do anything except to stare dumbfounded at the television, the door to the Oval Office swung open. A handful of cabinet officials strode past. Based on their demeanor—the blank looks, the tight whispers—they were caught off guard too. The only two who appeared unfazed were Hendrickson and Wisecarver. Wisecarver beckoned Chowdhury into his office, which in the previous week had been moved kitty-corner to the president's own.

"C'mon in," said Wisecarver, as he waved Chowdhury through the door. "We can get this done with a five-minute stand-up." Wisecarver's office was a chaos of neglect. A framed gradeschool portrait of the son he'd lost sat next to his keyboard, but this was the only personal object amid the binders and folders that piled his desk and every shelf, one open on top of another. Each cover sheet contained an alphabet soup of classification codes. He began to stack documents one by one in either Chowdhury's or Hendrickson's outstretched hands, depending on whether the action needed to originate from the executive branch or Department of Defense. Wisecarver, a master in the language of bureaucracy, talked his subordinates through their paper chase with a practiced enthusiasm. Each minor task Wisecarver assigned to Hendrickson and Chowdhury took the country one step closer to a nuclear war.

Before Chowdhury could ask a question of his boss, the five minutes were up.

The door shut. Both he and Hendrickson stood out front of Wisecarver's office with a stack of binders in their hands. "Did you know ahead of time about the speech?" Chowdhury asked.

"Does it matter?"

Chowdhury wasn't certain that it did matter. He also thought this was Hendrickson's way of telling him that, yes, in fact he had known about the changes. He'd been the senior official from Defense in the room, so it made sense that he would have known. It also made sense that this knowledge would've stayed within a tight circle, one that excluded much of the cabinet and nearly all of the White House staff. Nevertheless, it felt like a deception to Chowdhury. Which is to say, it didn't feel right. But then again, he thought, how else should a decision authorizing such a use of force feel?

"There's no way we'll follow through with it," said Chowdhury. But as he said this, he wasn't certain whether he was asking a question or making a statement. Although Chowdhury had been kept in the dark about the president's plan to draw a nuclear red line, he'd been kept in the dark about little else. For instance, he knew the latest disposition of Chinese forces near Taiwan; the noose they had drawn around the island was a combination of their navy, their land- and air-based missiles, along with a contingent of their special forces that could conduct a limited invasion. To stealthily execute this high-speed encirclement, they had used an impressive and still-mysterious combination of technologies. China's naval forces now hugged the Taiwanese coast, and given the danger of collateral damage, what, if anything, could an American tactical nuclear strike target?

"They've just got to believe we'll do it," said Hendrickson. "Right now, three of our carrier strike groups have orders in hand to transit the South China Sea. We need time. If we can get those ships on station, we can threaten the Chinese mainland. Then they'll have to pull resources away from Taiwan. A credible nuclear threat buys us time."

"It's also risky as hell."

Hendrickson shrugged; he didn't disagree. He began to gather his things, locking the binders and folders in a classified courier bag. He needed to return to the Pentagon. Chowdhury offered to walk out with him. He'd likely spend all night at the office and so wanted to get some fresh air. "I saw your friend Hunt got command of the *Enterprise* Strike Group," mentioned Chowdhury in an effort at small talk. The two stood outside the West Wing, a few steps from the last Secret Service checkpoint. Above them the sky was clear and thick with stars.

"Yeah," said Hendrickson, who was looking away from Chowdhury, across the street toward Lafayette Park. "I saw that too."

"Well," said Chowdhury, "good for her." He was smiling.

"Is it good for her?" asked Hendrickson. He didn't return Chowdhury's smile. He only stood there, alternating his gaze between the park and the clear night sky. It was as if he couldn't quite bring himself to take either a step forward or one backward. "If we do launch—because the Taiwanese cave, or because the Chinese misstep, or because Wisecarver gets his way—it's most likely Sarah who will have to pull the trigger."

This hadn't occurred to Chowdhury.

When Hendrickson tried to step out onto Pennsylvania Avenue, the Secret Service held him back a moment. The Metro Police were responding to an incident inside Lafayette Park, where an old man with a tattered beard was screaming frantically about the "End of Days." He had emerged only a few minutes before from a small, dirty plastic tent. With a smart phone clutched in his hand, he was listening to a streaming news channel, the volume turned all the way up. Chowdhury recognized the man as he scrambled past. He was part of the so-called "White House Peace Vigil," which had protested continually against all war, but particularly nuclear war, since 1981. As the police descended upon the man, he grew more frenzied, tearing at his clothes and hurling himself at the gates of the White House. While Chowdhury waited for the Metro Police to make their arrest, he heard one of the Secret Service agents on the other side of the gates mutter, "Old loon . . ."

The next morning, when Chowdhury opened the news on his tablet's browser, he clicked on a brief story in the metro section dedicated to the incident. The old man had been released without bail but charged, nevertheless, with a single count of disturbing the peace.

Chowdhury closed the browser; he placed his tablet on the table.

To read another word felt futile.

12:38 June 11, 2034 (GMT-7)
Marine Corps Air Station Miramar

They hadn't quite figured out what to do with Wedge. His orders from Quantico read only ASSIGNED, THIRD MARINE AIRWING with no specific squadron mentioned. What was worse was that when he checked into Wing Headquarters and they pulled up his ratings log, the file had been corrupted. They had no record of him being qualified on the F-35, the latest entry being three years old, before he'd transitioned out of the F/A-18 Hornet. It made little difference to the Marine Corps' bureaucracy that this discrepancy in Wedge's record was likely the result of yet another Chinese cyber hack. The Marine Corps couldn't put a pilot into the cockpit of a hundred-million-dollar aircraft if that pilot had no record of ever having flown it. That Wedge had been taken down in Iranian airspace piloting an F-35 and that the details of that incident had been widely publicized didn't matter. If it wasn't in his flight log, it hadn't happened.

This was why, in the weeks after the president's address, with the specter of a nuclear exchange on the near horizon, Major Chris "Wedge" Mitchell, a fourth-generation fighter pilot, found himself spending most of each day in the deserted officers' club trying to beat the high score on *Galaga*, the vintage arcade game. The console sat in the back, leaning against the wall between a chewed-out dartboard and the bullet-riddled tail section of a Japanese Zero, a trophy from another war. Wedge loved the game's controls. They were so simple. A stick. A button. That was it. The idea behind the game was equally simple: a lone starship holds off a swarm of invaders. The weapons held by the invader and defender are an equal match. The only advantage the starship had was the skill of its human pilot. The game had been in the Miramar officers' club for decades—since the early 1980s, Wedge guessed. How many hundreds of pilots had played? Guys who'd come home from Vietnam, who had flown in the Gulf War, in Bosnia, Iraq, Afghanistan, and Syria, even in the liberation of Venezuela—they had all touched these controls, striving for that high score. This little red joystick, it was like a holy relic, like the Sword in the Stone. Or at least this was how Wedge allowed himself to think over the quiet mornings and restless afternoons spent in the empty officers' club.

Every pilot was deployed or getting ready to deploy. Every staffer was working long hours. Which was why Wedge was surprised when a lieutenant colonel wandered into the club one afternoon. Wedge didn't notice him at first. His concentration was fixed on *Galaga*. That morning he'd come within a few hundred points of the impossibly high score before his concentration had lapsed. He'd broken for lunch and one fruitless meeting at Wing Headquarters about fixing his orders. He then returned to *Galaga*, from which he would take only the occasional break to pour over the newspapers for the latest developments in what was beginning to appear like a stalemate around Taiwan.

The lieutenant colonel was sipping a pale beer poured into a frosted glass, his massive shoulders hunched over the bar. His chest was littered with ribbons and badges, to include gold flight wings, and he wore his service alpha uniform, so he was either headed to or coming from a meeting with a more senior officer—probably the commanding general, Wedge guessed. And from the colonel's loosened tie and hangdog expression, Wedge intuited that the meeting had not gone well. The colonel lifted a newspaper that Wedge had left at the bar. "You mind?" he asked.

"All yours, sir," said Wedge, who took a break from *Galaga* to perch himself on a nearby barstool.

The lieutenant colonel began to read, his forehead drawn into horizontal wrinkles. He pointed to an editorial's headline: THE US MILITARY'S IRRELEVANT TECHNOLOGICAL ADVANTAGE. "You see this shit," he said, flicking the page. Wedge noticed the walnut-sized Annapolis class ring he wore. "They're calling us irrelevant."

Wedge leaned a little closer, scanning the editorial, which advocated for a reduced reliance on high-tech platforms as a centerpiece of America's defense strategy, particularly in light of recent "Sino aggression," as the article euphemistically referred to the destruction of more than a quarter of the ships in the US Navy and what appeared like the inevitable loss of Taiwan. "Their argument isn't that *we* are irrelevant," said Wedge. "The argument is that our technology is getting in the way."

The lieutenant colonel placed both of his hands, palms down, on the bar. His bushy Cro-Magnon eyebrows knitted together, as if he were having a hard time understanding how someone could be critical of his aircraft without being critical of him. "What are you doing at the o-club in the middle of the day, Major?"

Wedge nodded toward the *Galaga* machine. "Trying to beat the high score."

The colonel laughed deeply from his stomach.

"How about you, sir?" asked Wedge. "What are you doing here?"

He stopped laughing. His eyebrows came together in the same pre-historic way as before. "Until a few days ago, I was the CO of VMFA-323."

"The Death Rattlers," said Wedge.

The colonel shrugged.

"I thought you guys were deployed on the *Enterprise*," added Wedge. He glanced down at the paper, to the bottom of page A3, where there was a photo of the *Enterprise* accompanying a lengthy reported piece on recent events in the South China Sea, which concluded that the US was, at this moment, outmatched. "What happened?"

"A real bitch of an admiral runs the carrier strike group, that's what happened." The colonel took a long pull on his beer, emptying the glass. He ordered up another and began to talk. "Hunt's her name. She's the one that got all those sailors from the *John Paul Jones, Levin,* and *Chung-Hoon* killed. I guess losing three ships is what qualifies as combat experience in the Navy these days. One morning, she shows up in our ready room and says I've got to rip all the avionics out of my Hornets, that it's the only platform she's got that can operate offline. According to her, when the time comes my guys and I are supposed to 'fly by the seat of our pants' against the Chinese fleet with dumb bombs and our sights grease-penciled onto the canopies of our cockpits. No fucking way."

Wedge's mouth turned dry. "What'd you tell her?"

"Just that. I said, 'Ma'am, with all due respect, no fucking way.' So here I am."

"And who's running the squadron?"

The lieutenant colonel rubbed his chin, as though the question hadn't occurred to him. "Beats the shit out of me. No one, I guess. When I left, the *Enterprise* was cutting squares and the ground crews were ripping out the insides of our cockpits. No one was doing any flying."

"They don't have a CO?"

The colonel shook his head.

Wedge's eyes opened very wide. He reached in his pocket and pulled out a crumple of bills and a fistful of the quarters he'd been pumping into the *Galaga* machine. He picked through it to settle his tab.

"Where you headed?" asked the colonel.

"I got to make a phone call."

The colonel seemed disappointed.

"You want these quarters?" asked Wedge.

"What the fuck for?"

Wedge glanced over at the *Galaga* machine. "If you're killing time here, I thought you might like to try for the high score."

The colonel took a long pull on his second beer. He planted his near-empty glass on the bar. "Gimme that." He snatched up the quarters and stormed over to the *Galaga* console. As Wedge left the officers' club, he could hear the colonel cursing. The game seemed to be getting the better of him.

10:27 June 18, 2034 (GMT+8)
20 nautical miles off the coast of Taipei

Water sluiced through the creases of Lin Bao's raincoat as he stood on the flight deck. On a clear day he would've been able to see the gleaming skyline in the distance. Now all he could see were the storm clouds that shrouded the city. Minister Chiang was scheduled to land any minute. The purpose of his visit wasn't entirely clear; however, Lin Bao felt certain that the time had come to resolve their current stalemate with the Americans and the Taiwanese. The resolution to that stalemate was the news Lin Bao believed the minister would bring.

Flickering in the distance, Lin Bao made out a dim oscillating light.

Minister Chiang's plane.

Pitching and yawing, it catapulted out of a rent in the clouds. Seconds later it was reeling on the deck, the pilots having perfectly caught the three-wire, much to Lin Bao's satisfaction. The engines whined in reverse, decelerating. After a few moments, the back ramp dropped and Minister Chiang emerged, his round face laughing and smiling at the exhilaration of a carrier landing. One of the pilots helped the minister remove his cranial helmet, which caught on his large ears. The minister's visit hadn't been announced, but like a politician he began distributing handshakes to the ground crew, who eventually surmised who he was. Before any fuss could be made on account of his arrival Lin Bao escorted him off the flight deck.

Inside Lin Bao's stateroom, the two sat at a small banquette scattered with nautical charts. A holographic map of Taiwan was projected over the table, rotating on its axis. An orderly poured them cups of tea and then stood at attention with his back to the bulkhead, his chest arching upward. Minister Chiang gave the orderly a long, interrogatory look. Lin Bao dismissed him with a slight backhanded wave.

Now it was only the two of them.

Minister Chiang slouched a bit deeper into his seat. "We find ourselves at an impasse with our adversaries . . ." he began.

Lin Bao nodded.

"I had hoped the Legislative Yuan would vote to dissolve, so we might avoid an opposed invasion. That seems increasingly unlikely." Minister Chiang took a sip from his tea, and then asked, "Why do you think the Americans threatened us with a nuclear strike?"

Lin Bao didn't quite understand the question; its answer seemed too obvious. "To intimidate us, Comrade Minister."

"Hmm," said Minister Chiang. "Tell me, does it intimidate you?"

Lin Bao didn't answer, which seemed to disappoint Minister Chiang.

"Well, it shouldn't," he told his subordinate. According to the minister, the American threat of a nuclear strike didn't show their strength. Quite the opposite. It revealed how vulnerable they were. If the Americans had really wanted to threaten the Chinese, they would've launched a massive cyberattack. The only problem was they couldn't—they lacked the capability to hack into China's online infrastructure. The deregulation that had resulted in so much American innovation and economic strength was now an American weakness. Its disaggregated online infrastructure was vulnerable in a way that the Chinese infrastructure was not. "The Americans have proven incapable of organizing a centralized cyber defense," said Minister Chiang. "Whereas we can shut down much of their country's electric grid with a single keystroke. Their threat of nuclear retaliation is outdated and absurd, like slapping someone across the face with your glove before challenging them to a duel. It's time we show them what we think of their threat."

"How do we do that?" asked Lin Bao, as he clicked a remote that turned off the rotating hologram. He cleared away their cups of tea so as to reveal the nautical charts that covered the banquette table, as if the two might discuss a naval maneuver.

"It's nothing we do here," answered Minister Chiang, disregarding the charts. "We'll handle it up north, in the Barents Sea. The American Third and Sixth Fleets have left those waters to transit south. With the American fleets gone, our Russian allies have unfettered access to the subsurface 10G internet cables that service the United States. Our allies will help us to, gently, remind the Americans that their power is outdated, that bombs aren't the only way to cripple a nation—not even the best way. What I need you to do is simple: be ready. This will be a cyber show of force. It will be limited; we'll only cut a cable or two. We'll dip the Americans into darkness, allow them to stare into that void. Afterward, either the Legislative Yuan will invite us into Taipei, or we will go of our own accord. Either way, your command must be ready."

"Is that what you came all this way to tell me?"

"I didn't come to tell you anything," said Minister Chiang. "I came because I wanted to stand on this ship and see if you are, in fact, ready."

Lin Bao could feel the minister's gaze boring into him. In the days ahead he understood how much would depend on his command's ability to act quickly, whether through an unopposed landing in Taipei, or alternatively a ship-to-shore assault. Before Minister Chiang could deliver his verdict as to the perceived readiness of Lin Bao and his command, there was a knock at the door, a dispatch from the combat information center.

Lin Bao read the note.

"What does it say?" asked Minister Chiang.

"The *Enterprise* is on the move."

"Coming here?"

"No," answered Lin Bao. "It doesn't make sense. They're sailing away."

¬

11:19 June 18, 2034 (GMT+8)
220 nautical miles off the coast of Zhanjiang

These waters were a graveyard. As the *Enterprise* set its course, Sarah Hunt knew the countless wrecks she sailed over. The Philippines were to her east. To her west was the Gulf of Tonkin. She considered the names of the ships—the USS *Princeton*, *Yorktown*, the *Hoel*, and the *Gambier Bay*—whose blasted hulls rested on the seabed beneath her. And Japanese ships as well, battleships and carriers. Hunt and her crew passed silently above them, taking up a position—for what?

Hunt didn't know.

Her orders had come in quick succession. Every couple of hours she was summoned to the radio room, an antiquated closet in the bowels of the ship that a senior chief, who everyone called Quint, treated as his own personal fiefdom. The nickname Quint came from his uncanny resemblance to the captain of the ill-fated *Orca* played by Robert Shaw in the film *Jaws*. Working alongside Quint was his assistant, a young petty officer third class who the crew of the *Enterprise* called Hooper, not because he looked like Richard Dreyfuss's character, Matt Hooper—the intrepid, bespectacled, Great White–hunting marine biologist—but simply because he spent every waking hour with Quint.

Hunt, who had spent a career receiving her orders over lengthy briefings via secure video teleconference, accompanied by kaleidoscopic displays of PowerPoint, was slowly getting used to this fragmented manner of communications. With their Chinese adversaries having the upper hand in cyber, the *Enterprise* had gone into an internet blackout. Indo-Pacific Command, which was in direct contact with the White House, kept tapping out these minimalist communications to

Hunt in high-frequency radio bursts, the same long-range bandwidth employed by the US Navy in the Second World War.

Another of these messages had arrived, so Hunt traveled four levels down from her stateroom to the radio room, where she found Quint and Hooper surrounded by a tangle of electronics, the former with a pair of spectacles perched on the tip of his nose as he unsnarled some wires and the latter holding a smoking soldering iron.

"Gentlemen," said Hunt, announcing herself.

Hooper startled at her voice while Quint sat frozen with his chin tucked down as though calculating his share of the bill at a restaurant. Undisturbed, he continued to focus through his spectacles as his hands worked swiftly at the tangle of wires leading into the radio. "Mornin', ma'am," said Quint. An unlit cigarette dangled from his mouth.

"It's evening, Senior Chief."

Quint raised an eyebrow but didn't take his concentration away from the wires. "Then evenin', ma'am." He nodded for Hooper to pass him the soldering iron, which he quickly applied to a connection he was grafting onto a circuit board. For the past two weeks, ever since they got underway, Quint and Hooper had been retrofitting a suite of antiquated VHF, UHF, and HF radios into the avionics of the single F/A-18 Hornet squadron aboard the *Enterprise*. This made the Death Rattlers the only squadron that would be entirely immune to cyber interference. At least that was the plan.

"How many of those have you got left to install?" she asked.

"None," said Quint. "We finished the last Hornet this morning. This is an upgrade to our ship's HF receiver." Quint drew silent for a moment, mustering his concentration. "There," he said, a ribbon of smoke unspooling from the soldering iron as he handed it back to Hooper. Quint then screwed on the front panel of the radio they'd been tampering with. They powered it on. Its receiver was hooked to a speaker, which emitted a warbling sound.

"Can you turn that down?" asked Hunt.

Hooper glanced at Quint, who nodded, but kept his head canted slightly to the side, his one ear raised, like a maestro fine-tuning his instrument. While Hooper manipulated the dial, Quint gestured alternately with his left hand or his right as they cycled up or down the frequency ladder, searching for . . . what? Hunt couldn't say. Then, as if perceiving her curiosity, Quint began to explain himself.

"We're searching for long-delayed echoes, ma'am. LDEs. When you transmit an HF frequency, it loops around the earth until it finds a receiver. On rare occasions, that can take a while and you wind up with an echo."

"How long of an echo?" asked Hunt.

"Usually, only a few seconds," said Quint.

"We picked up some yesterday," added Hooper.

Hunt smiled at him. "What's the longest echo you ever heard of?"

While Hooper manipulated the dial, Quint made a gesture with his right hand, as though encouraging a piece of music. He was both speaking to Hunt and listening to the oscillations in frequency. "Old salts I served with said that in these waters they'd picked up conversations from fifty or even seventy-five years ago," explained Quint. With a wide grin that revealed decades of the Navy's shoddy dental work, he added, "There's lots of ghosts out here, ma'am. You just got to listen for 'em."

Hunt didn't return Quint's smile; still, she couldn't help but imagine the possibility of ages-old conversations lingering in the surrounding atmosphere—the lost pilots searching the darkness for their carriers off the coast of North Vietnam, the frantic gun crews calling out flights of incoming Zeros in the Philippine Sea. However, she needed to turn to the task at hand.

Quint reached across his desk to a piece of paper with the message he'd recently decoded from Indo-Pacific Command. "They aren't giving you much to go off of, huh?" he said.

The message was hardly a message, simply four latitudinal and longitudinal coordinates, so a box. There was no mission statement, no situation update; Hunt would place the *Enterprise* and its escorts within this box and then await further instructions. She tucked the scrap of paper in the pocket of her coveralls. As she went to leave, Quint stopped her. "Ma'am," he said, reaching onto a back shelf. "We fixed this up; thought you might be able to use it." In his large grip was an old travel radio. "If you tune it just right, you can get the BBC World Service, even a bit of music, depending on where we're at. The dial is a bit tricky. It takes some finesse. But it should do all right for you."

Quint and Hooper were still playing around with the HF receiver as she left, Quint making motions with his hands, Hooper manipulating the dial. With the decoded message in her pocket, Hunt bounded up the four levels to her stateroom. She set the slip of paper with the coordinates on her desk, already layered with an assortment of nautical charts. With a set of parallel rulers, a divider, a compass, and a sharp pencil, she sketched out the corners of the box. It was tight, but large enough to fit her carrier strike group. It was to the south of their current position, another eighty nautical miles further off the coast, a three-hundred-mile straight line overwater to Zhanjiang, the headquarters of China's South Sea Fleet. With the crisis around Taiwan, she wondered how many of the South Sea Fleet's ships were currently in port.

It wouldn't be many.

But it would be enough.

Hunt set her pencil down on the chart. She turned on the radio and managed to find the BBC World Service. With her arms crossed and her legs stretched out in front of her, she closed her eyes and relaxed. She tried to imagine the news reports—*USS* Enterprise *strikes Chinese naval facility with tactical nuclear weapons*—but she couldn't; it seemed too improbable. Although few Cold War precepts had aged well in the twenty-first century, the logic of mutually assured destruction was one of them. Even so, thought Hunt, her country had little to gain by wiping out the port at Zhanjiang. As she prepared to alter the course of the *Enterprise*, she couldn't help but recognize this maneuver for the theater it was—for the theater such maneuvers always had been—ever since man split the atom, unleashed its power, and nations coerced one another with the threat of that power. The current crisis would de-escalate, as crises always did. She felt certain of this.

That certainty gave her some peace of mind, enough so she dozed off in her chair. She slept dreamlessly, waking an hour later. Her radio was no longer playing the BBC World Service. It had lost the signal. All it emitted was static. Hunt fiddled with the dial, trying to retune into the news.

Then she heard something.

A weak, indistinct voice.

As quickly as she heard it, it disappeared.

She left her radio tuned to the static, set on the same frequency, wondering if she might hear the strange transmission again. She knew what it was; Quint had told her.

It was ghosts.

⌐

14:22 June 24, 2034 (GMT+2)
Barents Sea

This far north the sun held above them nearly twenty-four hours a day. The sky was clear, the weather unseasonably warm. The American fleet was nowhere to be found; it had sailed away. The Russian Federation owned these waters, and they knew it. Unencumbered by the looming threat of the US Navy, the crew of the *Rezkiy* and other ships of the flotilla indulged in bouts of recreation. On the battle cruiser *Pyotr Velikiy*, the crew descended its side boats to take plunges into the icy seawater. On the carrier *Kuznetsov*, the captain authorized sunbathing on the flight deck despite the cold. On the smaller *Rezkiy*, Kolchak allowed pop songs to play over the ship's intercom during the daily cleanup; most popular were classics like Elvis, the Jonas Brothers, and anything by Shakira. "Hips Don't Lie" was a favorite.

These little breaks with discipline, plus the general eccentricity of naval life, confounded Lieutenant Commander Farshad. His liaison duties consisted of little more than being a presence that evidenced two nations' faithfulness to one another, even though neither of those nations had ever been renowned for faithfulness to anything but themselves. Farshad had once said as much in the wardroom to Kolchak, who had asked in reply, "Has a nation ever been faithful to anything but itself?" Farshad had conceded the point.

Not long after this exchange, Farshad had been standing on the bridge of the *Rezkiy* when the watch spotted a school of sharks off the ship's port side. Kolchak had been manning that watch and he took an uncanny interest in the sharks, even adjusting their ship's course to follow them for several minutes. "Perfect," said Kolchak as he stared at their thrashing dorsal fins. As if sensing Farshad's confusion, he explained himself. "Those sharks are heading in the direction of the 10G undersea cables. They're attracted to the electromagnetic energy. Those cables connect to the United States, and sharks have been known to chew through them. Their presence will give us deniability."

Destroying a few of the undersea cables would send a powerful message to the Americans, slowing internet across the country by as much as 60 percent, or so Farshad had been told by Kolchak. This might be enough to de-escalate the crisis, to bring everyone to their senses. When it came to acting pragmatically, which was to say acting in their national interests, it seemed to Farshad that only his country—and perhaps the Russians—were capable of clear thinking. The Russians, like them, knew that any scenario that weakened the Americans was advantageous. In fact, a de-escalation of the current crisis wasn't really in the Iranian or Russian interest.

Disruption was in their interest.

Chaos.

A change in the world order.

The sharks disappeared beneath the waves, and for the remaining hours of the day the *Rezkiy* and its sister ships idled over the 10G cables. The mood on the ship turned businesslike. Farshad lingered on the bridge, where Kolchak and the captain kept a vigil, the two speaking exclusively in Russian, while Kolchak took the occasional break to explain the situation to Farshad.

"We'll circle around this area here," Kolchak said, pushing a yellowing fingernail at their navigation computer's interface. "The *Pyotr Velikiy* has a tethered submersible aboard that is going to place an explosive cutting charge on the cables."

"How large is the charge?" asked Farshad.

The captain brought his eyes out of his binoculars. From over his shoulder, he glanced at them warily.

"Just enough to do the job," said Kolchak.

The captain made a face, and then a transmission came over the radio in Russian. Kolchak snatched the receiver and promptly replied while the captain dipped his eyes back into his binoculars and continued to scan the open sea. The *Pyotr Velikiy* was recovering its submersible, the charge having been set. Planted on the horizon was the *Kuznetsov*, its decks crowded with aircraft. Kolchak continued to check his watch, the second hand making its steady orbit around the dial as they waited.

More minutes passed in silence.

Then an explosion, a geyser fountaining upward from the seabed. Followed by a shock. And a sound, like a clap. The entire ship rattled. The water splashed back onto the surface of the ocean. Another radio transmission came into the bridge. The voice was excited, congratulatory. The captain answered the call in the same congratulatory manner. The only person on the bridge who didn't seem pleased by the result was Farshad, who was confused. Grasping Kolchak by the elbow, he said, "That must've destroyed more than one or two cables."

The smile vanished from Kolchak's face. "Perhaps."

"Perhaps?" answered Farshad. He could feel the old familiar rage brimming up from the center of his chest, into his limbs. He felt duped. "That explosion must have destroyed every cable."

"And so what if it did?" answered Kolchak. "A de-escalation between Beijing and Washington hardly benefits us. It doesn't benefit your nation either. Let's sow a little chaos into this crisis. Let's see what happens then. The result will be advantageous, for both of our countries. Who knows, then we might—" Before Kolchak could finish the thought, the ship's collision alarm sounded.

Orders were rapidly shouted across the bridge—a new heading, a new speed ("Reverse right rudder, full ahead left!"), a reflexive set of impact-avoidance measures—while both Kolchak and Farshad scanned off the bow. At first, Farshad couldn't see the obstacle that threatened collision. There was no ship. No iceberg. No large object that assured catastrophe. There was only clear sky. And a mist of seawater that still lingered in the air after the explosion.

It was the mist that concealed the obstacle.

Sharks, dozens of them, an entire school, bobbing upward like so many apples in a barrel, their white bellies presented to the sun. The evasive maneuvers continued. Farshad could do nothing; a sailor in name only, he couldn't help the crew avoid the collision. The *Rezkiy* plowed through the field of dead fish, their bodies hitting the thin hull, reminding Farshad of the ice floes that had so often kept him awake at night—*dong, dong, dong*. Then a far sharper noise combined with this hollow thudding, a noise like a fistful of metal spoons tossed down a garbage disposal; the shark carcasses were passing through the twin propellers of the *Rezkiy*.

Farshad followed Kolchak out to the bridge wing. They turned to the stern of the ship to assess the damage. The seawater mist still lingered in the air. The sunlight passed through it, casting off brilliant rainbows—blues, yellows, oranges, reds.

So much red.

Farshad realized the red wasn't only in the air; it was also in the water. The slightly damaged *Rezkiy* set a new course, leaving a wide swath of blood in its wake.

Γ

21:02 June 26, 2034 (GMT+8)
300 nautical miles off the coast of Zhanjiang

The internet was out across the entire eastern seaboard. Eighty percent of the connectivity in the Midwest was gone. Connectivity on the West Coast had been reduced by 50 percent.

A nationwide power outage.

The airports closed.

The markets panicked.

Hunt listened to the updates arriving via the BBC World Service on the handheld radio Quint had given her. She immediately understood the implications. She scrambled down four levels to the radio room, where Quint was also listening to the news and awaiting her.

"Anything yet?" she asked.

"Nothing," he said.

Hooper wasn't there, he was asleep in the berthing, and Hunt was glad it was only her and the old chief. She knew the message she was waiting for, and she felt as though she wanted the fewest people possible around when it arrived. The idea of receiving her task in front of some-one from a younger generation, like Hooper, felt particularly difficult. Perhaps this was because he would have to live with the consequences longer than any of them. This was Hunt's train of thought as she sat in the cramped radio room with Quint, the two of them listening to static on the HF radio set, waiting.

And then the message arrived.

⌐

10:47 June 26, 2034 (GMT-4)
Washington, D.C.

Chowdhury wasn't in the room when they made the decision. To assuage his guilt about what followed, he would always cling to that fact.
In the years to come he would have ample opportunity to imagine the
discussion around the Situation Room conference table beneath the
dim generator-powered lights. He would imagine the positions taken by
Trent Wisecarver, by the various service chiefs and cabinet secretaries,
the tabulations of arguments *for* or *against* what they were about to do—
what they had all committed themselves to do when the president had
put down her "red line" and dared her counterparts in Beijing to cross it.

Which was what it seemed Beijing had now done, though not in the
way anyone had anticipated. The cutting of the undersea cables and the
resulting plunge into darkness was the demonstrable fact that, when
discussed around the conference table, proved Beijing had crossed the
red line. The question was the response. And even that was settled in
remarkably short order. Chowdhury envisioned the scene—a disquisi-
tion of US interests by Wisecarver, followed by a range of options (or
lack thereof) presented by the Joint Chiefs, and then formal nuclear
authorizations being granted by the president herself. Chowdhury
didn't need to imagine any more than that because he had seen the prin-
cipals as they exited into the West Wing, their dour expressions failing
to contain the knowledge of the decision they had settled upon, even
though they themselves didn't yet understand past intellectualization
the destruction they would unleash. How could they?

With the orders dispatched, Wisecarver set up a duty rotation
among the national security staff and Chowdhury was sent home, to

return the following morning. He expected the strike to occur sometime in the night. There would, of course, be a response from Beijing. And the national security staff needed to be ready for it. On Chowdhury's drive home, entire blocks were still without power. Only about half the traffic lights in the city worked; the other half were blacked out or shuffling their colors nonsensically onto empty streets. In only a few more days, the trash would begin to pile up. When he tuned in to his favorite radio station he was met with static.

So he drove in silence.

And he thought.

He thought the same thought all through that night—as he ate dinner with his mother and Ashni, as he carried the girl up to bed with her arms looped heavily around his neck like two ropes, and as he wished his mother good night in the guest room and she kissed him, uncharacteristically, on the forehead and then touched his cheek with her cupped palm as she hadn't done in years, not since his divorce. The thought was this: *I have to get my family somewhere safe.*

Chowdhury knew where that place was. It wasn't a bomb shelter (if those even existed anymore), or outside of the city (although that wouldn't be a bad start). No, he concluded; none of that would be enough.

He knew what he needed to do.

Who he needed to call.

In the quiet of his home, with his mother and daughter sleeping so near he would need to speak in a whisper, he picked up his phone and dialed. The answer came after the first ring.

"Admiral Anand Patel speaking. . . ."

Chowdhury froze. A beat of silence followed.

"Hello? Hello?"

"Hello, Uncle. It's me, Sandeep."

⌐

13:36 June 27, 2034 (GMT+8)
300 nautical miles off the coast of Zhanjiang

White light on the horizon.

That's how Sarah Hunt would always remember it.

⌐

11:15 June 30, 2034 (GMT+8)
Taiwan Taoyuan International Airport

Lin Bao believed he had known them, but he hadn't.

If he had once considered himself half American, he no longer thought so. Not after what they'd done at Zhanjiang three days ago. Every member of his crew knew someone who'd perished there, and almost all had family within the blast zone. Countless friends of his— from his academy days, to postings on other ships, to three cousins who had nothing to do with the Navy but who lived in that port city by the turquoise sea—each gone in an instant, in a flash. Others had not been so lucky. Lin Bao couldn't bear to linger on the details; they were too gruesome. But he knew the hospitals in Beihai, Maoming, Yangjiang, and even as far away as Shenzhen had already filled to capacity.

If the American strike on Zhanjiang had been swift and decisive, the invasion of Taiwan by the People's Army had proven its equal— though it wasn't Beijing's response to the 150-kiloton blast; that was yet to come. A discussion of that response was the reason Lin Bao was summoned away from his ship to a conference, so that he was now awaiting the arrival of Minister Chiang in the airport's international terminal, in what had once been the British Airways first-class lounge. Floor-to-ceiling windows allowed Lin Bao to marvel at his country's occupation of the island. Though the invasion had shut down the airport to civilian traffic, it was busy—if not busier—with military traffic, commuter jets having been replaced with fighters and transports, and vacationers and business travelers having been replaced with soldiers. When Minister Chiang at last arrived in the lounge, he was followed by a vast retinue of security, which, as he explained apologetically, was the reason for his delay. "They've become very protective of me," he said, and laughed nervously, offering one of his characteristically expansive smiles to his security detail, none of whom returned it.

Minister Chiang escorted Lin Bao into a conference room, a clean glassed-in cube designed for executives to use between flights. The two sat next to each other at one end of a long table. Lin Bao couldn't help but notice Minister Chiang's uniform, which wasn't his usual service dress but rather a set of poorly fitting camouflage utilities that still held the creases from where they'd been folded in plastic packaging. Like Lin Bao, the minister couldn't help but steal the occasional admiring glance at his troops as they moved efficiently through the airport, dispersing throughout Taipei and then beyond for the seizure and annexation of this stubborn republic, finally brought to heel.

However, when Minister Chiang's attention returned to the conference room, his expression turned severe, and he began to knead his chin, as if the action were a way to coax his jaw into motion. Eventually, he spoke, "Our position is becoming increasingly precarious. We have a week, maybe two, until the Americans will have massed their fleets so close to our mainland that we'll no longer possess free access to the sea. Which is unacceptable. If we allow that to happen, the Americans will strangle us as we have done here, to this island. With our access to the sea blocked, our entire mainland will be under threat of invasion, to say nothing of the nuclear threat. The Americans have crossed that threshold. Once a nation has dropped one nuclear weapon the stigma of a second or a third is less. The moment has come for us to settle on a course of action."

Minister Chiang was speaking imperiously, which caused Lin Bao to hesitate before replying, "Is that the reason for this"—and Lin Bao struggled for a word to describe the nature of their meeting, which was ostensibly why Minister Chiang had summoned him here, away from his ship, to the British Airways lounge, which increasingly felt like a strange, even illicit location—"I mean, the reason for this *conference*?"

Minister Chiang leaned forward in his chair, placing his hand affectionately on Lin Bao's forearm. Then he glanced out the window, to his security detail, as if making sure his dark-suited entourage observed the gesture. And Lin Bao saw that they did. Gradually, he began to intuit the subtext for their meeting as Minister Chiang confessed that their "conference" was a "conference of two." Yes, he could have invited the commander of the special forces task force, an unimaginative major general whose troops had already fanned out across Taipei, seizing strategic targets such as radio, television, and power stations, as well as gathering up probable agitators; and he could have also invited the commander of their air forces, a technocrat who was coordinating a vast logistical web of resupply while keeping his fighter and attack aircraft poised for any counterstrike; but to invite either of them would have disrupted their efforts. Also, Minister Chiang explained that he wasn't certain they possessed "the required competencies for what would come next."

Which begged the question of what that *next* would be.

When Lin Bao asked, Minister Chiang grew uncharacteristically reticent. He crossed his arms over his chest, turned his chin slightly to the side, so that he was observing Lin Bao from the corners of his eyes as if to confirm that he had appraised him correctly from the start.

"It seems I've been recalled to Beijing," said Minister Chiang. He once again glanced outside the glass conference room, to where his security detail lingered. Lin Bao now understood; those men were to ensure the minister returned—whether he wanted to or not. "After what happened three days ago in Zhanjiang," the minister continued, "certain voices are saying that our planning miscalculated the American response." He fixed his stare on Lin Bao, examining him for the slightest reaction to such charges of *miscalculation*. "Those same voices, both inside and outside the Politburo Standing Committee, are blaming me. Intrigue like this is nothing surprising. My enemies see a vulnerability and they strike after it. They claim I'm to blame for the actions of our unreliable allies in the Barents Sea, or for an American president whose greatest weakness is her fear of being perceived as weak. I haven't come as far as I have without possessing certain instincts that allow me to navigate such intrigues. And it is those instincts that drew me to you, Admiral Lin Bao. It is why I made you Ma Qiang's replacement, and it is why I am asking for your support now, against not only our enemies on the outside but also our enemies within."

"My support?" asked Lin Bao.

"Yes, for what comes next."

But Lin Bao still didn't know what came next. Perhaps they could hold their gains around Taipei and negotiate with the Americans. The devastation of Zhanjiang would be the price they'd pay to annex Taiwan. He said as much to Minister Chiang, reminding him that their original plan was based on a strategy of de-escalation, as well as Sun Tzu's wisdom about subduing one's enemy without fighting.

One of the dark-suited security men knocked on the glass with the knuckle of his middle finger. He pointed to his watch. It was time.

Minister Chiang stood, tugging down on his uniform, which had ridden up his soft belly. With all the dignity he could muster, he raised a finger to the impatient member of his security detail, insisting that he wait another moment. Then he turned to Lin Bao and rested his hand on his shoulder. "Yes, we all know that old bit of Sun Tzu. He was a master of asymmetric warfare, of defeating an enemy without giving battle. But he also tells us, *On difficult ground, press on; on encircled ground, devise stratagems—*"

The security man swung open the door, interrupting them.

Minister Chiang's eyes flashed in that direction, but then he fixed them determinedly on Lin Bao. *"And on death ground, fight."*

As improbably as he had arrived, Minister Chiang was gone.

5

On Death Ground

02:38 July 01, 2034 (GMT+8)
South China Sea

From the nose cone rearward, his eyes ran the line of the fuselage. He ducked under the flared wings and walked in a crouch to each of their tips, brushing their leading edge with the pads of his four fingers as he checked for a dent, a loose coupling, any compromise in their aerodynamics. He made his way back to the dark, gaping exhaust of the twin engines. He stuck his head inside each afterburner, inhaled deeply, and shut his eyes. God, how he loved that smell: jet fuel. Next, in a single leap, like a house cat assuming its perch on a favorite windowsill, he hoisted himself onto the back of the Hornet. Wedge walked forward to the open cockpit and sat inside. He placed one hand on the inert throttle, the other on the stick, leaned against the headrest, and shut his eyes.

It was the middle of the night and the hangar deck was empty.

Wedge had arrived on the *Enterprise* only a few hours before, after a brief layover in Yokosuka. On the flight in he observed the sun setting with a particular brilliance in the west, in the direction of Zhanjiang. It was the reddest he'd ever seen—red like a wound. He could think of no other way to describe this, his first glimpse of nuclear fallout. Although the strike had only used a tactical nuke, it was a significant escalation and the possibility of a strategic attack was on the rise. The Indians were making noises about trying to negotiate some kind of ceasefire, but that wasn't going anywhere. Wedge hardly considered himself a strategist, but he knew enough to understand that a single miscalculation on either side could take this whole war high-order nuclear—that meant the big stuff, the end-of-days stuff.

What a goat fuck, Wedge thought to himself.

Followed by, *Pop-Pop would've loved this.*

The jet lag had eventually brought him down to the hangar deck, to check out the aircraft assigned to his new command, VMFA-323, the Death Rattlers. Even without the time change, the excitement of this assignment would have likely kept him up. After the chance meeting at the officers' club in Miramar with the Death Rattlers' old colonel, he'd had the idea to call the master sergeant who'd played chaperone to him while he was in Quantico. When Wedge asked whether the air wing had assigned another officer to take over the underequipped and under-staffed Death Rattlers, the master sergeant explained that the vacancy was low-priority because the Corps' unchanged policy was to fill vacancies in its F-35 squadrons, not its antiquated Hornet squadrons. At that point their conversation went the same as nearly all of their conversations before ("Nobody's in command? Are you shitting me?" "Negative, sir."). With a few deft strokes of his keyboard and a phone call to a soon-to-retire general, the master sergeant was able to cut Wedge a new set of orders.

How long had he waited for those orders? Really, since he'd been a kid. He had a sense as he sat in the cockpit that his entire life—everything he had ever hoped to be—came down to this assignment. With his eyes shut, he continued to manipulate the Hornet's controls, juking the stick, stamping the rudder pedals, adding and easing off the throttle, while in his imagination he sequenced through a Split-S, a Low and High Yo-Yo defense, an Immelmann, and High-G Barrel Roll. As a child, he used to make a cockpit out of a cardboard box and wear one of his father's old flight helmets. He would visualize dogfights, as he did now (*Three-quarters throttle. Even rudder . . . closing, closing . . .*), epic battles in which sometimes he was the victor (*Full-throttle, break right!*), and other times he was blown out of the sky (*On your tail! Eject! Eject!*) facing impossible odds. But always there was glory.

When he was ten years old, he'd put his cardboard box cockpit on the top of the stairs. Wearing his prized helmet, he sat inside. He wanted to feel what it was like to fly. His mother told him it wasn't a good idea, and though she wouldn't stop him from trying, she refused to be the one to give him the push. So he balanced his box on the lip of the stairs and then he leaned himself forward. The box tipped over the edge. And he flew . . .

For about five stairs.

Then the front of the box caught the sixth stair. It pitched over, violently. Wedge went face-first into the floor. The crash landing split his lip open. He still had the scar, ever so slight, on the inside of his mouth. He ran the tip of his tongue over it now.

"Can I help you, Major?"

Wedge glanced over the side of the cockpit, to find a senior chief with an unlit cigarette dangling from his mouth. He introduced himself to the senior chief and explained who he was. As he was the new commanding officer of the Death Rattlers, these were, in fact, his planes, so there was nothing to worry about; he could sit where he wanted.

"Your planes, Major?" said the senior chief, gazing out at the Hornets. The ten aircraft were gathered nearest the elevator that led to the flight deck, in the ready position, and crowding out the dozens of F-35s that had proven useless. The senior chief laughed to himself incredulously as he pulled a ladder up to the side of the cockpit. "Your predecessor thought these were his planes too. Admiral Hunt didn't much appreciate that."

Wedge had an in-brief with the admiral scheduled sometime in the next week. At the evocation of her name, he chose to listen a bit more closely to the senior chief, who introduced himself only as "Quint" and who Wedge suspected might possess some shred of wisdom to keep him in the good graces of his boss, or at least from meeting the ignominious fate of his predecessor. Quint then powered on the avionics in the cockpit. Any interface with a computer, a GPS, or that could conceivably be accessed online, Quint had disabled. Munitions would be deployed via manual weapons sights and manual releases. Navigation would be performed off charts, with flight times calculated using a wristwatch, pencil, and calculator. Communications would be handled via a custom-installed suite of VHF, UHF, and HF radios. For Wedge, who already knew that his Hornets had undergone some modifications, the tour Quint gave of their streamlined cockpits both under- and overwhelmed him.

It underwhelmed him because—even though he should've known better—he couldn't believe the bare-bones nature of the onboard systems. It overwhelmed him because he couldn't believe that he would have the chance to fly how they used to fly, before pilots became technicians, which was to say on instinct.

Inadvertently, Wedge succumbed to a heedless smile.

"You all right there, Major?" Quint asked.

Wedge turned toward him, the expression still stamped to his face. "Fine, senior chief. Just fine." He ran the tip of his tongue on the inside of his lip, tracing the outline of his boyhood scar.

⌐

10:37 July 03, 2034 (GMT+2)
Gdańsk Bay

The destruction of the undersea cables was accepted with equanimity, if not a measure of outright enthusiasm, by Farshad's old colleagues in the Revolutionary Guard Corps. Major General Mohammad Bagheri, chief of staff of the armed forces, was somewhat more taciturn. A dispatch directly from the general arrived on Farshad's encrypted laptop within hours. It gave a single instruction: *Continue to keep us apprised of all developments*. Farshad couldn't help but wonder what the Russians would come up with next.

The following week, the *Rezkiy, Pyotr Velikiy,* and *Kuznetsov* altered their course southward, toward Kaliningrad. Farshad didn't believe this merited notification of Bagheri's staff in Tehran. They would, he assumed, be returning to their home port. But when the *Kuznetsov* held fifteen miles short of Kaliningrad and began preparing for flight operations in Gdańsk Bay, Farshad knew they weren't returning to port, at least not yet. When the first sorties of Su-34 Sukhoi attack aircraft catapulted off the deck of the *Kuznetsov*, their wings drooping with munitions, Farshad disappeared into his cramped quarters and quickly fired off another dispatch to his superiors, notifying them of developments but providing no analysis of his own. Farshad knew enough to know that an incorrect analysis of the situation could only be used against him later and that a correct analysis would gain him little. Before he could shut down his laptop, a cursory reply arrived from the General Staff: *Acknowledged. Continue to monitor.*

Farshad returned to the bridge to find Kolchak in command of the *Rezkiy* as they circled the *Kuznetsov*, screening for threats to the much larger carrier, close as they were to the coastline. Farshad could see the shore through his binoculars, a ribbon of dark rocks in the hazy distance. He estimated it was perhaps a dozen miles off. Not even an hour had passed since the first launch of Sukhois and already they'd returned across the coast and were "feet wet," safely over the water. Farshad observed them through his binoculars: their wings were empty. The Sukhois had dropped their munitions. When the aircraft came a little closer and entered the flight pattern to land on the *Kuznetsov*, he could make out soot-darkened smudges on the gun ports at either side of the cockpit. The cannons within those gun ports had been firing.

Kolchak saw it too. With his binoculars raised he watched the Sukhois as they landed. "Looks like they got in pretty close," he said, and then called out a new heading and speed to the helmsman before smiling triumphantly at Farshad, who struggled to know how he should react to his ally's apparent victory, given that his Russian counterparts had not as of yet taken him into their confidence as to their mission.

As the first sorties landed, refueled, and rearmed, all within sight of the *Rezkiy*, Kolchak explained to Farshad that aircraft from the *Kuznetsov* were flying close air support for an invasion force that, at this very moment, was "reclaiming ancestral territories that connect the *Ro-*

dina to its northern ports on the Baltic Sea." That these ancestral territories were part of present-day Poland mattered little. Weeks before in the wardroom, Kolchak had foreshadowed Russia's interests in seizing a ribbon of land that would connect its mainland to its Baltic port at Kaliningrad. While the world's attention was diverted to the Far East, they would use that crisis to their benefit. "Who will object?" Kolchak now asked Farshad rhetorically. "Not the Americans. They're hardly in a position to lecture us on 'sovereignty' and 'human rights,' particularly not after Zhanjiang. As for the Chinese, they understand our actions intuitively. In their language the word for *crisis* and *opportunity* are one and the same. Look at the map." Kolchak fingered it while his cigarette smoldered between his knuckles. "We carve this slice from Poland and connect it to us through Belorussia. The Poles will complain, but they won't *really* miss it. And it sews up a tidy ribbon around Lithuania, Estonia, and Latvia. They, too, will soon return home to the *Rodina*."

Farshad opened his mouth to speak, but his words were drowned out by another section of Sukhois catapulting off the deck of the *Kuznetsov*. Ribbons of dark smoke began to tower upward on the horizon as the fighters struck their targets and advancing Russian ground forces seized their objectives. Farshad thought to disappear to his quarters belowdecks, to check if he had received another message from the General Staff in Tehran. His Russian counterparts would have thought little of it. They wanted him reporting back their every move, particularly on a day like this, in which each move brought them greater success.

Farshad thought the operation was reckless, even by Russian standards. Poland was a NATO member nation. Perhaps President Putin, now an octogenarian, had made a disastrous miscalculation in his old age. He looked up at the jets and wondered when NATO would respond. American disinterest over the previous decades had crippled the alliance. It felt antiquated, irrelevant, a shadow of its Cold War self. This year it had celebrated its eighty-fifth birthday. But it still had teeth, surely? Maybe not. Maybe of the two octogenarians locked in this conflict, it was Putin who'd kept his teeth over the years.

Before Farshad could send a further report from his quarters there was a commotion on the bridge. A single fighter had threaded its way between the *Kuznetsov* and the *Rezkiy*. It had come in low and fast, at less than one hundred feet, so that its twin engines blew ripples across the water's surface. With the continuous comings and goings of the Russian Sukhois, it must've gotten confused in the mix. The aircraft was a MiG-29, its wings clearly marked with the red-and-white checkerboard pattern of the Polish Air Force. Everyone seemed to see it at once: Farshad, Kolchak, the entire crew of the *Rezkiy*. The collective shock of finding an enemy aircraft at so close a range caused them all to freeze, and in that moment a great silence enveloped them.

That silence was broken when the MiG-29 engaged its afterburners, arching upward, gathering altitude as it bled off speed. One thousand, two thousand, three thousand feet, it hung suspended above the flight deck of the *Kuznetsov*. Beneath the single Polish MiG, dozens of heavily armed Sukhois and their ground crews were, suddenly, exposed.

The MiG barreled over, nosing downward into its angle of attack.

Farshad glimpsed the MiG's belly as it pirouetted. It wasn't even outfitted with a full complement of munitions. Two bombs hung from a single rack; that was it. But that would be enough.

A flash and then a trail of smoke on the deck of the *Rezkiy* as it fired on the MiG.

The smoke coiled upward.

On the belly of the MiG, Farshad could see the bombs leave their rack, where they hung for a moment, suspended in air. Farshad could also see the profile of the pilot, a determined speck in the canopy. The last thing Farshad saw before the rocket fired from the *Rezkiy* destroyed the MiG and the twin bombs it attempted to drop, as well as the pilot who never had a chance to eject, was the gun ports on the aircraft.

They were clean, not soot-darkened like the returning Sukhois. Because in the end, after all of the commotion, the pilot of the MiG never got off a shot.

Farshad went belowdecks to send his report to Tehran.

07:55 July 06, 2034 (GMT+8)
Shenzhen

Lin Bao's summons from the Politburo Standing Committee had come in the middle of the night. The unmarked transport that flew him off the deck of the *Zheng He* an hour later wasn't one of his; it was sourced from another command. There were only two additional passengers aboard, both large, dark-suited men, clearly from one of the internal security branches. Lin Bao thought he recognized them from his last meeting with Minister Chiang in the British Airways lounge, though he couldn't be sure. Thugs like these usually defied differentiation.

By first light, Lin Bao was sandwiched between those two security men in the back of a black sedan as it wound up a long, twisting ribbon of driveway to its improbable location, the front entrance of the Mission Hills Golf Club and Resort in Shenzhen. To his surprise, when he stepped from the sedan, Lin Bao was met by a lithe twentysomething woman. She had an orchid pinned in her long black hair, wore a name tag that announced her title: *hospitality associate*. She handed Lin Bao a glass of cucumber-infused water. He sipped it, cautiously.

She escorted Lin Bao along the labyrinthine route to his junior suite, while the two security men disappeared amid the bland furniture of the echoing reception hall. When they arrived in his suite, the hospitality associate gave Lin Bao a quick tour, pointing out the mini-fridge and the sofa that pulled out into a second bed, then drawing back the curtains so he could appreciate the expansive green-lawned view overlooking the more than two hundred holes of golf at Mission Hills. Everything would be provided for Lin Bao, she explained, pulling out a drawer that contained a change of civilian clothes and gesturing to his fully stocked bathroom. She knew he had traveled a great distance, so it was now time to relax. If Lin Bao was hungry, he could order some lunch from room service. She would also send up the valet to clean and press his uniform, which wasn't appropriate attire at a resort. The hospitality associate was polite and methodical in her speech, missing no detail, her chin raised slightly, the tense line of her throat expressing her words with a practiced efficiency that by the end of their exchange had Lin Bao wondering whether she was employed by the resort or by the same branch of internal security as the darkly suited men who'd brought him this far.

It hardly mattered, Lin Bao concluded as she left him alone.

But not really alone. Lin Bao sat on the edge of the bed, his left hand on his left knee, his right hand on his right knee, his back rigidly straight. He searched the room with his eyes. The air-conditioning vent most likely contained a listening device and pinhole-sized camera. The mirror that hung above the bed most likely contained the same. The hotel phone was certainly monitored. He walked to his window, which overlooked the golf course. He tried to open it—the window was sealed.

Lin Bao returned to the edge of the bed. He took off his boots and his fatigues and wrapped a towel around his waist. He crossed the suite and turned on the shower. A fresh tube of toothpaste was balanced on its cap by the sink. He touched the bristles of the hotel toothbrush; they were damp. Lin Bao brushed with his finger. Before he could step into the shower, a valet knocked on his door.

Did he have any dry cleaning?

Lin Bao gathered his uniform and handed it to the valet, who told him that his colleagues would be ready for him that afternoon. Who those colleagues were, Lin Bao didn't know, and likely neither did the valet, who left with the bundle of clothes tucked beneath his arm. Lin Bao showered, ordered a light lunch for which he had little appetite, and dressed in the khakis and golf shirt that had been left for him. He sat in a chair by the window and looked out at the nearly vacant course, its acres and acres of grass rolling outward like an ocean.

For the first time, he allowed himself to wonder if he would ever gaze at the ocean again. Since being summoned here from the *Zheng He*, he'd disciplined himself against such thoughts, but his anxiety got the better of him as he waited in his room. He had heard of such "summonses" before. A national disaster had occurred in Zhanjiang, with millions killed, incinerated, while many others slowly perished in hospital beds around the country—in hospital beds not far from here. Someone would be held accountable. The Politburo Standing Committee would purge what it identified as the single point of failure. Which would always be a person.

Lin Bao suspected that he was perfectly positioned to be that person.

He continued staring at the golf course. What an improbable venue for it all to end.

Hours passed until there was a gentle knock on his door. It was the same pleasant young woman, the hospitality associate. "Were you able to get some rest, Admiral Lin Bao?" Before he could answer, she added, "Do the clothes fit all right?" Lin Bao glanced down at his khakis and shirt. He nodded, allowing himself to smile at the woman and restraining himself from thinking of his own wife and daughter, neither of whom he expected to see after today. Then the young woman said, "Your colleagues are ready for you now."

⌐

15:25 July 06, 2034 (GMT-4)
Washington, D.C.

Home felt lonely and Chowdhury was trying to spend as little time there as possible. His mother and daughter had left Dulles International two days before, bound for New Delhi. Young as she was, Ashni would've asked few questions, but Chowdhury felt compelled to give the little girl an explanation as to where she was going and why—an explanation that approximated the truth. "You're taking a trip to see where our family is from," was what Chowdhury had settled on, even though his mother still struggled with the idea that her own brother could be considered family, let alone trusted.

The idea of trust was very much on Chowdhury's mind as he considered what he had to do next, which was to inform his ex-wife, Samantha, that without her permission or foreknowledge he had flown their daughter across the world, to New Delhi, with an indefinite date of return. As he calculated what lay ahead, Chowdhury thought there existed a two-in-three chance of a strategic nuclear exchange with China. The idea that tactical nuclear exchanges wouldn't escalate to strategic ones seemed wishful thinking at best. And so, he needed to get his daughter a long way from Washington. What Chowdhury understood—

or had at least resigned himself to—was that no matter what his ex-wife said, no matter what custody court she dragged him into, no matter what international convention she evoked to have their daughter returned, he would fight and stall and writhe and obfuscate until he felt certain that it was safe for Ashni to come home. And if that day never arrived, then she would never return; he would simply alter his life accordingly.

But he didn't need to deal with the rest of his life now; he only needed to inform Samantha of what he'd done and brace himself for her reaction. He sent her a text message, asking if they could meet for dinner. It was an odd request, to be sure; the two of them could hardly get on the phone without one hanging up on the other. However, Samantha replied immediately to the invitation—that is, Chowdhury could see the floating ellipses on the message thread, which meant that Samantha was typing, or typing and then deleting, which was likely the case because her reply after nearly a minute read only: *Ok.*

To which he replied: *Name a place.*

More ellipses before she answered: *City Lights.*

He nearly threw his phone across his empty apartment. The choice was so typical of her. Typical of her passive aggression. Typical of her moralizing. Typical of her need—since his one, fleeting infidelity, which led to their divorce—to belittle him whenever the opportunity presented itself. City Lights was a Chinese restaurant.

The next night he arrived for dinner at precisely seven o'clock. Samantha sat discreetly in the back, though the establishment was empty. The hostess led Chowdhury to a corner booth and pulled out the table, as if he might sit next to Samantha. Samantha didn't stand to greet him, and Chowdhury didn't sit in the booth; he pulled out the chair across from his ex-wife. The hostess handed Chowdhury his menu and left

them alone. Chowdhury already knew what he wanted. He and Samantha used to come to City Lights weekly when they were first married
and lived only a few blocks away near Dupont Circle, in a condo she had
kept in the divorce settlement.

The decor hadn't changed in the intervening years, the plump gold-
fish in the gurgling aquarium, the reproductions of dynastic woodblock
prints on the walls. "Nice choice, Sammy," Chowdhury said flatly.

"You used to like this place," she replied, and then added, "Please
don't call me that."

When they'd been at graduate school together, her friends had
called her Sammy and her professors had called her Samantha, but the
further those years receded, the more she insisted on the formal name.

Chowdhury apologized—"Samantha"—and explained that given
the current geopolitical crisis and his role in it, her choice of a Chinese
restaurant seemed to be, "How shall I put this," he said, "a passive-
aggressive move."

"You're the one who asked me to meet you, Sandeep," she replied,
nearly spitting out his name. "Now more than ever, supporting businesses like this one is the right thing." God, she was insufferable, thought
Chowdhury, always so quick to tell you what was or was not *the right
thing*. "Ten million people are dead in Zhanjiang. Why don't you order
the Peking duck, asshole. It's the least you could do."

She flagged down their waiter.

Chowdhury cupped his hand over his mouth to conceal a smile.
Samantha's attitude and her sense of humor—the two were often one
and the same. What he appreciated in her and what repelled him about
her had always coexisted, so perhaps their relationship had been doomed
from the start. However, this didn't prevent him from admiring Saman-

tha for the seconds it took her to gain their waiter's attention and order an entire Peking duck. "What do you want?" she asked him.

"Just a wonton soup," Chowdhury answered as he handed the waiter his menu.

The waiter receded toward the kitchen.

"Are you kidding me?" said Samantha. "That's all you're going to—"

Chowdhury cut her off, "Just stop." He could feel his blood rising. "What organization have you got paying you minimum wage while I subsidize your do-gooding with alimony payments? What's it today? Human Rights Watch? Amnesty International? PETA?" She pushed away the table so she could climb from the booth and leave. It stuttered across the floor and jammed Chowdhury in the ribs, which was enough to bring him back to his senses. "Wait," he said sharply between his teeth. "Please," and he made a motion with his hands. "Sit down."

She glanced once at him.

"Please," he repeated, knowing that what he was about to tell her would likely cause her to get up all over again. She sat down, took a breath, and crossed her arms over her chest. "Thank you," he said.

"Why did you need to see me?" she asked. For the first time, Chowdhury wondered about the reasons she had imagined for their meeting: that he'd lost his job; that his mother was sick; that he was sick. Whatever it was, she was carrying the expectation in her rigid posture and the slight frown she wore.

He blurted out what he'd done with their daughter in a single long sentence: "I won't be dropping off Ashni to you on Thursday because she's with my mother in New Delhi staying with my uncle the vice admiral since it isn't safe here after what we did at Zhanjiang and if you or anybody else believes Beijing won't retaliate then you're wrong but we don't know where that retaliation will come but since we struck their homeland it only makes sense that they'll strike our homeland and I'm not going to play Russian roulette with what city Beijing decides to target you can judge me all you want and I don't care because even though I'm an American and even though I work in this administration I am a father first and I have to do what's best for my—sorry—for *our* daughter."

Chowdhury was breathing heavily by the time he finished. He sat very still. Samantha was equally still as she sat across from him. He watched her intently, searching for her reaction, hoping that she wouldn't again push back the table and bolt for the door, rushing home to call a lawyer and drag him in front of a judge as she'd taken every opportunity to do over the course of their bitter divorce.

If Samantha had wanted to get up and leave she was at least momentarily stymied by the arrival of the food. Several long moments passed.

Finally she said, "Eat your soup; it's getting cold." She tucked into her duck, tearing off a leg, peeling back the skin. "I suppose you thought I'd be angry at you about this?"

Chowdhury made a slight, deferential nod.

Samantha began to shake her head; she almost seemed amused. "I'm not angry at you, Sandy. I'm grateful that our daughter has someplace to go. Someplace that's safe. She only has that because of your family, not mine. If anything, I should be thanking you."

Chowdhury wanted to say, *But this means you might not see her for a long time,* and thought better of it. He knew Samantha understood this and was mustering her strength to accept the pain of that conclusion. Chowdhury couldn't help but admire her. And in this admiration, he couldn't help but reflect on one of life's great ironies: namely, how many divorced couples understood each other more completely than many married couples. They had seen each other at their best, when falling in love and constructing a life together; and at their worst, when falling out of love and dismantling that life. Which was particularly excruciating when children were involved.

"You aren't going to do anything?" Chowdhury asked her.

"Like what?"

Chowdhury knew there was nothing that could be done, for either of them. In Europe, in Asia, here, a crisis was playing out, a global re-alignment, or you might just call it a war. Events had been set in motion and they would need to resolve before he or Samantha could determine what to do next. But he felt relieved that the two of them, who hadn't agreed on anything for as long as Chowdhury could remember, had found it within themselves to agree on this one measure to protect their daughter.

Changing the subject, Chowdhury asked Samantha about her mother, who he knew was sick, or at least increasingly frail. Samantha was trav-eling one week a month to care for her. Then Samantha began to ask him about work, nothing sensitive, but more of a genteel checking in, the type of non-substantive professional chitchat that comprised most dinner conversations, at least in quieter times. She asked about "the Navy officer who was at school with us, what's-his-name, do you see him much?"

Chowdhury spoke with some pride about the work he'd done alongside Hendrickson, who had been a far superior student—as if the fact that the two were now colleagues was proof that he had not been the academic basket case his ex-wife discounted him for. "We've all been under a lot of strain," Chowdhury said between slurps of wonton soup. "Hendrickson is pretty close with the one-star admiral who launched the strike on Zhanjiang, Sarah Hunt." Chowdhury glanced over his bowl, to see if Samantha recognized the name, as here and there the papers had reported it. Her expression didn't register anything, so Chowdhury added, "She was one of his students when he taught at the academy. He's worried about her. It's a lot to ask of someone."

"What's a lot to ask?" replied Samantha.

"To have that on your conscience—all those deaths."

Samantha paused from pulling a strip of meat off a thigh bone to point a greasy finger at Chowdhury. "Aren't they on *your* conscience?"

Chowdhury flinched, almost as if the light of a projector had been turned on his face. "Stop it," he said.

"Stop what? It's a fair question, Sandy." And then Chowdhury's ex-wife began to hold forth on his moral complicity not only with respect to Zhanjiang, but also with respect to the entirety of American foreign policy, stretching back to the decades before his birth and before his parents' migration to this country. Chowdhury could easily have formulated counterarguments to the case Samantha laid against him. He could have pointed out that her family, a brood of purebred Texan WASPs, had settled this country centuries before his own, making her the inheritor of every crime from slavery to Manifest Destiny to fracking; but he'd made those arguments before, even though he didn't believe them himself and fundamentally disagreed with her worldview, in which history held the future hostage.

Instead he sat and said nothing, allowing her to say whatever the hell she wanted to say. He had gotten what he'd come for. Their daughter was safe. Samantha wouldn't fight him. This was the only thing that mattered.

They finished their food and the waiter cleared their plates. Chowdhury caught Samantha glancing at her watch. "If you've got somewhere else to be that's fine."

"You don't mind?" she asked.

Chowdhury shook his head. When Samantha reached into her purse, he told her to put her wallet away. "I've got this." She protested, and he added, "Please, I'd like to take you out." She nodded once, thanked him, and also elaborately thanked the staff of the empty restaurant. Then she was gone.

Their waiter presented Chowdhury with a little dish that contained his bill with a pair of fortune cookies on it. Chowdhury stared vacantly at the cookies and thought about what Samantha had said, about his complicity, about how each of us was bound together, from his ex-wife, to his mother, to his daughter, to Hendrickson and Sarah Hunt, and even to this waiter, who would likely only have one table to serve for the entire night.

"Is there anything else I can get you?" the waiter asked.

"Yes, actually," said Chowdhury. "I'd like to place an order to go."

He was returning to an empty apartment and ordered enough food to last him several days—another Peking duck, General Tso's chicken, mixed fried rice, the works. And as he added to his heaping order, the waiter's subdued expression raised itself into a smile. While the kitchen got to work, Chowdhury sat there waiting, either end of his fortune cookie pinched between his fingers. He then broke the cookie apart and ate it piece by piece, avoiding the fortune inside, which he didn't read but instead tore compulsively into little pieces.

His food was soon ready. The waiter brought out four bags, saying, "Thank you very much," as he bowed slightly and set them on the table.

Chowdhury nodded. He looked once more around the empty restaurant before replying, "It's the very least I could do." He lifted the bags and headed for the door. On the table all that remained was the little pile of shredded paper for the waiter to brush away.

Γ

10:32 July 06, 2034 (GMT+8)
South China Sea

The dream changed a little each time. Hunt would be back in Yokosuka, standing on the dock, all of her ships pulling in at once—the *John Paul Jones*, the *Chung-Hoon*, the *Carl Levin*. What altered was how many more ships kept showing up. Now the scuttled *Ford* and *Miller* arrived each night. So, too, did the ships from the South Sea Fleet sunk at anchor in Zhanjiang, the carrier *Liaoning*, the destroyers *Hefei*, *Lanzhou*, *Wuhan*, *Haikou*, as well as a blur of smaller ships—frigates and corvettes too numerous to count. Their dozens of gangplanks would fall, the boatswains would pipe their calls, and the crews—American and Chinese alike—would spill onto the dock.

Hunt would be there to meet them. In her dream she is always searching for familiar faces, people like Morris, and like her father. But ever since she gave the order for Zhanjiang, she hasn't been able to find him on the dock. There are too many ships pulling in at once. She asks for help, but the disembarking crews ignore her or can't see her—Hunt can't say which. Are they ghosts? Or is she?

She remembers what her father told her, the first time she had the dream. She remembers how young he appeared, and the way he took her by the arm and said, "You don't have to do this."

But it had been done.

The stream of ships, disembarking their thousands—they were the evidence.

Her father had once said to her that if you could snap your fingers and bring all of the dead sailors in the Mediterranean Sea to the surface, you'd be able to walk from the Strait of Gibraltar to the Port of Haifa stepping on the backs of sailors—Greeks, Romans, Carthaginians, Britons, Germans, French, Arabs, and on and on. War at sea began in the Mediterranean, but it might end here, in the South China Sea. Already, in one strike, Sarah Hunt had killed more people than had died across the millennia in the distant Mediterranean.

Among the thickening mass of ghosts, she can't find her father. She's calling out for him. But her voice doesn't carry far enough. And even if it did, what could he tell her?

Nothing—there is nothing he can say to make this crowd disappear so that it could be only the two of them standing on the dock. But she wants to find him, nevertheless. She remembers how he used to take her by the hand and squeeze three times and then she would squeeze four times back. And if she could just feel his hand in hers that might be enough . . . enough to bring back the dead? To forget what she'd done? To be forgiven? Enough for what?

Night after night she lay in her bed, not quite asleep but not quite awake, asking herself that question.

It was after one such night that Hunt had an in-brief scheduled with a new pilot who'd arrived on the *Enterprise*. When she saw who he was, she'd requested this in-briefing. She knew his history, how the Iranians had taken him down over Bandar Abbas in an F-35; knew that he'd spent some weeks in captivity, and that he'd pulled strings—a whole bunch of strings—to receive orders to the *Enterprise*, specifically to the one Hornet squadron that she had so controversially modified. She also knew, as she sat at her desk studying his personnel file, that Major Chris "Wedge" Mitchell, by either luck or his own design, would be the seniormost pilot in that squadron, making him the de facto commanding officer.

He stood in front of her desk, throwing out his chest in salute, his body magnificently still and his thumbs pinned to the seam of his flight suit, as he held the position of attention. Hunt let him stand there for a moment while she paged through not only his file but also a few media clippings her chief of staff had included, ones that spoke to his family history, those generations of Mitchells who'd flown fighters for the Marines. When she glanced up, she couldn't help but notice that his attention was fixed on the photograph hanging on the wall behind her; it was of the *John Paul Jones*, the *Chung-Hoon*, and the *Carl Levin*, sailing in a column. It had been taken less than six months ago, a fact she struggled to comprehend. She wondered if, perhaps, Wedge was struggling to comprehend the same.

"At ease, Major Mitchell," she said, shutting his file and welcoming him aboard the *Enterprise*. She dispensed some pleasantries, asking how his flight out had been and whether he was comfortable in his assigned quarters, to which he replied that everything was fine. Hunt then got to the point. "No doubt you're aware that I fired your predecessor."

Wedge was aware.

"He didn't agree with certain of my directives," she added. "I assume we're not going to have the same problem." Before Wedge could answer, Hunt explained how every vulnerable system had been stripped from the cockpits of his Hornets. "Even after your downing at Bandar Abbas and our defeat at Mischief Reef, there's still a whole swath of officers in our military who cling to a cult of technology. They cannot bring themselves to acknowledge that an overreliance on these systems has crippled us. They cannot imagine how this might ultimately be the source of our recent defeats." Hunt then described the situation as she saw it, a dire picture in which America's strike on Zhanjiang made a counterstrike on the continental United States inevitable. "An old friend of mine from the academy is on the White House staff. He insists that

Beijing will back down, that we've made our point and enforced our red line. He's as smart as they come . . . and he's been wrong about most things lately, to include this." And then she looked at Wedge hard and grim, as if she could see every step that was to come, one following another, events progressing like a dark figure stalking a narrow corridor toward an inevitable door. "They're going to strike at least two US cities. That'll be their escalation. We hit one. They'll hit two. Then we'll have to choose whether or not to de-escalate. We won't, of course. We'll strike back, at least three cities. We won't use strategic nukes; that's doomsday stuff, not practical. We'll keep the nukes tactical. Which means they'll have to come off a carrier. That means you."

A silence followed as she allowed this vision of hers to coalesce between them. Hunt was watching Wedge, closely observing his reaction to the events she'd described.

Slowly, his smile revealed itself.

"Does some part of this amuse you?"

The smile vanished. "No, ma'am."

"Then what's with the smile?"

"Nothing." He appeared to be talking to the corners of the room. "Just tension, I guess."

But she didn't believe him. For a certain type of pilot, flying by the seat of your pants on a raid deep into enemy territory held an allure. Romance always attended a particularly daring mission. It also attended a suicide mission. And Hunt needed someone who would regard it as the former instead of the latter. Hunt also needed someone who thought they could make it back—even if they never did. Because a pilot determined to survive would stand a better chance of success.

Hunt began to review with Wedge some of the modifications made to the avionics in his Hornets, but she didn't get far before he interrupted her, explaining that he'd already made an inspection of the aircraft.

"When?"

"The night I got here," he answered. "I met your communications senior chief, Quint. Nice guy. I was still on West Coast time, so I stayed up to walk around the hangar. The planes look good, ma'am."

She leaned back in her chair, pleased that he thought so. For what she suspected would not be the last time, she allowed herself to feel a measure of affection for Wedge. She also felt sympathy. A great deal would be asked of him. She thought of her own sleeplessness. "If you're having trouble getting rest, I can have the ship's doctor prescribe you something."

Wedge shook his head. "That won't be necessary, ma'am. It's never really been a problem for me. Plus, out here, I sleep like a baby." He popped back to attention, then disappeared from her office, into the bowels of the ship.

Γ

14:27 July 06, 2034 (GMT+8)
Shenzhen

The frail little man shuffled along the crest of the perfectly manicured grass hill, a golf club choked in his grip, the afternoon sun framing his silhouette. The same hospitality associate who'd taken Lin Bao to his junior suite now drove him toward the hill. Although Lin Bao had never met this man, he soon recognized him as Zhao Leji, member of the Politburo Standing Committee, secretary of the Central Commission for Discipline Inspection—the CCDI.

Those four letters, and the little man who embodied them—Lin Bao had feared both his entire professional life.

His golf cart arrived on the crest of the hill right as Zhao Leji was entering his backswing. Lin Bao sat completely still. If he had any lingering belief that the hospitality associate wasn't involved with the communist party and its internal security apparatus, if he held on to a hope that she was simply a young woman from the provinces who'd come to Shenzhen and found a good job at Mission Hills, it was dispelled when Lin Bao noticed how she, too, sat completely still, equally fearful of distracting Zhao Leji.

Now, at the apex of his swing, the head of Zhao Leji's club floated in the air, his entire body conforming to this upward articulation. With a *swoosh*, the club made a clean decapitation of the ball from its tee, his shot sailing out toward the horizon, where it disappeared into the mix of sun and afternoon smog. As Zhao Leji slid his club back into his bag, he noticed Lin Bao.

"Not bad for an old man," said Zhao Leji, hoisting his clubs onto his shoulder. He would walk to the next hole, preferring the exercise, while his security detail trailed behind in a squadron of golf carts. He motioned for Lin Bao to join him, and to grab a set of clubs off the back of one of the carts. As Lin Bao followed after Zhao Leji, he noticed that the hospitality associate would not look at him, as if she suspected Lin Bao was about to meet a fate she had long feared for herself.

It was soon only the two of them, Lin Bao and Zhao Leji, hoofing it across the golf course, each burdened by their bag of clubs. Eventually, Zhao Leji began to talk. "These days, hiking across a golf course is the closest I get to honest labor. . . ." He was breathing heavily. "I began my career during Mao's Cultural Revolution, digging trenches on a commune. . . . You do the work yourself. . . . There is satisfaction in that. . . . You grew up in America, yes?" When he turned to face Lin Bao, Zhao Leji's eyes became like tunnels. "That makes us very different, doesn't it. Take our game of golf, for instance. Americans like to ride around in a cart and play with a caddy. When they take their caddy's advice and win, they claim the win as their own. When they take that advice and lose, they blame their caddy. . . . It's never good to be the caddy."

They arrived at the next hole, a par-4.

Zhao Leji took his swing. It landed on the fairway.

Lin Bao took his swing. It landed in the trees.

Zhao Leji began to laugh. "Go on, my young friend. Try again." Lin Bao said that it was all right, he didn't need a second chance, he didn't want to cheat. But Zhao Leji would hear nothing of it. "It's not cheating," he insisted, "if I make the rules."

Lin Bao switched clubs.

He put his second shot on the fairway, a bit behind Zhao Leji's, and as they walked to their balls, Zhao Leji resumed their conversation. "Some might say that after what happened at Zhanjiang, it's frivolous for a man in my position to be out playing golf. But it's important for our people to know that life goes on, that there is steady leadership at the helm, particularly in light of what might be coming next. If our intelligence is correct—and I suspect that it is—the Americans will have three carrier battle groups in position to blockade our coastline within the next two weeks. You've worked very closely with Minister Chiang, but I feel that I must let you know that he's expressed some reservations as to your competence. He believes that you might have given him, and by that virtue the Politburo Standing Committee, bad advice with regard to American intentions. Your mother was American, correct? Minister

Chiang believes that your affinity for her country might have clouded your judgment when advising him."

The two gazed out at the next hole. The oblong fairway extended in front of them for almost two hundred yards. Then it cut sharply to the left, running between a copse of trees and a water obstacle. After reading the ground, Lin Bao concluded that if he hit too short, he'd wind up in the trees—which was recoverable. However, if he hit too long, he'd wind up in the water—which was not.

Zhao Leji stepped to the tee with a 3-wood.

Lin Bao stood behind him with a 2-iron.

As Zhao Leji sunk his tee into the green, he commented on Lin Bao's club selection, noting that a 2-iron wouldn't give him enough range. "It seems we've looked at the same problem and reached a different set of solutions," he said.

Lin Bao averted his eyes to avoid any outward disagreement with Zhao Leji. But if he thought to exchange his 2-iron for a 3-wood, something within Lin Bao wouldn't allow it; perhaps it was his pride, or dignity, or willfulness. Whatever it was, the defiance he felt when confronted by someone more powerful was familiar. He'd felt it as a naval cadet when older boys had teased him about his American heritage, or when he'd first been passed over for command of the *Zheng He* in favor of Ma Qiang, and now, staring at his 2-iron, he even felt that defiance when questioned by a man who with a single word could have a dark-suited thug put a bullet in his head. And so, Lin Bao explained, "A 3-wood is going to give you too much range. If you overplay, you're going to wind up in the water. There's no recovery then. If you underplay and wind up in the trees, at least you'll be in a better position for your next shot instead of all the way back here on the tee. When the range falls between two clubs, it's a better strategy to select the less ambitious choice."

The old man nodded once, planted his feet firmly on the ground, and, with his 3-wood gripped tightly, reached into his backswing. His ball exploded off its tee, the sound alone signaling a perfect connection, which arced ever higher. When its trajectory reached its apex, it became apparent that Lin Bao was right. The 3-wood was too powerful of a club.

Zhao Leji's ball sailed into the water with a *plunk.*

He bent over, picked up his tee, and then faced Lin Bao, who searched for any expression of disapproval or even disappointment in the old man. There was none; he simply made way for Lin Bao, who sunk his tee into the stubby grass. The thought did occur to him that he could angle his shot into the rough. He imagined that someone more obsequious—someone like Minister Chiang—might throw his game in favor of a senior official like Zhao Leji. But Lin Bao had only risen as far as he had because he'd never indulged the weaknesses of a superior, even when that superior could harm his career or—as was the case with Zhao Leji—end his life.

His 2-iron connected with the ball.

Its trajectory was low and fast, rocketing toward the bend in the fairway. His shot was gaining altitude, but it wasn't certain that it would be enough to clear the trees. It was like watching an overburdened aircraft attempt to climb above a particularly treacherous mountain face. Lin Bao found himself gesturing with his hands, *up, up, up.* And then he noticed that Zhao Leji was doing the same; it was as if the old man wanted to be proven wrong. When the ball clipped the top of the trees, it kept going, landing on the fairway right as a few agitated birds took flight from the topmost branches.

"Looks like I'm one stroke behind," said Zhao Leji through a broad smile. Then the old man stepped over to his golf bag and replaced his 3-wood with a 2-iron.

They spent the better part of the afternoon on the course. That would be the only hole Lin Bao won against Zhao Leji. Though Lin Bao played his best, the old man was a far superior golfer, and it soon became obvious how remarkable it was that Lin Bao had outfoxed him on even a single hole. While they made their circuit around the course, the conversation turned to Lin Bao's duties and "their natural evolution," as Zhao Leji put it. He would no longer report directly to Minister Chiang. The disaster at Zhanjiang had forced the Politburo Standing Committee to "reorganize the military command structure," a statement that Lin Bao recognized for the disciplinary euphemism it was. Zhao Leji then reminded Lin Bao that the People's Republic was "on death ground," in an echo of the language used by Minister Chiang, while not attributing that language to him or his subsequent conclusion: "We must fight." When it came to the details of that fight, Zhao Leji was prepared only to say, "We must take commensurate action to the Americans' strike at Zhanjiang."

Lin Bao had felt tempted to remind Zhao Leji of the lesson from only moments ago: when selecting between two nearly equal courses of action it was always best to choose the least ambitious, lest you overplay. But correcting the secretary of the Central Commission for Discipline Inspection on his golf game was one matter; correcting him on affairs of state was quite another. Lin Bao possessed enough gumption for the former but not yet the latter.

If he didn't speak up against a potential nuclear strike on the United States, he nearly spoke up when Zhao Leji explained what he had planned next for him.

"Some people within the party hold you responsible along with

Minister Chiang for Zhanjiang. I wasn't sure myself until today. My belief is that you advised him as best you could. Perhaps, if he'd kept you closer, we might have avoided that tragedy—provided he would've listened to you, which I also doubt. From this point forward, I have taken on his responsibilities in the Defense Ministry. And I will need sound advice . . . a caddy, as it were." And he smiled at Lin Bao. "Someone to provide an alternate viewpoint. So, you won't be returning to your carrier. You'll return to Beijing instead, to serve as my deputy within the ministry."

Zhao Leji flagged down a member of his security detail, who appeared swiftly alongside them in a golf cart. The wily old man surely knew that the loss of Lin Bao's command would be a demoralizing blow, which is why he didn't wait for his reaction. As Lin Bao climbed next to the driver, Zhao Leji said his goodbyes, telling Lin Bao only, "I will see you in Beijing before long." He turned to study the fairway and began to select the next club from his bag.

When Lin Bao arrived at reception, the hospitality associate seemed almost surprised to see him again. The member of Zhao Leji's security detail spoke a few words to her and she escorted Lin Bao back to his room. As she had checked him into Mission Hills, Lin Bao now asked what he would need to do in order to check out. She seemed confused, saying only, "I'll look into that," as if she were unfamiliar with the procedure herself and Lin Bao was the first person she had ever needed to check out. When she left him at his door, she asked if he required anything else. Lin Bao reminded her about his dry cleaning, the uniform he'd sent out that morning. He couldn't make the return trip in his golf clothes. The young woman again seemed unsure and repeated, "I'll look into that."

While Lin Bao packed up his few possessions in a shapeless bag, his mind began to wander. Despite Zhao Leji's obvious frustration with Minister Chiang, he and the Politburo Standing Committee agreed with Chiang's assessment of the situation. An American blockade off their coast was unacceptable. A counterstrike was the only option. But what form would that counterstrike take? Lin Bao understood that he would be required to have an opinion on the matter as he advised Zhao Leji. And like Minister Chiang, he would be held accountable for that opinion if it proved incorrect. The idea unsettled Lin Bao. He would be in Beijing soon and perhaps he would seek out Minister Chiang. Perhaps his old boss could quietly advise him, even if he had fallen out of favor with the Politburo Standing Committee and Zhao Leji. Perhaps Chiang could help him navigate his new role among these powerful and dangerous men.

A knock at the door interrupted these thoughts.

A young valet stood in the threshold. "This is the dry cleaning I have for your room."

Lin Bao thanked him and took the hangers covered in transparent plastic. He laid them on the bed next to his bag. As he tore off the plastic, he noticed that the first uniform seemed a larger size than what he wore. It was wider in the stomach. The sleeves extended almost to the jacket's hemline. When he read the embroidered name tape sewn above the breast pocket, it wasn't his own—but it was familiar, nevertheless.

It read, *Chiang.*

What a coincidence, thought Lin Bao—but he only thought this for a moment. He suddenly felt utterly alone. He wouldn't have his old boss to rely on for advice when he returned to Beijing. It was no coincidence that he and Minister Chiang had stayed in the same room. Nor was it a mistake that Minister Chiang's uniform had been left behind.

┌

By any objective measure Farshad had witnessed a spectacular success. His Russian naval counterparts had in a two-week period supported a land campaign conquering several hundred square miles, thus fulfilling a multigenerational strategic imperative: Russia now had direct overland access to its Baltic ports. Atrophied bodies of international governance and alliance, the United Nations and NATO, decried this "aggression," but Farshad suspected that woven between their declamations was grudging respect. Decades of miscalculation in Washington and Beijing had sown discord into the world order; all the Russians had done was reap the harvest. That other nations—namely Farshad's own—would try to reap a similar harvest in other locales seemed unsurprising. Equally unsurprising was that his countrymen would bungle it.

While Farshad was immersed in Russia's advance into Polish territory, pleased to have found himself useful to naval commanders supporting a ground invasion, a hawkish faction of the Revolutionary Guards decided it was time for Iran to assert control of the long-contested Strait of Hormuz. The Revolutionary Guards, using their smaller fleet of speedboats, had brashly chosen to seize the first large international ship making the transit, a freighter owned by TATA NYK, the company's name being an alphabet soup of meaningless letters that proved relevant to Farshad in only one way: the ship was Indian.

It was a particularly foolish choice for the Revolutionary Guards, who'd acted without the express approval of the chief of staff of the Armed Forces, Major General Bagheri, although his detractors speculated he'd known all along. Now Farshad's government was in the unenviable position of having to de-escalate tensions while also not losing face or delegitimizing its long-running claim over the strait. In short, what General Bagheri needed was someone who had ties to both the Revolutionary Guards and to the regular military. Someone who could speak credibly for both. And who was a naval officer. Farshad knew, before the message ever arrived for him from Tehran, that he was the single person who fit this description.

He had flown commercial out of Moscow direct to New Delhi. This wasn't because the Russian or Iranian military lacked the resources to fly him officially, but because neither his government nor the Indians had officially acknowledged they were willing to negotiate. He would, ostensibly, be traveling to New Delhi as a private citizen. Farshad's mission was a delicate one. He understood that India's old adversary, Pakistan, would be more than willing to aid his country if asked, and he also understood that the Indians could potentially throw their weight behind the Americans if pushed too far. The slightest misstep by either party could lead to a further escalation of what was already a global conflict, or, put another way, a world war.

Crammed into a center seat on his Aeroflot Airbus A330, he followed his flight's progress. On the monitor affixed to the seatback in front of him, an icon of their plane left a tiny trail of bread crumbs across the globe. As he considered the map, Farshad reflected on how quickly tensions had escalated between the Americans and Chinese, two nations, unlike his own, that had a major stake in preserving the world order. From the *Wén Rui* incident, to the succession of naval battles fought between the US and Chinese fleets, to the invasion of Taiwan and the US nuclear strike on Zhanjiang, so much of what had occurred since March defied the logic of both nations' interests.

Unless that logic had changed.

No one—neither politicians nor pundits—had yet to refer to this conflict as the Third World War. Farshad wondered if India's involvement, or perhaps even Pakistan's, would be enough to bestow on this crisis that grim name, with its apocalyptic connotations. Farshad doubted it.

The involvement of other nations wasn't what would make this a Third World War. It would take something else. . . .

At Zhanjiang the Americans had used a nuclear weapon, but it was tactical, its payload and the fallout both manageable and imaginable—the equivalent of a single, devastating natural disaster. No nation—America, China, or otherwise—had yet to dip into its arsenal of strategic nuclear weapons. The doomsday weapons.

Farshad's ears popped.

The engines on the Airbus A330 groaned as they hurried their descent.

The plane landed and Farshad passed through immigration without incident. He had brought only one carry-on bag and within minutes was standing in the overcrowded arrivals hall, surrounded by the joyful embraces of travelers reunited with their loved ones. However, no one was there to meet him. His instructions from General Bagheri's staff hadn't extended beyond this point. He'd been assured that his Indian counterpart would find him here. He sat at a crowded Starbucks without ordering. His mind wandered. Watching the crowd, he began to think of the many names the people in it had for one another—whether it be *mother, father, son, daughter,* or simply *friend*—and how that might all vanish in an instant, in a flash, because of that single, other obliterating name we give to one another: *enemy.*

Interrupting Farshad's thoughts, a stranger asked if he could sit in the empty seat at his table. Farshad gestured with his hand and the stranger, a man who was perhaps a decade older, joined him. Farshad continued to consider the crowd.

The stranger asked if he was waiting for someone. Farshad said that he was.

"Who?" asked the stranger.

Farshad considered him for a moment. "A friend, I guess."

The man extended his hand, introducing himself. "I am Vice Admiral Anand Patel, a friend."

⌐

22:46 July 19, 2034 (GMT+5:30)
New Delhi

Chowdhury was returning late to the US embassy. Diplomatic tensions being what they were, he was obliged to sleep there. His mother, however, had determined that it would be best if she and his daughter stayed with Chowdhury's uncle. Though his days had been busy, Chowdhury committed himself to having dinner every night with Ashni. He had been in New Delhi for almost a week and the routine of early mornings, full days, and late-night returns to the embassy from his uncle's house east of the Yamuna River was quickly wearing him out. He dozed in the back of the cab, remembering the last week as though it were a dream while he skirted Nehru Park. Within hours of the Iranians' claiming autonomous control of the Strait of Hormuz and seizing the tanker owned by TATA NYK, Trent Wisecarver had called Chowdhury into his office and told him he would be "heading back to New Delhi."

The way Wisecarver had said "back" hadn't sat well with Chowdhury. Amid this conflict, a resurgent nativism was beginning to possess the American psyche, as it had in other conflicts, a phenomenon Chowdhury had witnessed that night with Samantha at the empty City Lights restaurant. Perhaps Wisecarver hadn't meant anything by it; perhaps when he said "back" he was referring to his prior mission to New Delhi to retrieve the downed Marine pilot. But Chowdhury couldn't shake his suspicions.

After the strike on Zhanjiang, Wisecarver had cleaned house within the national security staff. The country, unlike in generations past, had failed to come together when confronted by the specter of a world war, even a nuclear one. A strike against the American homeland seemed inevitable, though no one could know where or in what shape it would manifest—a dirty bomb planted by a sleeper cell, a warhead on the tip of a ballistic missile, or perhaps both? Decades of partisan division had taken their toll, and the administration was under fire from all sides, from the hawks who believed the tactical nuclear strike hadn't gone far enough to the doves who believed America had abdicated its moral authority by employing such weapons. To respond to whatever came next, Wisecarver needed true loyalists. Which was to say he needed people who owed their positions in the administration not to their competencies, but to him alone. And so Chowdhury had been quietly sent "back" to New Delhi to deal with the new crisis in the Strait of Hormuz.

When Chowdhury arrived at the embassy, he checked his email a last time before heading to bed and saw that he had a message from another colleague who had been banished in Wisecarver's putsch, Rear Admiral John Hendrickson: Bunt.

The two had left Washington at about the same time, though Hendrickson's journey had been longer and more treacherous, and his mission equally complex. It was, in its way, also a diplomatic mission. Sarah Hunt, his "old friend and colleague" (this was how Hendrickson always referred to her), had at Zhanjiang launched the first nuclear strike in almost a century. On her orders millions had been killed. The strain must've been enormous. With the leadership in the White House bracing for the Chinese response to Zhanjiang, every commander in the field needed to be ready to deliver a swift counterpunch. Hesitation could be disastrous. Which was why Hendrickson was being sent to check on Hunt, to assess her state of mind. The fuzzy language Wisecarver had given him was "augment her command."

The message Chowdhury had in his in-box from Hendrickson read simply, *Arrived on* Enterprise. *Hope you're well. More soon.—Bunt.* Chowdhury and Hendrickson had made an arrangement when they'd both left Washington at the behest of Wisecarver, to help each other navigate the increasingly internecine politics of the administration they served. Chowdhury doubted their alliance would amount to much. But he needed all the friends he could muster. Hendrickson did too.

As he finished scrolling through his work emails, Chowdhury's cell phone pinged with a fresh text message. It was from his uncle:

Come tomorrow 08:00 for breakfast. Have a new friend you should meet.

20:03 July 19, 2034 (GMT+8)
South China Sea

Hunt couldn't believe it until she held the flight manifest in her hand. How had life conspired to deliver him here, now? His name on the manifest: *Hendrickson, J. T.* It appeared in the same order as when it had headed their softball team roster decades before at Annapolis. She checked her watch. From her stateroom she could hear flight deck operations underway. The Death Rattlers had been constantly in the air. Hunt had given Major Mitchell top priority to qualify his pilots on their low-tech avionics. At all hours, she could hear the fiery rumble and metallic screech of their Hornets launching and recovering. Now came an interruption, the hollow, raspy vibrations of a turboprop engine, a V-22 Osprey—the resupply flight with Hendrickson aboard.

Ten minutes or so passed and then with a knock at Hunt's door a junior sailor announced, "Admiral Hendrickson to see you, ma'am." When Hendrickson came in, he glumly stood there, his khaki uniform carrying the creases of the many layovers he'd had to endure as he leapfrogged from one base to another on his way out to sea. Dispensing with the naval courtesies, Hendrickson slumped into the chair opposite her desk, cradled his chin in his palm, and said only, "I want you to know that coming out here wasn't my idea."

"Why are you out here, then?" she asked.

The office rattled slightly as another Hornet catapulted off the flight deck.

Hendrickson, ever the company man, regurgitated the language Wisecarver had offered him.

"Augmenting my command?" Hunt replied, throwing back his words. "What the hell does that mean? Have you cleared this with INDOPACOM? Though, I guess respecting protocol has never been your thing." She was angry, and she felt she had every right to be angry. No one had listened to her, not from the start. Hendrickson and his cronies on the national security staff had been so certain of their superiority, of their ability to take on any threat, and that overconfidence had backed them into this corner, cutting squares in the South China Sea, waiting for the imminent strike against their homeland.

"Admiral Johnstone at INDOPACOM is well aware of my visit," answered Hendrickson. "You can call him on the redline if you want. I stopped in Honolulu and briefed him on my way out here—"

Another Hornet roared as it was catapulted off the flight deck.

"People are worried about you, Sarah." Hendrickson softened his tone. He couldn't manage to look at her as he said this, so he stared at his hands, fingering the obnoxiously large Annapolis class ring he still insisted on wearing. "You've been through a lot . . . been asked to take on a lot . . . emotionally." *Emotionally? Fuck him.* Was he referring to events since her command of the *John Paul Jones* and her central role in the strike against Zhanjiang? Or was he going beyond that, to her days at Annapolis? To what she'd given up—namely, a family, a life, him—so that they could sit here together these many years later, two admirals on the bridge of a US warship. She'd never know. And he'd never say. But she listened to him regardless. "We all realize what's coming. And it seems the *Enterprise* will be in the middle of our response. You shouldn't have to go through it alone. I am here . . ." And she hoped for a moment he'd leave it at that, a personal statement that affirmed the history between them, except he couldn't and so added, ". . . to augment your command."

Their conversation shifted to the overall readiness of the *Enterprise* and its ability to inflict a counterstrike. So long as the Chinese didn't engage with strategic nuclear weapons, the appropriate response would be a multipronged attack on their mainland with tactical nukes. Hunt had concluded that her one squadron of Hornets, the Death Rattlers, would be the most effective. She explained to Hendrickson the reworked avionics system, and her belief that a strike package should consist of the squadron's nine planes distributed over three target sets: three flights composed of three aircraft each. The squadron's new command-ing officer, Major Chris "Wedge" Mitchell, had been tirelessly preparing his pilots for such a mission.

Hendrickson said, "I thought it was ten aircraft to a Marine Hornet squadron?"

"Wedge lost one aircraft four days ago. We've had to modify their targeting computers so that the bomb release is now done manually. We were testing them at sea with live ordnance. One of the pilots had a bomb get stuck, so it was dangling from his wing off its ejector rack. He couldn't land like that, so he bailed out and put his plane into the drink. These pilots are young; they're not used to navigating with nothing but a compass and flight chart. He had called in his position and we di-verted there. We circled for an entire day, never found him. Maybe someone else picked him up—we were close to the mainland. . . . You can always hope."

After a long silence, Hendrickson cocked his head skeptically. "'Wedge?' What the hell kind of a call sign is that, anyway?"

09:37 July 20, 2034 (GMT+8)
Beijing

His wife and daughter were happy to see him, but home felt unreal to Lin Bao. He was living in the shadow of what was to come.

The *Zheng He* had already gone dark when Lin Bao returned to Beijing. He monitored it daily from the Defense Ministry as it made creeping progress toward the West Coast of the United States, its com-plement of stealth technology fully employed, its communications un-der a blackout. Lin Bao, better than anyone, understood the capabilities of that battle group. All they needed was a target set, which the ministry would transmit to Lin Bao's replacement, a younger admiral of high competence, once the *Zheng He* was in position. Although Minister Chiang hadn't lived to see his plan's implementation, Lin Bao recognized the plan when it came across his desk. It arrived preapproved by the Politburo Standing Committee in a single manila folder. Lin Bao took it into the secure conference room in the bowels of the ministry, the same conference room where Minister Chiang had once triumphantly received him with heaping bowls of M&M's. Lin Bao missed the doughy old bureaucrat; he missed his exuberant scheming and his odd sense of humor. Perhaps what Lin Bao missed most of all, as he tucked into Minister Chiang's old armchair at the head of the conference table, was his boss's company, the assurance that he wasn't engaged in this madness alone.

But he was, at this moment, very much alone, by design.

Although the Politburo Standing Committee had approved the plan Lin Bao was about to put into action, he would be the senior-most officer tasked with its execution—the only person in the room. All responsibility fell on him.

Tensely, he collected himself and opened the folder.

It contained two envelopes. The two target sets.

One or another of the junior staffers had left a letter opener on the table for him. He slid the dull blade into the first and then the second envelope. Inside each were four paper-clipped pages, exhaustively stamped, certified, and serialized. On the top was a signature line, confirming receipt. He wrote his name, the only actual name that would appear on any of these documents. Then he skimmed over the authorizations, a labyrinth of anodyne operational language with whole passages that he himself had drafted on behalf of Minister Chiang.

Every detail was accounted for.

Which was to say with Lin Bao's signature alone on the document, he was accountable for every detail: from the selection of the launch platform (whether it be surface-based, submarine-based, or aircraft-based), to the loading of the fissile material, to the readiness of the crews, to the accurate delivery onto the targets—

The targets . . .

For Lin Bao, this was the single unknown aspect of the plan. He imagined that Zhao Leji had chosen them himself. After their exchange on the golf course, Lin Bao half expected the old man to consult him as to their selection, to allow him again to assume the role of caddy. If given that chance, Lin Bao would've advised him not to overplay. A strike against the largest US cities—such as Los Angeles, or New York—would be too ambitious, the equivalent of choosing the 3-wood that day on the course. It should be two US cities for Zhanjiang, so an escalation. A parity should exist in the choice. Their South Sea Fleet had been based at Zhanjiang, so a similar military target would be appropriate, at least for one of the cities. The other target should be more industrial. Lin Bao thought of the advice he would have given had he been asked. However, Zhao Leji hadn't needed another advisor. What he'd really needed was a receptacle for blame if his plans unwound.

A fall guy.

A patsy.

Which is what Lin Bao had been reduced to. In that moment, he made himself a promise: This would be the last order he ever followed. He would retire from the Navy.

But for now, he had a job to do.

He flipped to the final page of each document, where he found the coordinates that would serve as ground zero:

32.7157° N, 117.1611° W
29.3013° N, 94.7977° W

He plotted the first on a chart: *San Diego*. Then the second: *Galveston*.

⌐

08:17 July 20, 2034 (GMT+5:30)
New Delhi

Traffic in the city didn't follow any logical pattern, or at least none that Chowdhury could decipher. During rush hour he'd find the roads empty and during the laziest parts of the day he'd find the roads congested to a standstill. He struggled to arrive at appointments on time. He would either show up awkwardly early, or woefully late. As was the case now, at nearly twenty past eight in the morning, as he struggled to navigate his way to his uncle's house for a breakfast appointment that the vice admiral, using his military vernacular, had set for 08:00.

Business with his uncle needed to remain "unofficial": retired Vice Admiral Patel didn't technically represent his government in any formal capacity, which was why Chowdhury found himself crossing to the east bank of the Yamuna in the back of a taxi as opposed to an embassy car. Chowdhury couldn't deny that his mother and daughter were safer now, staying with his uncle. But this placed him in an increasingly conflicted position, with the interests of his country not necessarily aligning with the interests of his family. So he reflected as he approached his uncle's home for the 08:00 breakfast that was now closer to 09:00. And if Chowdhury was tardy to this meeting, he was equally tardy when it came to figuring a solution to his conflicted interests. However, he accepted that certain things, like the traffic, moved with a logic all their own.

When his uncle greeted him at the door, he didn't mention the delay, and even explained that "his guest" had also arrived late, though not quite as late as his nephew. The house was empty aside from the three of them. At his uncle's behest Ashni had enrolled in the local primary school, a decision Chowdhury hadn't felt certain of but that his mother supported, leading to perhaps the first time in decades the two long-estranged siblings had agreed on anything. Chowdhury was glad that at this moment he wouldn't need to face his mother or daughter as his uncle escorted him into the den.

The room was furnished with a love seat, a wing chair, a bookshelf, and a television in the corner on whose screen a troupe of colorfully attired dancers gesticulated about a stage in what looked like the climactic third act of some Bollywood production. A man stood waiting in the center of the room. Before Chowdhury could catch his name, he noticed that he had only three fingers on his right hand. They shook. Chowdhury was introduced as "my nephew, Sandeep, who works for the American government," while his uncle introduced his guest as "Qassem, a Persian friend."

A slight duplicity existed in Patel's introduction, one which Chowdhury didn't mind but of which he was certainly aware. His uncle evidently assumed that Chowdhury knew nothing of this Iranian officer. Chowdhury knew a great deal. He had read Major Mitchell's debriefing from his captivity in Bandar Abbas, which included—among other details—a lengthy description of the three-fingered Iranian brigadier who'd beaten him senseless. What Chowdhury didn't understand was how Farshad, a former senior-level officer in the Revolutionary Guards Quds Force, had wound up here, on a somewhat quixotic diplomatic mission to negotiate the release of an Indian tanker.

The three of them sat in the den, with Patel strategically placed in the wing chair while Farshad and Chowdhury were forced to share the love seat, a seating arrangement that reminded Chowdhury of the interminable sessions he'd spent in marriage counseling years before. Farshad and Chowdhury had begun to speak of their nations' current dispute with the same low-level acrimony of one of those matrimonial sessions.

It was, said Chowdhury, unacceptable for the Iranians to claim control over the Strait of Hormuz. The consequences to the global economy, which had already suffered enormously due to the current Sino-American War and now teetered on the edge of a depression, would be devastating, to say nothing of the effects on Iran, which would surely suffer further censure and perhaps renewed sanctions, similar to what they'd endured two decades before during their failed nuclear bid.

At the mention of the sanctions, Farshad clenched his hands into fists. His face reddened. No doubt Farshad's career, in Iraq, in Afghanistan, in Palestine and Syria, and wherever else he'd fought over the past thirty years, had been inextricably linked to the West's punitive measures against his country, making Chowdhury's evocation of sanctions far more personal than a policy disagreement between two nations. And knowing how Farshad had lost control of himself during his interrogation of Major Mitchell, Chowdhury now wondered if he might be the victim of a similar episode. Might he find himself battered to unconsciousness in his uncle's den by this Iranian?

However, Farshad took a breath. His body language began to change. His shoulders relaxed. His fists opened. His complexion unreddened. Then, in his calmest voice, Farshad said, "I wouldn't be here if my nation didn't believe a solution existed to our current problem."

Chowdhury, seizing upon this, nodded agreement. "We feel the same way. Neither of our countries wish to see a further spread of hostilities. I believe I also speak for our Indian allies when I say that they don't wish to be brought into this conflict either. They've stayed out of our dispute with Beijing, as have our other allies like the Japanese, and it would be foolish for this conflict to take on an even broader dimension due to a"—Chowdhury paused a beat, searching for the correct word—"miscalculation."

The miscalculation, however, seemed to be in Chowdhury's choice to speak for Indian interests and in so doing to speak for his uncle, who glowered at him from his place in the wing chair and then silenced him with a dismissive wave. "The fact of the matter is," Patel began, "that neither of your nations has behaved in its best interest. America's hubris has finally gotten the better of its greatness. You've squandered your blood and treasure to what end?" He looked directly at his nephew but did not wait for an answer. "For freedom of navigation in the South China Sea? For the sovereignty of Taiwan? Isn't the world large enough for your government and Beijing's? Perhaps you'll win this war. But for what? To be like the British after the Second World War, your empire dismantled, your society in retreat? And millions of dead on both sides?" Then Patel turned his attention to Farshad. "Tell me, Lieutenant Commander, how does it serve your nation to provoke us, a neutral power with a population fifteen times the size of your own? We're more than capable of taking back our ship, if need be. And we're capable of far more, if further provoked." Then the retired vice admiral sat a little straighter in his chair, his shoulders rounded backward, his chest filling with air, addressing both Farshad and Chowdhury as though he were again in command on one of his ships and they were subordinates to whom he was issuing a course correction. "You both represent countries that began this war. I represent a country that is capable of finishing it."

Sufficiently chastised, Chowdhury and Farshad sat silently next to one another in the den. The only movement was from the television in the corner, where their eyes instinctively wandered. Patel turned up the volume. On the screen, the troupe of dancers had yielded to a single woman, hardly more than a teen, who wore a sari of green silk, with golden bangles on her wrists and henna on her hands, palms, and the bottoms of her bare feet, which she kicked in the air as she pirouetted in time with a quick drumming. Patel said, "This is the Tandava," as if Farshad, or at least Chowdhury, would be familiar with the dance. Their blank expressions made it clear that neither were. "Performed in a cycle, it channels the cosmic evolution of life."

"How so?" asked Farshad, his eyes fixed on the screen.

"The Tandava was first danced by Lord Shiva," answered Patel.

"Shiva?" said Chowdhury, as he reached back in his memory for the identity of that particular deity.

His uncle filled in the gap. "Yes, Lord Shiva. He is both the Creator and Destroyer."

A phone rang in the back of the house. Patel excused himself, leaving Chowdhury and Farshad alone in the den. Neither of them had an inclination to speak without Patel in the room, so they sat wordlessly while the tempo of the drum, flutes, and accompanying sitars continued to accelerate the dance that played out on the television.

Chowdhury believed that the situation would soon resolve itself. The Iranian position was untenable. They couldn't shut down the Strait of Hormuz for much longer. The risk of a broader Indian intervention was too great, not only for Tehran but also for Tehran's ally Beijing. Such an intervention would be enough to tip the scales decidedly in favor of the United States. However, as Chowdhury reached this conclusion, a certain melancholy came over him. His country was the one that intervened—whether in the First World War, or the Second, in Korea or

217

Vietnam, in the Balkans and later in Iraq, Afghanistan, and Syria. American intervention, if only occasionally successful, was always decisive among nations. But no longer.

His uncle, having finished his call, appeared in the doorway. His mouth opened slightly as if to speak, but then he sealed it. He sat back in his chair with whatever he had to say trapped inside of him. Before he could deliver his message, a ticker unspooled itself across the bottom of the television's screen. It was a news update in both Hindi and English. Before Chowdhury or Farshad could read further, Patel exhaled once, as if in anguish, only to say in a voice like doom, "San Diego and Galveston."

They sat, the three of them. In the room the only sound was the music. Not a word was spoken. The sole movement came from the television. The ticker continued to run, articulating the news, while above it was the girl, joyously articulating the movements of the Tandava. On and on she seemed to dance.

6

The Tandava

Lin Bao was alone when the first images came in. He'd arrived at the Defense Ministry three hours before the strike, sequestering himself in the conference room, and he waited. The *Zheng He* had dispatched long-dwell drones, whose radar and infrared profiles were the size of gnats, over San Diego and Galveston. The static-filled live feed projected ghostly gray onto a screen at the far end of the room. While Lin Bao sat in his armchair at the head of the table, he listened to the drone operator's disembodied voice as it described what it saw: the blast circumference of the crater; the black rain of several pyrocumulus clouds; the otherworldly annihilation of two cities, which appeared as though a wrathful deity had inhaled them up from the earth. The voice was giving words to this single greatest act of human destruction. The more

219

it spoke, the more it took on larger proportions, so that to Lin Bao it soon sounded less and less like the voice of a man and more as though it were the voice of God Himself.

If Lin Bao possessed any reservations about his decision to leave the Navy and government service, watching the fallout over San Diego and Galveston gave him complete conviction that his time as a military officer was through. The only question was how to extract himself safely—not a small task, he realized. After their meeting at Mission Hills, Zhao Leji had, by default, made himself Lin Bao's direct superior. Even though no table of organization existed that showed Lin Bao and Zhao Leji in the same chain of command, no official would accept Lin Bao's resignation without Zhao Leji's explicit approval.

And so Lin Bao could submit his resignation to one person alone: Zhao Leji.

However, since leaving Mission Hills, he and Lin Bao had had no direct communication. Not a telephone call. Not a meeting. Not an email. Zhao Leji had become a ghost, as distant and disembodied as the drones circling the destroyed American cities.

Although Lin Bao had heard nothing from Zhao Leji, he did nothing without the old man's tacit approval. That formal approval would, of course, never arrive with Zhao Leji's name on it, or anyone else's name on it for that matter. The Politburo Standing Committee expressed itself in the language of bureaucratic obfuscation. Direct intent from an individual (or a collection of individuals) was laundered through existing offices, and not infrequently through nonexistent ones. The routing on any memo—the "FROM:"—often took up the entire first page. Names hardly ever appeared, only those obscure office titles. If a decision from the Politburo Standing Committee went awry, one of these intermediary offices could take any or all of the blame.

As Lin Bao watched the live feed from the *Zheng He*, one of these bureaucratic messages sat on the desk in front of him. Like the strike's launch order, it had arrived in a sealed envelope. It, too, had an extensive administrative routing directive on its first page. Lin Bao wondered what would happen if he composed his letter of resignation with a reverse of this routing? Like a trail of bread crumbs, would it lead back to Zhao Leji and the Politburo Standing Committee? He doubted it. He knew, instinctually, that a matter as sensitive as the resignation of a senior admiral couldn't be handled through such channels. If only his departure was as simple as properly formatting a memo.

His thoughts inexplicably turned to the one-way radios on the Soviet tanks during the Second World War, that cautionary case study at the US Naval War College about overly centralized command structures. His wife and daughter had loved Newport, the winter snowstorms spent huddled by the fireplace and that single glorious summer when on weekends they would rent a dinghy from Goat Island and then let out full-sail, passing beneath the Claiborne Pell suspension bridge as they headed toward the hulking gray facade of the historic Naval War College, where they'd beach their dinghy and spread a picnic on a blanket in the sand. With his shoes off, reclining alongside his family, Lin Bao had talked about his retirement back then too. His idea: to teach at the war college.

He smiled self-consciously even thinking of it. How preposterous it seemed now.

The disembodied voice interrupted: "Twenty-two minutes on-station time remaining. Standing by for additional taskings. . . ." The combat information center on the *Zheng He* responded, sending the unmanned flight out into the spectral blast-scape to further confirm what was obvious at a glance: the destruction of everything.

I would have taught history, thought Lin Bao, his mind wandering as he considered the live feed. His dream to teach was one that he didn't speak of to anyone, not even his wife. Had he acted on it those years ago he never would have made admiral. He would have retired from the Navy as a commander, a respectable rank. His dual US citizenship and his doctorate would have been enough to land him a job. As a former Chinese naval officer, he would have brought a unique perspective to the faculty. He had never quite relinquished the dream. Over the years, he had composed a curriculum for a few classes in his mind. He never dared write them down; that would have made the dream too real, and deferring it too painful.

He imagined himself at the lectern discussing the ancient Greeks to his American students: "The First Persian War, in which Miltiades defeats Darius at Marathon in 490 BC, leads to the Second Persian War, in which the Athenian navy commanded by Themistocles destroys the Persian navy under Xerxes at Salamis in 480 BC. Ten years of war gives the Greeks fifty years of peace, a golden age. The Athenians secure peace on the Hellespont through the Delian League, a mutual-security pact in which the other Greek city-states pay Athens a tribute to protect them against future Persian aggression. Sound familiar?" Lin Bao would then imagine himself looking out at his class, at their blank expressions, in which the past held no relevance, in which there was only the future and that future would always be American.

Then, in his imagined class, Lin Bao would tell his students of their past but also of their future. He would explain how America's golden age was born out of the First and Second World Wars, just as Greece had found its greatest era of prosperity in the aftermath of the two Persian Wars. Like the Athenians with the Delian League, Lin Bao would explain how the Americans consolidated power with mutual-security pacts such as NATO, in which they would make the largest contributions in exchange for military primacy over the western world—much as the Athenians had gained military primacy of the then-known world through the Delian League.

Lin Bao would always wait for the question he knew was coming, in which one of his students would ask why it all ended. What external threat overwhelmed the Delian League? What invader accomplished what the Persian fleet could not at Salamis? And Lin Bao would tell his students that no invader had come, no foreign horde had sabotaged the golden age forged by Miltiades, Themistocles, and Greece's other forefathers.

"Then how?" they would ask. "If the Persians couldn't do it, who did?"

And so, he would say, "The end came—as it always does—from within."

He would explain this patiently, like a father telling a beloved child that the Easter Bunny or another cherished fairy tale didn't exist, and while his students' puzzled expressions fixed on him, he would tell them about the jealousy of the Spartans, the fear they felt for the broadening powers of the Delian League. He would also tell them about Athens, drunk on its own greatness, blinded by narcissism and decadence. "Look over the ages," he would assert, "from Britain, to Rome, to Greece: the empire always rots from within." Most of his students, he knew, would underwhelm him. They would stare back in disbelief, or even hostility. Their assumption would always be that the time in which they lived could never be usurped; it was singular, as they believed themselves to be singular. Endemic dysfunction in America's political life hardly mattered because America's position in the world was inviolate. But a few of his students, their faces clear in his imagination, would return his stare as if his understanding had become their own.

What Lin Bao wondered now, as he watched the last of the live feed, the skeletal remains of buildings, the rush-hour commute left incinerated on the highway, was what rank those few American students would hold today. Some would likely be admirals, like himself.

What if he had retired early? What if he had taught and reached a few of them?

Would there have been a Zhanjiang? A San Diego? A Galveston?

Probably so, but he allowed himself to conjure an alternative history, one in which the miscalculations of the past four months had not occurred, one in which incidents like the *Wén Rui* and battles like Mischief Reef and Taiwan had never happened. Perhaps a single dissenting voice, properly applied, had prevented this collective madness. The historian in him couldn't resist placing these events into a causative order, in which each became a link in an otherwise interruptible chain, one that had bound them to this moment, where Lin Bao—seated at the conference table, staring at the live feed—was witnessing the single greatest act of destruction in the history of mankind.

But there was nothing he could do about any of this.

The task before him was simple: to observe the last of the live feed and to pass along to the *Zheng He* the order that sat in front of him on the table. It tasked the carrier and its escorts to return from the Pacific to the South China Sea at best speed to "defend against the American threat in our waters."

Another fifteen minutes had passed.

The drone operator continued to survey the blast-scape. Then, with fuel running low, he announced that he'd be checking off-station in seven minutes. With his hollow, disembodied voice, the drone operator radioed to the *Zheng He*, asking whether they had any further taskings.

The *Zheng He* had none.

Next, the drone operator called to the Defense Ministry and asked if they had any further taskings. Lin Bao picked up the handset on the satellite uplink, connecting him directly to the drone operator. He said the Defense Ministry had no further taskings.

There was a moment of silence.

The drone operator again asked if the Defense Ministry had any further taskings. Lin Bao repeated himself into the handset.

Nothing.

There'd been some breakdown in communications. A member of Lin Bao's support staff rushed into the conference room, untangling wires beneath the table, toggling switches on and off at the back of the satellite uplink, while Lin Bao repeated over and over again that he'd seen enough, that he had no further taskings, that he didn't need to see any more.

There was no response.

Lin Bao kept repeating himself. He was frantic to deliver his message, frantic to hear a response on the other end of the line from that hollow, disembodied voice.

⌐

11:49 July 20, 2034 (GMT+5:30)
New Delhi

Vice Admiral Patel immediately ordered two taxicabs, one for Farshad and the other for his nephew. The three of them hardly spoke as they waited. Farshad never considered himself a prejudiced man—in his mind bigotry was a safe harbor for weaklings. However, all through his life, he'd noticed how on the few occasions he'd met an American he'd immediately recoiled at their presence (he had a similar reaction to Israelis, though had an easier time self-rationalizing this response as something other than bigotry). But when Farshad witnessed Chowdhury's palpable grief as the first reports came in from San Diego and Galveston, he couldn't help but feel something akin to pity. What he did next not only surprised his American friend but also surprised himself. As the two sat next to each other on the love seat in the admiral's den, Farshad reached over and placed his right hand consolingly on the American's left arm.

The first taxicab arrived. There was no question that Chowdhury would be taking it instead of Farshad. The American's need was more urgent. As his uncle shuttled him to the door, he turned to Farshad and said, "Thank you." Farshad said nothing in return. He suspected that the American was thanking him for the gesture from before, but he couldn't be certain. He reminded himself never to trust an American.

Farshad asked Patel when the second taxicab would arrive. Instead of answering, Patel invited Farshad to sit with him a little longer in the den. Farshad made a slight protest—he, too, had to check in with the officials at his embassy—but Patel ignored him. "How about a cup of tea?" he said.

Farshad's patience was running low, but he gathered up enough composure to accept the invitation. Somehow, despite himself, he trusted this old admiral. Patel disappeared into his kitchen and returned with the pot of tea. He sat next to Farshad on the love seat, their knees almost touching as Patel prepared Farshad's cup and then his own. Patel exhaled heavily. "A tragedy, this."

Farshad frowned. "Inevitable," he replied, and then blew curlicues of steam from the surface of his cup.

"Inevitable?" asked Patel. "Really? You don't think this could've been avoided?"

As he thought of the annihilation of two American cities, Farshad considered the ancient antipathies that existed toward the United States, deep antipathies, not merely those of his own nation but those of all the world. It was America's perpetual overreach that had led to today's events. How long could one country continue stoking up resentment before someone eventually struck a mortal blow? His word choice had been correct: *inevitable.*

He checked his watch and again asked about the cab. Patel ignored the request. "I can't say that I agree with you," he began. "This conflict hasn't felt like a war—at least not in the traditional sense—but rather a series of escalations, each one greater than the last. But a single break in this chain of escalation could defuse the entire conflict and halt this cycle of violence. That's why my word is *tragic*, not *inevitable*. A tragedy is a disaster that could otherwise have been avoided." Patel took another sip from his tea, and Farshad could feel the old admiral's gaze from over the rim of his cup. If Patel was searching for agreement, he would have none. Farshad sat rigid in his seat, his shoulders swept back, his hands in his lap. His face expressed nothing. Patel continued, "You above all others should know that today could have been avoided. You were on the bridge of the *Rezkiy* when the Russians sabotaged the undersea cables. The Americans never would have launched at Zhanjiang had that accident not occurred. That's another word for you: *accident.*" Instead of three syllables Patel spoke it in one, spitting it out, its falseness in his mouth like a bite into spoiled fruit.

Farshad became defensive. He offered other words, like *miscalculation* and *unintentional,* to describe what the Russians had done in the Barents Sea. But he knew they were lies and soon retired them, drawing silent and resigning himself only to, "How did you figure out that I was on the *Rezkiy*?"

"You just told me," Patel replied.

Farshad smiled. He couldn't help it; he liked this wily old man.

Placing Farshad on the *Rezkiy* was a simple act of deduction on Patel's part—Farshad had flown through Moscow, and how many Iranian liaison officers did Tehran have assigned to the Russian fleet? Not many. Patel now asked his Iranian counterpart to engage with him in a similar deductive exercise. The Indian government, Patel explained, wanted its ship back from the Revolutionary Guards. Patel understood that unlike the Russians in the Barents Sea, the seizure of the privately owned tanker was an actual miscalculation that had led to an impasse between their two governments. After laying out the facts as he saw them, Patel expounded on "the unique position of our two countries."

According to Patel, arbitration of the Sino-American War now fell to India. Among the nations of the world, events had conspired to make New Delhi the best interlocutor between Washington and Beijing, and it would take Iranian cooperation as well. Only their countries had a chance of ending the hostilities. He alluded to "sweeping actions" his government might be called upon to take in the coming days. "Without our intervention," Patel explained, "the Americans will counterstrike, and the Chinese will counterstrike the counterstrike. Tactical nuclear weapons will turn into strategic ones. And that will lead to the end. For all of us. . . . But our intervention can work and will only work if it's allowed to unfold freely, if no other nation interferes." Patel turned to Farshad. Like a spouse begging their partner to give up a lover, he said simply, "When I say *interference*, I'm talking about the Russians."

Farshad understood. He knew that Patel saw the Russians clearly, just as he and his government saw them clearly. Farshad found himself thinking of Kolchak, who could trace his lineage to the Imperial Navy,

"The driver will take you to the airport," said Patel.

"The airport?"

"I imagine you want to get back to Tehran, to speak with General Bagheri. We've booked a flight for you. Pass along my regards. Tell him that we're happily anticipating news that our freighter has been released and that we're very much looking forward to our partnership."

Outside the window, the driver stood by his taxi.

"What is this 'decisive action' you keep referring to?" Farshad asked. "General Bagheri is going to want to know." Farshad remained on the sofa, cemented in place as if his returning to Tehran might be contingent on this last piece of information.

Patel gave Farshad a long, appraising look. "What we're going to do next will be dramatic," he answered. "But it will end this war. Will you trust me?" Patel placed his hand on Farshad's arm.

Γ

12:07 July 20, 2034 (GMT+5:30)
New Delhi

Over and over again, Chowdhury kept calling her. Sitting in the back of the taxicab on the way to the embassy, he was in a panic. Samantha wouldn't answer her phone. He kept dialing and dialing.

Nothing.

His former mother-in-law, that Texan WASP Chowdhury had never felt any affinity for, lived in Galveston, her health failing, her only enjoyment the ocean air and those periodic visits from her daughter.

As he crossed from the east to the west bank of the Yamuna River, Chowdhury tapped out an email to Samantha: *Have tried you many times. Please call -Sandy*

A new email popped into Chowdhury's in-box, an out-of-office reply from Samantha. *I will be away from my desk and in Galveston on a family matter until Monday, July 24th. If the issue is urgent, please try my cell phone.*

Like that, she was gone.

The grief Chowdhury felt wasn't for the loss of her; the two hardly had a relationship. It was for his daughter—*their daughter.* How many times over the years had he secretly hoped that Samantha, his stalwart antagonist, might vanish in such a way? Lost in a plane crash. Incinerated in a fire. Killed in a car wreck. He had, guiltily, harbored such fantasies. However, had any of these fantasies proven true, it would've left Ashni motherless. And now that Samantha was gone, his guilt was as acute as if he'd killed her himself. In fact, he couldn't quite convince himself that he hadn't.

When he arrived at the embassy, it was eerily quiet. He had expected to find a hive of activity as the ambassador responded to this crisis. Instead, the halls were mostly empty. Here and there, clusters of staff gathered around one cubicle or another. From the hushed tones of conversations, Chowdhury assumed the cubicles' occupants had lost a loved one in the attack. Otherwise, the mood was stunned silence.

Chowdhury shut the door to the temporary office he'd been assigned. Though he didn't wish to admit it, he, too, was stunned. As he logged into his email, he hoped to find something that might recall him to his senses. At the top of his in-box there was a message from Hendrickson. The subject line was empty, and even though they were communicating on a classified system, the text was cryptic: *Our orders arrived. What do you hear? -Bunt*

Chowdhury knew those orders were for a counterstrike led by

the *Enterprise*. It would be against the Chinese mainland. The days of indirect strikes—at power grids, or disputed territories like Taiwan—were over. The counterstrike would follow this pattern of escalation. Zhanjiang had led to San Diego and Galveston, so the next logical step after the destruction of two American cities would be the destruction of three Chinese ones. The only question was which cities, a detail that Hendrickson had no doubt received in the recently arrived "orders."

While Chowdhury sat in front of his screen struggling to compose a response, his cell phone rang.

It was his uncle. "Our Iranian friend just left."

"To where?"

"Home," said Patel. "Are you at the embassy?"

Chowdhury told him that he was.

"Nothing's going to get accomplished there," said his uncle. "I'm on my way to the Defense Ministry. Come meet me."

Chowdhury made a half-hearted protest; he wasn't in New Delhi on an official diplomatic mission and a meeting at the Defense Ministry broke any number of protocols; he would first need to secure the appropriate authorizations. His uncle listened, or at least the other end of the line fell silent, before he said, "Sandeep, we know the *Enterprise* has its launch orders . . . and I know about Ashni's mother. For that, I am sorry; we can tell her together if you like. But first, we need you to come to the Defense Ministry."

Chowdhury glanced out his window, to the vacant corridors of the embassy. He knew his uncle was right. Nothing was going to happen here, or at least nothing that might avert a counterstrike by the *Enterprise*. We'll take out three of their cities for our two. Then what? They'll take out four of ours. Then we take out five more. Then come the doomsday weapons. . . . He could feel his loyalties shifting, not from one

233

nation to another, but between those who wanted to avert an escalation and those who believed that victory, whatever that meant, could exist along this spectrum of destruction. Receiving the appropriate authorizations to visit the Defense Ministry suddenly seemed like an irrelevance. He increasingly felt as though his allegiance didn't reside with any government but with whoever could reverse this cycle of annihilation.

"All right," said Chowdhury, returning to his desk. "I'll be there in thirty minutes."

His uncle hung up.

Chowdhury couldn't help but wonder how the Indians knew that the *Enterprise* had received their launch orders. It could have been a myriad of intercepts made by their intelligence services, but Chowdhury suspected they'd intercepted his correspondence with Hendrickson. If they had, their ability to hack into his classified email demonstrated a level of cyber sophistication beyond what he and his country had previously thought them capable. When Chowdhury crafted his reply to Hendrickson, he now did so with the knowledge that others might be reading it. In response to the question *What do you hear?* he wrote: *The Indians might do something.*

15:32 July 23, 2034 (GMT+8)
South China Sea

It was perhaps the loneliest moment of her life. Hunt stood on the bridge overseeing flight operations, but what she was really there to observe was Hendrickson departing to Yokosuka, then on to Honolulu, and finally back to Washington, where he'd been recalled via an immediate action request, originating from the White House. When Hendrickson received the message, he'd crumpled the sheet of paper, tossed it in a burn bag, and muttered, "Fucking Wisecarver."

Hendrickson had come to believe that he hadn't actually been sent to the *Enterprise* to check up on Hunt; he had been sent to the *Enterprise* so he would be out of the way when Wisecarver crafted the orders for the nuclear counterstrike. Now that the White House had dispatched those orders, he wanted Hendrickson back in Washington to keep an eye on him. He explained his theory to Hunt.

"But I thought I was the one they didn't trust?" she asked.

Hendrickson replied, "They don't trust you. It's just that they might not trust me either." In this way, by both being untrustworthy to the same authority, they were once again confederates in the hours that remained before Hendrickson's departure.

This may have been why, watching his plane dwindle into a speck on the horizon, Hunt felt so spectacularly alone. She returned to her flag cabin. The orders for the counterstrike were locked in her safe, whose combination she struggled with, preoccupied as her mind was. She couldn't quite bring herself to focus on the detailed planning that would be required of her. Before he'd left, Hendrickson mentioned that he had it "on good authority that the Indians might intervene."

"Cut the shit. On whose authority?" she'd asked.

Hendrickson would only answer, "A contact of mine from Washington."

The fantasy of the Indians—or of anyone—intervening proved such an escapist distraction that it took her four attempts to unlock the safe. Then at her desk she unfolded the orders, which totaled three pages, one for each of the targets, coastal cities that read from south to north: Xiamen (population: 7.1 million), Fuzhou (population: 7.8 million), and, lastly, Shanghai (population: 33.24 million).

To both Hunt and Hendrickson, the inclusion of Shanghai seemed chillingly disproportionate. It was China's most populous city. A strike on Shanghai would assure a counterstrike on New York, Los Angeles, or even Washington. Which wasn't to say that the staggering number of lives lost in a place like Xiamen or Fuzhou wasn't grim enough, but it would be difficult to imagine a scenario in which a strike on Shanghai wouldn't result in an escalation from tactical to strategic nuclear weapons. It was, Hunt thought, a suicide mission. Not that the pilot wouldn't make it back, though that was unlikely enough. No, it was a suicide mission in the broadest sense. Its accomplishment assured the suicide of much, if not all, of mankind.

As that thought lingered, there was a knock at the door. "Come in," she said. Wedge stepped across the threshold, wiping some grease from his hands with a filthy rag. He then tucked the rag into the pocket of his flight suit and presented himself to Hunt, snapping to attention. "Christ, at ease," she said. "I've told you that you don't have to do that."

Wedge again took the rag from his pocket, working the grease from his palms and beneath his fingernails. "Customs and courtesies, ma'am. A simple sign of respect."

Hunt held the three pages of the order in front of her. "I appreciate that, but I don't need the extra deference."

"It's not specific to you, ma'am. It's respect for your rank." He tucked the rag back into his flight suit. Hunt couldn't help it; she had come to like Wedge. He was insubordinate. But his insubordination didn't manifest itself in a refusal to follow orders, or disrespect for his superiors. He was, instead, insubordinate in the broadest sense. He was insubordinate to the time in which he lived. He refused to give up the old ways. Or, put differently, he refused to stop believing in them. Where did Wedge think all this would lead? wondered Hunt. Did he imagine that a bygone order would one day reassert itself? That he could somehow fly through the fabric of time to arrive in a different, better, and older world? Perhaps his insubordination was a form of denial, a rejection not only of the present but of all that was to come.

No matter, she thought cruelly, as she handed him the order for the counterstrike.

"What's this?" he asked, thumbing through the pages. Hunt didn't need to tell him; he could read it for himself: *Xiamen, Fuzhou, . . . Shanghai.* His left eyebrow ticked upward when he read the last one. Aside from that he sat across from her stone-faced.

"When can you be ready?" she asked.

"Day after tomorrow," said Wedge. That would give his pilots a full night's rest. The Hornets, antiquated as they were, could also benefit from the attention of a twenty-four-hour maintenance stand-down. Each crew chief could then conduct a full inspection of the avionics, airframes, and weapons systems, all of which had proven temperamental during their training runs.

"That's fine," said Hunt. "We don't need to launch any earlier than that."

"Three flights of three," answered Wedge. "That sound about right to you?"

Hunt glanced down at her desk and nodded. "Which flight will you take?"

"I figured I'd take Shanghai."

When he said the name, all Hunt could think was *33.24 million people.* The same with the other cities turned targets. Fuzhou wasn't Fuzhou anymore; it was *7.8 million people.* The same for Xiamen: *7.1 million.* "Wedge—" she said, his name catching for a moment in her throat. "A lot of folks are calling this a suicide mission."

Wedge folded up the three sheets of paper Hunt had given him and stuffed them in the same pocket as his dirty rag. "Ma'am, I don't do suicide missions. We'll get her done and make it back here." For a moment, Hunt thought to tell him that wasn't what she meant by suicide mission. But she thought better of it.

Wedge snapped to attention and was dismissed.

⌐

19:25 July 29, 2034 (GMT+8)
Beijing

It took four days before Lin Bao realized that his wife and daughter had fled the city. He'd last seen them when he left for work on a Tuesday. He had stayed that night at the ministry as well as the night that followed. He'd come home the following morning, a Thursday, and had slept from nine o'clock until three o'clock in the afternoon before returning to the ministry. He'd worked all the next day and through that night into Saturday. When he came home around lunch the house was empty. He began to wonder where his family was. When he phoned his wife, she answered on the third try. She and her daughter were staying in her mother's village in the countryside, hundreds of miles inland—"until this is over," she had said. Lin Bao asked to speak with his daughter, but she was out taking a walk with her grandmother. "I'll have her call you back."

"When?" Lin Bao had asked.

"Soon," answered his wife.

Lin Bao didn't protest. What right did he have to? If anything, he was jealous of his wife and daughter. Jealous of the time they had together; jealous of their safety, of their distance from the capital, and of their decision to leave it. He'd been indulging in escapist fantasies of his own, imagining what his life might be like when he left the Navy. He was indulging in one of these fantasies as he settled down in his empty house, rooting around the mostly bare fridge for some dinner. Early the next morning he would need to return to the ministry to monitor the reentrance of the *Zheng He* into territorial waters. He heated up a microwave meal, a burger and fries, his favorite indulgence, although it never cooked quite right in a microwave. The burger always wound up bland, the fries soggy. Not like it tasted in the States.

He watched the timer. He wondered again if perhaps he'd teach when this war was over. The idea of returning to the academy, or to any of his country's war colleges, was unappealing. Their curricula were merely programs of regurgitation. The professors had no input in their development. To teach the way he wanted to, he'd need to settle in the West. However, with each passing day of the current conflict that seemed more and more like an impossibility. And if he couldn't teach, he would at least use his retirement to refocus on his family, to reestablish his relationship with his daughter, which had lost the warmth it had known during their days in Newport almost a decade before. No one could take his family from him, he thought, as the timer on the microwave went off.

Lin Bao took his meal in its plastic container and settled down on the sofa in the living room. He uncapped a bottle of Tsingtao and took a long pull. With one hand he grasped his beer by the neck and with the other he held his remote as he scrolled through a series of unfamiliar television shows. How long had it been since he'd had a night alone like this? Feeling overwhelmed by his program choices and disoriented by being on his own, he struggled to relax. He couldn't quite bring himself to take advantage of his time off. Eventually, he rerouted his internet through an illicit VPN he'd downloaded, allowing him to watch an uncensored broadcast of BBC News from London.

The pasty-faced anchor led with a story, ". . . coming from the open waters south of Japan in the Philippine Sea . . ." According to reports, freighters transiting into and out of the Pacific had observed a massive fire. Ceaseless clouds of smoke billowed miles into the air. Early speculation leaned toward this being the result of an undersea drilling disaster; however, the BBC and other networks soon dispelled this theory. No energy companies had wells in that remote portion of the Philippine Sea. An intrepid private pilot had, with that afternoon's sun descending off her left tail wing, managed to fly the approximately two hundred miles southeast from the Japanese archipelago of Naha. The BBC was livestreaming video recorded by the pilot, while the anchor, mumbling away, attempted to make sense of the images.

Lin Bao set his beer on the floor and put his meal on a side table. He craned his neck forward, his face pressing closer to the television.

It couldn't be.

He would've heard.

There would have been a cry for help.

But then Lin Bao thought of them heading west, their stealth technology fully engaged while maintaining the discipline of a communications blackout. A student of history, he recalled the USS *Indianapolis*, which had gone down in the Philippine Sea almost a hundred years before, sunk by a torpedo fired from a Japanese submarine; it'd taken four days for the Americans to realize what had happened.

Lin Bao continued to watch closely, his eyes unblinking.

The pilot, who was narrating parts of the livestream, explained that she had to keep her distance. Secondary explosions made it difficult for her to approach any closer. Her plane rattled in the turbulent air. Then, through a break in the smoke, Lin Bao saw it. The familiar slope of its prow, the gentle arch where its anchor lay: his old ship, the *Zheng He*.

She was ablaze, listing hard to starboard.

The news anchor still didn't understand what he was looking at. He fumbled along through his broadcast, hypothesizing along with his coanchor as to what all this smoke and fire at sea could possibly mean. Lin Bao, however, was already up from his seat, out the door, and on his way back into the ministry. He forgot to switch off the television.

An hour later, when his daughter returned his call, he wasn't available to take it.

⌐

12:25 July 29, 2034 (GMT+5:30)
New Delhi

This was Chowdhury's second trip to the Defense Ministry in as many weeks. His first trip had proven eventful by way of introductions. Over lunch, Chowdhury had met the defense minister himself, the chief of staff of the armed forces, and an extensive retinue of staff officers. Sitting around an oval table in the minister's personal dining room, each of them had offered their condolences for "the atrocities at Galveston and San Diego." None of them knew about Chowdhury's ex-wife, or his recently motherless daughter, so these condolences felt impersonal, like one nation's theoretical expression of sympathy for another. No one had said anything of substance in that first meeting; it had served to open a dialogue.

Now Patel had recalled his nephew to the ministry for a second time. They met down by security. Despite Patel's retired status he had a badge that listed him as permanent staff, allowing him to come and go as he pleased. When Patel arrived, he cut to the front of the security line and was promptly handed a visitor's badge for his nephew. The two were waved through a turnstile by an alert, white-gloved soldier in his service dress.

Patel walked briskly, with Chowdhury trailing a half step behind. Unlike the day before, when they'd followed the long corridor toward the upper-floor offices of the senior ministry officials, Patel led Chowdhury down to the basement. With its low ceilings and flickering halogen bulbs, this was the domain of minor officialdom. Eventually, they found themselves at a small canteen. "Let me buy you a cup of tea," said his uncle.

Chowdhury followed him inside. There were only three tables, each empty. Patel explained that the woman at the cash register was the pensioned widow of a long-since-martyred soldier. Patel paid, dropped a few extra coins in her tip jar, and offered the elderly widow his most convivial smile.

"I was hoping we could talk unofficially," Patel began as they sat. "When I brought you here last week to meet the defense minister and chief of staff, it was to convey to you that I speak for the senior-most levels of our government. Understood?"

Chowdhury nodded. He didn't quite understand why he'd been chosen as the receptacle for whatever message his uncle seemed poised to deliver. Why wasn't this proceeding through official channels, through the ambassador, or even some lesser embassy official? As if in anticipation of these concerns, his uncle explained, "Within your government, certain parties have a strong interest toward escalation. They will knowingly misinterpret our actions. Because of this, it is important for you to convey clearly both what we have done but also what we are willing to do."

Chowdhury studied his uncle. "By 'certain parties,' who do you mean?"

"I believe you know who I mean," answered Patel.

"Wisecarver?" asked Chowdhury quietly.

Patel neither affirmed nor refuted Chowdhury's guess. He took another sip of his tea before explaining, "Our government, specifically the leadership in this building, is not choosing a side. We are not supporting Beijing. And we are not supporting Washington. We are allied with no one. Our support is for de-escalation. Do you understand?"

Chowdhury nodded.

"Good," added Patel. "Because what I'm about to show you might be confusing to your national security staff." From his pocket, Patel removed his government-issued cell phone. He began to scroll through a series of photographs taken along the surface of the ocean, with waves cresting in the bottom of the frame. Superimposed over each image was a reticle, as if from a gunsight, with crosshatched X and Y axes bisecting its width and length. As Patel scrolled through each picture the ship on the horizon drew closer, until Chowdhury could clearly observe an aircraft carrier. Patel paused for a moment, glanced once more at his nephew, and then cycled to the next photo. . . .

An inferno of smoke and flames obscured and consumed the carrier.

Patel paged quickly through the pictures that followed as if each were an image in a flip-book, animating the burning carrier as it slipped beneath the waves. When his uncle came to the last photograph, which was of the calm and consuming sea again at rest, he put words to what Chowdhury had witnessed. "These are periscope photographs from one of our upgraded Kalvari-class diesel-electric submarines. Their modified propulsion system affords them an essentially unlimited range, equal to any of your nuclear submarines. We've used one to sink the *Zheng He.*"

As his uncle had promised, Chowdhury was perplexed. "You sunk the *Zheng He* . . . but you are not allying yourself with the United States?"

"Correct," said Patel. "Our interests are to de-escalate this conflict. If your government takes any retaliatory action for Galveston or San Diego, it won't be a Chinese ship that we sink next but an American one." Patel presented his nephew with another image, a map that showed the approximate disposition of Indian naval forces in and around the South China Sea. "And as you'll see, this isn't a hollow threat."

Patel's map seemed an impossibility to Chowdhury. If accurate, it meant that dozens of Indian warships had infiltrated into the South China Sea undetected, representing a gross underestimation of India's stealth-cloaking and cyber capability by his own country. Chowdhury's thoughts shifted to a couple of days before, how his uncle had learned of the *Enterprise*'s receipt of launch orders against the Chinese mainland. He was increasingly certain that Patel knew this through Chowdhury's email exchange with Hendrickson. If the Indians possessed enough sophistication to hack into a state-of-the-art encrypted email system, was it not also likely that they possessed the sophistication to position their fleet clandestinely between the *Enterprise* and the Chinese mainland?

"Our defense attaché visited the White House and showed these pictures to your national security advisor. . . ."

"And?" Chowdhury asked his uncle.

"He was thanked and escorted out of the building."

Chowdhury nodded.

"It is my belief that your Mr. Wisecarver never passed along these materials or news of our attaché's visit to anyone else in the administration. It is also my belief that your Mr. Wisecarver has no intention of expressing the nuance of our government's position to your president."

"Your beliefs are likely correct," answered Chowdhury. "So why are you telling me this?"

They'd finished their tea. Patel gave his nephew a glance, then went back to the register where the cashier sat. She poured him another two cups, but this time Patel neglected to drop a coin in her jar. Patel returned to his seat, picking up their conversation. "I am telling you all of this because perhaps there is another way to convey our message." He handed Chowdhury his tea and fixed him in his stare, as if he were waiting for his nephew to speak. However, Chowdhury wouldn't say anything. By conspiring with his uncle in this way, he felt as though he were skirting a treasonous line. And so, Patel finished the thought for him: "Your friend Hendrickson might be able to communicate our message directly."

"Going around Wisecarver to the president would likely end his career."

"If the *Enterprise* launches a counterstrike," Patel answered gravely, "much more will end than the career of one man."

The two of them sat quietly. "Why are we meeting here, in this canteen?" asked Chowdhury. "Why not in a secure conference room?" He glanced at the cashier, who was nominally paging through a gossip magazine but who he suspected had been listening to them this entire time.

"Because we haven't had a meeting," answered Patel. "None of this is official. My government hasn't sanctioned my talking to you. As far as they're concerned, we're discussing my sister's health." For the first time, Chowdhury felt uncertain who exactly his uncle spoke for. As if he could sense his nephew's unease, Patel added, "To break certain impasses, sometimes we have to rely on a bond stronger than nationality. Sometimes the only bond that is strong enough is family." Patel clasped his nephew by the shoulder. "You will talk to your friend Hendrickson?"

Chowdhury nodded.

"Good," he said. "I'm late to a meeting. Can you find your way out?"

He nodded. "Yes."

"And don't worry about her," Patel added as he got up. "She's near deaf . . . a tragic story." On his way out, he glanced once more at the cashier. With that, his uncle was gone.

Chowdhury sipped slowly from his half-finished cup of tea, puzzling over how to outmaneuver Wisecarver. He likely had only hours until the *Enterprise* launched its counterstrike against the Chinese mainland. He had no idea what the Indian response might be. Or how his government might react. The task his uncle had placed before him seemed an impossible one. He must've appeared in pretty bad shape as he stood from his seat. He could feel the old widow at the cash register staring at him piteously. As Chowdhury passed by her, he reached into his pocket and took out some change, dropping it into her jar.

She took his hand by the wrist, startling him. Her eyes were wide and watery with what seemed like nostalgia. "Thank you," she said. "Thank you."

Chowdhury glanced down at her grip. "Think nothing of it."

For another long moment, she wouldn't let him go.

⌐

17:49 July 29, 2034 (GMT+4:30)
Strait of Hormuz

He had been walking in circles. At least that's what it felt like to Farshad. Day and night. Ever since he'd arrived on Hormuz Island. Going in one big circle. He would check a fighting position—say, an antiaircraft gun—then proceed to the next—say, a machine gun oriented on the beaches—then one of the new directed-energy cannons, which never seemed to work. On and on he'd go, viciously kicking stones out of his path as he followed the few miles of perimeter, his only break being the brief boat ride between this island and its twin, Larak Island, where he walked a nearly identical circle.

The defenses on the islands were paltry at best: a handful of antiaircraft guns, a few hundred poorly trained conscripts, some barbed-wire obstacles. That was about it. Did General Bagheri really expect him to defend these strategically critical islands with this? He couldn't be serious. And in fact, General Bagheri wasn't serious—or at least he didn't take the threat of a Russian invasion seriously. When Farshad had presented this prospect on his return from New Delhi, General Bagheri had sat behind his desk, plucking pistachios from a dish, knuckling open their shells while he listened patiently. Then with indifference he'd asked, "Is that all?"

What had followed was the greatest dressing-down Farshad had received in at least a decade. According to General Bagheri, the idea of a Russian invasion of the Hormuz Strait Islands was preposterous. Tehran and Moscow had been allied for decades. Furthermore, the information had come from the Indians, who were no great friends of either nation. Then, turning personal, Bagheri had said, "Lieutenant Commander Farshad" (annunciating his full rank as if to remind him how far he had fallen), "I placed you in the Navy so that you wouldn't cause more problems. But now, the Supreme Leader has himself read your warning of a Russian strike. Against my advice, he's chosen to release the Indian tanker and he has also ordered me to reinforce our islands in the strait. It seems I've been unsuccessful in keeping you out of trouble."

General Bagheri informed Farshad that he had no choice but to follow orders. He was compelled to reinforce the islands. But his reinforcement would be a single person: Farshad. When he departed General Bagheri's office, it was to a small dhow that was waiting to take him to his new, desolate posting. Since arriving on the islands, Farshad hadn't allowed himself to wonder how much longer he would remain there. If the Russian invasion—those Spetsnaz parachutists supported by their navy—never arrived, how long would Bagheri keep him postured to repel an assault? A week? A month? A year? The rest of his pitiful life? Farshad had come to realize that by delivering his message directly to the high command he had become the architect of his own exile.

The few hundred conscripts who manned these defenses had been enduring a similar exile, some of them for years. As Farshad mingled among them, he learned that most had a history of disciplinary infractions. These islands had become a dumping ground for hard cases. The supply depots sent them no fresh food, only packaged rations. They showered once a week. The tents they slept in were often blown away by the unpredictable winds that thrashed through the strait.

Unlike General Bagheri, the men on the island had accepted the idea of a Russian invasion, even if such an occurrence seemed like an improbability. What were the odds, one in ten? Even less? But what else did they have to do but prepare, and how long would the odds have to be on their lives for them to take no precautions whatsoever? And so they filled sandbags, they calibrated the ranges on their antiaircraft guns in precise intervals of one hundred feet, and they endured incessant inspections by Farshad while they waited for the invasion.

At night under his tent, with no special accommodations afforded him, Farshad began to think of home. He wanted to return. The desire entered his dreams. It wasn't the comfort of his bed that he envisioned, or the warmth of his house, or a good meal. It was his family's land, specifically his garden. With the fierce winds whipping against his tent, surrounded by the sleeping heaps of rejected soldiers, he concluded that he'd seen enough. If he ever got off this rocky island, he swore to himself that he would finally go home. And he wouldn't again make the mistake of leaving.

These dreams recurred fitfully each night, all except for this one. It was the only night that he slept the whole way through. It was also the only night that the wind shifted its course, dying down to a gentle breeze. This night he dreamed most intensely of all.

He is back in his garden, performing the routine he'd fallen into after his expulsion from the Revolutionary Guards. He writes his memoirs in the morning. He takes his walk at around noon, lunching beneath the elm tree on the far end of his property. When he finishes his meal, he leaves the scraps out for the pair of squirrels to eat. And he waits. He is conscious that he is dreaming, and he hopes that both squirrels might again appear. He thinks that this time he might restrain himself and not kill the squirrel if it bit him. Farshad waits a long while in this dream. The longer he waits, the more the landscape changes. The trees dry up, their brittle leaves falling around him. The thirsty grass turns to stubble and then to bleached rock. The rock is the same as the island's.

The next morning, right at dawn, the wind returned. He woke up to its howl. It stretched the fabric of his tent before yanking up the stakes and sending that same tent tumbling toward the sea. Farshad lay in the dawn with nothing between him and the sky except for the wind.

"Look!" one of the conscripts cried out.

He pointed to the east, in the direction of the rising sun. Farshad squinted, making a visor of his hand.

Dozens and dozens of them.

More than he could have imagined.

Arranged like a vast migration of birds.

"They are here!" he shouted to his garrison, but the wind drowned out his voice.

Γ

06:32 July 30, 2034 (GMT+8)
South China Sea

Weather had been erratic, thunderstorms appearing violently and then vanishing. Wild fluctuations in temperature. Golf ball–sized hailstones fell on the deck of the *Enterprise* one morning. That same evening, the temperature peaked at ninety-two degrees. The onboard meteorologist surmised that this erratic weather was the result of the atmospheric fallout from Galveston and San Diego. They had struggled to find a launch window for Wedge and the nine Death Rattlers. Each time they'd be given the all-clear and migrate to their ready room for a final mission brief, a fresh weather system would appear. Complicating matters further was the fact that they didn't need passable weather but perfect weather. The Hornets that Wedge and his crews would be flying didn't have GPS-guided bombs. Without that technology they'd have to drop their ordnance in the old way, which meant they needed clear skies over the three target cities.

After the fourth or fifth aborted launch attempt (Wedge had lost count), he found himself alone in his stateroom, sitting at his desk, trying to pass the time. Two levels above him, he could hear the ground crews working. Each iteration of stand-up-then-stand-down cost them several hours. They couldn't allow nine fully armed Hornets (particularly given the nature of their armament) to idle on a flight deck that was pitching through rough weather. Wedge took out his flight plan, reviewing it yet again:

*Nine aircraft launch, divided between three flights (Blue, Gold, Red)

*Arrive at release point (28°22'41"N 124°58'13"E)

*Set course and speed to target: Xiamen (Blue), Fuzhou (Gold), Shanghai (Red)

*For redundancy each aircraft armed with nuclear payload

*Only one aircraft per flight drops payload

*Return

He knew that last bullet point—despite being the shortest—was the one with the least probability of success. He could feel it in his gut. But Wedge didn't do suicide missions; that's what he'd told Admiral Hunt and he'd meant it. Instead of fixating on the slim probabilities of his return, he diverted his attention elsewhere. . . .

He began a letter.

It wasn't an *if-you-are-reading-this-then-I-am-gone* death letter. He'd always held those in low esteem, thinking of them as little better than suicide notes. Instead, he thought of it as a historical document. He wanted to capture his thoughts on the eve of victory. He addressed the letter to his father.

Wedge found himself writing in a sort of stream of consciousness, freed from the way he normally wrote, which was the composition of lists like the flight plan he'd just reviewed. It felt good to write in this way, a release. Although it was only him, alone in his stateroom, he wanted to bring all the world into this moment. The more he wrote, the more aware he became of his place in the universe. It was as though he could see his words being read by future generations of American schoolchildren before he'd even composed them. He could envision a child standing in front of the class, reciting portions of this note from memory in much the same way Wedge himself had recited the Gettysburg Address. This wasn't his ego at work; he knew that he possessed no remarkable gifts of expression—a C-minus in freshman English could attest to that. Rather, Wedge knew it was the moment itself that was remarkable, a moment in which everything was on the line. Then he thought, Christ, Wedge, get a grip.

Except for a single page, he crumpled up the many sheets of paper and pitched them in his trash can. The remaining page sat on the desk in front of him. He didn't read it over.

He didn't want to.

What remained were his thoughts, as pure as he could harness them, to be handed to his father.

Wedge found himself unexpectedly exhausted from the writing. He was soon asleep in his chair, his head on the desk.

Time passed, perhaps an hour or more. There was a knock on his door. Wedge felt disoriented, as if maybe it had all been a dream. Perhaps he was back in his stateroom on the *Bush*. Before Bandar Abbas. Before his stint in captivity. Back to when he was still trying to get close to *it*.

There was another knock.

"What?" he growled.

"Sir, it's time."

"Tell them that I'm coming."

He could hear the sound of departing steps as he sat up. Wedge gathered his things on the way to the ready room. His notebook. His sunglasses. A pack of Marlboro Reds. He planned to smoke one on his triumphant return. He also thought to bring the letter. After all, it wasn't a death letter. There was no reason to leave it on his desk, was there?

He glanced at it skeptically.

Wedge eventually chose to leave the letter where it was. What did it matter? Whether for bad weather, or a maintenance issue, he'd likely be back in his stateroom in a few hours after yet another aborted launch. He could mail it then. Walking toward his briefing in the ready room, he took his time down the ship's passageways, even as every other member of the crew rushed past as though in possession of some urgent piece of news. When Wedge came to an exterior hatch, he thought to take a minute to grab a breath of fresh air. What he saw caused him to hurry back inside the ship.

The day was sunny, clear, and crisp. The most beautiful flying weather he could remember.

⌐

06:42 July 30, 2034 (GMT-4)
Washington, D.C.

Hendrickson insisted Chowdhury catch the night flight. "Don't wait until morning," he said. "Get back here *now.*" On the phone Hendrickson confirmed everything Patel had said in the canteen. Wisecarver had rebuffed the Indian defense attaché when he'd come to the White House. The defense attaché had met with Hendrickson unofficially (at a Starbucks) to reiterate India's intention to take military action against either party—Chinese or American—who further escalated the crisis. Hendrickson and Chowdhury had this conversation over an unsecured landline between Washington and New Delhi. What did it matter if the Indians intercepted their call? They'd already intercepted their emails. Perhaps it would assuage them if they knew two national security staffers were taking matters into their own hands.

Chowdhury's flight had been bumpy, with heavy turbulence over the Atlantic. When he landed at Dulles, Hendrickson was there to meet him. On the drive in from Northern Virginia, Hendrickson told Chowdhury the one thing he hadn't been able to mention over the phone. "All that's stopping the launch at this point is the weather."

"The weather?"

"The *Enterprise* is ready," Hendrickson said gravely. "The planes are fueled and armed. The pilots are briefed. After Galveston and San Diego, the weather's been erratic."

"So how much time do we have?" asked Chowdhury.

"Like I said, we've got until the weather gets better. After that, they launch."

Chowdhury's flight had been virtually empty, which got him an upgrade to first class. Despite the upgrade, he hadn't slept a wink. Exhausted, he now leaned his head against the car window. His eyes grew heavy, and as they began to close, he noticed the traffic. It was early morning, D.C. rush hour. Except no one was on the road. He wondered when, if ever, they would return.

The drive in was quick, maybe thirty minutes, but Chowdhury felt he'd been asleep for much longer. They had no trouble finding a spot for the car across from Lafayette Park. In front of the office buildings, trash was piled up. Traffic lights flashed on mostly deserted streets.

When they crossed the park, they walked past the Peace Vigil. The tent was empty, though at a glance Chowdhury couldn't tell whether or not it'd been abandoned. The White House was, of course, in perfect order. The uniformed Secret Service agents stood at their posts. The morning's newspapers sat in reception, along with coffee and pastries. Chowdhury's surroundings began to reassume their familiar proportions.

To his surprise, Chowdhury's badge still worked. A part of him had assumed that when Wisecarver dispatched him to New Delhi it was with the expectation that he would never return. Soon both Hendrickson and Chowdhury sat outside Wisecarver's office door. On the other side they could hear the murmurs of a meeting in progress.

Chowdhury and Hendrickson had no plan beyond confrontation. They would explain to Wisecarver that they knew about the defense attaché's visit. They would demand that he disclose this information to the president. The pilots on the *Enterprise* needed to know about the Indian threat. They had no idea that it wasn't the Chinese defenses alone that they'd have to contend with. If Wisecarver still refused to divulge this threat, Chowdhury and Hendrickson would go to the press, which, admittedly, wouldn't do much.

The door to Wisecarver's office swung open.

One by one a group of staffers Chowdhury didn't recognize stepped into the corridor. They spoke in low tones, sharing sidebar conversations, even laughing here and there. In a word, these staffers—all hand-selected by Wisecarver—projected confidence. Last out of the room was Wisecarver himself.

He stepped across the hall, his hand on the doorknob to the Oval Office.

"Sir, do you have a minute?" asked Hendrickson.

Wisecarver froze, his hand still on the knob. At the sound of Hendrickson's voice, he slowly turned over his shoulder. "No, *Bunt*, I don't have a minute." If there was any doubt in Chowdhury's mind as to how much of a nuisance Hendrickson had made of himself over the preceding weeks, it was now obvious.

"Millions of lives are at stake," interjected Chowdhury, "to say nothing of an international radiation-induced pandemic and the collapse of the global economy, and you don't have a minute?" He was shaking, but managed to add, "You have an obligation to pass on what you know."

Wisecarver released the doorknob. "Do I have an obligation to pass along misinformation?" He took a step closer to Chowdhury, invading his personal space. "Also," said Wisecarver, as he ran his eyes intrusively over Chowdhury, "aren't you supposed to be back in New Delhi?"

That word again, *back*.

Chowdhury didn't hesitate this time. He knew exactly what it meant. Had he come this far, had his family endured so much, only to turn *back*? And back to what exactly? He was here; only a shut door separated him from the most powerful office on earth. He was in possession of knowledge that could save this country—*his* country—if only he could convince Wisecarver to step away and let him pass to the other side.

But there would be no convincing him.

Of this, Chowdhury felt certain.

That word, *back*—he conjured it into a necessary rage. If Wisecarver wouldn't step aside, Chowdhury would move through him. He reached for the doorknob. "Where do you think you're going?" snapped Wisecarver. Chowdhury shouldered into him. The two struggled, their arms hooking, their chests pushing against one another. Neither was a fighter, so the scene quickly turned sloppy, with both Wisecarver and

Chowdhury losing their balance and taking an amateurish tumble to the floor.

Hendrickson tried to separate them.

Chowdhury lunged upward for the doorknob, as though it were the rung of a ladder placed just out of reach.

Wisecarver swatted his arm down.

The commotion didn't last long. Three Secret Service agents charged toward them, pulling both Chowdhury and Wisecarver to their feet. Wisecarver was left by the door. Chowdhury was escorted to the other side of the corridor.

"Get him out of here!" shouted Wisecarver.

Before the Secret Service agents could lead anyone away, the door opened.

Chowdhury couldn't see inside, but he could hear her voice. That persistent and restrained voice of speeches. The voice that had, a long time ago, convinced him that staying in government was a good idea.

It asked, "What the hell is going on out there?"

⌐

06:52 July 30, 2034 (GMT+4:30)
Strait of Hormuz

The seconds passed with strange imprecision. Farshad stood steadily among his men, a panicked swarm of conscripts scrambling to their dugouts with boots untied and slung rifles jangling over bare shoulders. Farshad watched the incoming formations of planes, calculating their altitude and distance and factoring for wind. He would pass this along to the antiaircraft gunners who were already cranking at the elevation wheels that raised their barrels skyward, swiveling and locking themselves into position. Farshad then ran to his command post, nothing more than a hole with a radio dug into the rocky sand.

As he crossed the beach, a half dozen impacts struck behind him, blasting up fountains of earth. Then the shock wave. It brought him to his knees. Up again, he continued to run, calculating his steps. Twenty . . . fifteen . . . he was almost there. Another group of impacts, this time closer—close enough that the shock wave blew the shirt up his back. Then he toppled over the lip of his command post, landing on his radio operator, who was gathered in a knees-to-chest bundle in the corner of the hole. "Get up," he growled. The young conscript slowly stood, a pleasing confirmation to Farshad that among his men he remained more frightening than death.

A swift crosswind cleared the smoke from the last barrage. Farshad snatched the radio's handset. He called out range, altitude, and windage to his gun crews, his ability to triangulate the three being one of those refined soldier skills that proved useless elsewhere in life. All at once, his several antiaircraft batteries began to chug out their fat, egg-shaped explosive rounds. The sky peppered with little detonations. Immediately, Farshad could tell they were off target. He had one battery of directed-energy cannons, but when he looked at them, he could tell their generators weren't engaged. Another cyberattack? Or shitty maintenance? It didn't matter.

Another missile barrage fell, this time directly onto his position.

Farshad crumpled forward, hands on his head, eyes shut. He opened his mouth so his eardrums wouldn't rupture with the overpressure. And he waited, rolling the dice as he'd done so many times before. He could feel the alternating blasts, like a violent wind juking between two opposing directions. The back of his neck was covered in dirt. Then stillness. He lifted his head.

Range . . . altitude . . . windage. . . . Those were his first thoughts. He made his estimations and then gave another order to fire, noticing a slight tinge of desperation in his voice, which he swallowed away. This would be their last chance. The landing paratroopers would overwhelm the garrison if Farshad didn't take out at least a portion of their transport planes.

Out chugged the egg-shaped explosive rounds.

Again, the sky peppered with little detonations.

Off target—all of them.

Then Farshad realized what he'd done—the fatal mistake he'd made. He'd calculated for wind, but not for wind at altitude. The erratic weather had caused wild atmospheric fluctuations. The crosswind he was experiencing at sea level must not be blowing at several hundred feet—or it was at least blowing differently. Even though he now noticed the inconsistency, it was too late. Standing in his command post, Farshad could do nothing but look above as in quick succession thousands of parachutes blossomed open into tidy skyborne rows.

The antiaircraft guns continued to fire, though they proved ineffective against the dispersed paratroopers. Farshad placed his rifle on the lip of his trench. He glanced from position to position, to the upturned faces of his men. A few took potshots at the descending paratroopers, but most didn't, perhaps for fear of retribution. The seconds passed, as they had all morning, with strange imprecision.

Time bent.

A life's worth of consequences existed in the moments it took for a plane to pass overhead. Or for a gust of wind to blow over a dusty fighting hole. Or for a parachute to descend to earth, coming down at . . . *six hundred feet* . . . Farshad watched . . . *five hundred feet* . . . he fingered his trigger . . . *four hundred feet* . . . the radio clutched in his hand . . . *three hundred feet* . . . the crosswind on his face.

The swift crosswind.

Farshad couldn't believe it at first. Wouldn't allow himself to believe it.

The crosswind he'd felt all morning caught the first stick of paratroopers as they descended below two hundred feet. Their parachutes, snatched by this slipstream, now raced dramatically across the frontage of the island, yanked out to sea as if by invisible tethers.

They splashed into the water.

Within minutes, thousands of others fell on top of them, all into the water. Although a few paratroopers touched down on the beach, or near enough to swim in, Farshad's conscripts quickly rounded them up. Soon Farshad was out of his hole, standing on its lip, observing the miraculous expanse of parachutes dispersed across the open water like so many lily pads coating a pond.

Well into that afternoon survivors crawled onto the beach, many retching seawater. The garrison rounded them up one at a time, trotting them off at rifle point with a jaunty confidence that Farshad's conscripts had hardly earned. Although this battle had cost the Russians an entire Spetsnaz division, Farshad didn't feel he could count the victory as his own. He and his opposing commander had, after all, made an identical mistake, albeit with different consequences: both of them had incorrectly calculated the wind.

There was an unfairness to it, thought Farshad. But also, an irony. A miscalculation in one circumstance could win a battle, and in another lose it.

By the time the last of the paratroopers splashed into the water, the Russian missiles had stopped falling. Reports from Iranian reconnaissance aircraft scrambled from Bandar Abbas were that the Russian fleet, which was moving from the northern Indian Ocean to reinforce the islands after the paratroopers seized them, had retreated north, back toward the Red Sea and the Syrian port of Tartus.

The Russian prisoners mixed calmly among their Iranian captors, the two sides swapping cigarettes, speaking each other's languages in broken phrases. Because neither nation existed in a formal state of war with the other, it allowed each side to assume a posture of mea culpa: the Russian paratroopers for their misbegotten and opportunistic invasion, and the Iranian conscripts for inflicting on them the inconvenience of captivity.

Farshad's state of mind was neither apologetic nor hostile—he was numb. A bone-deep exhaustion had set in. After a battle—particularly a battle won—he had usually felt elation, a nearly uncontainable exuberance as he passed among his men, readying them for a counterattack and radioing his situation report to a congratulatory high command. Not this time. Farshad didn't have the energy to prepare his men for an unlikely counterattack. As for the high command, when General Bagheri's helicopter arrived from Bandar Abbas right after nightfall, Farshad could barely muster the effort to receive it.

When Bagheri stepped off the ramp, he walked with his arm extended, as if the congratulatory handshake he offered to Farshad had lured his entire body from Tehran. "Fine work," Bagheri muttered. The radius of his congratulations spread wider as he trooped the line, clasping the shoulder of every soldier who came within reach. Only when a member of Bagheri's staff handed out challenge coins did the befuddled conscripts realize they'd met the chief of staff of the armed forces.

General Bagheri and Farshad retired to the "command post." They sat on the lip of Farshad's hole, staring out into the spongy darkness. "Did they land over there?" asked General Bagheri, pointing in a vague direction, to where the night hid the thousands of parachutes littered over the surface of the water.

Farshad nodded.

General Bagheri gave a belly laugh. "You are the embodiment of Napoléon's most famous maxim. Do you recall it?" Farshad shook his head. Not because he didn't know the maxim (which he did), but because he didn't care. He could feel himself struggling to stay awake. General Bagheri prattled on, "When it comes to a general, Napoléon said, 'I would rather have one who is lucky than good.'"

Farshad leaned his head all the way back, his face flush with the stars. He felt a slight spasm through his body, as one feels when dozing off in a dull movie. General Bagheri continued to speak. His voice—and its message—only partly registered to Farshad as he listed further and further toward sleep. Bagheri was stumbling through a half-hearted apology, in which he conceded that he hadn't believed Farshad's report about the threat to these islands but in which he also congratulated himself for possessing the intuition to send Farshad to command the garrison. Farshad propped his elbows on his knees and cradled his head in his palms. General Bagheri didn't seem to notice, continuing to heap praise not on Farshad himself but on his remarkable luck. The importance of this victory over the Russians couldn't be overstated, explained General Bagheri. It would unite the nation and the nation would, of course, again recognize Farshad with the Order of the Fath. Schoolchildren would learn his name, which shouldn't be that of a lowly naval officer. No, this wouldn't do. General Bagheri then confided to Farshad that his staff had already begun to process the required paperwork to have Farshad reinstated to the Revolutionary Guards and, perhaps, even promoted.

This woke Farshad up. "You'll do no such thing."

"And why not?" asked General Bagheri, whose tone wasn't anger but bewilderment. "Your country needs to honor you. You must let it. Is there some other distinction you would prefer? Say the word and, believe me, it will be yours."

Farshad could see that General Bagheri was telling the truth. This was Farshad's moment to ask for what he truly wanted. And why shouldn't he? He'd given his country so much, everything in fact. From his father's assassination, to his mother's grief and death thereafter, to his own adult life spread across so many wars, everything he'd ever had or could have hoped to have had been laid on the same altar.

"What is it?" General Bagheri repeated. "What is it that you want?"

"I think," said Farshad sleepily, "that I just want to go home."

"Home? . . . You can't go home. There's work to be done. Your reinstatement must be accepted . . . then there's a new command to discuss . . . I have certain ideas . . ." As General Bagheri spoke, the sound of his words receded, as if he were speaking at the distant end of a tunnel down which Farshad had begun to travel. Farshad had stopped trying to remain awake. He leaned onto his side in the dirt, tucked his knees to his chest, and with a rock for a pillow drifted into the sweetest sleep he had ever known.

⌐

18:57 July 30, 2034 (GMT+8)
28°22'41"N 124°58'13"E

"Blue Leader, this is Red Leader; acknowledge arrival at release point."

"Roger, Red Leader. This is Blue Leader. We've arrived."

"Good copy, Blue Leader. . . . Gold Leader, this is Red Leader; acknowledge arrival at release point."

"Roger, Red Leader. This is Gold Leader. Arrival acknowledged."

"Good copy, Gold Leader. . . . Red Leader confirms all flights in orbit at release point." Wedge checked his watch. They were right on time. According to plan, they'd hold at the release point for five additional minutes. This would be his last communications window with the *Enterprise*. After that they'd go dark.

Wedge then glanced below, to the vast expanse of ocean beneath his wing.

The day was bright and clear, with perfect visibility.

The conditions were ideal for him to see the column of smoke corkscrewing toward him from the water's surface.

⌐

07:04 July 30, 2034 (GMT-4)
Washington, D.C.

"God help you if you're wrong."

That's all Wisecarver could say as Hendrickson was joined by Chowdhury in the Situation Room. The three of them sat at one end of the table while a single staffer dialed INDOPACOM and the *Enterprise* for an emergency video teleconference. The president waited in the Oval Office, while the White House operator scoured the switchboard for a direct line to the Indian prime minister.

⌐

07:17 July 30, 2034 (GMT+8)
Beijing

When Lin Bao arrived at the ministry, the lights in the conference room were out. Surprised, he switched them on one at a time and began to poke his head into the adjacent offices, trying to find his support staff, that platoon of junior officers who set up his video teleconferences, his live drone feeds, his numerous secure calls.

They were nowhere to be found.

Stillness pervaded the large, empty rooms. Not sure what to do, Lin Bao installed himself at the head of the table. With perfect timing, the phone next to him rang. He startled. He would have been embarrassed if someone had been there to see him. Then the thought occurred that perhaps he was being watched. Putting this thought from his mind, he picked up the phone.

It was Zhao Leji: "No doubt you've heard the news."

The attack on the *Zheng He* was part of the American response to Galveston and San Diego, replied Lin Bao. Sinking the *Zheng He* demanded a reprisal. However, Lin Bao cautioned, it should be proportional. Perhaps they could use their surface-based missiles to strike at American interests in Japan or the Philippines. Such a response would be immediate. Also, there was always the opportunity to launch another cyberattack, perhaps this time against more critical US infrastructure, like their electrical grid, or water system. "There are many options," Lin Bao explained. "The key is that our response to the Americans be carefully considered."

The line went silent.

"Hello?" said Lin Bao.

A sigh. Then, "The Americans didn't do this."

Now it was Lin Bao's end of the line that went silent.

Zhao Leji added, "It was the Indians who sunk the *Zheng He*."

"The Indians?" Lin Bao's mind went blank. "But . . . why would the Indians . . ." He struggled to find the right words. "They've allied themselves with the Americans?" Lin Bao had already begun placing one alliance against another as though canceling out the numerators and denominators in a complex equation whose solution would solve for how the American-Indian alliance might shift the global balance of power. "This doesn't change anything with the Russians . . . nor the Iranians. . . . With the Indians in play we will, of course, need to keep the Pakistanis in check. . . ."

"Lin Bao—" Zhao Leji cut him off. "India's involvement in the conflict is because of a strategic miscalculation. The sinking of the *Zheng He* is a disastrous consequence of that miscalculation. The Politburo Standing Committee is meeting later today in a secure location. There's a man outside who will take you to us. We need you to help with our response. Do you understand?"

Lin Bao said that he did.

Zhao Leji hung up.

Silence returned to the room. Then a knock. A man opened the door; he wore a dark suit, and had a powerful build and a blank, anonymous affect. Lin Bao thought he recognized him from Mission Hills.

⌐

19:16 July 30, 2034 (GMT+8)
South China Sea

Thirty-seven minutes since launch. Sarah Hunt hadn't moved in that time. Fixed in the middle of the combat information center, she stood with her arms folded across her chest, staring at a digital display that plotted an approximation of Wedge's progress from the *Enterprise* toward his mission's three targets. Behind her sat Quint, along with Hooper, the pair of them tuning their radios through a desert of static, searching for a return signal.

"Are you sure you've got the right frequency?" Hunt asked Quint, trying to restrain her growing impatience.

Quint, lost in his task, didn't reply.

Beside the digital map was a video teleconference split between two screens. The first screen was INDOPACOM, a conclave of admirals with furrowed brows calling in from Hawaii, none of whom had much to say. The second screen was the White House Situation Room, a smaller group that comprised Hendrickson, another staffer who Hunt didn't know but who introduced himself as Chowdhury, and in the background Trent Wisecarver, who she recognized from television and who kept getting up to refill his cup of coffee. "Are you sure he's arrived at the release point?" Hendrickson asked gently.

"Am I sure?" Hunt countered. "No, I'm not sure. That's only where he's supposed to be." Wedge was also supposed to have come up for a last comm check with the *Enterprise*, but they couldn't raise him. They were thirty-seven minutes into the mission. At the twenty-eight-minute mark Hunt had received the call from Hendrickson in which he had, with little explanation, ordered her to abort the strike. When Hunt had asked on whose authority, as she was obliged to do, Trent Wisecarver entered the video teleconference's frame and answered flatly, "On the president's authority."

For the past nine minutes they had been trying to contact Wedge. They'd been met by nothing but static.

"Quint," snapped Hunt, "are you sure you're on the right frequency?"

Quint glanced up at her very slowly, his unlit cigarette calmly dangling from his lip. "Yes, ma'am," he said in a whisper, as if he were consoling her. "I'm sure. He ain't there."

"He wouldn't miss a comm window. It makes no sense," she said.

Quint replied, "What if it's exactly what it seems. Maybe he just ain't there. Maybe those Chinese or those Indians, or whoever, maybe they took him and the whole mission out before they ever got to the release point. Ma'am, it might be they're all gone."

On the video teleconference, there was a sharp exhalation, almost like a laugh. It was Wisecarver. He was reclined in a chair, so only half of his body appeared on the screen. He leaned forward. "Well," he said, "since we're trying to call off their mission that would simplify things, wouldn't it?"

The only sound in response was radio static.

Г

18:58 July 30, 2034 (GMT+8)
28°22'41"N 124°58'13"E

Wedge broke hard right, taking on altitude. The corkscrew of smoke climbed from the surface, chasing him skyward. "This is Red Leader, missile launch, my two o'clock!" He was banking hard—as hard as he could—five G, six G, then seven. . . . He flexed his legs and abdomen, making little grunts as the G-forces sucked the blood downward in his body. . . . He held there; any more G and he'd black out. Little pinpricks of light burst in his vision like paparazzi cameras as his aircraft pirouetted almost as violently as the missile that he'd lost sight of. He popped chaff and flare from ports on his fuselage, the shards of burning magnesium tumbling in a celebratory arc to confuse the missile's sensors.

Then a flash behind him, in the direction where the three Hornets that comprised Gold Flight had been assembled. He called out over the radio, trying to confirm what he already knew, which was that he'd lost one aircraft. There was no response. "Gold Leader, this is Red Leader," he repeated . . . and then he tried, "Any station, any station, this is Red Leader, over." For a handful of seconds he spoke into this emptiness until one of the other Hornets formed on his wing. The two held even like a pair of drivers idling at a traffic light. At a glance, Wedge couldn't tell which of his pilots this was. All he could see was the silhouette gesturing toward its ear, making the universal sign for *I can't hear you.*

And another flash.

Smoke enveloped his cockpit. Debris collided with glass. As quickly as the smoke engulfed him, it released him. His aircraft was fine, again flying straight and level. Off his wing, the other Hornet had vanished—incinerated in that flash. He craned his neck forward and could see little flaming pieces of its fuselage drizzling over the ocean, on whose surface Wedge now observed a half dozen other smoking corkscrews, their white tails ribboning skyward. Then behind him in his mirror, Wedge glimpsed a section of four aircraft forming near his six o'clock.

He could see their markings, a green, white, and orange roundel.

Not Chinese—Indian.

Wedge didn't quite understand. Since when were the Indians allied with the Chinese? Then two more flashes, one off his left wing and another off his right. An alliance between the Indians and Chinese didn't make any sense to Wedge, but he didn't have time to consider it. The shock wave from the two explosions came from separate directions, jarring his aircraft. His radio remained silent. He didn't know who he'd lost or understand who he'd lost them to. He still had a target to reach, and his only chance to reach it was to use these seconds of confusion to slip away, hug the contours of the earth, and head north. His radio was surely being jammed, but he nevertheless called out to whatever re-

mained of the *Death Rattlers*, ordering all ships to proceed to their targets. And as if in rebuttal to his words, he tracked another explosion
high above him as a fifth Hornet was destroyed.

Nose down, afterburners screaming, Wedge descended to below
one hundred feet, pulling up so low that his engines blew ripples across
the ocean's surface. Above him, three of the Hornets remained tangled
with a gathering number of Indian fighters—perhaps a dozen—which
Wedge tracked as the superior Su-35. His Hornets didn't stand a chance;
his pilots' skill would count for very little, maybe nothing. He knew that
they understood this. Even though he couldn't communicate, he hoped
they appreciated that the seconds they remained fighting in the air
would be put to good use by him. With the Indians occupied, he'd make
his escape, heading north toward Shanghai.

Another explosion behind him.

Then a second.

And eventually a third.

Wedge had the head start he needed. If he stayed below one hundred feet, with luck he'd slip the coastal defenses. Flight time was another twenty-two minutes. He checked his watch. It'd been forty-three
minutes since their mission had launched. Even if his radio had worked,
his communications window with the *Enterprise* had closed.

⌐

07:14 July 30, 2034 (GMT-4)
Washington, D.C.

No one could get in touch with Major Mitchell. Admiral Hunt's decision to strip the Hornets of any overridable communications system
had left the aircraft without any functioning communications at all.

Without too much trouble, the Indians had jammed the low-tech UHF/ VHF/HF receivers the aircraft relied on. From the White House Situation Room to the combat information center on the *Enterprise*, the only sound was Quint as he continued to call out to the flight of nine aircraft, his voice echoing across the video teleconference. In the Oval Office, a separate conversation was in process: the president requesting that her counterpart, the Indian prime minister, recall his fleet.

The prime minister obfuscated. Was Madam President certain the aircraft that engaged her were Indian? The prime minister would, of course, need to confirm this with his defense minister and his armed forces chief of staff before recalling any of his assets. And what was the mission of these aircraft that had allegedly come under fire from the Indian fleet? Could Madam President kindly pass along the exact location of this flight of nine planes? Nearly a dozen staffers—from CIA, NSA, the State Department, and Pentagon—listened on the line, furiously jotting down their notes on the prime minister's obvious stonewalling.

That was also the word Wisecarver used when he stepped back into the Situation Room from the Oval Office. On hearing this, Chowdhury exited into the hallway and pulled out his phone. There was only one other thing he could think to do.

Patel answered on the first ring. "Quite a corner we've painted ourselves into," he said, without waiting for his nephew to speak.

"You need to call off your aircraft," answered Chowdhury. He had cupped his hand over the receiver, concerned that he might be overheard. "Switch off your jammers so we can talk to our pilots."

"*Pilot*," corrected his uncle. "Our interceptors report that only one of them escaped. Two of our aircraft are giving chase."

"Recall your interceptors," pleaded Chowdhury. "Let us get in touch with our pilot to abort his mission." Even as he said this, Chowdhury wasn't certain it was possible. Would they be able to contact the pilot? Was he even listening?

The line went silent. Chowdhury glanced up and noticed Wisecarver standing in the doorway of the Situation Room, watching him.

"Too risky," answered Patel. "If we call off our interceptors, how can we be certain that the pilot won't strike Shanghai?"

Chowdhury glanced once more at Wisecarver, who'd taken a menacing step in his direction. "We'll abort the strike; you have my word. The president will—"

Wisecarver slapped the phone from his grip. In the time it had taken Chowdhury to utter his first sentence and then half of his second, Wisecarver had covered the distance between them. "You don't speak for the president," Wisecarver snapped, planting the heel of his shoe on the phone, so that when Chowdhury reached after it, he appeared as though he were groveling at Wisecarver's feet, which in a way he was.

"Please," said Chowdhury. "You've got to give us a chance to call it off."

"Not after Galveston," he answered, shaking his head. "Not after San Diego. Do you think this administration or this country will tolerate"— for a moment he struggled for the appropriate word, and then found it, plucking it like fruit from a branch—"*appeasement.*"

Chowdhury remained on his knees, his hands still reaching pathetically for his phone as he glanced up at Wisecarver, who, with a halogen bulb from the ceiling framing his head, seemed to glow strangely, like a vengeful saint. "There's only one pilot left," Chowdhury said weakly. "What are the chances he'll even make it to his target? If we call the Indians off, we could save him . . . we could stop all of this."

Wisecarver reached down toward his foot. He picked up Chowdhury's phone and tucked it into his own coat pocket. Then he offered

Chowdhury a hand, hoisting him up from the floor. "C'mon," said Wisecarver. "On your feet. No need to stay down there." The two stood next to one another in the empty corridor, sharing a quiet second as if to diffuse the tension between them. Then Wisecarver glanced up toward the lights that had framed his head a moment before. "There's a quote from the Bible," he began, "or maybe it's the Talmud or Qur'an? I can never remember which. But it's one I've always appreciated. It goes, *Whosoever destroys one life has destroyed the world entire, and whosoever saves a single life is considered to have saved the whole world.* . . . Or at least I think that's how it goes. Tell me, Sandy, are you a religious man?"

Sandeep shook his head, no.

"Me neither," said Wisecarver. He walked off with Chowdhury's phone.

⌐

19:19 July 30, 2034 (GMT+8)
Shanghai

At first the shore was just a smudge on the horizon. Then the contours of the skyline formed. At one mile out, Wedge would begin his ascent, climbing to his attack altitude. Everything would depend on altitude and time. He needed to take on at least ten thousand feet so that when he activated and then dropped his payload it would have sufficient time to arm. He needed to do this quickly so that the antiaircraft systems that lurked below couldn't find their mark. As he approached the city, his thought pattern was simple, almost primordial: *Here it comes, here it comes, here it comes,* each breath seemed to say.

At five miles out he could see traffic on the roads.

At three miles he could see the waves breaking on the beach.

At two miles the individual windows in the skyscrapers winked at him as they caught the sun—

Then he rocketed his stick, hard back.

The Gs pressed on his chest like an enormous hand. Pinpricks of light did their familiar Tinker Bell dance in his vision. Had anyone been listening, they would've heard his grunts, which were like a tennis player hitting from the baseline. A long stream of tracer fire arched toward him from the shore as he careened above Shanghai. Wedge rolled his plane belly skyward. With his cockpit hung toward the ground, he glimpsed two wispy missile launches, whirling upward toward his head. He deployed the last of his chaff and flares, dumping the white-hot magnesium beneath him and hoping it would be enough to confuse the missiles.

His altimeter orbited past three thousand feet.

Behind him, the pair of Indian Sukhois now appeared. He'd flown low enough and fast enough that they couldn't have tracked him. They must've figured he was heading here.

His altimeter passed four thousand feet.

The Chinese systems didn't distinguish between him and the Indian pilots. All three of them corkscrewed and juked through the antiaircraft fire that chewed up the sky while their engines, with a dismal rumble, forced them ever higher. Wedge struggled to reach his drop altitude of ten thousand feet while the Sukhois kept up the pressure, slotting into position on his tail. Any second they'd take their shot. Wedge knew he needed to deal with the Sukhois if he was ever going to get up to altitude.

He barreled right.

We'll decide it here, he thought, at five thousand feet.

Beneath the three aircraft, the city was lit up, spitting tracers in every direction. When Wedge had barreled right, the Sukhois had barreled left. The two sets of aircraft traveled in opposite directions along the circumference of a shared circle whose miles-long diameter was nearly the size of Shanghai itself. Wedge couldn't help but admire the Indian pilots, who had made an astute tactical move. By giving up their position on his tail they'd each be able to make a head-on pass, leveraging their two-to-one advantage.

Wedge made his orbit around the city and prepared to meet the pilots somewhere along that path. They would come at each other like jousting horsemen of another era—lances down, forward in their saddles, the issue decided in a blink. Events were playing out in seconds and in fractions of seconds. This is *it*, Wedge thought—the *it* he'd been chasing for the entirety of his life. He was ready. His thoughts returned to his family, to that lineage of pilots from whom he'd descended. He could feel his father, his grandfather, and his great-grandfather, their presence so close it was as if they were flying off his wing. A certainty possessed him: the advantage in numbers wasn't with the two assholes in the Sukhois but with him, Wedge.

Odds are four to two, motherfuckers, he thought—and almost said it aloud.

He locked onto the first Sukhoi, releasing a sidewinder from his wingtip, while simultaneously firing an exhalation's worth of rounds from his cannon. The Sukhoi did the exact same to him, so that their air-to-air missiles passed one another in mid-flight. However, the first Sukhoi had made a mistake. When Wedge diverted toward the second aircraft, so, too, had the sidewinder fired by the first. Wedge was out of chaff and flares to confuse the sidewinder, but if he could bring it in close enough to the second Sukhoi, that might disorient it.

The second Sukhoi observed the threat of the incoming sidewinder. From its fuselage, it deployed chaff and flare.

Wedge could see the sidewinder spiraling toward him as he rushed closer to the second Sukhoi, like a three-way game of chicken. Then the sidewinder dipped on its axis, following a burning piece of chaff. Simultaneously, both Wedge and the second Sukhoi released bursts from their cannon. When the two passed one another, there was a sound like a limb snapping off a tree. . . .

. . . *Blue sky everywhere, it turns to black, then rushes back to blue.* The wind on Wedge's face.

When he bolted awake, the stick had flopped out of his right hand. Wedge grabbed it, snatching back control of his Hornet. Checking his instruments, he hadn't lost much altitude. He couldn't have been unconscious for long, maybe a second, like an extended blink. A puddle was growing beneath his legs. He touched his right thigh and could feel a protrusion. A piece of steel—likely from the fuselage—had embedded below his hip. Two thumb-sized holes—around thirty millimeters, a little larger than his own cannon—had pierced the front-left and back-right of his cockpit, hence the wind on his face.

He glanced behind him, to where the second Sukhoi would've passed. He found it easily, a brackish trail of smoke heaving from one of its engines. In the same direction, a little farther on, an oil-black smoke cloud lingered in the otherwise perfectly clear sky. This could only be one thing—the other Sukhoi. His sidewinder must have found its mark. He'd tallied his first-ever air-to-air victory. He felt dizzy, which might have been loss of blood and might have been his body's response to the thrill of this achievement.

Wedge now needed to climb to ten thousand feet. He still had his payload to deliver. Then he would figure out how to get home, or at least how to get far enough out to sea to bail out. Slowly, he climbed. His left rudder was shot out, making the plane skittish in its ascent and hard to control. Neither of his engines were at thrust capacity; the pair of them were bleeding fuel. Whatever damage he'd done to the second Sukhoi, it had done about the same to him. And as he climbed, that stubborn second pilot slotted in behind him, giving a limp chase.

Won't matter, concluded Wedge. He was already past eight thousand feet.

He glanced down at the city spread before him. Little pits of light appeared in his vision. He tried to blink them away. Then a vertiginous darkness crept inward from his periphery as though he might black out again. The puddle he sat in kept deepening. When he looked at his altimeter, it was blurry too, but it soon read ten thousand feet. Wedge went through the arming sequence. His hands felt as though he wore several sets of gloves as he clumsily toggled through the switches and buttons and lined up his aircraft into its angle of attack. The Sukhoi was behind him, but he had thirty seconds, maybe more, until he'd need to deal with that.

A lot was going to happen in those seconds.

Everything was set. Wedge's finger hovered over the button. Whatever wooziness or confusion he'd felt moments before had yielded to a perfect clarity.

He hit the release.

Nothing.

He hit it again.

And again.

Still, nothing. And now the Sukhoi was coming up to altitude, notching in behind him. Wedge struck the controls in his cockpit in frustration. He recalled the tenth Hornet in their squadron, the one that'd gone down in training days before. He thought they'd fixed this problem with the release mechanism. Apparently not.

Didn't matter. He had a job to do.

Wedge pushed the stick forward, angling into a dive. The payload was going through its arming sequence, and if it was stuck on his wing he'd take it in himself. The Sukhoi didn't follow but instead broke away, understanding the maneuver and evidently wanting no part of it. Not that it would've made a difference. The Sukhoi wouldn't be able to put enough distance between itself and what was to come.

A sensation of weightlessness overtook Wedge as he dove.

The details below—buildings, cars, individual trees, and even individuals—were filling in fast. This business, war, the business of his family and of his country—he'd always accepted that it was a dirty business. He thought of his father and his grandfather—the only family he had—hearing the news of what he'd done. He thought of his great-grandfather, who'd flown with Pappy Boyington. And, strangely, he thought of Pappy and the old stories of him staring out through his canopy, scanning the horizon for Japanese fighters, a cigarette dangling from his lip before he'd toss it into the vastness of the Pacific.

The city was rushing up toward Wedge.

He'd told Admiral Hunt that he didn't do suicide missions. Yet this didn't feel like a suicide. It felt necessary. Like an act of creative destruction. He felt like he was the end of something and in being the end he would achieve a beginning.

Wind from the broken canopy was on his face.

At five hundred feet, he remembered the pack of celebratory Marlboros he'd tucked into his flight suit, in the left chest pocket. Though it was futile, he reached for them. This was his last gesture. His hand placed over his heart.

⌐

19:19 July 30, 2034 (GMT+8)
Beijing

Three more men from internal security waited in the lobby of the Four Seasons Hotel. They stepped onto the elevator with Lin Bao. Not a single introduction, no one speaking. His escort, the dark-suited man who'd taken him from the ministry, had the number of the suite where Zhao Leji and other key members of the Politburo were clandestinely meeting to discuss the appropriate strategic response to the sinking of the *Zheng He*.

Lin Bao had ideas as to what that response could be. He chose to focus on those ideas as opposed to why they were meeting at the Four Seasons and not some more secure location, or why they'd stepped out of the elevator on only the fifth floor and were now walking down a corridor with closely spaced rooms as opposed to suites. India's involvement might prove a positive development, if leveraged correctly. An Indian intervention would make it so that the strikes against Galveston and San Diego would be the last of the war. If his country struck the final blow, they could make the argument—at least to their own people— that they had been the victors. And they could avoid what at this moment seemed like an inevitable counterstrike against another of their major cities—Tianjin, Beijing, or even Shanghai.

He would explain this to Zhao Leji, and to whoever else from the Politburo attended this meeting. Lin Bao imagined that Zhao Leji would place some of the blame for the *Zheng He* on his shoulders. After all, it had been his name on the deployment orders, not Zhao Leji's, or that of any other member of the Politburo. They would likely accuse him of having exceeded his authority in a time of war, but nothing more than that. They would want to be rid of him. After peace was negotiated with the Americans, it would be easy for Lin Bao to convince Zhao Leji to turn the other way while he defected. If anything, a defection would help prove the substance behind the accusations Zhao Leji would surely level, which was that Lin Bao was untrustworthy, a secret ally of the Americans. Good riddance, they'd say. And he would return to the country of his mother's birth. Maybe even to Newport, with his family. To teach.

By the time Lin Bao had walked to the far end of the corridor on the fifth floor, these ideas had calmed him, so that when the security man swiped the key card and gestured with a low wave of his hand for Lin Bao to step inside, he did so without any trace of fear.

He took a half dozen steps into the empty room. It wasn't a suite. It was a single. There was a queen-size bed.

A console.

A dresser.

Everything, including the carpeted floor, was covered with plastic tarps, as though the room were undergoing a renovation.

Lin Bao stepped toward the bed.

Resting on its edge was a golf club, a 2-iron. He lifted it up. The familiar weight was pleasant in his hands. A note was attached to the shaft with a piece of string. He took a deep breath, filling his lungs, knowing it was likely the last such breath he might take. The writing on the card was blocky, the symbols formed by an untutored hand, the hand of a peasant. It read, *This time you picked wrong. I am sorry.*

It was unsigned. That's how they survive, he thought. They never sign their names to anything.

From behind Lin Bao, a series of steps squished over the plastic. He could feel the presence of the large security man at his back, plus the three others who no doubt stood by the door, waiting to help clean up the mess. Lin Bao had an instinct to shut his eyes, but he fought it off. He'd watch, until the very end, in this grim room where there was little worth seeing. He peered out the solitary window, to the equally grim Beijing skyline. The idea that this—not his daughter's face, nor the open ocean he loved—would be the last thing he ever saw filled him with self-pity and regret. He felt his throat constrict with those emotions in the same moment he felt the cold press of metal against the soft hairs at the base of his neck.

Keep your eyes open, he demanded of himself.

He continued to stare out the window, which faced to the southeast, generally in the direction of sunrise and the Pacific. Though it was late, a brilliant light like twenty sunrises all at once kept expanding unrestrained from that direction, as though the light itself had the potential to consume everything. This was coupled by an incredible noise that shook the windows and assured that no one heard the single gunshot.

What is that on the horizon? Lin Bao wondered. It was his last thought as he toppled forward onto the bed.

CODA

The Horizon

Finally, he was home. The trip to Bandar Abbas had been the first of any kind Major General Qassem Farshad had made in the past year since his promotion and subsequent retirement. He dropped his bags by the front door, went straight to the bedroom, and stripped out of his uniform. He'd forgotten how much he hated wearing it. Or, put another way, he had forgotten how much he'd come to enjoy not wearing it. He thought over the difference between the two as he showered and changed into the polyester tracksuit that had become his new uniform around the house. While he tied on his sneakers, he reminded himself that he didn't harbor any real grudges against Bagheri and the others in the high command. He simply wanted to embrace this new life.

On the return flight from Bandar Abbas, he had worked on his memoir, as he did most every morning, and now he was looking forward to his customary walk around his property and to settling back into the comfort of his routine. When the invitation to Bandar Abbas had arrived some weeks before, Farshad had initially refused it. Ever since the Victory of the Strait, as the high command had anointed his last battle, his country had heaped honor after honor on his shoulders, from his second awarding of the Order of the Fath to a mention by the Supreme Leader in a nationally televised address to the Parliament. Had such recognition arisen from another battle, one where the difference between victory and defeat hadn't come down to which direction the wind was blowing, perhaps Farshad would have felt otherwise about accepting the invitation.

Now, finally home, he first thought to unpack but then decided he would do it that night. He would instead have a long walk, to stretch his legs. He went to the kitchen and prepared himself his usual simple lunch: a boiled egg, a piece of bread, some olives. He placed the meal in a paper sack and set out across his property. Trees canopied his route. The first autumn colors already touched the rims of their leaves, and in the early afternoon the cool air hinted at the passing of the seasons. Late-blooming wildflowers lined his path as he headed along dirt-packed trails toward the ribbon of stream bisecting his property.

Farshad could hardly believe it had been more than a year since those Russian paratroopers had been blown out to sea. He couldn't quite decide whether a great deal of time had passed or not very much at all. When he thought of the specifics of the battle in the strait, it felt like not very much. When he thought of how much the world had changed since then, it seemed as though far more than a year had passed. Farshad now understood himself as a small actor in a far broader war, one that had resulted in a profound global realignment.

When Farshad was bracing for a Russian attack against his island fortifications, he had no inkling that the Indians had intervened on the side of peace by sinking a Chinese carrier and destroying an American fighter squadron. Tragically, a single pilot from that squadron managed to slip both the Indian interceptors and Chinese air defenses, dropping his payload on Shanghai. These many months later the city remained a charred, radioactive wasteland. The death toll had exceeded thirty million. After each of the nuclear attacks international markets plummeted. Crops failed. Infectious diseases spread. Radiation poisoning promised to contaminate generations. The devastation exceeded Farshad's capacity for comprehension. Though he'd spent his entire adult life at war, not even he could grasp such losses.

Compared to the trilateral conflict between the Americans, Chinese, and Indians, his country's contest with the Russians felt in retrospect like little more than an intramural squabble. In Parliament and among the high command, there had been some question as to whether the captured Russian prisoners qualified as "prisoners of war," seeing as the two nations were not in a state of formal hostilities. In Tehran, zealots within the government had threatened to classify the Russians as "bandits" and execute them accordingly. However, when as part of the New Delhi Peace Accords negotiated by the Indians, the United Nations announced its reorganization, the Supreme Leader astutely leveraged clemency for the imprisoned Russians as a way to secure a permanent Iranian seat on the Security Council, which the Indians had already insisted on relocating from New York City to Mumbai as a precondition of delivering a direly needed multiyear aid package to the United States.

Out on his walk, Farshad arrived at the stream on his property. He stepped onto the footbridge, leaned against its balustrade, and gazed into the clear glacial melt that passed below. His thoughts turned from the last year to the last few days, to his trip to Bandar Abbas and the final, albeit somewhat absurd, honor that the Navy had bestowed on him: the dedication of a vessel in his name.

Admittedly, Farshad had been quite flattered at first. Although he was technically retired as an officer in the Revolutionary Guards, the Navy had taken him in when his career was in tatters, and now, bedecked with his newfound glory, they proved keen to claim Farshad as their own. He pictured the sleek prow of a frigate or cruiser with his name emblazoned on its side. He could envision the teeth of its magnificent anchor, and its decks bristling with rockets, missiles, guns, and a crew that kept the ship, and thus his name, gleaming as it crossed horizon after horizon.

Several weeks passed while arrangements were made for Farshad's travel to Bandar Abbas. Then the Navy forwarded along the specifications of the vessel that would bear his name.

Not a frigate.

Not a cruiser.

Not even a puny yet swift corvette.

A photograph of the undedicated vessel accompanied the announcement; the shape of its hull was like a wooden shoe, wide in the front, narrow in the back, functional but not something anyone would wish to be seen in. The decision had been made to dedicate a newly laid Delvar-class logistics ship in his honor.

Standing on the footbridge over the stream, Farshad leaned forward and considered his reflection as he thought of the many photographs that had been taken of him over these past few days. When he'd arrived in Bandar Abbas, the Navy had scheduled an ambitious itinerary. After dedicating the ship, he accompanied it out to sea for its maiden voyage, which took them to the now heavily garrisoned islands in the Strait of Hormuz where he'd fought his famous battle. As a surprise— and a signal that Iran would lead the nations of the world in the process of reconciliation—there was a guest visitor aboard: Commander Vasily Kolchak. Kolchak, it turned out, had been part of the Russian invasion fleet a year before.

The two were scheduled to sail through the Strait of Hormuz together—allies turned adversaries, then allies again. He was pleased to see Kolchak, who had also been promoted since their last encounter. The dedication ceremony was on the whole a pleasant affair, except when the seas rose late that afternoon. The pitch and roll of the little, flat-hulled logistics ship that bore Farshad's name soon proved too much for him. He spent the final hours of the maiden voyage locked in the latrine, retching, while his old friend Kolchak stood vigil outside the door, doing Farshad one last favor. He made certain nobody witnessed the greatest naval hero in a generation bent over on all fours debilitated by seasickness.

As Farshad rested on the footbridge, recalling these past few days, he felt reassured to know that in all likelihood he would never again see a body of water larger than the little stream that babbled pleasantly be-low his feet. He continued on his walk. The leaf-filtered sun fell along the path and on Farshad's upturned and smiling face. It felt good to have the steady earth beneath him. He breathed deeply and quickened his pace. Soon he was at the far end of his property, near the elm where he was in the habit of taking his lunch.

He sat with his back against the trunk. On his lap, he spread out his meal: the egg, the bread, the olives. Since his bout of seasickness, his appetite hadn't quite returned. He only nibbled at his food. He thought of Kolchak. When the two had a quiet moment on the ship that bore Farshad's name, the Russian had asked him what he would do now that he was retired. Farshad didn't mention his memoirs—that would've been too presumptuous. Instead, he talked about this land, his walks, a quiet life in the countryside. Kolchak had laughed uproariously. When Farshad asked what was so funny, Kolchak said that he never took Farshad as one for the quiet life. He had expected Farshad to try his hand at politics, or business; to use his notoriety to vault toward the topmost rungs of power.

Farshad finished his lunch. He wondered what his old mentor Soleimani would think of his decision to strive for a quieter life. It was, after all, Soleimani who had wished a soldier's death for his young protégé, as opposed to the withering away he himself had feared and so narrowly avoided. How many times and on how many battlefields had Farshad cheated death? Too many to count. But as he thought of this, he began to wonder whether he'd cheated death or if it was death who had cheated him, never granting the end that Soleimani had wished for Farshad. Still, sitting beneath the elm at the edge of his property, Farshad couldn't quite bring himself to wish that he'd died on a battlefield. Didn't a soldier deserve the fruits of his labor? It seemed fitting that at the end of his days a soldier would become an intimate with peace. One might argue that the highest achievement for a soldier wasn't to die on the battlefield, but rather to pass away quietly in a peace of his own creation.

A few morsels of his meal remained. Farshad flattened the paper sack in front of him on the grass, placing a piece of egg, a crust of bread, and two olives in a neat arrangement.

He waited. Waiting as he'd done nearly every day since his return home the year before. He dozed off. When he awoke, the afternoon sun held just above the treetops. The shadows had lengthened. Now he saw what he'd been watching for. Standing in the open grass was the single squirrel, the white-tailed one whose partner had bit Farshad long ago.

He placed the crust in his hand, offering it to her.

She wouldn't come. Yet she wouldn't run away either.

On many an afternoon, the two of them had sat fixed in a similar impasse. It always ended when Farshad walked off and the squirrel safely ate what he left behind on the paper sack. But Farshad wouldn't quit. Eventually, he would convince her to trust him enough to eat again from his open palm. What would Kolchak, Bagheri, Soleimani, or even his father think if they could see him now, reduced to this, an old man coaxing this helpless creature toward him.

But Farshad no longer cared.

"I'm not giving up," he whispered to the squirrel. "Come closer, my friend. Don't you believe even an old man can change?"

Γ

07:25 October 03, 2036 (GMT-4)
Newport

New home. New city. The loss of her father. The overworked guidance counselor at their local middle school had told the girl's mother that the first year would be the hardest. Yet the second year was proving harder still. When they'd left their home in Beijing for the countryside, her mother had said it would only be for a few days. The girl had repeatedly asked to speak to her father on the phone, and her mother had tried to call but couldn't reach him. According to her mother, he had been doing important work for their government. She was old enough to understand that there had been a war on, that this was the reason they'd had to leave the capital. However, she wasn't quite old enough to understand her father's role. That understanding would come later, after Shanghai, when she and her mother were recalled to Beijing.

She remembered the old man who'd come to their apartment. Several of his large attendants in dark suits had waited outside the door. The old man carried himself like a well-dressed peasant. When her mother told her to go to her room so they could speak, the old man insisted that the girl stay. He cupped her cheek in his hand and said, "You look very much like your father. I see his intelligence in your eyes." The old man went on to tell them that their home wasn't their home anymore. That her father—intelligent as he was—had had bad luck, he'd made some mistakes, and he wouldn't be returning. Her mother would cry later, at night, when she thought her daughter couldn't hear her. But she didn't betray a single emotion in front of the old man, who suggested they go live in the United States. "This will help things," he said. And then he asked if there was anywhere in particular that they would like to go.

"Newport," her mother answered. That's where they'd been happiest.

And so they went. Her mother explained to her that they were lucky. Her father had gotten himself into trouble and they might have found themselves in prison, or worse. Except the government needed someone to blame for what had happened in Shanghai. They would blame her father. They would tout his disloyalty. They would accuse him of having conspired with the Americans. The proof of this would be his family's abrupt departure to the United States. Her mother told her these things so that she would know that they weren't true. "This new life," her mother had said, "is what your father left us. We have become his second chance."

Her mother, the wife of an admiral and a diplomat, now worked fourteen-hour days cleaning rooms at two separate chain hotels. The girl had offered to help, to also get a job, but her mother placed limits on her own humiliation, and seeing her daughter's education sacrificed to menial labor would have breached those limits. Instead, the girl attended school full-time. In solidarity with her mother, she helped keep the studio apartment they shared impeccably clean.

Her mother never settled for menial labor. When she wasn't working, she was searching for a better job. On several occasions, she reached out to the local Chinese community, those immigrants who'd arrived on American shores within the last one or two generations, her presumed allies who now owned small businesses: restaurants, dry cleaners, even car dealerships sprouting up around Route 138. Although America was a place where people came to make a new life, for both mother and daughter their old lives followed them. The Chinese community had to contend with the suspicions of other Americans, many of whom assumed their complicity in the recent devastation. Unfair as that assumption was, such assumptions in times of war were an American tradition—from Germans, to Japanese, to Muslims, and now Chinese. Helping the wife and daughter of a deceased Chinese admiral would only heighten suspicions against anyone foolish enough to assume the undertaking. The community of Chinese immigrants rejected the girl and her mother.

So her mother continued with her menial labor. One day a week she had off from work, but it didn't always fall on a weekend, so it was the rare occasion when mother and daughter could spend a free day together. When they had their day, they always chose to do the same thing. They would take the bus to Goat Island, rent a dinghy from the marina, let out full sail, and head north, tucking beneath the Claiborne Pell suspension bridge up toward the Naval War College, the same route they'd taken years before, with Lin Bao.

They never spoke his name around the house, fearful of who might still be listening. Out here, however, on the open water, who could hear them? They were beyond reach and free to say what they pleased. Which was why it was on the water, shortly after they passed beneath the bridge and two years after they'd first arrived, that her mother admitted she'd finally stopped looking for a different job. "Nothing better is coming," she conceded to her daughter. "We must accept this. . . . Your father would expect us to be strong enough to accept it."

"No one here trusts us, not even our own people. We'll never be Americans," the girl said bitterly. She sat slumped next to her mother, the two of them side by side in the stern of the dinghy. Her mother held the tiller; she didn't look at her daughter, but at the horizon, trying to keep them on course.

"You don't understand," her mother eventually said. "We are from nowhere and have nothing. We have come here to be from somewhere and to have something. That is what makes us American."

The two sat silently for a time.

A spray of water came over the bow as they crossed the wake of a much larger ship, the uncaring wave almost swamping their small dinghy.

When they arrived off the coast of the Naval War College, they drew in the sail, lifted the tiller, and dropped their small anchor. Their dinghy bobbed in the gentle swells. The two of them, mother and daughter, didn't speak. They watched the shore, the familiar pathways, the office where he had once worked, the life they'd once had and, perhaps, would someday have again.

Г

**17:25 June 12, 2037 (GMT-6)
New Mexico**

The ranch house was built in the center of her one-hundred-acre plot. The renovation had taken three years and most of her savings, but Sarah Hunt was starting to feel as though it was home. The house itself wasn't much, a single floor with exposed timbers and rafters. She still didn't have anything to hang on the walls and wondered if she ever would. Most of her photos she kept in storage. On a few occasions since retiring, after one sleepless, sweat-soaked night or another, she would go out to the shed in the back of the house and consider burning the single box that contained the photographs.

But it hadn't come to that, at least not yet.

After Shanghai, the dreams got worse. Or not necessarily worse, but more frequent. Night after night she would be standing on the dock with the seemingly infinite parade of ships offloading their cargo of ghosts, while she searched for her father. She never found him, not once. Yet she remained unconvinced that her searching in the dreams was futile. For a long time, she hoped that when she finished her new home, the dreams might stop. And if they never stopped, she at least hoped to find something or someone recognizable in them. That hadn't yet proven the case.

She had gone on and off medication to no effect.

She had spoken to therapists who only seemed to want to bury her beneath the weight of her own words, so she'd stopped talking to them. Each day, she walked the perimeter of her property, though it made her bad leg ache. Eight miles from her nearest neighbor, her plot of high desert brought her a modicum of peace. Despite the dreams, out here she could at least sleep. After the strike on Shanghai, she'd gone nearly a week with no sleep at all, her nerves so frayed that Hendrickson had to fly out to the *Enterprise* and relieve her of command himself, in the midst of the ceasefire negotiations being brokered by New Delhi. He had been gentle with her then, and he had remained gentle with her in the three years since. Predictably, he'd stayed in the Navy, pinning on a third star in his ascent to its highest ranks. A reward—and a deserved one—for the role he'd played in brokering the peace.

On his visits, which had become less frequent, he always assured her that there was nothing she could've done to prevent Shanghai. She hadn't been the one to issue the launch order. Once the nine Hornets had departed the *Enterprise* there was nothing she could have done. If anything, the one Hornet getting to its target might have proven crucial to ending the war. During the ceasefire negotiations that followed, it had been essential for hawks like Wisecarver to make the face-saving claim that they had avenged the attacks against Galveston and San Diego. Without that claim, Hendrickson felt certain no ceasefire agreement would have been signed.

"This wasn't your fault," he would say.

"Then whose fault was it?" she would ask.

"Not yours," and they would leave it at that. For the first year and into the second, Hendrickson would offer to help her in the ways he thought she needed help. "Why don't you come stay with us for a bit?" or, "I'm worried about you out here on your own." He thought it might be good for her to get back on the water again. *Healing* was the word he'd used. Hunt had reminded him that it was no accident she'd bought property in New Mexico, a landlocked state.

In the third year, on one of his now-rare visits, the two had decided to take a stroll around her property before dinner. During a lull in their conversation, she finally asked, "Will you help me with something?"

"Anything," he answered.

"I'm thinking about adopting."

"Adopting what?" he replied, as if he were hoping she might say a cat or a dog.

They continued to walk in silence, until, eventually, Hendrickson muttered, *"Whosoever destroys one life has destroyed the world entire, and whosoever saves a single life is considered to have saved the whole world. . . ."*

"What the hell is that supposed to mean?" she asked.

"Isn't that why you want to adopt?"

"I never thought I'd hear you quote scripture."

Hendrickson shrugged. "I heard Trent Wisecarver say it once. Though I don't think he believed it. Do you?"

They had come to a portion of her fence that needed mending. Instead of answering, Hunt bent down and cradled one of the heavy joists in her arms. She lifted with all her strength, exhaling sharply as she jammed its end into an upright. It would hold, at least temporarily, until she could make a permanent fix. She did this again with the joist's other end. Then she wiped her dirty hands on the front of her jeans. "I've already started the adoption process," she said matter-of-factly. "I'm not asking for your opinion. I'm only asking for your help. They require letters of reference. You're a war hero; one from you might mean something."

Hendrickson didn't answer. They finished their walk, had their dinner, and the next morning he left. A week passed, a month, and then several more. She fixed the fence on her property. She remodeled the ranch house, turning her study into a nursery. Her application for adoption continued its slow, bureaucratic progress. She provided bank statements. She submitted herself to interviews, to home visits. She knew the odds were stacked against her. She was a single woman and over fifty years old—or "of an advanced age," as phrased by the New Mexico Children, Youth, and Families Department. But none of this would disqualify her. What would disqualify her, she feared, was what had happened on the open ocean three years before. Would her government entrust her to nurture a single life after entrusting her to end so many? She didn't know.

Then, quite by surprise, a sealed letter arrived in the mail. She didn't need to open it. Hunt understood what Hendrickson had done for her. She forwarded along this letter to the adoption authority. The process continued. Step by step she moved through it, transforming herself into a prospective mother and transforming her isolated ranch into a suitable home. The social worker assigned to her case, a no-nonsense official who seemed impervious to chitchat and who wore a modest gold crucifix outside her turtleneck, reminded Hunt of Commander Jane Morris, which reminded her of the *John Paul Jones*. Hunt was so haunted by the resemblance that on the home visit she'd chosen to sit alone in her living room as opposed to walking through the house with the social worker, a breach of manners that likely didn't work to her advantage. When the social worker finished her hour-long inspection, she exited the nursery and commented, "You'd never know you'd been in the Navy walking around this house. You don't have a single photo out."

Hunt hadn't had a response, or at least not one she felt prepared to give.

Before she left, the social worker told Hunt she would receive a phone call in the coming days as to her eligibility to become an adoptive parent. In the days that followed, Hunt hardly slept. Her dreams returned with a ferocity she hadn't known since immediately after Shanghai.

The ships unload their cargo. . . .

Panicked, she searches for her father, knowing she'll never find him. . . .

On and on the dream spirals, only increasing in intensity. Until, one morning, in the midst of her dream she is released from her familiar terror by a sound. . . .

Her phone was ringing.

⌐

17:12 November 24, 2038 (GMT-6)
Kansas City, Missouri

The bedroom hadn't changed in two decades. Posters of fighter jets, from the Corsair to the Phantom to the Hornet. A Super Bowl victory poster from 2017, the year Tom Brady became the GOAT. Varsity trophies littered the desk, a football player rushing, a batter hitting, their shoulders blanketed by a thickening layer of dust. History books were piled beside the trophies, including a dog-eared paperback of *Baa Baa Black Sheep*, an autobiography by Colonel Gregory "Pappy" Boyington. In the center of the desk was a letter first opened four years before, the envelope yellowing with age at its corners. It had come back from the *Enterprise* with the rest of his personal effects. His father kept it there. When missing him became too much, his father would sit vigil at the desk and reread the letter.

Hey Dad,

You'll probably hear from me on the phone before you get this letter. But in case it's much longer than that before we talk, I wanted to put pen to paper. These past few days, I've been thinking a lot about Pop-Pop. My first-ever memory is of him telling me stories from the Pacific. Later on came Pop's stories about Vietnam. And, of course, your stories. (If you were here, I'd ask you to tell me the one about the camel spider and sheet cake again.) But more than my memory of all those stories is my memory of wanting a story of my own. One that I could tell you. And goddamn if I haven't gathered a few out here.

We've been waiting to launch for days now (the weather's been bad) and that's given me time to think. I want you to know that I went into this clear-eyed. All I ever wanted was to hold my own in this family. And I feel like I've done that. But I suspect something else will soon be asked of me, something more than what you, Pop, or even Pop-Pop had to do. And if I have to do that thing, I want you to know I'm okay with it. If I'm the last in our family ever to fly, it makes sense that I'd have to give the most. When you build a chain, you cast the last link a little thicker than the rest because that's the anchor point. The most punishment always falls on the anchor point.

That's it—that's all I've been thinking about.

Be sure to keep taking your heart meds.

And thanks for the carton of Marlboro Reds.

I love you,

Chris

The old man finished reading. He gazed out the window, to the fields they used to play in. It was late autumn. The leaves were collected in great piles. He carefully refolded the letter and placed it in its envelope. He sat alone in the chair as the afternoon moved toward darkness. Occasionally, in the distance, he could hear the dull sound of a plane as it passed invisibly overhead.

07:40 April 16, 2039 (GMT+5:30)
New Delhi

Sandeep Chowdhury had a flight to catch. His taxi to the airport would arrive in a few minutes. The night before, he'd packed meticulously. This would be his first trip back to the United States since he'd left Washington as part of the peace delegation five years before. He brought an assortment of clothing, including a suit he would wear to formal meetings, but mostly he packed items to wear in the camps around Galveston and San Diego, which were filled with the internally displaced who had yet to resettle. It was strange for Chowdhury to wonder whether or not he should bring extra soap or toothpaste to an American city, where once you could buy anything. But no longer. At least that was what the security officer at UN headquarters in Mumbai had said.

Truth be told, Chowdhury's distancing from America started when he'd resettled his mother and daughter in New Delhi. His mother, who had now reconciled with her aging brother, was reluctant to leave him. And if his mother was reluctant to leave her brother, Chowdhury couldn't leave his mother—particularly in light of Ashni's attachment to her grandmother. The girl had already been through so much with the loss of her own mother. This tally of familial obligations led Chowdhury to resign from the administration and stay on in what his uncle insisted on calling "your home country." Once Chowdhury had made that decision, he was pleasantly surprised to discover that his expertise was in high demand. After the New Delhi Peace Accords, both the political world and business world opened up to him in a way he could never have anticipated. Not only had he served in the highest levels of the US executive branch; he was an India expert (or simply Indian, if the offending party hadn't read his CV). International lobbyists, think tanks, venture capitalists, sovereign wealth funds—they aggressively courted him with board seats, stock options, and prestigious titles such as "Senior Distinguished Fellow" as they vied for his expertise as part of a general clamor to understand India's ascendance as an economic and political juggernaut.

For Chowdhury, this meant that he'd had no reason to go back to America. However, packing for this trip, that word, *back*, came to mind again. Although success after success had come to him since resettling in New Delhi, a certain bitterness remained in how he had left home. How often had he replayed the events of five years before in his mind, wondering if a different set of decisions might have led to a different set of outcomes. He thought of Wisecarver too, whose obstruction of the Indian defense attaché had eventually come to light, a scandal that cost the administration its next election, so that even had Chowdhury stayed on he would've soon been out of the job. But none of that had ever alleviated the deeper wound, which wasn't the loss of life, as tragic as it had been, but rather the sacrifice of America itself, the idea of it.

Chowdhury had packed one suitcase and a carry-on, a daypack

he could take when he traveled into the camps. His office at the UN High Commission for Refugees had also advised he bring a sleeping bag. Depending on road conditions and available accommodations, the chance existed that his delegation might need to stay one or two nights in the wretched camps, a detail that Chowdhury kept from his mother, who wouldn't have approved. Cyclical outbreaks of typhus, measles, and even smallpox often sprouted from the unbilged latrines and rows of plastic tenting. These diseases had ravaged communities far and wide, only heightening the cost of the war. Their own hometown of Washington, D.C., had lost nearly fifty thousand residents to a vaccine-resistant strain of rubeola two years before. Chowdhury had wanted to return then to help, but his mother had convinced him not only to remain in New Delhi but to submit his application for Indian citizenship. Which he reluctantly did. "You need to accept that this might be your home," she had said. Still, he couldn't quite believe that the America he remembered, the America that Kennedy and Reagan had both called "the city upon a hill," might vanish.

Except America was an idea. And ideas very seldom vanish.

Whenever he despaired, he reminded himself of this.

With his bags set by the front door, he stepped into his study, which had once been his uncle's study, the very room where he'd learned of the attacks on Galveston and San Diego. At the corner of the desk sat a photograph of his great-great-grandfather, Lance Naik Imran Sandeep Patel of the Rajputana Rifles. This wasn't the photo from the Delhi Gymkhana that his uncle had shown him years before, but a photograph from later on in his great-great-grandfather's life, after his career in the army, once he'd made a modest fortune selling arms during Partition to the newly formed Indian government. Although the forty years between photographs had obscured the resemblance of the young and old versions of the same man, the gaze was unmistakable. It was unrequited, hungry for more—to do more, achieve more, to make a better, safer, more secure, more dignified life. It was, in Chowdhury's estimation, a distinctly American gaze, though the man had never set foot in America.

When he considered his great-great-grandfather, and considered Reagan and Kennedy—who felt like grandfathers of another sort—and their shared vision of "the city upon a hill," he felt assured by the notion that America, as an idea, did not depend upon any particular set of borders to endure. In fact, on this UN-sponsored humanitarian trip, he would be doing his part to restore American ideals to its very shores.

Outside, his taxi pulled up. Chowdhury messaged the driver to wait a minute. Another idea rang discordantly in his mind, an idea from another of America's forefathers. These were words spoken by a young Abraham Lincoln two decades before the calamity that became the American Civil War. *All the armies of Europe, Asia, and Africa combined*, Lincoln had said, *with all the treasure of the earth (our own excepted) in their military chest, with a Buonaparte for a commander, could not by force take a drink from the Ohio or make a track on the Blue Ridge in a trial of a thousand years. . . . If destruction be our lot we must ourselves be its author and finisher. As a nation of freemen we must live through all time or die by suicide.*

A nation of freemen.

Chowdhury counted himself among that nation, no matter where it might exist, in Washington, New Delhi, or elsewhere. And so he would travel back to America, hopeful that the spirit of that nation had yet to abandon the place. He had one last item to pack. Opening his desk drawer, he reached for his two passports: Indian and American, different shades of the same blue.

His hand hovered indecisively over them both. He had a flight to catch. Time was growing short. The taxi began to blare its horn. He stood, the seconds bleeding away. For the life of him, he couldn't decide which to choose.

"Because no battle is ever won. . . . They are not even fought.
The field only reveals to man his own folly and despair,
and victory is an illusion of philosophers and fools."

—William Faulkner

Acknowledgments

Elliot Ackerman would like to thank Scott Moyers, Mia Council, PJ Mark, and, as ever, Lea Carpenter.

James Stavridis would like to thank Andrew Wylie, Captain Bill Harlow, Scott Moyers, Mia Council, and the Fleet's best spouse, Laura Stavridis.